"You have a hankering for my DNA?"

Nick paused, undecipherable emotion in his eyes. "You're serious."

More than Sage wanted to admit. She'd been trying to work up the nerve to approach him since the first time they'd hit the sheets. And it was no wonder. It wasn't just his mesmerizing sky blue eyes, thick dark hair or masculine good looks. But intelligence and kindness, practicality and innovation, compassion and heart...

And that something special that was all his own. But she couldn't tell him that. Not without sounding like she'd really gone round the bend.

"You are everything I'd ever want in a baby daddy."

His sexy grin encouraged her to go on.

"Big. Strong. Handsome."

He tilted his head, the edges of his lips curving seductively. "And here I thought you liked me for my brain."

"I do." She batted her lashes flirtatiously. "Your sense of humor, too."

He grinned. "We do know how to make each other laugh."

Which was the way th
Uncomplicated.

This could be, too. If c

HOME ON THE RANCH:
TEXAS FAMILY RESCUE

———————— ⚒ ————————

CATHY GILLEN THACKER

PATRICIA THAYER

Previously published as *Wanted: Texas Daddy* and *Dylan's Last Dare*

HARLEQUIN HOME ON THE RANCH

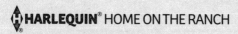

⊞HARLEQUIN® HOME ON THE RANCH

ISBN-13: 978-1-335-00867-1

Recycling programs for this product may not exist in your area.

Home on the Ranch: Texas Family Rescue
Copyright © 2020 by Harlequin Books S.A.

Wanted: Texas Daddy
First published in 2017. This edition published in 2020.
Copyright © 2017 by Cathy Gillen Thacker

Dylan's Last Dare
First published in 2004. This edition published in 2020.
Copyright © 2004 by Patricia Wright

This edition published by arrangement with Harlequin Books S.A.

For questions and comments about the quality of this book, please contact us at CustomerService@Harlequin.com.

Harlequin Enterprises ULC
22 Adelaide St. West, 40th Floor
Toronto, Ontario M5H 4E3, Canada
www.Harlequin.com

Printed in U.S.A.

CONTENTS

Cathy Gillen Thacker is married and a mother of three. She and her husband spent eighteen years in Texas and now reside in North Carolina. A popular Harlequin author for many years, she loves telling passionate stories with happy endings and thinks nothing beats a good romance and a hot cup of tea! You can visit Cathy's website, cathygillenthacker.com, for more information on her upcoming and previously published books, recipes and a list of her favorite things.

Books by Cathy Gillen Thacker

Harlequin Special Edition

Texas Legends: The McCabes

The Texas Cowboy's Quadruplets
His Baby Bargain
Their Inherited Triplets

Harlequin Western Romance

Texas Legends: The McCabes

The Texas Cowboy's Triplets
The Texas Cowboy's Baby Rescue

Texas Legacies: The Lockharts

A Texas Soldier's Family
A Texas Cowboy's Christmas
The Texas Valentine Twins
Wanted: Texas Daddy
A Texas Soldier's Christmas

Visit the Author Profile page at Harlequin.com for more titles.

WANTED: TEXAS DADDY

CATHY GILLEN THACKER

Chapter 1

"You want to have my baby," Nick Monroe repeated slowly, leading the two horses out of the stables.

Sage Lockhart slid a booted foot into the stirrup and swung herself up into the saddle. She'd figured the Monroe Ranch was the perfect place to have this discussion. Not only was it Nick's ancestral home, but with Nick the only one living there now, it was completely private.

She drew her flat-brimmed hat straight across her brow. "An unexpected request, I know."

Yet, she realized as she studied him, noting that the color of his eyes was the same deep blue as the big Texas sky above, he didn't look all that shocked.

For he better than anyone knew how much she wanted a child. They'd grown quite close ever since she returned to Texas, to claim her inheritance from her late father and help her mother weather a scandal that had rocked the Lockhart family to the core.

So close, in fact, the two of them had been "friends with benefits" for several months now.

Nick's gaze drifted over her, creating small wildfires in its wake.

With a click of his reins, he turned his horse in the direction of the wide-open pastures behind the Triple Canyon ranch house. He slowed his mount slightly, while waiting for Sage to catch up. "You're still having second thoughts about using an anonymous donor from the fertility clinic?"

She nodded, enjoying the warm autumn breeze blowing over them. It was a perfect Indian summer afternoon.

Swallowing around the knot of emotion in her throat, Sage admitted, "On the one hand, picking out a potential daddy for my baby via a set of statistics and characteristics seems easy enough."

Squinting at her, he settled his hat on his head. "Kind of like reading a menu of options."

"Right." If only it were that simple, she thought wistfully. Because her mom had been right. Having a baby was an emotional—not a scientific—proposition.

"But?" He kept the pace slow and steady as they threaded their way along a path that took them down a steep ravine, across a wildflower-strewn canyon and up the other side.

"It's a lot more complicated than I thought it would be." Mostly, because the only person she could see fathering her baby was the ruggedly handsome rancher-businessman beside her.

She drew a deep, bolstering breath. "The idea of a

complete stranger fathering my child is becoming increasingly unappealing." When they reached their favorite picnic spot, she swung herself out of the saddle, watching as Nick tied their horses to a tree.

Together, they moved into the warm early September sunshine. Spread a blanket out on the ground. "What if the donor profiles aren't exactly accurate?"

Nick set down the rucksack containing their meal. "I thought the clinic had everyone go through extensive background checks."

Sage settled cross-legged on the blanket. watching as he did the same. "They do."

He opened up the bag, brought out the containers from her café-bistro. Two individual thermoses of chicken tortilla soup. Luscious squares of jalapeño-cheese cornbread. And for dessert, triple-berry tarts that she'd gotten up at the crack of dawn to make especially for him.

"Then…?"

Sage shrugged. Aware that Nick was carefully weighing his options—the way he always did when the talk turned to anything personal—Sage forced herself to abandon the hopelessly idyllic notions that had dictated her actions for years, and speak what was on her mind, rather than what was in her heart.

"The more I think about it, the more I have to wonder. Do I *really* want some stranger's DNA swimming around inside me?"

Nick grinned, as if pleased to hear she was a one-man woman, at least in this respect.

He looked at her from beneath the brim of his hat. "Which is why you're asking me?" he countered in the rough, sexy tone she'd fallen in love with the first second she had heard it. "Because you know me?"

Sage locked eyes with him, not sure whether he was teasing her or not. One thing she knew for sure: there hadn't been a time since they'd first met that she *hadn't* wanted him.

And that, too, was unusual. Prior to meeting Nick, she hadn't considered herself a particularly sexual person.

He'd changed all that. Fast. Thanks to the times they'd spent in bed, she now knew how much she loved the physical side of affection.

Even *without* the heretofore requisite falling in love.

"Or because," he continued flirtatiously as he unscrewed the lid on his thermos, "you have a hankering for my DNA?"

Aware the only appetite she had now was not for food, she quipped, "How about both?"

He paused, spoon halfway to his lips, undecipherable emotion in his eyes. "You're serious."

More than she wanted to admit. She'd been trying to work up the nerve to approach him since the first time they'd hit the sheets. And it was no wonder she felt he was the perfect man for the job. It wasn't just his mesmerizing sky blue eyes, thick, dark hair or masculine good looks. Or the way he made her feel in bed, all woman to his man. At six foot four inches tall, with broad shoulders and a fit, muscular body, he was the quintessential Texas cowboy. A man who was as much at ease running his family's business as he was this ranch. He radiated not just boundless energy and good health, but intelligence and kindness, practicality and innovation, compassion and heart...

But she couldn't tell him any of that. Not without sounding like she'd really gone round the bend. "Well…" With a wistful sigh, she flashed him a teasing look. "You are everything I'd ever want in a baby daddy."

His sexy grin encouraged her to go on.

"Big. Strong. Handsome."

He tilted his head, edges of his lips curving seductively. "And here I thought you liked me for my brain."

"I do." She batted her lashes flirtatiously. "Your sense of humor, too."

He grinned. "We do know how to make each other laugh."

Which was the way they both liked it. Nice. Easy. Uncomplicated. This could be, too. If only she could make him see so…

She covered his big hand with her own. Gave it a squeeze. "And since we're already friends, with benefits, conceiving wouldn't require us to do anything we're not already doing. Except," she added, unable to prevent a self-conscious flush, "forgetting to use protection."

Clearing his throat, he looked her in the eye. "Nice as that sounds…"

Her heart took on a rapid, uneven beat.

Fearing rejection, she persuaded swiftly, "You want kids, too." She removed her hand from his, sat back. "You've said so, at least half a dozen times."

He nodded, his beautiful mouth set in a sober line. "When the time is right. Yeah, Sage, I do."

Restless, she leaped to her feet. Hands knotted at her sides, she began to pace. "What if it's never right?" She whirled back to face him then watched as he rose, too.

"What if, like me—" her tone grew as strangled as the hopes inside her "—you don't find someone and fall madly in love? What if we wait too long and then something happens and we find we're no longer as fertile as we once were and we suddenly *can't* have children? I don't want to live with that kind of regret, Nick. Especially since I've already wasted so much time."

"Chasing after Timothy Wellington."

"Terrence Whittier," she corrected, aware that was the one thing he could never get right, her ex's name. "And you're right, I don't want to do that again. Live so far in the future that I don't appreciate the here and now. I don't want that for you, either, Nick." She trod closer, hands raised beseechingly. "And since…"

She stopped, aware in her eagerness to convince him, she may have spoken a bit too bluntly.

"I've already had two broken engagements?"

Knowing she had no room to talk, given her own relationship failure, she wrapped her hand around his bicep. Felt it swell beneath her touch.

"My point is," she continued, her fingers curving intimately around the hard-packed muscle, through the soft chambray of his shirt, "you've been no more successful at finding the perfect match than I have." She stepped back, jerked in a breath, gave it one last shot. "So why not accept that the odds are against us? And simply make it happen, on our own terms."

Sage had a point, Nick knew.

Waiting might bring them everything they wanted. The kind of fantastic, enduring love he knew Sage still dreamed about—even if she wouldn't admit it. And it might bring them nothing. Hadn't he put off pursuing his long-held dreams for too long? An orphan since age ten, he knew better than anyone how short life could be. Still, there were problems with her proposition. The least of which were his growing feelings for her. Compared with the way she still felt—might always feel—about him. As a friend. A bed buddy. Nothing more.

And although their casual arrangement was fine for now—more than fine actually, since he had so much else going on, work-wise—he wasn't sure that would always be the case.

Because like most deeply ambitious souls, he knew this about himself. He always wanted more.

And that was never more true than when it came to Sage Lockhart. She was five feet nine inches of nonstop energy and enthusiasm, her slender body as feminine as it was curvaceous. With a breathtakingly beautiful face, mesmerizing golden-brown eyes, soft pink bow-shaped lips and a thick mane of wheat-colored hair that fell in soft waves to her shoulders, she drove him wild with lust. It didn't matter if she was dressed in fancy cowgirl attire, like she sported now, or the white chef's coat she wore to work, he was constantly wanting to pull her into his arms and make love to her.

Unfortunately, making her physically his wouldn't solve this dilemma.

Sobering, Nick put on the brakes. "As much as I want a family of my own, too, you know I'm married to the Monroe family business right now."

As always, at the first hint of conflict, a wall went up. "That's just it, Nick. I'm not asking that marriage be part of this equation. Not now. Not ever."

"Even when you become pregnant and/or the baby is born."

"Even then."

She said that, but did she actually mean it? Nick studied Sage skeptically. "Yet, to hear your family talk, you're one of the most hopelessly romantic women ever born."

"I used to be. Before I met you."

Ouch.

She waved an airy hand. "You made me realize that reality is better than romance any day," she confided in a sweet, matter-of-fact voice.

He tamped down his disappointment. Faced her with his legs braced apart, arms folded in front of him. "How so?"

"You and I started out as just friends."

Only, he thought, because she would have refused to date him in the tumult of the family scandal that had brought her back to Texas in early June. Then, she had wanted to concentrate on helping her shell-shocked mother clear the Lockhart name of any wrongdoing, while also figuring out what to do with her own inheritance from her late father—a commercial building, complete with a personal residence, on Laramie, Texas's historic Main Street.

Over the course of the summer, Sage had accomplished both, while her "friendship" with him had morphed into a no-strings-attached affair.

She had opened a thriving café-bistro, The Cowgirl Chef, which was just down the street from his own family venue, Monroe's Western Wear. She'd also moved off her mother's Circle H Ranch and into the apartment above her coffee shop.

"And because we got to know each other platonically first before we fell into bed, we never viewed each other through rose-colored glasses." She stepped close enough he caught the intoxicating scent of her perfume. "The point is, Nick, we were honest with each other. About everything from Day One."

Except for one thing, he thought.

How much I wanted to be with you.

Sage might have *fallen* into a sexual relationship with him, but he had known all along that he wanted to make her his woman. Luckily, she had felt the chemistry between them, too. Sighing, she looked up at him from beneath her lashes and went on, "I've never had to pretend to want things I didn't want, just to be with you. The way I did with Terrence."

Instead, he realized ironically, it was him, pretending he didn't want the things he did. Not that this current roadblock was going to stop him. He would win her heart, no matter how long it took.

"Like marriage," he guessed, keeping his attitude as ultracasual as hers.

The soft swell of her breasts rose and fell. "It's not for me." She gripped his forearms beseechingly. "And since you're as wedded to your family business as I am to my new café-bistro, we make a perfect pair."

That much he could agree on. He'd never met a woman who fascinated him the way Sage did.

That being the case, maybe he should be a gentleman, try it her way. "So how would this work?" he asked curiously. If there was anything his own joke-of-a-love-life had taught him, it was never to crowd a woman. Never jump the gun. It was slow and steady patience that would win out in the end. A tact that had moved them from friends, to lovers and possibly parents, thus far. He took her all the way into his arms. "Us having a baby together?"

Sage splayed her hands across his chest. "As you might imagine..."

Oh, he could imagine, all right, he thought, body already hardening.

"...first, we get me pregnant," she teased, her golden-brown eyes gleaming with excitement.

Nick savored the feel of her soft body pressed up against his. "Can't say I mind working on that part..." he admitted huskily, kissing her temple. It would give him ample opportunity to make love with her again and again.

And every time he made love to her, he felt her stubborn resistance to real, enduring commitment slip, just a little bit.

Sage shrugged. "Then we have the baby and parent him or her together."

"Under one roof?"

She stepped back, clamping her arms in front of her. "Well, I don't think we have to go that far..."

What if I want to go that far?

She lifted her hand before he could interject. "I think it would be smart to maintain separate residences. You can live at your family ranch, I'll keep my apartment in town. And we can care for the baby at both places. Be together as much or as little as we want."

That sounded okay, since he knew better than anyone how one thing could easily lead to another, with Sage.

Soberly, he warned, "You know, if my quest for venture capital comes through, and I can expand into half a dozen new stores in different locations the way I'd like, I'll be traveling some."

Sage smiled, unperturbed. "That's the beauty of my being here in Laramie. I have my whole family, you have yours. Between the Monroes and the Lockharts, we'll have more backup with this baby than we know what to do with whether you're in town or not."

That was true.

Was it possible they could both have everything they wanted?

Especially since marriage per se didn't mean all that much to him, either. What he really wanted was to be with Sage. Having a baby with her, well…that was the stuff of dreams, too.

"Sounds like you've got it all figured out," he drawled.

"We can have it all, Nick. Friendship. Sex. Family. Plus, the freedom to live our lives exactly as we want and pursue our careers without constraint." She toyed with the top button of his shirt. "So what do you say?"

The only thing he could if he wanted to make Sage his. He lowered his head and took possession of her lips. "Darlin'?" He kissed her again, more tenderly and persuasively now. "Consider me 'all in'…"

Chapter 2

Four months later

Nick put the closed sign on the door of Monroe's Western Wear and turned back to Sage.

Wheat-gold hair swept up into an untidy knot on the back of her head, her face glowing with the unmistakable light of happiness and maternal good health, she looked more gorgeous than he had ever seen her.

But the time for avoiding this conversation was over.

He walked through the rustic interior of the store, his attitude as stern as hers was stubborn. "Enough of this evading, Sage. We have to tell people." The sooner the better, as far as he was concerned.

Sage ducked her head to avoid meeting his gaze, and continued sorting through the stack of women's jeans. "In a couple of weeks," she murmured, zeroing in on another size up from her normal.

He resisted the urge to direct her over to the small but well-outfitted area containing denim maternity wear. Settling with his back against the heavy wood display rack, so she would have no choice but to look at him, he asked, "You really think you can keep hiding this?"

Her lower lip thrust out into a kissable pout. "The chef's coat and colorful aprons have worked so far."

Actually, Nick thought, his gaze sliding down her newly voluptuous body, they hadn't. It wasn't just the waist and hips of the garment that were snug—the double row of buttons over her newly luscious breasts were so tight, they threatened to pop off.

Deciding, however, that might not be the best thing for him to point out, he merely inclined his head. "Your family has been giving me looks."

"So?" She shrugged again. "They give everyone they think has designs on me looks."

Not, he thought, the kind of looks they'd been giving *him*. He cleared his throat, regarded her severely, tried again. "Sage…"

She started to dart past him, then stopped, spying a Bullhaven Ranch pickup truck parking in one of the slanted spaces in front of the store. Her pretty mouth dropped into an O of surprise.

"Oh, heck!" she swore, darting off in the opposite direction toward the back of the store. "There's Chance!" She ducked through the curtain that led to the storeroom, calling over her shoulder. "If he asks, I'm not here!"

Well, this ought to be fun, Nick thought wryly, as a second, then third pickup pulled up next to the first. Three tall men emerged from the driver's seats. Headed toward the front of the store.

Chance Lockhart peered around the closed sign. Gestured. He wanted in. So did his two brothers.

Figuring they may as well get this over with, Nick obliged. Garrett, Wyatt and Chance Lockhart stalked in. Not surprisingly, all three of Sage's older brothers looked loaded for bear. The only sibling not there was her Special Forces brother, Zane, who was as usual off on assignment. Garrett nodded perfunctorily at Nick. "Monroe."

This was not looking good. "What can I do for you?" Nick asked.

Wyatt jumped in with a suspicious glare. "For starters, tell us what in blazes is going on between you and Sage."

"Not sure what you mean."

Chance squinted. "Are the two of you a couple? Or what?"

It took everything Nick had to suppress a groan. "I imagine Sage would classify us in the 'or what' category."

Garrett's frown deepened. "Not funny, Monroe."

"Mom is worried sick," Chance added.

Lucille Lockhart was a wonderful woman. Kind and generous to a fault. Nick did not want to cause her grief.

"She needn't be." He would care for and protect Lucille's only female child with every fiber of his being.

"Really?" Wyatt demanded, slamming his hands on his waist. "Because from where we're standing, it looks as if Sage has some pretty big news to share."

So they did suspect, just as Nick had figured. Pushing aside his irritation that Sage had let it come to this, he said, "Then maybe you should be asking her."

The brothers' expressions turned even grimmer. "We have," Wyatt groused. "She won't tell us anything."

Sounded familiar.

Suddenly, he felt sympathy for her family, even as he remained boxed in by his first obligation, which was to Sage. "What do you want me to do?" he demanded impatiently. It wasn't like he could control Sage. No one could.

"Cowboy up," Chance said.

Garrett nodded. "Show some responsibility."

The intimation that he hadn't stung.

Nick thought about all the times he'd held Sage while she cried—uncharacteristically—over the silliest things. How he'd taken it in stride when she'd fallen asleep, mid-just-about-anything, and/or asked him not to touch her breasts because her nipples were just too sensitive. Surpassed what he really wanted—like sizzling fajitas or a big juicy rare steak—and instead dined on what she was having, even if it was ginger ale and crackers.

Resentment knotted his gut. "How do you know I haven't been?"

A skeptical silence fell.

Finally, Garrett said, "Have you asked her to marry you?"

Without warning, the curtain behind them was ripped aside. Sage stormed out, temper flaring.

This, too, was par for the course. Since conceiving, her emotions had frequently skyrocketed out of control.

"Whoa, Nellie!" Hormones raging, she marched toward her brothers, shooing them away with both arms. "You guys need to back the heck off!"

Her brothers remained where they were.

And suddenly, Nick knew what had to be done. Whether Sage liked it or not.

"They're right." He pivoted back toward her, wrapping an arm around her shoulders. "The time for pretending there's nothing going on with us has passed, darlin'."

Giving her no chance to protest, he swung back to her three brothers. "Sage is pregnant." He paused to let the words sink in. Aware in that moment he had never been prouder, or happier. "And the baby is mine."

"Well, that went badly," Nick admitted, the moment Sage's brothers had left, more than a little disappointed to find out the two of them had no plans to marry.

"You think?" Sage paced back and forth between the aisles. She'd thought Nick was on her side in this! Fuming, she gave him a sharp look. "Now it's only a matter of time before they tell Mom I'm pregnant with your child."

His eyes lit up the way they always did when he knew he'd gotten under her skin. "First of all—" Nick shrugged, as if not sure what the big deal was "—you *are* pregnant. And your brothers are right—you can't hide it much longer. So unless you cowgirl up and have that talk with your mother—and soon—they'll be forced to spill."

As always, his ultramasculine presence, the sun-warmed leather scent of him, made her feel protected and intensely aware. In an attempt to keep her equilibrium, she kept her distance from him. "That's not really a comfort to me, Nick."

He rubbed his hand across his closely shaven jaw, then lazily dropped it again, his eyes never leaving hers.

"Hey, I call it like I see it. And for the record, Sage? I'd like to tell *my* family you're carrying my baby, too!"

The bell above the door dinged.

Sage moaned, thinking it was probably her brothers, back for Round Two of Convince Sage To Do The Traditional Thing. Instead, the interloper was a gorgeous, elegantly dressed young woman Sage had never seen before.

Nick looked surprised but pleased as he moved to shake the lady's hand. "MR! What are you doing here? I thought our meeting wasn't until tomorrow."

This was the lauded MR? Sage thought in shock. From the way Nick had talked about the venture capital executive, she had imagined someone older and stodgier. Not some auburn-haired beauty sporting stylish black eyeglasses who could double as a Hollywood starlet.

Not that Nick had indicated he had noticed MR's stunning good looks.

He turned back to Sage, backtracking long enough to make introductions. "Sage, this is MR Rhodes, from Metro Equity Partners. She's the venture capital exec I've been working with. MR, this is—"

"Your fiancée?" the exec guessed tartly.

So she was stodgy after all, considering her disapproving tone as her gaze moved knowingly to Sage's tummy.

"Ah—" For the first time since the other woman had entered the store, Nick looked flummoxed.

"Baby mama?" MR guessed again, with a candid smile that did not reach her eyes.

The set of Nick's mouth was suddenly as tense as

his shoulders. "Did you want to talk business this evening?" he asked brusquely.

MR got the hint. "Briefly, I do. We're very close to getting approval from the other partners for the deal you and I have been negotiating."

A long, slow back and forth of ideas that had been going on as long as Sage had known Nick. "That's great news!" he said.

MR scowled, suddenly seeming as reluctant and unhappy as Nick had a second ago. "It would be, if you weren't in the midst of a *situation*."

Oh, dear. "Maybe I should leave," Sage said.

"No." Nick clapped a possessive hand on her shoulder. He gave her a look that said they had nothing to hide. "You stay."

Okay, then.

He turned back to MR. "What do you mean by *situation*?"

MR huffed and looked at Sage as if she were a spoiler. "The plan is to make Nick the public face of the new Western-wear stores. Have him featured prominently in every ad, with personal appearances at every location. But we can't do that if he's a deadbeat dad."

Deadbeat dad? "Nick is not shirking his responsibility," Sage said hotly.

"I know my partners. They are old-school, family men. There is no way they're going to go for the new company spokesperson—the brand representative, if you will—having a kid out of wedlock. It's just not going to happen." MR looked Nick in the eye. "So unless you want to be trapped here in this one-horse town, in this one-horse store, in perpetuity, the two of you need to get hitched. Pronto."

Sage turned to Nick in a panic. She didn't want him to lose everything he had been working so hard to achieve, any more than she wanted to be backed into a corner herself. To her relief, he reached over and gave her hand an understanding squeeze.

"What if we had the rest of my family—my three sisters and brother, and all my nephews and nieces—in the ads?" Nick proposed. "Maybe even use photos of the rest of the Monroe clan. We could go back as far as the store's beginnings, which is four generations."

"No. You are the one they want to see in all the ads. And you can see why, right?" MR turned to Sage in full business mode. "He's like a younger, hotter, tall-dark-and-handsome Ralph Lauren. Our vision and the success of the new venture hinges on Nick's sex appeal, his image as an upstanding cowboy and devoted family man. And with you pregnant, Sage, regardless of how either of you feel about it, that means marriage. ASAP."

"We can't make a decision like that on the fly," Nick countered.

"Understandable. You all need to talk about it. In the meantime, my assistant, Everett Keller, is checking into the Laramie Inn. We'd like to have dinner locally. So if you could recommend a place with fresh fish. Shrimp. Scallops. Salmon." MR picked up on Sage's distaste. "Something wrong?"

Sage shook her head. Nope. Nothing to see here.

But the ever-probing venture capitalist wouldn't let it go, so Nick placed a comforting hand on Sage's spine. "Sage got sick on shrimp early in her pregnancy. Just thinking about it makes her ill."

An understatement if there ever was one. She couldn't even look at recipes. Never mind photos of the cooked food. And she was a chef! Hopefully, the malady would pass. But for now, a simple whiff made her toss her cookies. Pronto.

"I see," MR said.

When clearly she didn't.

Eager to discuss something other than her continuing battle with morning—or in some cases, evening—sickness, Sage wrote down the name of a bed-and-breakfast located a short distance away. "They have an executive chef that's on par with the best in Dallas, and the menu and wine list to go with. You'll need reservations. But if you tell them you're here to do business with Nick and he recommended it, I'm sure they'll find a way to fit you in this evening."

"Thanks." MR looked grateful.

"No problem," Sage said.

She'd do whatever she could to help Nick.

Short of ruining everything and marrying him, of course.

"MR is right," Hope Lockhart said, a short time later, when Sage and Nick went over to her brother and sister-in-law's home. The four of them gathered in the kitchen of the Victorian, while one-year-old Max sat in his high chair and ate his dinner of green beans and diced meatballs.

A crisis manager and public relations expert, Hope had guided the family through several calamities since first meeting them the previous summer. "While there are many customers who won't care whether you or Nick ever tie the knot, there are others who will be up in arms over it," Hope told them gently. "You don't want to lose any potential business right out of the gate. Not if you want this venture to be a success."

"Think of the plus side," Garrett added, from his place at the stove. Winking, he gave the boiling pasta and spaghetti sauce another stir. "Mom will be delighted."

It was all Sage could do not to groan. "Did you all tell her yet?"

Garrett shook his head. "Like we said a while ago at the store, that news is yours to deliver, sis. I just wouldn't wait too long."

"Want to do it now?" Nick asked, as he and Sage turned down an invitation to stay for dinner and left.

The sun had set, leaving the quiet residential street bathed in the yellow glow of the streetlamps. Stars shone overhead.

Feeling the need for some support, Sage tucked her hand in Nick's and rested her chin on the solid warmth of his upper arm. "First, we need to talk about what we're going to do."

He caught her other hand and turned her to face him. "I don't expect you to marry me, Sage."

But clearly, she thought, it was what he wanted. A simple solution to a very thorny problem. "You heard what MR said. If we don't, your deal with her firm is likely off."

Nick shrugged, a distant look coming into his eyes. Sage felt about a million miles away from him. She didn't like it. In an effort to understand what was going on with him, she asked, "Did you ever tell MR you felt trapped here in Laramie?"

His broad shoulders tensed. "Not in so many words."

"So she inferred it?"

He nodded curtly.

Which had to mean, she knew Nick pretty well. Pushing aside a surge of unexpected jealousy, Sage gently pushed for more information. "Why would she do that? What did you tell her?" *That you haven't told me?*

"When I first approached Metro Equity Partners we talked a lot about the fact that the store, the custom boot-making operation and the ranch have been in my family for four generations. The fact that the women have always run the mercantile operation, the men the ranch."

"But at some point all that changed."

"When my mom and dad died in the accident when I was ten, my oldest sister, Erin, took over everything. She sold off all the cattle, but she ran the store."

"She also raised you and your three older siblings, right?"

Nick nodded gratefully. "Along with her own kids, yeah. But when she married Mac Wheeler and they added a set of twins and another baby to the three they were already raising, Erin needed to take a break from running Monroe's for a while, and just concentrate on her family life and custom boot-making—which she really loves." He released a breath. "So at my suggestion, she spun her custom boot-making operation off into a separate business entity, while I took over at Monroe's. And when she and Mac moved to Amarillo for his work, I put aside my own plans to work for a big corporation in Dallas or Houston, and stepped in permanently to run things here."

"No one else could do it?"

"It wouldn't have made sense. I was the business major in the family. My brother, Gavin, studied medicine. My twin sisters, Bess and Bridgett, are both nurses. Plus, the three of them all needed to be closer to the hospital and their patients, so while they got places in town, I moved back to the ranch to take care of the horses, too."

This was something he rarely talked about. "Doesn't sound like you had a lot of choice," Sage said.

He shrugged. "I'm the youngest. It's my turn. And the way I figure it, a business is a business. And since my goal is to build Monroe's Western Wear into what it could be—not just what it is—I'm okay with it."

She understood concessions, because she had made more than a few of her own. Often unhappily. Knowing the kind of resentment that could fester, long-term, she asked, "Would you be okay with losing this venture capital deal because of conditions I put on our arrangement?"

His expression inscrutable, he worked his jaw back and forth. "I'll find other investors."

It wasn't that easy. If it had been, she sensed he would have done this five years ago, when he first took over the family business.

She ignored the quiver, low in her belly, her need to comfort him in a very elemental way. "How long did it take you to interest Metro Equity Partners?"

"Eighteen months or so."

Which, Sage knew, could feel like a lifetime when you weren't getting what you wanted. She couldn't bear to see him disappointed. Not when she was getting everything she wanted—primarily, his baby. "It's unacceptable for you to have to go back to square one," she told him firmly.

"It's just the way it is." Shouldering the burden stoically, he exhaled. "After all, we're not talking pennies here."

She recalled what he had shared with her of the proposal, thus far. "We're talking six additional stores, opened two months apart, over the course of a year. We're talking about the many years of work you've already put in on this business plan, which is…"

"Four, give or take."

"Four years." Sage shook her head in silent remonstration, more determined than ever to make him as happy as he'd made her. "You're not giving that up. And you're especially not giving that up on account of me. Got it?"

She tapped his sternum with her index finger.

Vowing softly, "They want you married? We'll get married. ASAP. And it doesn't have to change a thing."

But, of course, Sage quickly learned, matrimony changed everything, in the blink of an eye. Not only was her mother—who'd been frankly disapproving about Sage's initial plans to have a baby on her own via artificial insemination—delighted to hear that Sage was carrying Nick's child, she was even happier when she learned that her daughter was planning to marry him right away.

"That's wonderful news!" Lucille said, tears shimmering in her eyes as she hugged them both. "But, pregnant or not, you need to do this right—"

Meaning have a big fancy wedding, Sage thought in consternation.

"—and make this a special day reflective of your enduring love for each other," Lucille finished firmly.

Except, she thought with a wince, that would make

the nuptials feel real, and she and Nick knew they weren't.

At least not the way her mother was assuming, since she hadn't told Lucille why they were suddenly heading to the altar. And she had made Hope and Garrett promise they wouldn't, either.

"If you want me to call my event planner," Lucille continued, already reaching for her phone, "I'll get right on it."

Sage gently touched Lucille's forearm. "Actually, Mom, I think Nick and I want to make all the decisions ourselves."

"All right," her mother conceded, smiling at Sage's rounded tummy. "But if you, or Nick, or the baby need me—"

"We know where to find you," she promised.

"Well, that went okay," Nick said, when they left the Circle H Ranch.

Sage savored the intimacy of being alone with Nick. She loved the steadfast way he always backed her up. "Mom's always up for more grandchildren." There were four now, and with two of her four siblings married, another engaged, hints of more to soon be on the way.

Looking as if he wouldn't want to be anywhere else, Nick drove the country roads with the same masculine ease he did everything else. "This is going to work out," he told her reassuringly, then took her hand and kissed the back of it.

Tingling all over for no reason she could figure, Sage looked over at him. "Are you sure you don't feel trapped?"

He dropped his hold on her hand. "No." Steering the car over to the berm, he put it in Park and turned to look at her. His glance sifted slowly over her face, lingering on the flush in her cheeks and her bare lips, before returning slowly to her eyes. Sage caught her breath. As their gazes locked, he rubbed a strand of her hair between his fingers. The corners of his lips curved upward. "Do you?"

Insides quivering, Sage took a moment to consider. At times like this, all she wanted to do was make love with him. Maybe because that was the one place where they felt the closest.

"Yes. No. I don't know?" she said honestly at last, meeting his playful smile with one of her own. Taking off her seat belt, she moved to wrap her arms around his broad shoulders and kiss him. "But if this will help you make all your business dreams come true," she promised tenderly, wanting to give him as much as he had given her, "I'm all for it…"

"Good to know," Nick replied, a sexy rumble emanating from his broad chest. Taking her all the way into his arms, he covered her mouth with his own. And though she had promised herself she would keep their relationship in the friends-with-benefits category, it was darn near impossible to hold back the rush of feelings inside her as she melted into his embrace. He kissed her like there was no tomorrow. Only today. Like the future would always belong to them if only she had the courage to see where the relationship between them led.

And for the moment that was enough.

More than enough, she thought wistfully. Their plans to keep their nuptials simple, and under their control, quickly went out the window, however, when they met with MR late the next morning.

"You need a big, splashy, over-the-top romantic wedding. With plenty of photos we can release to the press later, if need be. And we need to get it done in three days," the venture capital exec said.

To help with that, MR had summoned her assistant, Everett Keller, a nerdy-looking young man who was clad in spit-shined wing tips, neatly pressed slacks with suspenders and a starched purple shirt with a wildly patterned bow tie. He hovered nearby, taking notes on an electronic tablet.

Sage's eyes widened in shock. "There's no way we can pull together a wedding in that time frame!"

Nor would she want to do so.

MR arched a perfectly plucked brow. "There is if I call in every favor I'm owed, and you all and your families do the same and we have it at Nick's ranch." She paused to let her words sink in while Everett typed furiously. "Saturday evening is perfect."

Sage and Nick exchanged exasperated looks.

Neither of them liked being railroaded into anything, and MR was being awfully pushy about what was, in the end, a very personal matter.

"Let me put it another way," the elegant redhead stated bluntly. "The partners meet on Monday to hear the presentation and vote on whether or not to fund the initial phase of Nick's proposal. I can't delay the vote on this project without explaining to them why. If I do that, and you're still not married, it's over. Done. On the other hand, if you're married, and wildly in love and expecting a baby, it's not really going to matter. So you decide. You want it done by Saturday evening? Or not?"

Sage looked at Nick.

Once again he wore that poker face. But just for a second, she had seen that flash of disappointment in his eyes. The look he evidenced every time he hit a road-block in his plans to expand Monroe's Western Wear. It was the same look she'd had whenever her own dreams of having a baby incurred another snafu. The one her ex had worn whenever she talked about getting engaged, when Terrence was perfectly content with things the way they were. She was not going to be the reason for Nick's unhappiness the way she had been with her ex's.

"We'll do it," she said, forcing herself to match MR's enthusiasm. She turned to Nick, took both his hands in hers and squeezed fiercely. "Just promise me one thing." She looked deep into his eyes. "All of this won't dam-age our friendship." Because she didn't think she could live without that.

"Come on now, darlin'." He gave her a long, searing look, then wrapped an arm around her shoulders and leaned forward to buss the tip of her nose. "You and I both know I would *never* let that happen."

She heaved a sigh of relief.

Out of the corner of her eye, she saw Everett Keller pause in bemusement. Like he couldn't believe he had to stand around and witness this. MR had an intense, watchful expression on her face, too. Almost as if she were waiting for a time bomb to go off.

Sage hoped it wasn't Nick.

Splaying both her hands across his broad chest, she relaxed into his easy embrace. Met his eyes. He seemed to be taking this all in stride. But was he really? She drew a deep breath, warned, "Preparing for a wedding, even in a normal amount of time, can be really stress-ful."

She only had to recall Terrence's reaction to their brief engagement to know that.

Nick nodded. Still appearing confident, unperturbed.

So, why, Sage wondered, was *she* suddenly completely on edge?

Again, MR observed the emotion simmering just beneath the surface and stepped in to assist. "That's why Everett and I are here," she soothed. "Not just to help but to make sure that absolutely everything goes according to plan. I promise you both…this is one wedding that will go off without a hitch."

Chapter 3

Sage snuggled against Nick, luxuriating in the safe, warm feel of his big strong body. "It's a good thing we're not getting married today for real, otherwise seeing each other like this would be bad luck."

"How can seeing each other ever be bad luck?" Nick regarded her with a devilish glint in his blue eyes.

Sage inhaled the unique masculine scent of him. On impulse, she kissed his cheek, found her way to his mouth. "You know what I mean."

"I do." He studied her as if he found her as endlessly fascinating as she found him. Stroking a lazy hand down her spine, he confessed huskily, "It's been a crazy three days."

"No kidding." She sighed, her cheek brushing delectably against the sandpapery roughness of his morning beard. She so loved having him in her bed, even though his six-foot-four frame took up so much room they barely fit on the queen-sized mattress.

A problem that, now that she'd entered her second trimester, sometimes left her with a tiny backache. "So many decisions…"

He turned toward her so they had full body contact. Lower still, his hardness pressed against her. "So little time."

A spark of arousal unfurled deep inside her. "We saved some headaches by delegating a lot of them out."

MR had arranged for a justice of the peace friend to preside over the civil ceremony. She'd also provided the caterer, tent and chair setup crew—all within the budget Nick and Sage had set. Assembling the guest list and sending out last minute e-invites had gone to the sisters-in-law, Hope and Adelaide, and the seating chart delegated to Chance's fiancée, Molly. Lucille had been in charge of the flowers and the menu for the reception. While Nick and Sage had selected the DJ and the songs.

This morning, she was going to have the final fitting for her dress—a gown from her cousin Jenna Lockhart's bridal salon—at her mother's ranch while Nick picked up his tuxedo. Her brother Wyatt's wife, Adelaide, was her maid of honor. Nick's brother, Gavin, was best man.

Nick reached for Sage playfully as the first light of dawn fell through the window blinds of her second-floor apartment. "I think we have time to make love one more time…" He kissed her shoulder.

Sage wished. She eased away and went to find a thick fluffy robe to ward off the chill of the late-January morning. "Actually, we don't." Computer tablet in hand, she climbed back into bed. "We haven't written our vows yet."

Reluctant, Nick scowled. "Sure you want to do that?" he asked, practical as ever. "Instead of going with the tried and true?"

The thought of promising to love him until death do them part seemed like tempting fate. Sage swallowed. "Given the fact that we're not…" Her voice trailed off. She didn't know how to finish without insulting him. Or the connection they shared, which she had to admit pretty much defied description.

He studied her, as determined to understand her as she was him. "In love?"

Sage caught his hand in hers, and pressed it against the center of her chest. "Maybe not in the traditional way, but I do love you, Nick. As a friend. A *best* friend."

His expression was as veiled as hers was open. "I adore you, too," he said softly.

She sensed there was more. Unsure, however, as to whether or not she wanted to hear it, she murmured, "Okay, then, that's what we need to say." She settled a pillow across her lap, to use as a desk. Opened up the leather computer tablet case, turned on the attached mini keyboard and logged on.

While she got comfortable, Nick folded his arms behind his head. He lounged against the pillows, his gaze drifting over her lazily. "There's no way I can memorize anything this late in the game. I mean, I'm the kid who always flunked the English class assignments where we had to get up and recite a poem."

Although she was wearing an old-fashioned button-front nightshirt that concealed her baby bump, he was clad only in his boxer briefs. Hence, with the sheet draped low across his abdomen, she had a very nice view of his broad, masculine chest.

Too nice, if she were to remain on task.

"Public speaking pressure?" she teased, turning her gaze away from the sinewy muscle and crisp dark hair that arrowed across his pecs, and narrowed, on the way to the goody trail…

"Procrastinating, and making up excuses, are we?" she taunted.

"Mmm-hmm."

"Not going to cut it, cowboy," she retorted sternly. "We have to get this done. Right now."

His sensual lips compressed as he ran a hand through the tousled layers of his dark hair. "Maybe you should tell me yours."

"I would. Except I haven't written mine yet, either."

His low laughter filled the bedroom. He rubbed a hand beneath the sexy-rough stubble on his jaw. "Aha."

"But I will now." Cuddled up in bed, beside him, sitting against the headboard.

He rested his chin on her shoulder. "This should be interesting."

"I take thee, Nick, for my parent-in-arms?"

He shook his head. "Sounds like we're forming a club."

Sage used the mini keyboard to type in some more. "May the joy that brought us together hold us in good stead through the days ahead."

Nick wrinkled his brow, sexy as ever. "That's going to have people scratching their heads and saying *huh*."

Sage opened a new document window on the screen. "Okay, Smarty-pants. You try."

He thought a moment. "I don't know what I did to get you to look my way," he drawled finally, "but I'm sure grateful you did."

Sage snickered. "Aren't those song lyrics?"

He grinned back, allowing, "Maybe."

Only able to imagine the grief she'd get from her brothers if they went that route, Sage decreed, "I think we should be a little more original."

Nick's brow rose in annoyance. "Then we should have started this weeks ago."

"Okay," Sage said hastily. "There's no need to get testy. How about I say, 'There are no words to describe how I feel about you. I just know this feels right, and I want to be with you,' or something like that."

Nick tilted his head. "Pretty good. Vague. But truthful."

Sage grinned, glad an argument—which would have been their first—had been averted. "Now all we have to do is add to it. Refine it a little. And then come up with something equally reassuring for you to say, too."

Nick wasn't sure who Sage was trying to pacify with this whole writing-their-own-vows stuff, but if it made her feel better, then he was all for it. The hectic nature of the last three days had been hard on her. She looked weary. And that couldn't be good for her or the baby.

So when she declared them done, a short while later, hit the print command and then ran over to her printer to pull out two sheets of paper, one for her and one for him, he celebrated by kissing her again.

One thing led to another.

The next thing they knew she really was late, and so was he. They split up, heading their separate ways. He did not see her again until she walked down the aisle on her eldest brother Garrett's arm.

As she glided toward him, looking like a princess out

of some Disney movie, his heart caught in his chest. She was so damn gorgeous in that ball gown–style wedding dress. So sweet and innocent and glowing. He felt like the luckiest man in the world. And would have even if she hadn't been carrying his child and on the verge of giving him the family of his own he had always wanted.

"Who giveth the bride away?" the JP asked.

Garrett lifted Sage's veil, kissed her cheek and answered, "Her family and I do."

Sage's lower lip quivered.

In that second, Nick realized what a disservice he had done. This was hard enough without his deceased parents and her late father here to see this. But to secretly be doing it all for a business deal… He swore silently to himself as he took her hand, vowing he would make it up to her. Some way. Somehow.

The distinguished-looking sixtysomething justice of the peace welcomed everyone to their nuptials. He spoke briefly about the grave responsibility entailed in entering into a marriage.

A speech that only made Nick feel all the guiltier.

"And now we will turn it over to Nick and Sage, who have written their own vows. Sage, would you like to go first?"

She nodded, hands trembling as she unfolded the page. Looking down, she began reading nervously, "Nick. There are no watercress…"

A few smothered chuckles.

The justice of the peace gave everyone a sharp look.

Aware of the solemnity of the occasion, everyone fell silent once again.

Sage shook her head, her brow pleating worrisomely as she squinted. "Sorry. There are no *words* that would adequately describe how I feel about you, Nick." She looked up with a smile, then read confidently from the paper in her hand, "So, I'm just going to say, I think yeast…"

Another undercurrent of nervous giggles.

Sage blushed.

Nick slid a hand beneath her forearm to steady her, aware she wouldn't be the first bride to wilt from a combination of nerves, and in their case, guilt. Resolved to help her through this, he encouraged under his breath, "Just calm down. You got this."

Sage nodded. Jerking in a deep breath, tried again. "I think *you* are the most wonderful mango…" She looked up, clearly mortified. "I mean, *man* I've ever known. And…" She swiftly scanned the page, looking even more distressed. "I think I'm going to just say I'm really happy to be marrying you today. And *stop* right there."

Radiating embarrassment, she gestured at him. "On to you."

Nick had never known Sage to fall apart like this. But given how quickly everything had happened, he figured she was entitled to suffer the same kind of public speaking phobia that had haunted him as a kid, and cut her speech short.

With a grin, he removed the paper from the inner pocket of his tuxedo jacket and unfolded it. Still holding her eyes, wordlessly promising that he would make this okay for both of them with the best recitation he had ever given in his life, he looked down at his vows. And began. "Sage. You are the most brioche…" He stopped and shook his head while trying to quickly remember what should have been there.

If this is what "his bride" had been dealing with, no wonder she'd panicked!

Ignoring the faint titters in their audience, he tried again. "The most um…most…*beautiful* woman I've ever met, inside and out."

Whew! High five on that one!

"And if there is one thing today is going to show us," he continued determinedly, glad to be back on track, "it's that we will otters have each other."

Otters?

What the hell?

And then, amid the muffled rumble of new laughter, he realized what had happened. There was no need to go on reading from the pages Sage had printed out for them. Not unless they wanted this to turn into even more of a comedy skit.

He turned to face their guests and held up the page for everyone to see. "So much for writing our vows on an electronic device with autocorrect," he announced, grinning from ear to ear. "Seriously, folks—" getting into the spirit of the hilarity he crumpled it up dramatically, and tossed it to one of his sisters in the front row "—proofread!"

With a mischievous grin, Sage crumpled up her vows, and tossed 'em to family, too.

Taking both his bride's hands in his he made an executive decision and decided, "We're just going to have to do this on the fly."

Ignoring her prior worry about the results of any extemporaneous speech, he paused and looked deep into her eyes, then said what had been on his mind since the day they'd decided to risk this.

"I used to think that life had to be lived in stages. If

I was going to have a family, I needed to find someone compatible and get married right out of college." He paused ruefully, to let his prior idiocy sink in. "A plan that did not work for so many reasons…"

He hadn't been anywhere mature enough. Hadn't known the first thing about love. Might still not…at least when it came to the traditional variety.

Aware the world had shrunk to just the two of them, he looked deep into her eyes and continued, "And then, and only then, would I focus on my career goals. Secure the future. And when that was all set, then I could have kids."

Understanding lit her eyes. She'd had similar expectations. It was one of the things that had drawn them together.

"But despite my ambition, it didn't work out that way. And I began to think that my work dreams and goals were all I was going to have." His throat tightened unexpectedly. He forced himself to go on hoarsely. "Then I met you, Sage, and I realized things didn't have to happen in any specific time frame or in any particular order. We could be friends. And then more than friends. And now parents-to-be of the no doubt most amazing child who will ever be born in Laramie County!"

Laughter rippled through the attendees as the world around them crowded in once again.

Happiness roaring through him with the force of a white-water river, he squeezed her hands and said, "In the seven months we've known each other, you've brought so much happiness to my life, I can imagine just how fantastic the rest of our time together will be. And darlin', I can't wait to experience it all with you," he finished soberly, a lump rising in his throat.

* * *

Because she could see Nick meant every single word he said, Sage's eyes misted over, too.

Grinning, she continued to hold on to him as fiercely as he was holding on to her. "Okay, cowboy." She heaved a sigh of relief. "If you get a do over with our vows, so do I! So here goes…" Taking comfort in the encouragement his steady regard offered, she jerked in a bolstering breath. "I never thought after everything that happened to me leading up to this point that I would want to be involved again." *Or risk a relationship that could stomp my soul to pieces.*

"But then I met you, and everything changed for me, too. I wanted friendship." *Deep, abiding, tell-each-other-almost-everything friendship that was eventually supplemented by deliciously sensual, mind-blowing passion.* "And then, a baby, and now here we are getting married," she exclaimed excitedly.

Her nerves calmed as she went on. "We've laid the right groundwork."

The corners of his lips quirked up in a way that let her know he could not have agreed more with her assessment.

Their eyes still locked, Sage pushed on, promising Nick, "We're going to have a happy life together. And when our baby gets here at some point close to Father's Day—" an astonishing present in and of itself "—you're right, we're going to be even happier than either of us ever dreamed."

Nick leaned in as if to kiss her.

Her heart fluttered.

The JP clamped a restraining hand on Nick's shoulder. "Whoa, there, pardner. We're not done yet. We've still got the rings and the official pronouncement to go."

Nick grunted, his lips hovering just above hers, then reluctantly drew back.

"You're right," he said finally to one and all, as everyone smiled and laughed yet again. "We've definitely got to get this done right."

No kidding, Sage thought.

This was beginning to feel like a whole lot more than the extension of their previous arrangement that they had privately agreed it would be.

Following their purposefully abbreviated next steps, Nick slid the wedding ring on Sage's finger. "Sage, I take thee to be my lawful wedded wife."

Sage followed suit and put a simple gold band on Nick's left hand. "Nick, I take thee to be my lawful wedded husband," she said.

"Then by the power vested in me," the JP said finally, "I pronounce you husband and wife."

Nick gathered her in his arms.

As he kissed her, a roar of approval went up, matched only by the relief and joy whisking through Sage.

Several hours later, Sage stared in the master suite bathroom mirror. "You really think my tiara is crooked?"

Lucille shook her head, tears abruptly misting her eyes. "No. I just wanted a moment alone with you before the evening ended."

"Oh, Mom." Sage turned and gave her mother a hug. This was a big day for both of them. All of it happening a little too fast for comfort.

On the other hand, had they had more time to consider, Sage wasn't sure she would've been able to go through with it. Because, no matter how fond she and Nick were of each other, at the end of the day, it all felt a little dishonest.

Lucille perched on the edge of Nick's bed and patted the place next to her.

Carefully arranging the poofy skirt of her wedding gown, Sage settled beside her mother. "What is it?" she asked softly.

"I just wanted to tell you how happy I am for you tonight."

"You mean that?"

Lucille nodded. "I confess, I had my doubts when you told me you and Nick were going to get married. I thought it all might have been related to his business somehow. Especially when the venture capitalist he's been working with—"

"MR Rhodes."

"—and her assistant, Everett Keller, became so involved in the execution of the wedding plans."

Sage tamped down her guilt. It was bad enough she and Nick were being disingenuous. They did not need to bring anyone else into it who wasn't already. "We kind of needed everyone to pitch in to make this happen, Mom."

"I know, and MR and Everett have both been wonderful, as has everyone."

"But…?"

Lucille worried the diamond necklace around her neck. The one Sage's father had given her mother for their fortieth wedding anniversary. "I'm just concerned you and Nick were going into this the same way you did having a baby together. Hastily and without forethought."

Her mother's elegant brow furrowed. "And that feeling was confirmed when the two of you started your wedding vows. But—" she paused, shaking her head "—then you started speaking what was in your hearts. The way you looked at each other—with such tenderness, faith and affection—I knew those feelings the two of you have worked so hard to keep private are genuine."

Lucille took Sage's hands in hers. "Bottom line... your dad would have been *so proud* of you tonight."

But would he really have?

Sage was still worrying about that throughout her and Nick's final dance of the evening.

Still wondering if she and Nick had done the right thing after all, when he pressed a kiss in her hair and then drew back to look down at her tenderly.

"Ready for one last surprise?" he asked huskily.

Chapter 4

Sage looked at Nick in much the same way he imagined he had looked, half an hour earlier, when he had received the news.

"A honeymoon?" she repeated as if she couldn't possibly have heard him right.

He continued slow dancing with her. She felt so good in his arms, and he lamented the fact that their just-best-friends-slash-lovers rules had made this romantic activity off-limits, until now. "Three nights at The Mansion, in Dallas."

Sage drew in a shuddering breath. "One of the most romantic hotels in the city."

So he'd been informed. "It's a gift from Metro Equity Partners. MR told me about it a few minutes ago. The limo is out in the drive. Your brothers are decorating it with the Just Married stuff now."

Sage winced. "Not tin cans."

"And the obligatory sign designating us as newly-weds," he told her with barely checked amusement.

As the last song stopped, so did they. She covered her face with her hand, then peered at him through spread fingers. "We're supposed to go tonight?" she asked, aghast.

There was no debating it. She looked dead on her feet.

Belatedly, he realized what a long few days it had been for her, in her pregnant state. They'd both been going since well before dawn. To expect her to endure another two-and-a-half-hour drive was probably way out of line. "We can wait until tomorrow," he soothed. "Drive there ourselves. Check in then."

Sage looked tempted, but remained careful of his feelings and commitments as always. "How is that going to be perceived?"

Hard to say, since he had yet to meet most of the partners who would be voting on his proposal.

"You know what, forget I even said that." Sage squared her slender shoulders, as if she were going into battle. "It's never a good idea to look a gift horse in the mouth. Particularly when you have the biggest business deal of your life pending."

Bless her generous heart. "You're sure you want to do this?"

She nodded, then said with her newfound practicality, "What's the alternative, anyway? Go back to our original plan, spend the night in my apartment and forego any celebration of our nuptials?" She rose on tiptoe and whispered seductively in his ear, "If we go to Dallas, at least we'll have our privacy."

Given the scrutiny they'd been under all evening, there was definitely something to be said for that.

"Wake up, sleepyhead," Nick murmured in Sage's ear, several hours later.

With effort, she opened her eyes. They were indeed at the luxury hotel. Apparently, she'd slept the entire journey. "What time is it?" she asked, blinking herself awake.

"Two thirty."

He still looked good. More than good, actually, in that dark tuxedo.

She smothered a yawn and tore her eyes from the hard sinew of his chest beneath his snowy white shirt. "Sorry I was such bad company."

He hugged her close, then kissed her temple and the top of her head. "I slept, too."

She drew back slightly and tipped her head up to his. He was definitely wide-awake now. With plenty of energy. The kind that usually presaged incredible lovemaking.

She tingled all over, just thinking about it.

His sexy grin widening, he teased, "Ready for the best part of the entire festivity?"

She placed a hand flirtatiously across her heart. She did not have to pretend to feel swept away. "Oh my."

His low masculine laugh filled the interior of the limo. "Oh my is right." He brought her close for a long lingering kiss, ended only by the intrusion of their driver opening the door. Nick emerged first, then assisted her in getting out, not an easy thing, given the fact that they were still in their wedding finery and the silk chiffon skirt of her dress was poufed enough to disguise her pregnancy. The driver followed them with the bags they had hastily packed before leaving Laramie County. Nick at his ranch house, she at her apartment on her way out of town.

They swept through the lobby, getting grins from everyone who saw them. "Congratulations!" more than one person called out as they signed in.

The bellhop escorted them to their suite and set their suitcases in the bedroom. He returned with a flourish, announcing, "Metro Equity Partners thought you might be in need of a late-night supper. So…" Another uniformed attendant rolled a room service table into the living room.

Silver-domed dishes were placed on an elegantly made-up table for two, next to an ice bucket containing a bottle of exquisite champagne, sparkling water and ginger ale.

Which was good, Sage thought.

Because now that she was awake, she was feeling a little nauseated. She wondered if there were any crackers in the minibar. If not, the elegant dinner rolls in the basket would probably take the edge off.

She smiled appreciatively as Nick tipped the attendants. "Seems like the partners have thought of everything."

"Let us know if we can do anything else." The attendants disappeared.

"I don't know about you, but I'm starved," Nick said.

He took off the lids with a flourish.

The roasted filet mignon and butter poached lobster tail had her feeling a little iffy, but it was the garlic prawns with Cajun aioli that really sent Sage over the edge.

* * *

"Sage, come on, open the door."

She leaned over the toilet bowl, arms folded over the cool porcelain. "No."

"I sent all the fish away."

She closed her eyes against the husky rumble of his voice. "You didn't have to do that."

"Ah, actually, Sage? I kind of think I did."

How could he maintain his sense of humor when she had just ruined everything? She moaned again, in even more distress. "I'm sorry."

The other door that opened up off the bedroom, the one she hadn't time or foresight to lock, swung inward. Nick strolled in. "What do you have to be sorry about?" He knelt down beside her.

He cupped a hand beneath her chin, and regarded her tenderly. "You're pregnant. I'm the one who should have thought to ask what was in there first, before lifting the room service domes and treating you to all those aromas."

The memory of the sights and smells made her shudder with distaste.

"I'm guessing it was the shrimp."

"Prawns," she admitted with difficulty. "And yes." My heavens, yes.

He stroked a hand through her hair—or tried—the elegantly upswept curls were still heavily lacquered into place. "I've seen people throw up before, you know." He wet a washcloth with cool water, wrung it out and placed it on the back of her neck.

She wallowed in her misery. "You haven't seen me."

He gazed at her possessively. "If we're living together, that is going to change."

What was he talking about? Sage sat back on her haunches and stared at him. "Living together?" she repeated.

"Well—" he shrugged, pausing to get comfortable, too "—now that we're married, I figured we'd spend the night together whenever I am in town, and then when the baby comes, and I don't have to travel so much…"

As much as Sage wanted to lean on him then, the way she was now, she wasn't sure it was a good idea. "You know this isn't a real marriage." More like a convenient arrangement. For business reasons.

"It can still be any kind of union we want it to be."

Why did he have to look so sexy? Especially under these circumstances? He should be irritated. Repelled. Not ready to move in with her!

Proceeding cautiously, she asked, "What kind of union do you want it to be?"

Mischief twinkled in his deep blue eyes. "The kind where we have a lot of great sex."

Sage rolled her eyes. "You would say that now." *When I've just finished throwing up and feel and look like death warmed over.*

Chivalrously, Nick helped her to her feet. "And have long talks," he said. "The kind that last all night."

She could go with that. It was what brought them together in the first place.

Tilting her head to study him closely, she murmured, "Or times when we say nothing at all, and it's still okay."

"Sounds good to me."

Shakily, she headed for her suitcase to get her toiletries bag. Nick stood by, ready to help if need be, as she removed her toothpaste and brush and then returned to the bathroom. Still fighting residual waves of nausea, Sage tried not to think how intimate this all was. "What else?"

He lounged a short distance away as she brushed her teeth, then handed her a towel. "I'd like to know we could be apart and still do our own thing and still be okay."

Sage blotted her mouth. "We will be."

He smoothed a stray curl from her cheek and admitted softly, "And I'd like to think that when the baby comes, we'll also enjoy spending lots of time together as a family, as we adjust to those new roles."

Strangely enough, she'd been able to picture that from the first, even before they'd made love or she asked him to father their child.

Sage glanced in the mirror, noting her tiara really was askew. She wondered for how long it had been. Perching on the cushioned stool, she began working the pins out of her upswept hair.

When she still couldn't get the glittering headpiece free, he moved to help her. His fingers moving gently in her hair, he worked it out and then set it on the bathroom counter. "What about you?" he asked gruffly. "What kind of parameters do you think our marriage should have?"

"I guess I want pretty much what we had before. We're only together when we want to be. We don't owe each other phone calls. Or have to check in. Or feel in any other way constrained. What is yours is yours, what is mine is mine."

The smile on his lips reached his eyes. "Except for this baby we're having."

"Which is *ours*," Sage agreed wholeheartedly.

A comfortable silence fell.

"Feeling better now?" Nick asked.

Not exactly. But rather than dwell on the ever-present queasiness, Sage drew a deeply constrained breath and gestured at the formfitting bodice. "I will be as soon as I get out of this damn petticoat and dress."

He laughed, low and deep. "I think I can help you with that."

Unfortunately, no sooner had he started to ease the zipper down, than Sage felt that unmistakable urge to be sick. Again.

Hand to his chest, she shoved him back out of the bathroom, and slammed the door in his face.

And was sick, sick, sick…

Finally, the retching stopped.

Some honeymoon, Sage thought miserably, still hugging the porcelain.

This time Nick didn't ask to come in.

As soon as the commode flushed, he opened the door and walked in. All big protective male. "Your stomach empty?"

Sage nodded weakly. "I think so."

Once again, he assisted her to her feet. "You need to go to bed."

"Nick…"

He rolled his eyes. "Not for that, sweetheart. For some much-needed sleep." He turned her around. Eased the rest of the zipper down, and assisted her out of the skirt and petticoat.

His brows lifted appreciatively at her sexy wedding lingerie. Sage hadn't thought it necessary at the time. Although what else she would have worn under such a romantic dress, she did not know.

Now, however, if they hadn't been dealing with the

catastrophe of evening sickness, she could see where it would have come in handy.

But certainly not now.

Once again, he rushed to her aid. He grabbed a thick and fluffy white spa robe from the hanger in the bathroom, eased her arms into it, then guided her to the bed.

Appreciating the warmth and softness of the garment, almost as much as she appreciated his kindness, Sage wrapped it around her. "Could you do me a favor and see if you can find me some saltines?"

"Sure thing." He looked in the minibar, then slammed it shut. "Be right back." He eased out of the hotel room.

She changed into her light-blue-and-white floral pajamas, then climbed beneath the bed covers.

It took fifteen minutes and a personal visit with the manager to the room service kitchen, but Nick rushed back with a big bowl of crisp saltine crackers, and another bottle of chilled ginger ale in hand. Only to find Sage curled up in the big hotel bed, fast asleep.

Aware, despite everything, that this was one of the best days of his entire life, he got ready for bed and climbed in beside her, wrapping her in his arms.

She snuggled against him.

The next thing Nick knew the bedside phone was ringing. Loudly.

Sage moaned in distress. He felt the same.

He reached across her to answer it, thinking this better be good. "Yep?"

"Nick, MR."

What the…

"Who is it?" Sage slid up on her elbows, looking so

delectably tousled he had to tamp down the desire to make love to her then and there.

She blinked furiously. "Is anything wrong?" she continued.

"Our families are all fine," Nick immediately reassured Sage. So far as he knew, anyway.

Still struggling to wake up, he rubbed the sleep from his eyes, asked, "What's going on, MR?"

"My assistant and I are in the lobby."

A lot of words went through Nick's mind. None of them pleasant. He shoved a hand through his hair. "Why?"

"We need to talk. Can we come up?"

Only able to imagine how his new wife might take such an intrusion, Nick said gruffly, "It might be better if I came down there."

Sage shook her head, grabbed his arm. As always, not one to put herself first. "It's fine," she mouthed and slipped from the bed.

Nick swore silently. There went his plans to really pamper Sage this morning. Make up for the horrendous sickness the night before.

Figuring they might as well get whatever-this-was over with, he ordered tersely, "Come on up."

He had just finished dressing when the knock sounded outside the suite. Barefoot, angry, he walked to the door.

"Yeah?" he said, as MR brushed by him, Everett in tow. Both were clad in the type of business attire they usually wore. While Sage had come out of the bathroom and was standing there in her pajamas and robe.

She'd brushed her hair, or tried. Whatever they had done to it before the wedding had left it a glorious curly mess. Her cheeks were bright pink, too, although he sensed that was as much from embarrassment as anything else.

MR looked stunned. "You were still asleep?"

Nick wrapped his arm protectively about Sage's waist. "It's barely nine in the morning." And given the fact that Sage hadn't stopped throwing up until almost 4:00 a.m., hell, yes, they were still asleep!

MR said, "We have a partner meeting tomorrow afternoon to prepare for."

As if he could forget. Still…

He had just gotten married last night.

Even if it was, to his regret, purely for business purposes.

The business proposal for Metro Equity Partners, on the other hand, was something they had been fine-tuning for months.

Nick felt Sage slip away and move to a chair to sit down. "You want to do that now?" It was an effort to remain professional.

MR nodded briskly. "At the office. Sage can stay here, of course."

"How long do you think it will take?" He worked to keep the irritation out of his voice.

"Until we're finished." MR shrugged. "I didn't think this would be a problem, since you only married so this deal would go through."

"It's not," Sage returned shortly. "Take care of business. You don't need to worry about me."

MR brightened. "Thank you for your professionalism, Sage."

"We've got a car and driver on standby to take you wherever you would like to go today," Everett said.

For Sage, that decision seemed easy. "Then I'd like to go home. To Laramie, Texas."

Disappointment roiled through him.

The last thing they needed was to start their marriage off on the wrong foot, as this certainly would.

Nick pivoted to Sage, determined to salvage what they could. "Look, I know it's not ideal. But you could go back to bed now, get some more sleep. Maybe go shopping or to a movie this afternoon. Or enjoy some of the spa services the hotel offers." He paused to let his suggestion sink in. "And we could still have dinner tonight."

For a moment, Sage was tempted. She and Nick'd had so little time together over the past few days prepping for their nuptials, and their wedding night had been a total bust. She had been hoping to make up for it this morning, to leave them both with better memories.

But before she could agree to his proposal, MR cut in briskly. "I'm not so sure about your being back in time for an intimate dinner, Nick. But Sage could join us at the office for our meetings. That is—" she turned back to Sage "—if Nick is okay with your knowing that much about his business."

This was becoming way too complicated, Sage thought. Furthermore, she did not want to put him on the spot. She'd rather leave things as they were. With him sharing whatever he liked about his work situation, and no more.

Plus, she sensed his "work session" with MR and Everett, would go better without anyone else present to distract them. So, reluctantly, even though she sort of felt like a coward for deserting him, she bailed.

"Honestly, Nick," she fibbed, "I just want to go back to my apartment."

He pulled her aside, the concern in his eyes almost as thrilling as his sexy presence. "You're sure about this?"

Her heart pounding, even as her spirits sank, Sage nodded. "I have to work tomorrow. So do you. So... I really do have to go back."

Noting he seemed ready to argue, she curved a hand around his forearm. "This proposal is important, Nick." She looked deep into his eyes. "You need to be here with MR and Everett to prepare for the pitch. And be ready for any questions the other partners might have."

MR nodded her approval. "When do you want to leave?"

"Ten minutes?" Sage returned.

She slipped back into the bathroom, bag in tow, washed her face and brushed her teeth, and put on her jeans, shirt and boots.

"I'll walk you down," Nick said when she was ready.

The last thing Sage wanted was an emotional goodbye. And given the way she was feeling...she was just pregnant enough, just hormonal and disappointed enough, to burst into tears at the slightest provocation. So, she faked courage she couldn't begin to feel. "Not to worry, cowboy." She slipped her bag over her shoulder and looped her wedding dress over her arm. "I've got this."

"Actually..." Everett stepped in dutifully to take her suitcase. "I've got it."

Was it her imagination or did Nick look as torn as she felt inside about her leaving? Enough to ask her— once again—to stay? Because if he had...

Oblivious to her secret yearning, he leaned over to kiss her brow and promised instead, "I'll call you."

Not trusting herself to speak, Sage merely nodded, then slipped out the door.

Once again, she got a lot of looks as she walked through the lobby, her wedding finery folded over her arm.

This time, none of them were envious.

Maybe because her mood wasn't exactly celebratory.

Luckily, the town car was waiting at the curb, as promised. Everett held the door for her, while the driver set her bag in the trunk. As the chauffeur climbed behind the wheel, Everett motioned for Sage to roll her window down.

She obliged. MR's trusted assistant paused, still looking young in the face, but suddenly much, much older in the eyes. Like he had seen too much. "You seem like a really nice person," he said at last.

Perplexed, Sage smiled. What was going on here?

She shrugged. "I hope so."

He seemed to struggle with something. Finally, he looked her right in the eye and said, "Everyone is going to tell you that you gained a husband last night."

She kind of had, Sage thought. Although no one but she and Nick knew just how unconventional their arrangement was.

"But that's not what happened," Everett continued.

Sage sensed a warning underlying his low, almost cordial tone. It was as if he knew something she didn't. Her pulse skittering, she pulled herself together and asked nervously, "Then what did?"

He sobered even more. "You lost your best friend."

Shock reverberated through her. "Nick?" she repeated in disbelief.

The young man nodded pityingly, the grimness of his conviction making her lose her breath.

"And don't let anyone tell you any different." He stepped back and, before she could ask him to clarify further, directed the driver to go.

Chapter 5

"Hey," Luisa Vasquez said, stopping in shock as she walked through the back door to The Cowgirl Chef kitchen Sunday evening to get a jump start on the baking for the following day. As usual, the gifted baker was wearing a denim skirt, T-shirt and sneakers, and had her long inky black hair in a French braid. "What are you doing here? I thought you weren't going to be back from your honeymoon for a couple of days."

Sage tried not to blush. "Neither Nick nor I can afford to take that much time off right now."

"You sure?" her assistant manager said. "Because I can handle things here for as long as necessary. It's not like I don't know all your recipes by heart. Or have enough help to carry us."

Sage knew that. She had hired two full-time baristas to handle the coffee and tea machines, another part-time bakery chef in addition to herself and Luisa, and four rotating cashiers/waitstaff, who arranged their hours around family responsibilities and/or college classes. All together, they were quite a team.

"I'm not planning to stay much longer." Sage cut rich and buttery triple-berry scone dough into wedges, and put them on parchment paper–lined baking sheets that would go in the walk-in until morning, when they'd be freshly baked.

Luisa took over rolling out the buttermilk biscuit dough. She eyed Sage carefully. "Nick doesn't mind?"

"He's working, too. In Dallas."

Silence fell. "You sure you're okay?"

"Why wouldn't I be?"

"Post-wedding blues. I had them when I married Carlos."

Sage put the ready-to-bake goods in the walk-in and began spooning out the nutrition-packed breakfast cookies. "That's hard to believe." She sent her assistant an admiring glance. "Sixteen years, six kids later, and you two are still so much in love."

So much so, in fact, they almost made Sage think happily-ever-after endings were possible for couples, after all.

"I know. But back then—" Luisa shook her head ruefully "—when we returned from our honeymoon, which was only a couple of days, and moved into our first home, which was in dire need of renovation, I hit the wall, hard. I kept thinking, is this all there is?"

Sage understood that. It was exactly how she felt right now.

"Plus—" Luisa sighed "—we had wedding bills that

had to be paid so Carlos and I were both pulling extra shifts. It was tough going for a while."

Sage observed, "You seem to have recovered nicely."

Luisa gave her a brief hug. "And you will, too, *if* that's all it is."

Despair coiled within Sage, but outwardly she shrugged. "What else could it be?"

Luisa squinted. "Why don't you tell me?"

Sage knew she had to tell someone her fear or she would burst. She helped Luisa cut out mini rounds for the quiches she was preparing and press them into individual pans. "Can I ask you something?"

"Always."

"You and Carlos are more than husband and wife. You're best friends, aren't you?"

"Have been from the first day we met," Luisa said proudly. "It's one of the things that makes our marriage so strong."

Sage bit her lip. "You don't think that could ever change?"

"No. Why? Are you worried your friendship with Nick might?"

Sage paused. "I want to believe nothing could ever endanger the bonds Nick and I have forged over the last seven months. And that with time, our relationship will only grow stronger…"

But Everett's partings words that morning bothered her.

She still couldn't figure out why MR's assistant had felt the need to warn her as she left Dallas. The efficient, fashionably dressed young man had not struck her as a busybody. Rather, the opposite. Which made his behavior seem all the weirder. Since he really didn't know her or Nick.

Sage knew she should let it go, the way she would have any other attempts to meddle in her life.

And she tried.

All night Sunday, and most of Monday, while working at The Cowgirl Chef. She was still trying that evening when her mother stopped by her apartment around dinnertime, a couple of stray wedding gifts in hand.

Sage thanked her and set them on the counter.

Looking as gorgeous as usual in one of her stylish outfits, Lucille eyed the stacks of yet-to-be-opened presents. "You haven't looked at *any* of those yet?"

"I'm waiting for Nick." But the truth was, it felt almost dishonest opening them, given the reason why she and Nick had tied the knot.

Her mom glanced around. "Where is he?"

"Meetings in Dallas."

Lucille blinked. "That couldn't have been delayed?"

Sage shrugged. "There was no reason to do so."

Lucille worried the pearls around her neck. "How about the fact that the two of you just got married less than forty-five hours ago?"

"It's just business, Mom."

Scoffing, Lucille returned, "That's what your father used to say to me."

Sage folded her arms in front of her, resentment like a river running through her. "I don't remember you complaining at the time." Her dad's devotion to the hedge fund he created had allowed them all to live a life of luxury.

Lucille's gaze turned troubled. "Maybe I should

have. Frank didn't have nearly enough time with me or you kids when you all were growing up."

Sage knew that, too. And lamented it. But since there was nothing that could be done about it now, she tried to look on the bright side. "He made up for it the last few years of his life, Mom." In fact, their whole family had grown closer during her dad's illness.

"I know," Lucille said softly. "And I'm glad he had that opportunity to really get to know each and every one of you before his heart gave out completely. But it would have been better if he'd been present more when you were little, too."

A lump formed in Sage's throat. She had missed her dad at the wedding. She missed him now. She suspected her mother did, too. She moved in to give her mother a brief, reassuring hug. "Nick's going to be a good father, Mom."

Lucille returned the hug, then stepped back to look her in the eye. "But what kind of husband is he going to be?"

Another good question. One, she felt, because of the deal she and Nick had made to maintain independent lives, that she shouldn't even be asking herself. Sage's phone rang. She smiled when she saw the caller ID. "Speak of my handsome husband! There's Nick now..."

Lucille patted her arm. "I'll let you talk to him, dear. But when you're finished, if you want to have dinner at the ranch with the rest of the family tonight, come on out."

Sage nodded and put the phone to her ear.

Lucille left.

"Hey," Sage said, wishing for a moment she had gone

against instinct and stayed on in Dallas for a few days, so she could be with Nick now.

He chuckled warmly. "Hey, yourself."

The sexy rumble of his voice did funny things to her insides. Immediately, she felt both better—and more hopelessly lonely, too. Which again was something she had promised herself she would not do—tie her happiness to someone else's presence in her life.

Attempting to maintain some emotional distance, she asked casually, "How'd it go?"

"They voted yes." Nick's triumph resonated between them.

Sage could not help but smile.

"With some stipulations, of course," he added.

"That's great news!"

In the background, she heard a throat clearing. Then Everett's distinct voice, "MR wants you to know your reservation has been extended at The Mansion for the rest of the week."

Did that mean Nick wasn't coming back to Laramie? Sage wondered with a stab of disappointment.

She guessed it made sense.

"MR will have my head if you don't get back in there," Everett continued.

Nick said something she couldn't quite catch.

Aware she did not want to be the ball and chain dragging him down, even if they were now "married," she forced herself to sound chipper. "Listen, I can tell you're busy, so I'll let you go."

Unexpected tears pricking her eyes, she ended the call.

The silence in her apartment had never seemed louder.

She sat slumped on the sofa, aware she hadn't felt this bereft since she'd been living with Terrence. Waiting for what seemed an eternity for him to come home from his IT job. Only to have him shovel in the dinner she had so lovingly made for him, get right back on his computer and go back to work, again.

He'd said he was doing it so they could live well, and since he made a lot more money than she did, she had not felt she could complain.

And she never had, not even on the day he had told her he wanted out of their relationship, out of their engagement, out of their living together arrangement.

Because he had felt trapped.

The ironic thing was, she had been trapped, too. Albeit of a situation of her own making. And she had not realized it until Terrence blurted out the truth of what he was thinking and feeling.

She could not go back to that loneliness and misery.

Not with Nick.

Not with anyone.

Furthermore, Sage decided resolutely, she wasn't going to. So she had an evening ahead of her. It was the perfect time to relish the solitude and pamper herself. And, by heavens, she would.

Three hours later, Sage was deep into relaxation. Conditioner slathered in her freshly shampooed hair, pore-cleaning face mask on, she settled down on the sofa with a pint of Blue Bell's Rocky Road and a spoon.

And that was when the knock sounded. Figuring it was one of her brothers, sent by her mother to check on her, she shouted, "Go. Away."

Another knock.

She ignored it and turned up the volume on the TV instead.

A more persistent knock. Followed by what she thought might have been "Sage!" although it was hard to tell, the sound on the program she was watching was so loud.

More knocking.

Sage sighed and closed her eyes. "I don't need—" *or want*, she added silently "—company!" she shouted again.

This time the lock clicked.

Only a few people had keys to her place.

Her mother.

And…

Oh, no no no no no!

The door swung open.

Nick stood framed in the portal, wearing a Hugo Boss suit and tie. Which was odd. She'd never seen him dress city slick. But then, he'd never been pitching a deal to a venture capital group, either. Although his expression was maddeningly inscrutable, she'd never felt so utterly embarrassed.

Seeing each other at their absolute worst had never been part of their arrangement.

It was all fun, fun, fun!

At least until she had become pregnant. Then, there had been a few all-too-real moments. Crowned by her wedding night hurling episode. Which, she was sure, even though he had been utterly decent about it, had left him feeling "charmed."

And now, to follow that humiliation, with this?

Oh, my heavens. He was never going to want to make love with her again.

And what woman in her right mind could blame him?

Doing her best to appear casual, Sage leaned forward and set her ice cream and spoon on the coffee table in front of her. Belatedly aware the neck of her thick white spa robe was gaping, she pulled it closed at her nape. Great. Now, he probably guessed she was naked beneath the robe, too. Something he might not have known, given the thickness of the terry cloth, if she had not just flashed him.

She regarded him coolly, doing her best to hide her mortification. "What are you doing here?"

An affable grin splitting his handsome face, he shut the door behind him and sauntered across the width of the living room. "I came to see you."

Despite her efforts to contain it, her temper rose. "Well, you can't—" she waved an airy hand "—not when I'm in the middle of all this."

"Too late." His gaze drifted to the wedding gown hanging from the bedroom door, still waiting to go to the specialty cleaners, then he chuckled and yanked loose the knot of his tie. Unfastened the first two buttons on his shirt. "I already have." He sank down beside her on the sofa, to her relief appearing more friend than unexpected "husband" at the moment. He made a perplexed face. "What's the stuff in your hair?"

Didn't the guy have three sisters? Surely, they had used it. "Deep conditioner," Sage enunciated clearly.

His eyes tracked lower to the aqua-green substance now hardening on her face. Lifted an inquisitive brow.

Was she going to have to explain everything? Lord help her, now she was really going to lose her temper.

"A face mask," she said even more clearly.

He kicked off his Italian loafers—another thing she had never seen him wear. "Hmm."

As always, he smelled like soap and man and sun-warmed leather and spice.

He also needed a shave.

Although the rim of evening shadow on his jaw made him look faintly dangerous, in the pirate-about-to-ravish-a-fair-maiden way.

Sage didn't know whether to nudge him with her elbow for showing up unannounced—or kiss him for showing up. How was it he always knew when she needed to see him and be with him? Even when she said she didn't?

Finding refuge in their repartee, she propped an elbow on her hip and echoed wryly, "Hmm? That's all you've got to say?"

He paused to get more comfortable, stretching his long legs over her coffee table. "Well, I could tell you that you look fetching…" He grinned, folding his hands behind his head. "And you kind of do…in a sort of un-wrap-the-present-to-discover-just-what's-underneath way…"

She imagined he did want to get her naked.

As much as she wanted to wait—until the usual barriers around her heart were firmly resurrected. Still, it was time for the mask to come off.

She shook her head at him. Rose wordlessly, disappeared into the bathroom and removed the face mask.

Her face pink and glowing, she walked back into the living room.

"What happened to the weeklong reservation at The Mansion?" she asked curiously, aware she still had nothing on beneath her robe.

And suspected he still knew it, too.

"Canceled."

Needing to do something besides throwing herself into his arms, or worse, inviting him into the shower with her, Sage picked up the ice-cream container, took one last bite of Rocky Road, then offered him the same. "You're not going to be in Dallas?"

Smiling appreciatively, he savored the decadent mixture of chocolate, nuts and marshmallow on his tongue. Then handed the spoon back. "At the end of the week, but I'm not going to be staying at that hotel."

"Why not?" she asked, curious.

"Way too expensive. And way too much room for just me."

Sage had grown up with people who turned up their noses at anything but the most elite accommodations. That was one of the things she liked about Nick, the fact that he could be so practical and down-to-earth. Jealousy clenched inside her. "What did MR say to that?"

A few days ago, he'd been worried about offending the venture capital folks.

Nick sobered. "She understands that under normal circumstances I prefer to make my own arrangements. Even if she and her partners are picking up the tab for all travel, per our agreement.

"The only reason I let them gift us with a couple of nights stay there in the first place was because I thought you might like it—having grown up in a swanky neighborhood in Dallas and all—and because I forgot to arrange for a honeymoon for us."

Surely that wasn't guilt she saw reflected in his gorgeous blue eyes. It wasn't as if she had planned anything for their wedding night, either. Or even stayed around to enjoy the spoils of the proffered luxury.

She re-capped the ice cream and put it away. "It's not as if we were getting married in the real sense."

Silence fell.

"I'm pretty sure it was legal."

The thought of being tied to him forever made her catch her breath. "You know what I mean."

Mischief sparkled in his smile. "I do…"

"Then…?"

He shrugged his broad shoulders nonchalantly, but there was nothing detached about the look on his face. He sauntered closer. All hot, hungering male. His come-hither grin widened. "Seems like hot sex is one of the perks of saying our I Do's."

It certainly should have been.

Hiding her disappointment about how her recent pregnancy-induced aversion to shrimp had eliminated that on their wedding night, Sage shrugged. "Oh, well…" Maybe those days were about over with, any-way. With the sexual mystique gone and her waistband expanding…

He sobered. "So how are you feeling? Overall?" His gaze drifted over her kindly. "Any more nausea?"

Aware she was close to falling for him in the tra-ditional way they had both wholeheartedly agreed to avoid, she squared her shoulders and said, "No."

Satisfaction radiated from him. "That's good."

Silence fell between them. The kind they usually filled with hot kisses, and more. But not when she had a headful of goop.

Figuring maybe she should at least offer to whip

something up for him, before sending him on his way, she said, "Did you have dinner?"

"On the road. You?"

She nodded. "One of the requirements of pregnancy. You have to eat regularly." She amended self-consciously, "Something more than ice cream."

He nodded, understanding a craving was a craving. Particularly in her state.

Suddenly aware she wasn't in a hurry for him to leave after all, she paused. "You mind if I jump in the shower and rinse this goop out of my hair?"

His gaze drifting over her lazily, he shook his head. "Mind if I make myself at home while you do?"

Trying not to read too much into her suddenly racing heart, Sage murmured, "Go right ahead."

Nick waited until Sage had disappeared into the bedroom, then eased back out into the hall outside her apartment. There, he had everything he needed.

And it was a good thing, too. Since his bride was every bit as overwrought and worked up as he had figured she would be. She might tell him everything that had happened to them the last week or so was no big deal. But he knew it was.

What lay ahead of them was even more important, he thought, as he quickly made preparations. Which was why he had to take the reins in their relationship. At least for now…

He had just finished setting up when the door to the bedroom eased open once again.

Sage paused in the portal, blinking as her eyes adjusted to the candlelight. She finished running the towel over her wet hair, then let it fall limply to her side. "What are you doing?"

"You really don't know?"

For a moment, she looked as if she might hazard a guess, then pulled back and said warily, "Haven't a clue. So suppose you tell me, cowboy."

Once again, all the barriers around her heart were up.

He smiled. Her feistiness didn't deter him in the slightest. He ambled toward her, slowly and purposefully, then said, "I'm here to claim our wedding night."

Chapter 6

Sage jerked in a quavering breath. "That's really funny, Nick."

He let his gaze drift over her, taking in her sweet lusciousness from head to toe. She had put on a pair of soft gray leggings that ended just below her knee, leaving her shapely calves, trim ankles and delicate bare feet in full view.

An oversize blue denim shirt fell past her hips, disguising the budding changes in her lithe body nearly as well as the chef's coats she wore to work.

Her hair was still damp, falling in silky dark gold waves to her shoulders. Her lips bare and soft and mutinous.

He could hardly blame her for acting guarded. Spiriting her off for an unexpected honeymoon, which he stupidly hadn't planned, and then ditching her early the next morning to go to work had *not* been cool. Regret lashed through him. She'd tried to hide it but he'd seen the stricken look on her face. The forty-eight hours since the wedding had been a total and utter disaster. And he had no one to blame but himself.

But he had every intention of making it up to her. Right here. Right now.

He spread his arms wide on either side of him, forcing himself to be the gentleman he had been raised to be. "I'm not joking."

Her chin lifted indignantly. "Well, you should be. Because need I remind you?" The color in her cheeks deepened. "We aren't really joined in the state of holy matrimony, at least not in the usual sense."

"Which ought to make this all the more entertaining. Since—" he let his gaze drop to the nipples pearling beneath the soft fabric of her shirt "—we won't be constrained in any way."

"Except one." She walked over to examine the bottles of sparkling apple juice and water, on ice. She opened the fruit beverage and poured some into two of the champagne flutes he had provided. Walking over to where he stood, she handed him one. "I'm really not in the mood for any faux romance."

Wow, she was prickly tonight. Pregnancy hormones? Or pissed-off woman? Luckily, he was braced for both.

"Neither am I." He took their empty glasses and set them aside. "Still, I think it's important to get back in the saddle as soon as possible, and replace some not-so-great recollections with new and improved memories."

Wrapping one arm around her waist, he hauled her closer. Dropped his head and kissed her neck.

He murmured, "Perhaps some mood music?" Reaching for his phone, he scrolled down the playlist. Found the song that made her laugh every time.

The sound of Marvin Gaye's "Let's Get It On" filled her apartment. She groaned and dropped her head comically to the width of his shoulder. "No."

He searched some more. Hit the more upbeat "Lookin' For A Good Time" by Lady Antebellum.

She chuckled in defiance and glided away from him. Propping both her fists on her luscious hips, she said, "I'm sensing a theme here."

So was he. He two-stepped closer. "And the answer is…?"

Wary stubbornness glittered in her eyes. "No…"

Of course that was her answer.

Because she knew if she relented, let the guard around her heart down just a little bit, what would happen. What he had long hoped would happen.

Determined to end the unexpected tension that had sprung up between them, he hit Stop and then Play again.

The first strains of John Legend's "All Of Me" floated in the air. The beauty of the music brought forth tears. Something he had seen before. And remembered.

She caught her breath, and he knew he had hit a home run. Wordlessly, he closed the distance between them and took her hand.

The beautiful music surrounded them. She melted against him as he wrapped her in his arms again.

He'd half expected her to keep holding back on him,

out of both residual anger and disappointment, and her ever-present need to keep them from getting too close. But she wreathed her arms around his neck, opened her mouth to the plundering pressure of his and let her body soften against him.

He'd thought the times they had made love, up to now, had been sweet and incredibly satisfying. But those times were nothing compared to this, as he tangled his hands in the silky dampness of her hair, and she kissed him back with a wildness beyond his most erotic dreams.

She trembled in his arms, and he moved his lips to the lobe of her ear, the hollow beneath. "Let's go to bed," she whispered.

Not an invitation he would refuse. Keeping his arms around her, he danced her slowly backward into her bedroom, kissing her all the while. Her lips were ravenous against his, and for once she didn't try to hide how she felt. Nor, as she moaned softly and curled up against him even more, did he.

And yet, he thought, as the sweet urgency of desire swept through him, making love with Sage had never been a simple thing. Much as she might wish it so. By her own admission, she had kept the need in her locked tightly away. And put her own romantic yearnings aside, too.

Their marriage was supposed to be a means to an end, nothing more.

Yet, as he felt the soft surrender of her body pressed against the rock-hard demand of his, their union felt all too real.

And that gave him pause.

He had been raised to never take advantage. To put his cards on the table and let the chips fall where they may. And he knew he had deceived her about the depth of his feelings from the very first. He lifted his head and looked into her eyes. "You know I never meant to mislead you," he began.

She bent her head and concentrated on unbuttoning his shirt. "You haven't."

He tried again as she opened the fabric and ran her hands lovingly over his chest. "Our relationship—"

Her hands dropped to his belt. "Is exactly the way we want it to be," she purred.

Sage didn't understand what was with Nick tonight. All she did know was that she did not want to see the guilt and regret suddenly reflected in his deep blue eyes. Any more than she wanted to feel the conflict that had been rising up within herself since the moment they had said their I Do's.

It was as if everything had changed. And nothing had changed. And she wanted things that were both frustratingly undefined, and just out of reach. She wanted them to be together for more than just business. Or their baby. She wanted them to love each other with wild romantic abandon, and make a commitment to each other that lasted the rest of their lives.

But this was not what they had promised each other. And she did not want Nick to feel as trapped—by her demands—as Terrence had.

So she returned to the things that bound her and Nick together from the very first. Friendship and fun, explosive sex.

Slipping back into the role of carefree vixen, she eased his pants away from his waist. Or tried. He caught her palms in his, and held them out on either side of her. Eyes gleaming, he decreed, "Ladies first."

She both hated and loved it when he took charge like this. It made her feel far too vulnerable, too ripe for his taking. Her breath caught in her throat. "Nick…"

Too late, he had let go of her wrists and was already busy divesting her of her shirt and stretchy cotton bra. With her breasts bared to his view, he looked his fill, in a way that had her nipples crowning all the more.

Sexy grin widening, he stripped her leggings and panties down her legs. Knowing by now it was hopeless to fight it—she would be battling against the flame of desire that could only be doused one way—she rested her hands on his shoulders and stepped out of both.

Then, instead of rising, he wrapped his arms around her and pressed his lips against her for the most thrilling of kisses. Her knees buckled, just like that. He chuckled in masculine satisfaction, and kept right on exploring. While she held on for dear life, he dallied provocatively, finding her every sweet spot with ease. Trying not to think about what the newly proprietary nature of his lovemaking meant, or how close she was to surrendering every ounce of her fast-dwindling independence, Sage drew in a shuddering breath. Aware she felt both ravished and cherished. "Nick…" *My Lord, Nick!*

Eyes glimmering with mischief, he gave her body one last affectionate squeeze, then rose. "You're probably right," he teased, "we do need to get more comfortable."

Not exactly where she'd been going. But…who was she to quibble with success? Or near success, anyway?

Her insides melting like butter on a hot stove, Sage watched him hungrily. Tall frame radiating barely leashed energy, Nick dispensed with his own clothes, shifted her backward and stretched out next to her on the bed.

"Now…where were we?" he growled.

As if he didn't know.

"I think it's my turn, cowboy." In an effort to regain control, she attempted to flip him onto his back. To no avail. It was like budging a boulder. A very hard, very big boulder of intense male energy.

She swallowed as right before her eyes, his arousal grew. "If you're ready…"

"We're taking our time." A decision, not a request.

Sage gulped. What was going on with him? "Nick." She tried again to assert some control.

"Sage." He mimicked her low tone perfectly.

Her throat went even drier.

"Let me."

Two words. One indomitable, hungry, oh-so-male look. And she opened herself up to him like a flower in the spring.

He kissed his way up and down, over every inch of her body.

When she came apart in his hands way too soon, he held her until the aftershocks stopped, then moved upward, as resolute and unstoppable as the general of a conquering army. Palms beneath her hips, he rested his weight on his knees. Lifting her gently, brought her up flush against him.

Just that quickly, she found heaven.

She could feel his body pulsing with the same fierce, unquenchable need she had seen etched on his face, as they began to kiss again. Passionately at first. Then more gently. She arched against him in abject surrender. His mouth moved inexorably over hers, tempting, teasing, claiming. She moaned as he gave another kiss, more soulful and exciting than the last. And then, without warning, he brought her closer still, and they were one. Moving toward a single goal, climbing ever higher. Until unable to help herself, she soared over the edge, this time taking him with her.

Long moments passed, as they continued to hold each other in replete silence. Shuddering. The sound of their ragged breaths still meshing, their heartbeats slowing in unison.

Nick ducked his head. As if savoring the way she felt in his arms. The essence that was just her.

Sage found herself doing the same.

She didn't want to want her new "husband" with this incredible, soul-deep intensity.

But she did.

She didn't want to need him in ways that she sensed could never be undone.

And yet she did. And that could be the ruin of them both.

For long moments after, Nick and Sage snuggled close. As always, neither of them was in any hurry to move away and Sage felt the surge of contentment and inner peace that only he could give.

Yet as he stroked her hair and continued to hold her

close, Sage could sense something was on Nick's mind. Finally, he asked, "Feeling better?"

Sage cuddled closer, the heat from his body still engulfing hers. She knew the effective businessman in Nick liked to identify and address problems before they snowballed out of control, but it unnerved her when he put the same skill set to their relationship. Hoping to avoid any serious talk, she lifted her head. Smiling. Shrugged. "What makes you think I wasn't okay when you got here?"

He held her eyes. "Call it 'husbandly' intuition."

His candid words unsettled her in a way she didn't expect. Maybe because, deep down, a part of her wished that they did have the potential for something more than friendship. Passion. And now a child they would share, and love, together.

But the boundaries in their relationship had been established early on. And there was no sense in fixing what wasn't broken, she told herself sternly. Especially now, with so much at stake.

She eased from the bed, and to keep them from making love again when she was suddenly feeling so vulnerable, began to dress. "I admit I've been feeling a little depressed."

His dark brow furrowed. "How come?"

Sage turned away from his searching gaze, as always leery of revealing too much. "Luisa calls it the post-wedding blues. She says it's the way all brides feel after the big day and the honeymoon, or in our case, the one that wasn't."

Reluctantly, Nick followed her lead. Putting the charcoal gray suit pants and shirt on.

Tenderness and understanding radiated in his gaze. "Listen, I know the past forty-eight hours haven't been the best, but I promise, I'll make it up to you."

She bet he would. The way he just had. In bed.

As for the rest…

His business was going to have to continue to take priority for him. As would the oft-unexpected rigors of her pregnancy for her.

Which meant, married or not, she couldn't let herself expect more—from either of them.

She walked into the other room of her apartment and headed for the small but well-outfitted kitchen.

He took a seat at the island and watched her move about the work area, doing what she always did when she was stressed-out. Cook.

Nick rested his forearms on the granite countertop. "So what is the cure for the post-wedding blues supposed to be?" he asked, in that low, husky voice that melted her from the inside out.

Sage got out a loaf of sourdough, ham, eggs, spinach, onion, gruyere and cream. "Settling into normal married life, realizing that it can be even more wonderful and magical than the ceremony."

He considered Luisa's theory dubiously. "Sounds like a lot of pressure on day-to-day living."

Which they both knew, especially when they weren't together, could be as dull as watching paint dry.

"My thoughts exactly. The thing is, I don't know how we're going to avoid dealing with it," she said as she layered torn pieces of bread into the bottom of a glass casserole, than began to whisk the eggs and cream.

"There's already so much expectation for us to personify the ultimate in passionate romance because we're…"

"Newlyweds?"

Sage added butter to the skillet on the stove and began to sauté the onion, Once again aware how cozy and right this all felt. "It was one thing to be expecting a baby together. I mean, no one knew for a few months but the two of us and my doctor. But still, there is a happiness associated with the coming birth of a child that we both felt."

"And still feel," he murmured affectionately.

Sage forced herself to continue. "And it wasn't hard, because until we announced our happy news to everyone last week, we weren't having to *pretend* the way we are now."

He gave her a quizzical look.

"About the marriage and everything," she explained self-consciously, putting the rest of Nick's favorite breakfast strata together. "The real reason behind us getting hitched in the first place."

"We're both consenting adults, Sage. I don't think anyone thinks it was a shotgun wedding, even if you are pregnant."

He paused to let his words sink in. "Whether our families approved or disapproved, we could easily have not gotten married, if that was what we wanted. People who know us—know how strong-willed and independent we both are—know that getting hitched was a *choice* we both made."

Except there hadn't been a choice, Sage thought unhappily, given the way MR and the other venture partners had insisted.

"And we made that choice happily," he finished emphatically.

She could see that was true—for him.

For her, the decision was a lot more complex, in retrospect.

Which was really ironic. She'd gone from being the woman who once "unfairly pressured and ensnared" her ex into a long-term relationship—at least to hear Terrence tell it—to the one in the equation who felt imprisoned by circumstances way beyond her control. At least if she wanted the man in her life to be as happy and fulfilled as he could be…

Aware Nick still didn't seem to get what the problem was, she covered the prepared dish and put it into her refrigerator to bake first thing the next morning.

She brought the dirty dishes over to the sink, as did he, and began putting them in her dishwasher. "I don't want the intimate details of our decision to wed to be common knowledge." As she straightened, her hip bumped against his.

Swallowing, Sage lifted her chin and continued, "It's bad enough Hope and Garrett know." Although both her brother and sister-in-law had been sworn to secrecy, and she knew they would keep their confidence, it still rankled, realizing she and Nick had been pushed into this.

It had seemed so simple and easy at the time.

Now…

Was Everett Keller, right?

Was she on the verge of losing her best friend? And all because she'd made Nick her husband?

His mood as quietly accepting as hers was troubled

and pensive, Nick went to her fridge. He helped himself to the Texas beer and a container of spicy mixed nuts, which she kept on hand just for him. While he lounged against the counter, enjoying his own snack, she got out a spoon and the carton of Rocky Road she had been working on when he arrived.

Together, they moved to the sofa. As she settled cross-legged next to him, Nick continued to study her curiously. "I agree that we're entitled to our privacy."

Good, Sage thought, relieved.

"So...why do you think we have to do anything besides make it clear to people that we're good together and really happy about the coming baby? Why do you think we have to *pretend* anything?"

Sage spooned up some of the frozen treat with more than her usual concentration. "I guess we don't, but..." With effort, she looked up into his imploring blue gaze. "We live here. And I at least will still be working here full-time, even if you're gone a lot." Sage paused, and as her next thought occured, she confirmed, "You *will* be gone a lot...?"

Nick nodded.

"For the next three or four months," he affirmed matter-of-factly. "After that, I plan to be here a lot more than I'm gone."

Relief filtered through her. Again, she pushed it aside.

She didn't *need* a husband. She didn't *need* Nick. She could want him, and cherish him, and she did...but she had to be as okay without him as she was with him if she wanted to be happy from here on out.

His mood turning sultry, he ran a hand lazily down her thigh to her knee. "So what else is on your mind?"

He was going to get wind of the rumors she'd begun to hear that morning, whether she told him or not. So maybe it was better it came from her. "Until I moved to town you were a very eligible bachelor."

"Not sure I'd put it that way."

"Trust me. Women were lined up to go out with you." She mugged at him playfully. "You were just too busy plotting your next business maneuvers to notice."

"And your point is...?"

She fought a flush with only partial success.

"Now that the news about our pregnancy has spread, I feel like everyone is looking at me, wondering if I trapped you into this situation via my pregnancy."

"You didn't."

"I know that. And you know that..." But now that the rings were on their fingers, it was open season on the speculation.

Nick set his beer aside. "Do you want me to take out an ad in the *Laramie Bugle* newspaper? It could say something like 'I, Nick Monroe, impregnated this woman with all my heart and soul...'"

She couldn't help but laugh.

Shaking her head, she leaned forward to elbow him lightly in the side. "I don't think that's going to solve our problem, cowboy. But you're right, it would definitely end the 'ensnared' storyline."

He squinted comically. "I could tell everyone *you* proposed joint parenthood to *me*."

Which was, unlikely as it might seem to outsiders, the truth. Sage put a hand to her temple to mime ward-ing off a migraine. "Ah. Please don't. My mother would hang both of us out to dry!"

And after arguing bitterly with her mom the previous summer about her proposed plans to have a baby on her own, Sage did not want to do that.

Her mom was the only parent she had left.

She did not want to disappoint Lucille, even if it meant concealing the truth. Something she also did not want to do. Which left her between a rock and a hard place.

Nick reflected, "We could just amp up the whole newlywed routine. Appear ecstatically happy." He removed the pillow behind her and lifted her over onto his lap. "Make out in public and stuff."

Back to sex again. As always. Not that she usually minded. She set her ice cream aside and wreathed her arms about his neck. "You're a dangerous distraction, you know that, cowboy?"

He flashed a wicked smile, kissing her temple, her cheek, her lips, then said softly, seductively, "There's a lot more where that came from, darlin'." Excitement roared through her as he found her mouth, indulging in a long, hot kiss that quickly had passion sweeping through her.

Long moments later, they drew apart. Sage had only to look into his eyes and feel his hardness to know he wanted to table this discussion indefinitely and take her to bed again. And while she fully intended to take him up on that invitation eventually, she put a staying hand to his chest. "As tempted as I am, let's get serious here for a moment, Nick. How are we going to quash the scrutiny? 'Cause with you gone, I really don't want to be pitied." *Or feel reason to be.*

Nick lifted her wrist to his lips, and kissed the inside of it. "You could travel *with* me some of the time."

And depend on him even more than she already was? Ignoring the new tingling the kiss engendered, her own growing need, Sage shook her head. "I did that once."

He tensed but his expression did not change. "With Terrence?"

Finding she suddenly needed her physical space, Sage got up to put her ice cream away again.

"I spent seven years following my ex from job to job. I lived in Silicon Valley, San Francisco, Portland and Seattle. And quit job after job, all to be with him."

He lifted his shoulder in a hapless manner. "You were engaged, weren't you?"

"In the end. Because I really wanted to be, and we both felt obligated, because of all the time we had spent together, to make it work. Only to find out…" Her voice caught. Suddenly, she was glad they had the width of the living area between them.

"What?" he asked gently.

Maybe she needed to tell someone. Maybe then the unbearable humiliation would end. She began wiping down the counters. "That Terrence had never really wanted to be with me that long, after all," she said in a low, choked voice. "He just hadn't known how to break up with me. So he'd let himself remain trapped in the convenience of it all."

A muscle ticked in Nick's jaw, the way it did over any injustice that was done to her. His gaze seemed fixed on her hand. "Sounds like a real jackass," he growled.

Sage sighed and put the spray bottle of cleaner and paper towels away. "I was at fault, too. I saw the signs, but I just kept thinking if I could somehow keep the romance in our relationship alive, I could make it all work in the end." She paced the length of her kitchen restlessly. "We'd have this grandiose happily-ever-after life that I know now doesn't even exist."

Slowly, deliberately, Nick got to his feet. "What do you mean 'it doesn't exist'?" he asked casually.

He neared her, his big body filling up the space.

Sage lounged against the counter. "You know, the fairy tale most of the girls I grew up with…believed in." She had to tip her head back to see his handsome face. "You grow up thinking that you'll go to college and get the perfect job, and find the perfect mate, and get married and have kids and live happily-ever-after." She shook her head sadly. "But nothing is ever perfect, Nick. Not even close. Because in reality, I have to create my own happiness. Not make it contingent on anyone else."

Even you, Nick.

Nick knew when he was in trouble, and he was in big trouble now. Calling on every ounce of persuasiveness he possessed, he moved toward Sage and said, "Look. I understand your disappointment over a failed relationship. I felt it too when both my engagements went bust."

The tension in her shoulders eased slightly. "You never said why exactly that happened."

There wasn't much to tell. "I did the same things,

both times. Pushed too hard, too fast, to achieve the kind of happiness you say doesn't exist."

Her lower lip forming a delicious pout, Sage folded her arms in front of her. "It doesn't. At least not outside of fairy tales."

In no hurry to engage her in further argument, he studied her for a good long time. "Well, let's just say after losing both my folks in an accident at age ten, I wished like hell that it had, back then. So I could have the complete family life I lost." And in fact, he still wished it.

Only now the fantasy had a particular woman starring in it, and she was standing right in front of him, her heart suddenly on her sleeve.

"Oh, Nick…"

Figuring if she had heard this much, she might as well know the rest, he looked her in the eye and said, "It was foolish to try to take a simple infatuation and turn it into more. But the fallout made me slow down. Temper my expectations just a little bit."

"Which is when you met me."

He couldn't help but grin at the feisty memory. "Who also had 'tempered' expectations." To the point, she'd told him flat-out she wasn't going to "date" anybody. Hence, he'd detoured onto the just-friends zone.

"See?" She smiled despite herself. "We're a match made in practicality."

Nick just wished that was all he wanted from Sage. But even being her lover and husband in name only wasn't enough.

Her soft hands lifted in a conciliatory manner. "And now we're having a baby together."

He ignored the erratic intake of her breath and the clear definition of her breasts beneath the loose shirt. "That's right, sweetheart. We've got an awful lot to be thankful for right now. So, maybe we should just use that—" *and our increasingly intense feelings* "—to keep the gossip at bay."

She blushed prettily and kept her eyes on his. "What do you mean?"

He moved toward her and planted a hand on the counter on either side of her. "I suggest we give everyone as much truth as they can handle. And let 'em know how happy we are, and have been for months now, even before the whole baby and marriage thing. Tell them we didn't say anything to anyone because we didn't want to risk jinxing the best thing that had ever happened to either of us." Which was, for him at least, the complete and honest truth.

"You think that will work?"

Loving the warmth and softness of her, as much as the yearning in her lovely eyes, he said, "I think relaxing about everything is always worth a try." Unable to keep himself from touching her, he plucked a stray curl from her cheek and tucked it behind her ear. "And speaking of upcoming events..." He paused to let his gaze rove her upturned face. "Didn't you tell me you had an ultrasound coming up?"

Sage radiated with excitement. "When I hit the five-month mark."

"Still want me to be there?" Thus far, she hadn't seen the need to invite him to any of the appointments. Except that one.

Sage merely nodded. Then she bit her lip, looking almost afraid to hope for too much again. "Do you think it will be possible?"

He wrapped both his arms around her and hugged her close. For a moment appreciating the soft surrender of her body against his. "I'll be certain that it is," he told her gruffly. "Wild horses couldn't keep me away."

Chapter 7

Sage sat next to Nick when he talked with his four siblings at Triple Canyon Ranch late afternoon the following day. As his wife, he'd explained, she was now expected to attend the Monroe family business meetings, whenever possible. "Although I originally hoped to expand Monroe's Western Wear into a multi-location corporation, with venture capital money, it's become clear that is just not going to work. So, the new business is going to be an entirely new and separate entity."

"Your new business partners were okay with that?" Gavin asked his brother with his usual directness.

Nick slanted Sage a self-assured look, then turned back to his sibs. "They understand all five of us inherited equal shares in Monroe's Western Wear and the ranch. And that although I draw a salary for running the store, the profits are already split five ways, and will continue to be. There simply wouldn't be enough re-turn on their investment for them to be involved, as is."

Nick passed out the papers the lawyers had prepared. "Hence their decision to go with something entirely new, while still utilizing my knowledge of the Western-wear clothing business."

Pretty, blonde Erin scanned hers. "How much money are you putting in?"

"None," Nick reported succinctly. "In exchange for my work in getting the projected six new stores up and running, I'll get a 49 percent share, while Metro Equity Partners will retain 51 percent ownership. The eventual profits will be split the same way."

"You're okay, not being in control?" Bess asked with a heartfelt concern Sage shared.

Nick shrugged haphazardly. "I've got a son or daugh-ter on the way."

Which wasn't exactly an answer to the question, Sage thought. Not sure that aspect of the deal was going to be as easy for Nick as he seemed to think now.

"Not to mention a wife to support," Gavin added.

As all eyes turned to her, Sage flushed. She had tried to tell Nick that she did not belong at what was in essence a private Monroe family meeting. That she could sign the necessary legal papers at another time, but he had insisted. Even though his two older married siblings hadn't brought their spouses.

"Nick and I agreed before we married not to share our assets," she explained, looking everyone in the eye, "so I won't be laying claim to any profits he reaps. And vice versa."

Her pronouncement was met with a mixture of un-derstanding and approval from the two younger unmarried siblings, and skepticism from the two older married ones.

As if sensing she felt more ill at ease than ever, Nick reached over and squeezed Sage's hand. "The bottom line is I'd prefer not to empty my bank accounts for a start-up. I'm happy just to put in my time and effort and have all my travel expenses paid. If it's the success everyone expects it to be, I'll be making plenty of money in the long run."

Sage hoped so. She knew how much financial success meant to Nick. As much as it had to her dad.

"I'm guessing you'll have to travel a lot?" Bridgett asked.

"In the beginning," Nick confirmed.

"What about the ranch?" Gavin queried.

"I've already hired a married couple to take care of the property and the horses."

Erin's glance drifted to Sage's tummy and the baby she was carrying. "Where is Sage going to stay?" she asked with maternal concern.

As all eyes turned to her, Sage spoke up. "In my apartment, in town."

"When I'm gone," Nick said, with a clarifying look aimed her way. "When I'm here, she'll be with me, at the ranch."

This was news to Sage. But again, was something everyone would expect in a happily-married couple. So she nodded agreeably, even though she and Nick hadn't actually come to a consensus. Generally, they just did whatever they felt like at that moment.

Silence fell.

"So what do you need from us?" Erin asked.

"Your signatures on the partnership agreement, stating your rights extend only to the ranch and the flagship business, not any new ventures. Sage, as my wife, you will need to sign, too."

The pages were passed around.

Signatures gained.

Nick collected the papers, and collated them into one neat stack. He looked at his siblings. The dining room was so silent you could have heard a pin drop.

To Sage's acute disappointment, there was none of the happiness or congratulations she would have expected. And Nick needed.

"Okay," he said shortly, unable to completely conceal his hurt. "Obviously, you all have reservations. Let's hear 'em."

"Life is really short," Bess, a nurse who worked with rehabbing vets said. "Are you sure you want to spend it on the road?"

Her twin, Bridgett, an NICU nurse at the hospital, predicted worriedly, "You're not going to want to leave that little baby, once he or she is born."

Erin, the oldest, who had run the store and the ranch herself a number of years, said, "I know it can look easy, from the outside, but running the store in Laramie is pretty time-consuming on its own."

Which was why, everyone knew, Erin'd had to step down and just focus on her young family and custom boot-making business.

Gavin, an ER physician, added, "The money sounds great."

"But...?" Nick prodded with a frown.

Gavin shrugged. "I just can't see you kowtowing to someone else's business plan."

Wow. Sage blinked. Before she knew it she was on

her feet, her hands flat on the table in front of her. Aware she had never felt more protective of anyone in her life, she chastened all four of Nick's siblings with one sweeping glance. "I think this is an incredible opportunity for your brother. He's worked hard and is deserving of your congratulations." *Not your private reservations!*

"You're absolutely right," a chastened Erin swiftly agreed. With an apologetic smile, she rose and walked around to embrace Nick warmly. "Sorry, little brother."

His three sibs followed suit, offering handshakes and hugs, too. The meeting over, everyone left to return to their own obligations. Nick lingered on the front porch of the ranch house beside her. The evening stretched out ahead, breezy and cool. He turned, his emotions locked up tight as a drum. "You didn't have to jump to my defense like that."

Yes, Nick, I did.

I couldn't bear to see you so momentarily beaten down.

"Hey," she teased softly, wary of coming on too strong for fear of pushing him away or further adding to his misery. "What are wives for?"

Sadness tinged his smile. "You've got a point," he returned.

He'd been there for her, so many times. It was her time to be there for him. Sage stretched out her hand. "Come on, cowboy." She winked. "I've got just the thing."

An hour later, they had taken his pickup to the highest point on the Triple Canyon ranch. "I can't say I'm surprised your idea involved an intimate dinner for just the two of us, given how much you like to cook. But can I say how glad I am it involved the kind of food only you can prepare?"

Sage grinned.

"And the back of a pickup truck." He gestured magnanimously. "And the view of the three canyons at sunset." For which his family's ranch had been named.

Sage leaned against the back of the cab, her legs stretched out on the thick layer of blankets lining the truck bed. "I've never seen anything this beautiful," she murmured as they polished off the last of the steak tacos. "How come you never brought me up here to see the sunset before now?"

He put their dishes into the basket. Tucked her into the curve of his arm and kissed her temple, teasing, "'Cause I figured you'd fall in love with the land and not me."

Love.

She just wished their emotions were that intense.

"Sorry." He mugged. "Bad joke."

Sage drew a deep breath, and looked out at the purple-and-pink streaks against the backdrop of the slowly darkening Texas sky. "No offense taken."

The only reason she was even the tiniest bit upset was that this whole adventure was so damn romantic. To the point that the promise of never bringing anything as problematic as love into their relationship was getting difficult.

Nick moved far enough away to see her face, and took her hand. "Something's off."

"I was just thinking about your sibs' reaction," she fibbed.

Nick took her hand in his. "From their point of view,

they probably have a right to be worried. I am the baby of the family, you know. After my folks died when I was ten, everyone had a part in raising me."

She liked it when he confided in her like this. It made her feel closer to him. "Let me guess. You were the rebel."

He squeezed her fingers companionably. "More like a wannabe Warren Buffet."

Trying not to think how handsome he was, or how much she always seemed to want to make love to him, Sage sighed. "Back to money. Lots of it." Just like her father.

"And success. But I have to admit, the money would have been great to have back then. We struggled, trying to hold on to everything after Mom and Dad died. Sold all the cattle. Went through what savings there was, trying to pay the taxes on the land, and still fell woefully behind." He released a breath. "If it hadn't been for Mac Wheeler coming to town, putting the wind energy turbines on our land, we might have lost everything, including the store, despite all our best efforts to the contrary."

"But now you don't need the money. The ranch pays for itself and the store is doing a booming business."

His brows took on a determined slant. "I do need more of a challenge. This could be it."

"Could be?"

He frowned. "There are some things I didn't tell my sibs."

Curious, Sage tensed. "Like what?"

"They're planning to make the stores a lot more high-end and seat them only in urban areas."

Sage blinked in surprise. "I thought the idea was to

link them in some way to the success of the original mercantile. Have you as spokesperson."

"They are still going to do that, although in a round-about way. Meanwhile, the Monroe name and four generations of expertise selling Western wear will help them promote the venture."

So he was being used. Willingly, albeit, but…she had to ask, "You think you're going to be happy with the finished product?"

As darkness descended, Nick turned on the camping lantern. It filled the bed of the truck with a soft, intimate light. Whatever demons he had had been put to rest. "MR has assured me that I'll still have a great deal of input."

Sage looked on the bright side. She might not believe in his new partners, but she definitely believed in him. She smiled. "So then it can't help but be a success. 'Cause I'm sure you'll handle whatever comes your way."

"Like I 'handle' you?" Nick teased, shifting her over onto his lap.

Sage settled intimately against him. "Ooh, sexy, cowboy!"

Nick stroked a hand through her hair, down her spine. "Ever made love in the bed of a pickup truck?" he asked huskily.

Sage shook her head, ready for the pleasurable diversion he offered. "Can't say that I have." She pressed her lips lightly to his. "Is that about to change?"

"Let's see." Nick rubbed his thumb across her lower lip. Slanted his head. "First we'd have to kiss…"

Sage opened her mouth to the insistent pressure of

his, savoring the heat and taste of him. "Very nice so far…" she decreed.

Nick smiled and reached for the buttons on her blouse. "Then we'd have to get a little closer still."

She quivered as he undid the clasp on her bra, and bared her to his touch. "Also nice," she whispered, unfastening his shirt, too.

"And touch." He shifted her over onto her side, and stretched his frame alongside hers. Facing each other, they kissed and stroked until his sinewy chest tautened and her nipples pearled and her blood ran hot and heavy through her veins.

Needing more, they kicked off their jeans.

Sage lay on her back, knees raised. "And become one…"

Resting his weight on his forearms, he slid home. Sage caught her breath, the force of her own desire driving her to wild abandon. Excitement racing through her, she ran her hands through his hair and held his head. "Good thing we fit together so nicely…" she murmured, her breath coming raggedly.

Nick paused, searching her face. "And in every other way," he affirmed in the rough sexy voice she loved. He flashed her a deliberately provocative grin, and took her mouth again in a long, hot, tempestuous kiss. As desire swept through her, he settled on top of her, his weight as welcoming as a blanket on a cold winter's night.

Savoring the intimacy, the emotional connection that only seemed to get more intense every time they were together, she wrapped her limbs around him, pulling him deeper still.

"Nick," she whispered. *Oh, Nick…*

He went deep. And slow.

She arched up to meet him.

And then all was lost in the swirling passion, their climaxes merging as irrevocably as they were beginning to merge their lives.

"Come with me today," Nick encouraged the following morning, after another bout of sweet and sensual lovemaking—in the shower at her apartment this time—had left her body humming.

Aware she didn't want to leave him, either, Sage shrugged on a thick terry-cloth robe. "Back to Dallas?"

He wrapped his arms around her and pressed a kiss into her hair. "We could work in some honeymooning in the evenings."

The days, Sage already knew, would be spent working on the new business venture. She slipped away from him and picked up a wide-toothed comb. "I bet MR would really like that."

Frowning, Nick finished drying his body. "You're not jealous of her, are you?"

Only in the sense that the exec was suddenly spending a lot more time with Nick than she was, Sage thought, as she began detangling her wet hair.

Yet the question reminded her of what Everett had told her as he escorted her to the town car at the hotel, indicating she was not gaining a husband, but instead losing her best friend.

She met his glance in the bathroom mirror. "Should I be?"

Grinning, Nick replied, "What do you think?"

Sage shrugged. *If I knew, I wouldn't have asked.*

Nick turned her gently around to face him. Planting his hands on the counter, on either side of her, he leaned over her and delivered the kind of long, soulful kiss that left her breathless and trembling and in no doubt of how much he desired her.

When he finally came up for air, he paused, his gaze drifting over her. As always, seeing far more of her inner vulnerability than she wanted him to see. "What's really bothering you?"

Something stupid someone else said.

But not about to become the kind of clinging woman who needed constant reassurance from her man, Sage pushed aside her niggling uncertainty.

"Sage?" Nick pressed, his gaze narrowing in concern. "Come on. Level with me. What is it?"

Actually, Sage thought, there were about a hundred little things. She picked one. "I know it's silly, but... I'm a little nervous about the sonogram."

A lot could go wrong with a pregnancy, and although hers was progressing nicely to date, according to her obstetrician, Sage had also read enough online to know that could change at any time.

Complications cropped up. Perfectly laid plans were forced to be abandoned...

Nick laced a reassuring arm about her shoulders and pulled her in close to his side. "I'm still planning to be there. Two fifteen, right? A week from Friday? Your OB's office?"

"Dr. Johnson. Right."

"It'll be amazing," he predicted with a grin as wide as all of Texas.

"I know." *I hope. I wish...*

"Our first glimpse of our new baby!"

Thus far. Although she had heard her baby's heartbeat, loud and strong, at her last appointment, Sage had yet to feel him or her kick. She had been told it could happen at any time in the fourth or fifth month, and several times she'd almost thought she felt something, only to wonder if she had only imagined it.

She drew a breath and tried to get a grip on her soaring emotions. This was all hormones, she promised herself, nothing more.

"Speaking of our little one, I need to purchase a crib and a changing table." She paused at Nick's inscrutable expression. Frustrated to find she still couldn't read him anywhere near as well as he could read her, she said, "I wasn't sure if you wanted to go with me for that…or…?"

He paused, looking completely at a loss. Why, she wasn't sure.

Sage moved away. "Actually, never mind. I think it might be better if I went with Molly and Adelaide, since they have already outfitted nurseries, and know exactly what to buy."

Nick's relief was palpable. "I'd be happy to put it together," he volunteered happily, looking around. "The larger question is, where are you going to put it?" he asked. Her apartment consisted of two large rooms and a bath.

Sage grimaced. "Not sure yet."

Nick tugged on jeans and a shirt. "Do you want to go ahead and get two cribs then? One for your place? One for mine? I'll reimburse you, of course."

Yep, they were definitely back to the business side of their relationship. Trying not to feel disappointed—this was what they had agreed upon after all—Sage smiled. "Do you want them both to be identical or different?"

He deferred again. "You decide."

O-kay. Wishing he were a little more enthusiastic

about setting up an infant space, Sage watched Nick's glance cut to the clock. Suppressing her frustration, she asked, "Need to get a move on?"

He drew her toward him and dropped a tender kiss on her forehead. "Unfortunately, yes." He smoothed the hair from her face. "But—" he paused to kiss her one last time "—I'll be back before you know it."

Chapter 8

"You're in a hurry."

Sage put the closed sign on the door. "Shows, huh?"

Luisa nodded. "Nick coming home tonight?"

Finally! "He should be in at about eight this evening," Sage reported. Which gave her roughly four hours…

"Cooking dinner for him?"

Shutting down the coffee machines, Sage feigned nonchalance. "I told him I'd throw something together."

"Which means…?"

"Man food. Steak. Baked potatoes. Salad. And of course the quintessential apple pie."

"Just make sure you don't get too tired to give your man a proper welcome home." Luisa winked.

Sage rolled her eyes, although she was expecting their reconnection to light up the sky with fireworks.

"Seriously, I'll finish up here. You go get ready for your man."

Sage hugged Luisa. "Thanks." She whipped off the barista apron, let herself into the hallway adjacent to the back alley and headed up the staircase. Inside, her apartment sparkled from a recent cleaning. Her fridge was filled with fresh ingredients. And she was brimming with excitement.

Nick had been gone ten days, most of which had been spent on the road with MR and Everett, meeting with potential suppliers. She hadn't heard from him yet today, but he had called or texted or emailed every other day. Just to see how she and their baby were doing. It had felt good, being connected to him that way, even if their communications had sometimes been rushed. So she was eager to catch up completely.

And that excitement stayed with her as 8:00 p.m. came and went. Still with no word from Nick. No call or email or text. Which really began to worry her. It wasn't like him not to let her know he was going to be late. Never mind *this* late.

Finally, around eleven, she texted his sister Bridgett. Her phone rang a few seconds later. "What's going on?" Bridgett asked.

Sage explained. "But, now that I'm saying all this out loud, I feel like I'm being silly, contemplating worst-case scenarios."

"I'm sure Nick's on his way," Bridgett soothed. "Otherwise, he would have let you know. Maybe he's out of cell phone range. You know there are a lot of dead spots between here and Dallas. But listen, if you want me to call all the other sibs…"

"No. You're right." Sage shook off her increasing

sense of dread. "I'm letting my imagination get away from me. He'll be home before I know it."

At midnight, Sage went to sleep. Sometime after that, her cell phone rang.

It was MR Rhodes, requesting a FaceTime chat with her.

Heart jumping with anxiety, Sage switched on the bedside lamp, drew the covers over her chest and accepted. MR appeared on screen, dressed in her usual elegant business attire. "Sage. Sorry to wake you."

Sage shoved the hair out of her eyes, glad she had worn a demure sleep shirt to bed. "Is everything all right?"

"We're just behind schedule. Which is why Nick asked us to get in touch with you."

That was weird. Embarrassing or not, she had to ask. "Is there some reason he couldn't contact me himself?"

"He's still meeting with the Santa Fe artisans who are trying to get their goods in our new venue. They've been coming to the hotel all day to show us what they can provide exclusively for us, and since Nick is the expert on Western wear, he's riding point on the discussions."

Made sense. Sort of.

MR smiled. "Anyway, he wanted you to have his flight information for tomorrow morning. Everett, can you please give it to Sage?"

The phone changed hands.

Everett appeared on screen. There was a second's pause, as he took Sage in, with what might have been a flash of remorse or indecision in his expression. Then he glanced down at the tablet in his other hand and read out the airline and flight number. "Departs at 6:07 in the morning, and arrives in Dallas at 9:20."

"Thank you, Everett. Text that information to Sage."

Everett disappeared from view.

MR came back into the picture. "So even if there is traffic Nick should easily be able to make your ultrasound appointment tomorrow afternoon. He wants you to know that. So…you're good?" MR said crisply.

Sage forced a smile. "I am. Thanks for calling."

They ended the call.

As much as Sage wanted to, she couldn't go back to sleep for several hours after that. Her mind kept replaying the warning Everett had given her the morning after she married Nick, the way he hadn't quite wanted to look her in the eye during the FaceTime chat.

Did he know something she should?

Or was it just the way the venture capital/start-up business worked that had MR's assistant so sure trouble was brewing for her and Nick?

One thing was for certain. You couldn't build any kind of successful relationship if you rarely interacted with the other person. And, Sage thought miserably as she wrapped her arms tightly around her pillow and sought comfort where she could, that was certainly becoming true for her and Nick.

"How many texts have you had this morning?" Luisa asked, sliding another tray of apple Danish into the oven to bake.

Sage spread a thin layer of jalapeño cream cheese on some tortillas. "Thirty-two." *In five hours.*

Luisa cast a look toward the front of the shop. Just after eleven, the lunch crowd had yet to come in. Satisfied the part-time counter help could handle things for the moment, she turned back to give Sage a concerned look, "All from Nick?"

Sage layered thin slices of mesquite-smoked chicken overtop, then added slices of avocado, heirloom tomato and red onion. "Every last one."

Luisa added cooled brownies to a display case tray. "Bad news?"

"He's still fogged in, in Santa Fe." Which meant he would miss the ultrasound.

"Can you reschedule?"

Sage rolled the sandwiches, sliced them in half, then covered them with plastic wrap. "Not without twenty-four hours advance notice," she admitted glumly. "Besides, I really want to take a look myself and see the baby is okay."

"Still not kicking?"

"Not that I can tell." Sage fell silent. And though she knew from her readings that it could be as long as the twenty-fifth week before a first-time mother felt her baby kick, she still worried. The anatomy scan would show them definitively that everything was okay.

So Sage went to her obstetrician's office alone, at the appointed time. Signed in, turned off her phone and drank the water they gave her. Twenty minutes later, Sage's bladder was uncomfortably full, and she was reclining on the exam table, a pillow beneath her head.

Dr. Johnson walked in. "Ready?"

Feeling unbearably excited and incredibly sad to be experiencing this moment without Nick at her side, Sage nodded. She turned her head toward the black-and-white monitor while the gel was smeared over her midriff.

"Here we go," the obstetrician said, picking up the

transducer wand and moving it over her belly. And suddenly, there, on screen, were lots of wavy, fluid lines. And through the shifting movement, the poignantly beautiful image of their baby's head.

She stared at the screen in wonder and relief. It was all just so incredible…

"Here's the baby's heart."

She could actually *see* it beating, steady and strong.

"And legs and arms…" Which were indeed, Sage noted, *moving*, even if she couldn't yet feel the motion inside her.

"Everything is looking good," Dr. Johnson said with satisfaction as the last of the measurements were taken and recorded. He turned to her, kind as ever. "Do you want to know the sex?"

Bad enough Nick was missing this. To miss that, too…? Sage felt a burst of generosity that far surpassed her anger and disappointment with her baby's daddy. "No," she said firmly. "We'll wait until the baby is born to find that out."

After a day of travel hell, and many unanswered phone calls to Sage, Nick got in close to 9:00 p.m. Friday evening. He found Sage right where he expected she would be. In her bistro kitchen, working on the next day's offerings.

In white capris and a loose-fitting dark blue shirt that covered her baby bump, her wheat-gold hair upswept in a clip, she looked gorgeous, and ticked off as all get-out.

Though she had to have heard him use his key and come in through the service entrance off the back hall, she ignored him steadily.

He couldn't blame her. He was wracked with guilt at

not being able to keep his promise, forcing her to go to their baby's ultrasound alone. He felt even sadder about missing such an important milestone in their relationship and their child's life. This was more than just a missed opportunity, it was a moment in time he could not get back. And he would make up for that.

But first, he had to make amends.

He set his bag down. "Sorry can't begin to cover it, I know."

She stared him down, growing even more flushed. "Do tell."

Damn, she was ticked off. "I'm as frustrated as you are."

She arched an elegant brow. "Somehow I doubt that."

"Okay." He girded himself for the worst. "Let me have it."

Even icier. "I'd rather not."

Nick tried again but could not quite keep the exasperation from his voice. "I sent you a message."

Sage set her rolling pin down with a clatter. "Yeah, that was great. Having MR and Everett call me at *midnight.* Four hours after you were supposed to be here for dinner. Really nice, Nick. *Really nice.*"

She thought he had stood her up without a word? "What are you talking about?" Nick moved closer. "We knew we weren't getting out of there last night *at noon* yesterday."

Sage wiped her hands with a towel. "Well, that's news to me."

With a weariness that went soul deep, he said, "I thought you had been called."

She tilted her head to one side and kept her eyes on his. "You really couldn't have done it yourself?"

Hell, yes, he wished he could have. But this was what happened, he was beginning to realize, when you gave up control of a business venture.

He shoved a hand through his hair. "If you had any idea how crazy it was the last ten days. How many vendors I've met, and spaces I've toured. Meetings I've been in."

All for you, Sage. And our baby...

Because if it hadn't been for the two of them, he would have said to hell with it all and pulled out of this mal-fated venture long ago.

But he couldn't.

Not if he wanted to give Sage the kind of ultraluxurious life she had grown up with.

She wanted to believe in him, in them. He could see that. She just wasn't sure she should.

Shoulders stiff, she finally looked right at him and allowed in a low, strangled voice, "I know you've been busy, Nick." Her chest heaved with each breath. "I've been busy, too." Amber eyes glistening with tears, she swallowed and pushed on. "I don't fault you for working hard," she murmured, clearly distraught. "But I still would have made it to our baby's ultrasound." She reached into her pocket and pulled out a black-and-white photo. Their fingers brushed as she thrust it at him. "I still would have moved heaven and earth not to have missed this."

He stared down at the ghostly image of a baby. Their baby. The miracle of it nearly slammed him to his knees. For a moment, he could barely breathe, let alone speak. "Is that the head...the legs...?" he asked, his heart bursting with love.

Affirming proudly, Sage pointed. "Arms..."

Of their kid! *Their kid!* "Sucking a thumb?"

Sage allowed in a low, proud voice, "The nurse said that happens in utero all the time. And if they pacify themselves that way while they are inside their mommy's tummy, they usually do it as soon as they get out of their mommy's body, too."

How cute was that going to be? Amazing.

They stared at the image some more in wonderment. Moving nearer, he wrapped one arm around Sage. Finally, he pulled himself together enough to ask, "Do we know if it's a girl or boy?"

Still holding herself stiffly, Sage shook her head. "I told Dr. Johnson I didn't want to know yet. I thought you should at least be there for that."

He turned her so she had no choice but to face him. He felt like a kid who was telling a teacher the dog ate his homework, but she needed to understand just the same. "I tried like hell to be here."

"I know," Sage said wearily, recalling the gist of the many text messages he had sent her that morning. "But the Santa Fe airport was fogged in this morning, and all the flights were delayed until almost noon, and the one you were supposed to be on eventually got canceled due to mechanical problems."

It had been the Murphy's Law of Travel day for him. He held her by the shoulders, needing, wanting to understand her. "So why did you stop responding to me? Why didn't you pick up when I called?"

She slipped out of his light grasp.

Her lower lip slid out in the delicious pout he knew so well and could never stop wanting to kiss. "Because I was too angry, and I shouldn't have been. And I knew that," she confessed in a thick voice. "And I didn't want to say something I would regret."

He studied her sullen expression, figuring she'd earned the right to have her say. And truth to tell, he wanted to hear it all. So they wouldn't find themselves in this place again.

She stomped closer, arms akimbo. "We made a deal, Nick, when this all started. That you could be around as much or as little as you chose, and I would never ever put any kind of pressure or expectation on you, or leave you feeling trapped in any way. Yet I was doing just that." She shook her head in silent remonstration, then aimed a thumb at the center of her chest. "And that made me angry at myself. And then add in a few pregnancy hormones…" Her voice broke. She waved a dismissing hand. "I needed to calm down."

He studied her upturned face. "And have you?"

For a moment he thought she was going to lie, then she sighed. "I'm working on it."

"Then you're ahead of me," he returned with grim honesty, moving closer. "Because I'm probably going to be upset with myself for a while."

Her eyes widened in surprise.

Obviously, she hadn't expected a mea culpa from him.

"I should have left yesterday as planned. MR and Everett could have stayed and handled the remaining business meetings. But I didn't. And I missed something I never should have missed." He put his hands on her shoulders and waited for her gaze to meet his. "I'm really sorry, darlin'," he said in a low, tortured tone. "More sorry than you'll ever know."

She could see that.

Her anger evaporated.

"I'm sorry, too." Sage ran her hands through her hair. "I didn't think things through. I should have explained the situation and rescheduled. Since there was no medical emergency precipitating the ultrasound, we could have just waited until you were available. So—" she drew in a ragged breath "—I'm at fault here, too."

Nick helped Sage put the baked goods into the walk-in for the next day. "So, truce...?" he said as they walked out, shutting the door behind them.

Sage nodded, taking off her apron. "Truce."

"Only one problem with that," Nick said.

Sage's delicate brow furrowed in confusion. "What?"

"This is no way to make up after our first fight as a married couple."

"Actually," Sage corrected, flashing an impish smile, "it's our first real fight."

"You're right. It is." And he never wanted to have one like this again. So...

He stepped forward, tucked one hand beneath her knees and swung her up into his arms. She let out a low squeal and held on to his shoulders.

"Well, this is getting interesting."

He returned her grin. "You think so?" He bent to kiss her cheek. "Just wait."

He headed out the service door of the bakery and carried her easily up the back stairs to her apartment. Set her down long enough for her to unlock the door, then picked her right back up again.

She gave him a mock-stern look. "You know I may be pregnant, but I can still walk."

Sensing they were at a turning point in their relationship, he cradled her in his arms. "But should you have to?"

She chuckled, clearly as turned on as she was exasperated.

"Seriously." He looked down at her adoringly. "During those long, long hours when I was waiting to get home to you, it occurred to me I never carried you over the threshold."

She hitched in a breath.

"And now seems like the perfect time." He walked through the front door, through the living area and into the bedroom, before setting her gently down next to her bed...

Sage wanted to continue to keep things simple with Nick.

But the moment his hands lifted her shirt and moved higher, his thumbs running over the tender crests, she felt herself begin to lose herself in him all over again.

She hadn't allowed herself to want anything as much as she wanted him in a long time. Hadn't allowed herself to hope that they could have anything close to a fairy tale.

Wise or not, she wanted to lose herself in the bliss, the intimacy only he could bring. She wanted the explosion of heat and hunger his kiss wrought. Overwhelmed by the pleasurable sensations, she returned his kiss with everything she had.

His need and yearning mirrored hers.

She surrendered against him one moment.

He took total control the next.

Until they dropped down on the bed, and she arched against him, the need in her an incessant ache. And still it wasn't enough for either of them, as she ran her hands over hard muscle and smooth skin. He was absolutely beautiful. So beautiful, she couldn't take her eyes from his sculpted pecs and abs, and lower still…

Yes, he wanted her.

Oh my, he wanted her.

He rolled her onto her side, so they were facing each other. And still they kissed, until her heart filled and her entire body throbbed with searing heat.

Flush with victory, he slid a hand between her legs, making her blossom, sending her quickly to the brink. Knowing this was no time to be selfish, she guided him inside her. Together, they soared. Found. Conquered. And came slowly, inevitably, back down.

And Sage knew all was right between them once again.

Chapter 9

"Look, I'm sorry," MR said, the following morning, over FaceTime with Nick. "I thought it would be better to wait and call Sage when we had the flight change nailed down. And that took a while."

Nick supposed that was true. The storms that had hit Santa Fe the previous day had wreaked havoc throughout the West Coast, leaving a lot of people stranded, scrambling to get home.

"Luckily, I was finally able to reach a VP friend at the airlines and he was able to manage it for us. But—" MR paused, her expression penitent "—the next time we need to get a message to her, I'll make sure Everett does it right away, even if we don't yet have everything worked out."

"That won't be necessary," Nick said. "From now on, any communications between me and Sage will be handled by me."

MR frowned and moved on tersely. "When can we expect you here?"

"I won't be returning to Dallas until Monday afternoon."

Another pause, while MR stared him down.

"Nick, with a Father's Day weekend opening, we really don't have 48 hours to waste. The lease for the space in Dallas has to be signed *today*."

"So, sign it," Nick returned implacably. "Metro Equity Partners has 51 percent control. You don't need me to finalize that."

Nick looked up to see Sage standing in the doorway of his office. He repeated, "I've got to go."

"One sec." MR snapped her fingers. Everett appeared in the background, computer tablet in hand. "We at least need to schedule a daily call."

No. They didn't. "Whatever it is, we can do it Monday afternoon." He ended the call and turned off his phone.

Sage lingered in the doorway. "Am I interrupting?"

He shook his head, wondering if she had any idea at all how much he missed her when they were apart, or how glad he was to be with her now. "Never."

He moved away from his desk, brought her into his arms and kissed her. She surrendered against him, basking in the fierce tenderness flowing between them.

When they finally drew apart, he paused to take her in. Instead of the white chef's coat he expected to see her in, she was wearing a pretty green shirt over her jeans, and the comfy sneakers she now usually chose over her boots. "I thought you were going to work this morning."

Sage grinned. "I decided to take the day off since

you're here. Unless—" she paused, glancing with trepidation at his phone "—you're leaving again?"

Nick shook his head. "Not until Monday."

Her amber eyes glowed with the same happiness and contentment he felt. "So you're footloose and fancy-free?"

Steps sounded in the hall. Nick's twin sisters, Bridgett and Bess, appeared in the doorway.

"Not exactly," they said.

"A baby shower?" Sage echoed in surprise.

"We knew Nick was coming in for the ultrasound yesterday," Bess said. "So we planned it for this morning. It's going to be held at your mom's ranch. Everyone from both families is going to be there."

Sage wasn't sure whether to well up with joy or groan in distress. The happiness she and Nick shared was so fragile, she wasn't sure it could hold up under intense familial scrutiny.

"It starts in forty-five minutes, so get a move on," Bridgett advised. "And bring the photo!"

As Sage had feared, no sooner had she and Nick arrived at the Circle H and were passing around the very first photo of their baby than the questions began. "So, what did you think of the ultrasound?" Nick's older brother, Gavin, asked.

"It was amazing," Sage said.

Erin looked at Nick, curious.

Never one to dance around a problem, Nick grabbed the bull by the horns. "I missed it due to flight delays," he said. The room fell silent.

Sage's mother was the first to recover. "That's a shame," she said sympathetically.

Nick took Sage's hand. "It's the last thing of importance I'm going to miss," he vowed protectively. "From now on, I plan to be at every obstetrics appointment with your daughter."

Now, it was Sage's turn to be surprised. "That's really not necessary," she said. Especially since at most of them all she did was step on a scale, pee in a cup and have her abdomen palpitated.

"Yes," Nick said firmly, "it is."

At that, everyone smiled.

And although she had promised herself she would not allow herself to rely on Nick too much, Sage couldn't help but feel really happy, too.

Her ebullience lasted throughout the party. Nick remained content in a way she had never really seen him, too. They were both still smiling as they arrived back at her apartment.

"Is that the last of it?" Sage asked, several trips from the vehicle later, as Nick walked in, his arms laden with baby gifts.

"Yep." He carried the bassinet over to the corner of her living room. "You want this here, too?"

Sage nodded. Between this and the wedding gifts, much of which was still in boxes, awaiting a decision— her place or his—it was beginning to feel more like a storage facility than a home.

Starting to feel overwhelmed, she knotted her hands in front of her and stared at the mess. "I thought I was going to have plenty of room to have our baby here. Now… Nick, we don't even have a crib or a changing table yet!"

His brow furrowed. "I thought you were going shopping for baby furniture for both our places."

"I special ordered identical sets. They won't be delivered for another few weeks, but when they do arrive…"

Nick caught her wrist. "We'll figure it out."

Ignoring the tingling in her arm, she slid out of his light grasp. Moving away from him, she put her hand to her lower back, rubbed restlessly. "When?" She walked a short distance away. "The baby will be here in another four months!"

A long thoughtful pause followed. "Which gives us plenty of time. What's the matter?" Nick cocked his head. "Did you hurt yourself carrying those packages up the stairs?"

"No." Sage stopped pacing.

The truth was, he'd barely let her carry anything.

He came closer. "Then why are you rubbing your lower back?"

Sage jerked in a deep, enervating breath. Realizing what she had been doing, she dropped her hand. "It's been bothering me since I hit the three-month mark."

"Did you tell your obstetrician?"

Sage waved off his concern. "Yes, and Dr. Johnson said, that pelvic and or lumbar discomfort is common in pregnancy. It's due to the growing uterus and hormonal changes."

He gave her a telling look. "What are you supposed to do to alleviate it?"

"Stretching exercises. Walking. Pelvic tilts. Prenatal yoga."

His gaze caressed her face. "What about massages? Do those help?"

"I'm sure they do," Sage retorted, "but I can't exactly do that to myself."

He grinned at her wry tone. "Which is why you have me here."

The heat within her intensified, but it was the kind of heat that usually presaged their lovemaking. "You're kidding."

"Nope." He tucked his hand in hers. "Luckily, these days, there's a how-to video for everything." Ten minutes later, Nick had watched enough to feel educated. "All right, first thing we have to do is get you to lie on the floor, and we'll turn you slightly on your side, and put one pillow beneath your neck and head, the other between your knees."

Sage knelt on the thick quilt they'd spread out in her living room. "You sure you want to do this?" She didn't know why but she was suddenly feeling very shy.

The grooves on either side of his lips deepened. "Hush, woman."

"Hush, woman?" What had gotten into him!

With gentle hands, he guided her into position. "You can't relax if you're talking."

Her back to him, Sage struggled to get comfortable. She tossed him a quelling look over her shoulder. "When did you get so bossy?"

"The day I realized you—and our baby—needed me."

He was so right about that. The funny thing was he looked like he needed them as much as they did him.

Sage was still trying to wrap her mind around that as Nick knelt on the floor behind her.

"Okay, we're going to start on one side of the neck." With an unclenched fist, he massaged his way magically down to her hips, on one side of her spine, then slowly worked his way back up again. His touch was so purposeful and heavenly it was all she could do not to groan in ecstasy. "Now we're going to try both sides," he soothed.

As he worked his way downward, this time she did moan out loud. He chuckled. "Feel good?"

Her muscles were warm and fluid. Sage sighed. "You have no idea…"

"Good. We'll keep doing it until you're…"

And then, out of nowhere, Sage realized, there it was. A flutter, a movement, a… "Nick!" Sage gasped.

He jumped back slightly. "Did I hurt you?"

"Give me your hand," she whispered. Staying very still otherwise, she beckoned him to comply. He reached over her. Sage captured his palm and settled it slightly above her navel.

His dark brow furrowed in confusion. "You want me to massage you there?"

Oh, no, please don't make me laugh, not now…

"Shh!" She stayed still, waited, and then there it was again. The slightest flutter, then nothing, then a kick.

Nick went very still, too. Amazement shimmered in his deep blue eyes. "Was that…?"

"Our baby is kicking!" Sage said, tears of sheer joy starting to flow. She turned her head slightly to look at him. Saw he was overcome with emotion, too.

"Was that the first time?" Nick asked in a rusty-sounding voice.

Sage nodded, her heart so full it was practically bursting. "I guess Little One was just waiting for you to be here, too."

"Still nothing?" Nick asked in obvious disappointment, several hours later.

Sage shook her head.

They'd gone to the ranch to check on the property and had dinner outside on the porch. Now, replete and relaxed, they sat together in the chain-hung swing and watched the sun go down. Sage curved her hand over her blossoming belly. "I guess our little one has decided once again to do things on his or her own time."

Nick rested his open palm next to hers. He leaned down to kiss her neck, then murmured playfully in her ear, "What do you think we're having? Girl or boy?"

Sage shut her eyes, quivering, as he kissed her again, this time on the sensitive spot just behind her ear. "No idea."

He shifted her masterfully onto his lap. "Which do you want?"

Aware it really didn't matter, Sage wrapped her arms around his broad shoulders and nestled against him. She kissed the nape of his neck, too. "I'll be happy either way," she confessed softly.

He turned his head toward hers. "Me, too."

Once again, a contented silence brought them together. Their lips met. And when they started kissing, it was impossible to stop. All coherent thought fled and a lightning bolt of desire swept through her. This, she thought, was what it felt like when it was right.

This was what she had always wanted...

Nick hadn't intended to make love to Sage out on the swing, but with the moon shining brightly down at them from a starlit sky it seemed foolish to waste such a perfect setting. Especially when he wanted her so much.

She shuddered as his hands swept over her. Before they knew it, they were naked from the waist down. Coming together once again, with Sage astride him.

134 Wanted: Texas Daddy

Kissing. And when he lifted her, the sensation of filling her left them both quaking and breathless.

He couldn't get enough of her softness and warmth. While he held her right where he wanted her, right where he wanted her to be, their lovemaking turning from pure passion to a deep all-encompassing need.

He held her close, closer, savoring every delicate caress, each sweet surrender. Every tremble. Every kiss. Connection. As they met each other stroke for stroke, her newly voluptuous body cradled him tenderly. Until finally, they surrendered to the blazing heat, the need, the intimacy.

To their mutual pleasure, the aftershocks were as potent as their lovemaking had been. And though this was the only time Nick ever felt Sage was all his, he knew, for now, it would not only have to be enough. It would be.

Sage woke to an empty bed. Nick was downstairs in the living room, clad in a T-shirt and jeans, laptop open on his lap, cell phone beside him. "Why are you up so early?" She ambled closer, wearing socks and one of his big shirts. "I thought we agreed to sleep in this morning."

They'd been planning to eat a leisurely brunch she cooked especially for him, then tour the ranch by jeep, checking out the property.

He set his laptop on the coffee table in front of him. "I didn't mean to wake you."

Not really the point. Sage folded her legs beneath her and cuddled up next to him. He looked so serious and so stressed. "What's wrong?"

His lips twisted unhappily. "I noticed last night before bed the voice mail box on my phone was full, and it looked as if I'd received even more emails, so I figured I'd better check."

"I gather there's some sort of emergency?"

Nick draped his arm along the back of the sofa and drew her against his side. Leaning over, he pressed a kiss in her hair. "MR and Everett were updating me on the partner meetings yesterday."

She turned toward him, appreciating how ruggedly handsome he looked in the early morning light streaming in through the blinds. "Were you supposed to be there?"

A terse nod.

Then he had skipped them, for her.

Sage wasn't sure whether to feel elated about that, or guilty. From the looks of it, he felt conflicted, too. Happy to be here, with her, worried about not being there, with them.

Nick rubbed his fingers through the mussed ends of her hair. "They were all playing golf yesterday morning…and then had a working lunch afterward at one of the partner's homes." He exhaled. "A lot of key decisions were made."

"Such as…?"

"The new name of the store." He retrieved his laptop and situated it so she could see the screen.

Sage blinked in surprise at the logo. "Upscale Outfitters?"

"It was either that or City Cowboy. Of the two that market-tested the best among their target customer, the former won."

Sage turned so they were facing in the same direction, and her body was pressed right up against his.

She rested her head on his shoulder, reveling in the brisk masculine scent of him. "What are they going to be selling?"

With a click of the mouse, he pulled up several more windows on the screen.

Sage paused thoughtfully. "I recognize some of the brands." They were the kind of thing she had worn, back in the day when growing up a very wealthy Dallas teenager. But...

"They're not exactly ranch gear."

Nick shut his laptop, and set it aside once again. "You're right. It's all for the elite. People who are making a fashion statement rather than going out to round up cattle." He rose, and made his way into the ranch house kitchen.

Sage stood and lounged against the counter. "How do you feel about that?"

He began making coffee—decaf, on account of her.

"Since they just signed a lease on a storefront in the Galleria mall, it's a good business decision." Nick went to the fridge and brought out the makings for breakfast. "No working rancher is going to go there to purchase their work clothes."

"For that, they would come to the original Monroe's Western Wear."

"Right." He layered bacon in a skillet, while Sage whisked half a dozen eggs. "What happens next?"

"MR has set up a meeting with the interior designer who's going to design the look and layout of the flagship store."

Sage put four slices of oatmeal bread in the toaster. "When does that happen?"

"Three o'clock this afternoon."

Which was certainly doable, if he canceled their plans and left before noon. Sage studied him. "Do you want to be there?"

A conflicted expression crossed his handsome face as he turned back to the stove to flip the sizzling meat. Finally, he said, "To tell you the truth, I'm not sure what difference it really makes. With 49 percent share, I'm being outvoted on everything. Whatever MR wants, the partners back. Period."

And MR and Nick were not thinking the same way.

"Still...you must have some ability to sway things."

He dipped his head, acknowledging quietly, "Sometimes. When I'm there."

Instead of in Laramie, with her.

As much as she wanted to continue spending time together, she also knew how important this was to him.

Sage added a touch of cream, salt and pepper, and poured the eggs into the pan. "Then you've got to go to that meeting," she said quietly. *Or end up looking back in regret at what might have been.*

He shook his head, determined now. "This is our day together, Sage."

"And we'll have plenty more of them," she argued.

He went still.

"You won't have another day to shape the feel and mood of the flagship store. So have breakfast here, like we planned. Then shower and go. Get it done." She rose on tiptoe and kissed him. "You can call me tonight and tell me all about it."

He wrapped his arms around her and pulled her against him, for another longer, deeper kiss. "You really are the perfect woman for me."

Sage was certainly trying to be.

If only they loved each other, too, then life really would be perfect. But that wasn't part of their deal, she reminded herself, so she would be happy the way things were. And so, hopefully, would he.

Chapter 10

"You're really leaving to go back to Laramie," MR said as Nick gathered up his things, a couple months later. "Again."

Nick zipped his laptop bag. "Sage has an appointment with her obstetrician."

"Routine appointment," MR clarified. "And there's still much to do to get ready for the grand opening next month."

He was well aware. It was also Mother's Day weekend. His and Sage's first. "That's five weeks away."

"And half the orders of merchandise have yet to arrive. Plus, we need to talk about the advance interviews you've been doing. Without our approval or consent."

Getting more than a little tired of the constant haranguing, Nick gave MR a long, level look. "You asked me to talk to every local TV station, newspaper and magazine, as well as the publications that cover the high-end Texas consumer."

"In June."

Nick exhaled. "I may not be available then," he explained patiently. "So I'm doing everything I can *in advance*."

MR scowled. Behind her, Everett looked up. Briefly, the assistant regarded Nick with a mixture of surprise, respect and pity, before resuming his usual poker face.

MR looked at him as if he were a dollar short and a day late. "The publicity needs to herald the advent of Upscale Outfitters. And, hence, appear in the days *immediately leading up* to Father's Day weekend."

Nick exhaled. "I've explained my situation, MR. Everyone's been very accommodating in doing the preliminary interviews with me now about the Western-wear business, and the tour and photos of the new store a few days before they go to press in June. They also know that if unexpected events occur and I'm unavailable for that, you and/or Everett will be happy to show them around and provide them with any further information they need."

MR stalked closer. When she spoke again, it was in a much more conciliatory tone. "I appreciate your diligence, Nick, but Sage isn't due until July first."

Nick looped his computer briefcase over his shoulder. "That's an estimate. She could give birth before or after that day."

"Unless her doctor induces her." MR flashed a winning smile. "Then you would know exactly when the baby would arrive, and could plan for it."

Not sure what to say to that suggestion that would be remotely polite, a fuming Nick fell silent.

Seeming to realize she had crossed a line, MR shrugged. "Plenty of couples do it."

"For medical reasons, sure."

"For *convenience*," MR emphasized.

Not going to happen, not with our child. Hanging on to his temper with effort, Nick retorted curtly, "Our baby comes into the world when he or she is ready. And not a second before."

For a moment, MR seemed taken aback. Angry color appearing in her face, she gripped the pen in her hand. "You will be at the grand opening, regardless," she decreed.

Nick wasn't going to promise what he could not predict. So he merely said, instead, "I'll be back in Dallas on Monday." His heart already with Sage and the baby she carried, he headed out the door without a backward glance.

"So what do you think?" Sage asked her brother and sister-in-law the same morning.

Molly and Chance toured her apartment above the bistro, studying everything with a general contractor's and interior designer's eye.

"Is there any way I could make a separate nursery?" Without moving out to Nick's ranch? An act that still seemed like a risky endeavor, for so many reasons.

Chance measured the front room, a combination living, dining and eat-in kitchen, with a hidden laundry closet off the entryway. "This is fifteen feet by twenty."

Molly emerged from the bedroom. "It's fifteen by twenty, too. And the answer to your question, Sage, is yes." She pulled out a pad and pencil, and quickly sketched a rough design. "It would mean putting up a partial wall on either side of the divide with pocket doors."

"So I'd have room for a crib, changing table–dresser and rocker-glider in the new 'nursery.'"

Molly nodded. "And still maintain the walk-in closet and the bathroom on your side of the suite."

Sage put one hand on her lower back, which was aching as usual, and the other on her tummy, where the baby was attempting to ride a bucking bronc inside her. "Next question." She paced back and forth, wondering if she would ever get truly comfortable again. "Do we have time to get the construction done before the baby arrives?"

It hadn't been such a big deal before Nick had begun spending the night with her, whenever he was in Laramie. But now that he had, she wanted them to be able to have the privacy to make love comfortably, whenever he was in town. And just as important, she wanted their baby to have a cozy nursery to call his or her own, too.

Chance gave her a brotherly hug. To her joy, he fully understood her nesting. "Molly and I can have our crews knock it out in a day or two early next week."

Sage smiled in relief. "Great."

"Don't you have an OB appointment this afternoon?" Molly asked.

"Yup, at four thirty."

Chance squinted like the protective older brother he was. "Nick coming in?"

Sage reported happily, "He hasn't missed an appointment since the ultrasound."

"I'm glad," Molly said.

She glanced at her watch. "I better get back down to

the bistro kitchen. Nick should be arriving any minute and wanted me to meet him there."

"How come?" Molly asked.

"Not sure. He just said it was important."

Fifteen minutes later, Nick had arrived. But Sage was not allowed to see him until he gave the signal. Which seemed to be taking forever to come, Sage thought, in mounting frustration. She wanted to throw herself into his arms, hug him close and give him one hell of a welcome-home kiss that would make them both breathless for more.

Instead, she was stuck in a corner of the bistro kitchen, as far away from the service entrance as possible, while her employees chuckled behind her.

"Eyes covered and closed?" Nick asked sternly.

"Yes," Sage replied, for what seemed like the fourth time.

"Okay." He was suddenly beside her, his arms around her, warm and encouraging, while she kept her hands over her eyes. "This way…" He guided her forward, then said triumphantly, "Open your eyes!"

Sage did.

In front of her was a tall beribboned chrome work stool on wheels, with a cushy black leather seat.

He grinned. "Happy Mother's Day!"

"It's…" She was speechless.

She had expected, if he gave her a gift, that it would be something like a necklace. Or flowers. Not…furniture.

On the other hand, it showed the depth of thought and concern she hadn't expected, either. And in that sense was incredibly sweet, as well as practical.

"It's completely ergonomic, with lumbar support, and adjusts dozens of ways. So you can cook in comfort, and won't have to be on your feet quite so much." He lifted a hand before she could interrupt. "I know. I know. We talked about this, and you have to do a lot of your prep work like chopping and dicing standing, but there are some tasks that can be done sitting, and if that helps you be more comfortable, or less physically stressed…" He nodded at her hand, which had, as it had so many times lately, unconsciously gone to her lower back.

"Thank you." Sage embraced him.

Exuding tenderness, he cuddled her close. "You like it?"

"So much that I have a feeling in a few weeks I'll be wondering how I ever lived without it!" Aware the more time went on, the more happily married she felt, she stepped back far enough to prop her hand on her hip and tease glibly, "My only question is where are you going to sit, cowboy?"

Grinning widely, he walked back out and came back rolling an identical fancy stool. "Problem solved."

She couldn't help but laugh, as around them her employees cheered his ingenuity, then exited to give the newlyweds coveted alone-time.

Sage went back into Nick's warm embrace. "You really do think ahead."

He lowered his lips to hers. "You have no idea, sweetheart." He started to kiss her, then drew back slightly to cup her tummy with the flat of his hand. The baby was kicking so hard her tummy was popping outward. "What is he or she doing in there?" he asked, astounded.

"I don't know. But it's been going on for about two days now…"

Sage's OB noticed the change, too. As soon as he had finished the exam, he ushered them into his office. Never a good sign. Sage and Nick took seats while he circled around his desk. "Is there a problem?" she asked anxiously.

"The baby is breech."

Nick clasped Sage's hand. "So if Little One were to be born right now...?"

"He or she would try to come out bottom first."

Which wouldn't work. Sage drew a quavering breath. Suddenly cold, she began to shiver. "What do we do?"

"Initially, we wait and see," Dr. Johnson told her encouragingly. "You still have plenty of room inside of you for the baby to turn on his or her own, and get back in the right position."

Nick held tight to Sage. "And if that doesn't happen?"

"Worst-case scenario, we may need to do a C-section and deliver the baby that way. But there are still seven weeks until the due date so it's way too premature for us to talk about that. Right now, we just need to wait and see."

Aware her first task as a mom was to stay calm, Sage sobered. "What can we do to precipitate that the baby gets back into position on his or her own?"

"There are some at-home turning methods to try but they aren't recommended for women who've had pelvic or back pain during their pregnancy, so I strongly caution you against those."

Briefly, Nick looked as disappointed as Sage felt. "Then there's nothing to be done?" he asked.

"Except relax, and let nature take its course," Dr. Johnson soothed.

Sage and Nick left the medical office, hand in hand.

They walked wordlessly over to his pickup truck and climbed in. He started the truck, but made no move to drive anywhere just yet.

With cool air blowing out of the vents, he turned to her. His deep blue eyes were as worried as she felt, and tension etched the planes of his handsome face. "Are you okay?"

Sage caught her breath, trying not to cry. Finally, she swallowed. "Are you?"

He didn't answer, but then he didn't have to. She could see he was just as overcome with emotion as she was.

They sat for another moment in silence. "It's funny," Sage said finally. "I've been worried about how I'm going to manage in such a close space and where the baby is going to sleep when he or she does get here. Even though I knew problems could occur, I took for granted everything would go smoothly with the actual birth."

The irises of his eyes turned a darker blue. "Me, too."

Another silence, this one more fraught with emotion than the last. Finally, Nick cleared his throat. "Maybe it still will."

Sage drew a shaky breath. "What if it doesn't?"

"We have each other, sweetheart. And our baby has us." He flipped up the seat divider in his pickup truck, and moved across the space to take her in his strong arms. "Whatever happens," he promised her resolutely, "we're going to get through this."

Nick appeared in his bedroom doorway, that evening, looking ruggedly sexy in a chambray shirt and jeans. "How is the relaxation going?"

Sage lounged against the pillows on his king-sized bed. She put down the novel he had insisted she read, in lieu of helping him with their dinner dishes. "How do you think?"

He handed her a bowl of praline ice cream—her newest craving—and settled beside her. "Is the baby kicking?"

Sage savored a spoonful of the rich delicious treat, then fed him one. "I feel movement every now and again but it's all up near my rib cage."

Nick stroked a tender hand over her baby bump. "Which means Little One is still positioned bottom first, near the birth canal."

"Probably." Sage sighed and ate some more ice cream.

Nick lifted the hem of her blouse and rested his head against her tummy.

Sage knew what Nick felt and heard. Absolutely nothing. "Where's our stunt-riding rodeo darlin' when we need him or her?" Nick asked, perplexed.

Sage sighed. "No kidding…" Of all the times for Little One to be content hanging out, doing absolutely nothing.

Nick pressed a soft kiss against her tummy, then sat up. "Seems to be sleeping now."

Sage gave Nick the last bite of ice cream, then set the bowl aside. Wondering what she had ever done without him, she informed him of their baby's schedule. "That's usually the case, early evening. It's in the middle of the night, when I'm trying to rest, Little One typically goes hog wild."

Nick's eyes twinkled. "Well, you know what they say

about smart parents taking advantage of their kids' nap times…" He began to unbutton her blouse.

A thrill swept through her. When Nick kissed her, he made her feel cherished and adored, as if nothing mattered but the two of them, and what they felt now. With a soft exhalation of breath, she asked, "You really want to make love?" Earlier, neither of them had been in the mood.

His eyes sparkled with mischief. "I want to kiss. The making love can come later, or not. Depending."

She chuckled at his exaggerated sternness. "On…?"

He waggled his brows. "How relaxed you are…"

"Nick…" He only looked at her like that when he intended to give her an amazing climax. He only gathered her in his arms, the way he was now, when he wanted them to feel connected, body and soul.

Smiling, he let his eyes drift over her, then lowered his lips to hers. "Just kiss me, Sage."

So she did.

Once. And then again. And again…

Afterward, they clung together. Feeling like husband and wife. Bonded as only worried parents can be. Which made their coming together all the sweeter. And Sage was very glad she did not have to face this alone.

Chapter 11

"Is that better?" Nick asked his wife, two weeks later, as he adjusted the pillows and heating pad behind her.

Sage nodded, turning to make sure the heating pad against her lower back was set on the lowest setting. Satisfied, she settled back into the cushy nest he had made for her. "Oh, yeah..." She gave his hand a squeeze and sighed luxuriantly, leaning back to wiggle her toes. "I can feel myself beginning to relax already."

Aware she only seemed to get sexier the further into her pregnancy she got, he lifted her hand to his lips and rubbed his lips across her palm. "I can think of another way."

She turned their twined hands over, and bent to kiss the back of his wrist with sensual accuracy. "You already gave me a back massage."

His body stirred. Lower still, he felt himself hardening. "Another way..."

"We did that, too," she reminded him. When they had turned in, the night before, and awakened this morning.

As if he could forget how good she felt, wrapped in his arms, her body pliantly entwined with his. He met her smile indulgently. "So how is Little One today?"

Sage curved a hand protectively over her rounded tummy. "Sleeping, I think, after being up most of the night." Which, he knew, had become typical in her third trimester.

But with only five and a half weeks left before the due date, it was something she swore she could handle. He tucked a strand of hair behind her ear, then stretched out next to her on the queen-sized bed that never seemed quite big enough. "Is that why you were so restless?" he asked, wishing he could take on some of the discomfort of pregnancy for her.

She nodded, sweeping her hair into an untidy knot on the top of her head. "I'm sorry if my tossing and turning kept you awake."

He wouldn't trade his time with her and their child for anything. Being awake with her just made him more present. But knowing she still wanted and expected them to keep things easy and casual, he shrugged off her restlessness and only said, "Gives me a chance to cuddle with the two of you."

Sage moved her head to rest against his shoulder. "You're getting pretty good at that."

He chuckled. "Nice to know…" He lifted his arm, shifting his body to accommodate her already cozily ensconced form, until he had brought her all the way into the curve of his body, without moving her off the pillows and heating pad that brought relief to her aching lower back.

Sage caressed her delectably rounded tummy. "I just wish I knew how to communicate to Little One it's time to do another 180 degree turn."

Nick had been doing some reading while he was away. The more he learned about breech presentations, and pregnancy and birth in general, the more worried he became. He'd never known so many things could go so wrong. But he had also made it his business to learn what to do in case of an emergency.

Knowing a positive attitude couldn't do anything but help, whatever the outcome, Nick soothed calmly, "There's still time for it to happen naturally. In any case, we've got a great hospital, with doctors and nurses that are prepared to handle everything."

Deliberately, Sage shook off her fear. Smiled, and said, "So true. And in fact..." She chuckled softly as her brows knit together in surprise. "I think someone else very important wants to weigh in on this discussion." She took his hand and put it just beneath her breasts. Just that suddenly, he felt it, too. A kick or punch... then another...

"See, even Little One is saying we should follow the doc's advice and try to relax about everything, so..."

Sage put a hand behind her, and awkwardly scooted toward the opposite side of the bed. She threw her legs over the edge, as restless now as she had been ready to take it easy a few minutes ago. "I think the best thing we can do is to stay busy. Because..."

Knowing how difficult it could be for her to change positions, he rose and walked around to assist her to her feet.

"It seems as if the more active I am, the more active Little One is."

Her delicate fingers encircled his bicep as she steadied herself. Lifting her face to his, she said, "And, the more likely he or she is to turn…"

Belatedly, Nick realized they should have gone out to the ranch to sleep the night before. Sage would have had much more room to maneuver in his king-sized bed. He also knew, now that she was starting to get closer to delivering, that she wanted to stay in town, near the hospital, as much as possible, just in case. "Is this your way of saying you want to tag along while I do inventory at Monroe's?"

She beamed. "How'd you know?"

Because like me, when we do have the opportunity to be together, you seem to want to be together nonstop. And that, too, was something new. Before they'd married, they'd both cherished their alone time, too.

"You sure you shouldn't stay here and rest, while I go look at the sales results?" He knew there were some problem areas with the current stock of Western wear. Apparently, the sales staff didn't have the same feel for the projected marketability of items as he did. Hence, they wanted him to review the orders for summer. Make sure they were as on track as they should be.

But none of that was Sage's problem. Protecting herself and her baby was her first priority. And the two of them, were his. Sternly, he reminded, "After all, this is your only full day off, every week…" And only because The Cowgirl Chef was closed. "Maybe you should take advantage of the quiet and just lounge about while I work."

She wrinkled her nose. "I don't really feel like napping." She sashayed closer. "And since I don't think you'll have me climbing up on ladders to check the stock on the higher shelves…"

He caught her in his arms and spun her around. "Definitely not." He dipped her playfully, righted her slowly.

"Then, I think I'll be perfectly safe, tagging along with you and lending a hand. And—" she pirouetted as he spun her around one last time, and then rose on tiptoe, to kiss him slowly and leisurely "—let's not forget, spending time with my favorite guy, to boot."

The words echoed in Nick's head long after they were spoken. *Favorite guy.* The endearment had been said with affection, he ruminated as they showered and dressed, and walked the short distance to Monroe's. So why was it rankling?

Maybe because he had figured they'd be really and truly married by now. Able to confess how much they had come to mean to each other. Because unless he was wrong, and he admitted ruefully he had been wrong in the past when it came to matters of the heart, Sage was as head over heels for him as he was for her. And had been for a while now…

Mistaking the reason behind his concern, Sage asked as they reached Monroe's, "Are you really worried about how the store has been doing in your absence?"

Yes and no, Nick thought, as he punched in the security code and let them in the back way. "Actually, sales have been good overall, but then, they always are, given what we carry."

She waited while he swung the door wide and held it for her. "The essentials for every working rancher. Male or female."

"Right." He closed the door behind them and hit the

lights. "We price merchandise fairly every day, so we don't do big sales."

Which meant business was reliably steady, all the time.

Sage stopped abruptly in the middle of the store. Stood, with her hands on her hips. "Do you know that man, standing on the sidewalk, peering in?" she asked.

Nick turned to the front windows and saw a trim, fortysomething man with a long brown braid, and a stone-colored Resistol hat. His shirt and jeans were nothing out of the ordinary, but the handcrafted solid silver-and-gold belt buckle holding together his rich leather belt radiated pure artistry.

"Yes, I do," he answered in surprise, staring at the noted silversmith. Although what Ed Durango would be doing here, on a Sunday afternoon, no less, was a mystery. Curious, Nick went to let the Santa Fe businessman in.

"Glad I finally tracked you down." Ed shook Nick's hand.

Nick rocked back on his heels. "I wasn't aware you'd been looking for me."

Ed Durango frowned. "I left a dozen messages for you with Everett and MR. Never got a return call."

Not good. And not surprising, unfortunately, given MR's need to control every tiny little aspect of the launch.

Figuring he would deal with that later, however, Nick asked kindly, "What's the problem?"

Ed rubbed his jaw. "Maybe you can tell me," he countered grimly. "I don't understand why Upscale Outfitters sent back the entire order of custom belt buckles."

Inwardly, Nick reeled. "I didn't know we had."

"Well, you did. And now I'm not going to get paid."

Nick bit down on a string of swear words. Resolved to get the other side of the story before he acted, however, he said, "Can you give me a chance to make a call?"

Ed nodded.

Nick took his phone out of earshot, while Sage chatted up Ed. As usual, MR answered right away. He did not like what he heard. Taut with anger, he returned to the noted craftsman. "Apparently, some changes were made without my knowledge."

Ed frowned. "Can you do something about it?"

Reluctantly, Nick explained he only had a 49 percent share in the new business, and had apparently been outvoted on a matter he had not even known was up for discussion. "But I'll make some calls and do everything I can for you," he promised.

Sage lifted a hand, looking like the down-to-earth hedge-fund heiress she was. "I know a family who owns a chain of jewelry stores in Dallas," she said, looking from Nick to Ed Durango, and back again. "I know they're always looking for high-end gifts with a Western flair. Particularly with Father's Day coming up. Perhaps if I put in a word…?"

"I'd appreciate it," Ed said, handing over his business card. "I really can't afford this kind of a loss."

"Thanks for doing that," Nick said, when the silversmith had left. "Ed and I go way back. I met him several years ago, when he came to see if I would carry his belt buckles in Monroe's. The quality is far superior to anything I've ever seen, but it was way too pricey for the average cowboy."

"I'm guessing several thousand per buckle."

"As a starting point, since they're all solid silver and

hand-engraved, and accented with 14-carat gold. Anyway, that's exactly the kind of item Upscale Outfitters should be carrying, so when we met with him in Santa Fe we placed a very large order. Enough to carry his company for the year."

Sage shook her head in sympathy, her heart going out to Nick. "And now it's been canceled. Without your knowledge. For heaven's sake, why?"

"MR and the partners decided the store was too Southwestern, so they called in upscale buyers from LA and NYC to consult. They've apparently made changes to the inventory. Not with just Ed Durango, but others. MR tasked Everett with sending me a list." Grimacing, he shoved his hands through his hair. "I'll have to personally call them all…"

Sage followed him back to the office, where the facts and figures awaited him. "I'm guessing these are all alterations in inventory that you don't agree with."

Nodding tersely, he slipped behind the desk and turned on the computer. "Then again, I don't know that much about what the socialites and inherited-money crowd buys."

"So you have to trust your partners," she guessed.

"I've put in too much time, effort and energy in this venture not to. But I hate letting the artisans and vendors I've personally contracted to do business with down."

Sage hated to see him betrayed, too. But there wasn't a whole lot she could do to help. Except be there for him.

"Nick went back to Dallas?" Lucille asked the following day, when she arrived to help Sage set up the nursery.

"Early this morning." Usually he left late Sunday evening, but this time he had delayed until the last possible moment and departed Monday morning. Part of it had been what she sensed was his reluctance to go back and deal with MR and the partners. The other half had been his continuing concern over her and the baby.

"How's Little One?" her mom asked sympathetically.

Sage sighed. "Still breech."

Lucille hugged her. "How's your back?"

With a shrug, Sage admitted, "Always kind of achy and uncomfortable, but the stretching and the prenatal yoga classes are helping." As was Nick's doting care. There was literally nothing as heavenly and soothing as one of his back massages. Except maybe a back massage followed by a hot lovemaking session...

Now, if only they could be together more than just the weekend, life might really start to be as perfect as she wanted it to be...

"Ready to get started?" Lucille paused at the sight of the blanket and pillow Sage had forgotten to take off the sofa.

Sage lifted a hand, before her mother could read anything further into it. "I couldn't get comfortable last night, so Nick finally came out here to give me a little more room."

Her mother scanned Sage's queen-sized bed, where the covers were already neatly in place. Stacks of freshly laundered infant wear, blankets and crib sheets laid out.

"Nick's a big man."

No kidding. And handsome and sexy and kind and loving, to boot. "Six foot four." As well as way too big for her bed, even without her pregnant self in it. Casually, she told her mom, "I've been thinking about getting him a king-sized bed for Father's Day, for my apartment."

It would take up most of her bedroom, but they'd be able to sleep together just as comfortably here as they could at his ranch house. Always a plus. And still have their baby nearby.

"*Your* apartment," Lucille echoed, as if she had never heard the phrase.

Sage returned her mother's odd look. "Yes. The one we're standing in? You know, the one Dad gave me…"

Her mother did not look any happier.

Sage went still. "What about that bothers you?"

For a moment, she thought her mother wouldn't reply. Which again, was no surprise, since they had made a promise to each other, when the big scandal with the family foundation had hit the previous summer, to stop arguing so much about inconsequential things, and do their best to simply love and support each other.

Finally, Lucille said, "You want to give each other more furniture? For Mother's Day? *And* Father's Day?"

Why did everyone think it strange Nick had given her a set of ergonomic cooking stools for Mother's Day? she wondered. What should he have given her? A diamond engagement ring—albeit, a little belated?

"That was a sweet and thoughtful gift, Mom," she defended hotly. "Mine would show him that I care about his physical comfort, too."

Lucille shook her head as if that would clear it. "Physical comfort…" she repeated.

"Yes, Mom, what's wrong with that?" Sage winced at her snappish tone, aware her pregnancy hormones were getting out of whack again. Plus, the stress of the argument was causing her back to begin to ache!

Her mother's expression gentled. "I know Nick is concerned about you, sweetheart, and that you are equally concerned about him."

"Good." Because they were.

"What I'm curious about is, what kind of a Faustian bargain did you make?"

Sage flushed.

Her mother went on, "I never hear you say you love each other. For heaven's sake, you didn't even allude to it on your wedding day!"

So what? Sage tried not to huff. "Love isn't everything, Mom."

Lucille disagreed. "Then you married for what? Expedience? Propriety?"

Sage really didn't want to get into this, but since her mother had brought it up, she had no choice but to remind archly, "You were the one who didn't want me to have a baby on my own, if you remember."

Lucille laid a hand across her chest. "Because I wanted you to *have it all*, Sage. The kind of romantic love and friendship that provides a foundation for a solid, enduring family."

The implied criticism stung.

Sage folded her arms in front of her and propped them on her rounded belly. "What makes you think Nick and I don't have that?"

Lucille picked up the diaper hanger and began filling it. "The fact that the two of you are still maintaining separate residences, with no apparent plans to merge into one. You still haven't told me—even now—that you love the man you've chosen to have a baby with."

Sage didn't know what to say to that.

Because although her feelings for Nick were deep

and enduring, she also knew they had promised each other they wouldn't muddy the waters with impractical, elusive emotions and "fleeting" romance.

She and Nick had sworn they would stay in the best-friends zone. She couldn't—wouldn't—risk changing that at this late date. Not when they both had a baby they already adored on the way.

Sage picked up a stack of newborn undershirts and carried them to the changing table–dresser. "I don't know what to tell you, Mom," she said stiffly, opening the drawer. "Except that what Nick and I have together works. And will continue to work."

As long as they didn't change the rules at this late date.

The following Friday, Sage walked out of her prenatal yoga class to find MR standing in the hospital annex hallway. Surprised, she walked over to greet the statuesque Dallas executive. "Nick's not with me for this."

MR's glance raked the abundant maternal curves revealed by the clinging leotard and tights. "I know. He's over at Monroe's, with Everett and the PR people, getting photographed for the advertising backstory. I wanted a moment with you alone." MR held out a chai iced tea. "It's decaf."

Sage slung her rolled mat over one shoulder, then drew the thigh-length jersey cover-up closer to her body, momentarily forgetting the sultry heat she would face when she exited the building.

"Where would you like to go?" she asked with a resigned sigh.

"I have an air-conditioned car and driver, waiting."

Like that wouldn't draw a lot of attention.

Reminding herself this was for Nick, not the venture capitalist who had been making him miserable, Sage forced a smile. "Sounds good."

They walked in silence among the other pregnant women, until they got to the limo. MR gestured for Sage to go first.

Not sure she wanted to know what her rear view looked like, even with the cover-up, Sage climbed in.

The elegantly thin MR settled opposite her. "As Nick has probably told you, the grand opening of Upscale Outfitters will be on Saturday of Father's Day weekend. Many local dignitaries and celebrities, including the mayor of Dallas will be invited. The ribbon cutting will be at 9:45 that morning. We'd like your family to attend, Sage."

"Are you sure?" The store wasn't that big. "There are a lot of us. Nick has a brother and three sisters, plus in-laws and—"

"We're only talking the Lockharts, Sage."

Sage just looked at her, sure MR had to be kidding. She was not.

MR removed her black eyeglasses. "The Lockharts have ties to the Dallas community, and it's those very wealthy customers we are coveting."

"But it's Nick's venture. Surely his family should be there."

"The Monroe clan is 'small town.' They'd feel out of place. Plus, they'd add no value."

With effort, Sage managed not to tell MR what she thought of her. "Have you told Nick this?"

MR smiled tersely. "I was hoping, given your background, and position as his wife, that you could explain it to him."

"I don't agree with it. So, no. I'm not going to do that. It's either both full families are invited," Sage stated firmly. "Or no one is."

MR shrugged. "If you choose not to attend…"

Sage lifted a silencing palm. "I didn't say I wouldn't be there. I will," Sage told MR firmly. Nick was not just her best friend, he was her husband, and the father of her unborn child. She would support him all the way.

"So. When are you going to tell me what's going on with you?" Nick asked later that evening as the two of them walked the town green, ice-cream cones in hand.

Sage'd had a craving for hand-churned butter pecan. Nick had selected chocolate almond.

"You've practically had steam coming out of your ears all evening," he continued.

Sage hadn't realized he had noticed. But then, Nick always realized more than she would have preferred. It was what had initially drawn her to him, and what kept her from completely lowering her guard, too.

He pushed on. "Did MR say something to upset you?"

She always upsets me. But I'm not about to upset you, too. "My lower back is bothering me," Sage fibbed. For once, it wasn't.

Nick squinted at her playfully, not fully buying it, but willing to play along—for the moment. "There's a cure for that, you know," he drawled.

Oh, she knew. Just thinking about making love with him again made her mouth water and her insides tingle.

"Ice cream first," she said. Then they could go back to her apartment, or maybe his ranch…

Catching her coveting his chocolate, Nick switched

cones with her. For a moment, they savored the flavors in silence. "So what else?" he said eventually.

I'm tired, she was about to fib, when she felt something weird inside her. Very weird, as a matter of fact.

Nick squinted. "Sage?"

She sucked in a breath, took his free hand and put it on her waist, left of her navel. "Feel that," she whispered.

He went still. "Is that the baby?"

Sage nodded. "Kicking," she whispered, almost afraid to move for fear she would stop whatever was going on inside her.

"Or punching," she guessed with a grin. "And that can only mean one thing…"

Nick laughed, triumphant. "Little One is on the move!"

Chapter 12

"You're right," Dr. Johnson confirmed with a smile during Sage's checkup, Monday morning "Your baby is no longer in breech position."

"Which means all is well." It was all Sage could do not to break out into a happy dance. Beside her, Nick looked just as relieved.

Her obstetrician nodded. "Your weight is also on track, and the baby is growing at a healthy pace."

Nick, who was standing on the other side of the exam table, squeezed Sage's hand. Appreciating the way he supported her, Sage squeezed his hand back affectionately, then confirmed cautiously, "So a C-section won't be necessary."

The doc paused to make a note on her chart. "Never say never, but probably not, given the way things stand today."

Sage wasn't surprised to see that her overprotective husband still remained concerned. "Is there a possibility Little One could go back to a breech position, the same way he or she just turned around?" he asked.

Dr. Johnson paused. "It's possible, but unlikely. However, if you do feel the baby on the move again in the next day or so, Sage, let us know. Otherwise, the only thing this little tyke will do is grow bigger and heavier, and drop farther down into the birth canal to get ready for the big day." Which was now less than one month away.

Sage and Nick exchanged glances, giddy with excitement.

"I have another question," Sage said. And it was an important one. She told the doctor about Nick's grand opening in Dallas, Father's Day weekend. "I know it's a little less than two weeks away from the due date, but I'd like to go." She drew a bolstering breath. "Can I?"

Minutes later, Nick and Sage exited the hospital annex. Looking prettier than ever in a summery pale peach dress that brought out the healthy hue of her cheeks, Sage stepped out into the bright sunlight.

Sage shot him a sidelong glance, as determined as he was wary. "I know you don't agree with my plan, but—" her lower lip slid out in the stubborn pout he knew so well "—you heard what Dr. Johnson said. It will be all right for me to go with you, *providing* I don't show any signs of early labor, and am checked by one of the obstetricians in his office the morning of departure, and get plenty of rest while I'm there."

She came closer, inundating him with a drift of perfume. "He's also going to give us the name of an obstetrics group and hospital close to the Galleria mall, and fax our records over in advance, so if anything does happen while we're in Dallas, we'll have someplace to go."

Nick knew all that, but it didn't stop him from worrying. "I don't want you to put yourself or the baby in jeopardy," he countered, all too aware how life could change in a heartbeat.

She winced as she stopped next to his pickup truck, and paused to rub the small of her back. "I'm not going to do that. I am, however, going to be at your side on what could be the biggest day of your life."

The three biggest days of his life had already happened. The first time they'd kissed and made love, thereby going from friends to lovers in one lightning moment, the day she had asked him to father their child and the day she had agreed to marry him.

Nick opened the door to let the heat out. Then reached over and massaged the tight muscles she'd been working on until she relaxed in blissful relief.

Sage smiled in the soft contented way she always did just after they'd made love.

His body reacted in kind. He wanted to make her his, then and there.

Sage smoothed a hand across his chest. She looked up at him cajolingly. "Besides, if I were going to go into early labor, wouldn't you rather I be with you, then two hours away by car?"

She had a point.

One he could not argue.

He had missed the ultrasound and he was sure as heck not missing the birth.

Just as important, this was what she wanted.

"Okay," he said gruffly, "you've convinced me."

She stood on tiptoe, wreathed her arms about his shoulders, and kissed him soundly. "Come back to my apartment," she whispered with a seductive smile, "and I'll let you convince me to do whatever pleases you, too."

She wasn't kidding, Nick found out a short time later.

They'd barely shut the door behind them, when she had toed off her flats, unzipped and shimmied out of her dress. Her pretty pink nipples tented the soft cotton fabric of her bra and her matching panties hit just below the enticing swell of her belly.

She came closer, already undoing the buttons on his shirt. "You can say no, you know."

He laughed at the notion as the blood pooled low. "Not much chance of that, sweetheart," he told her hoarsely, taking her hand and putting it over his fly.

Her golden-brown eyes shimmered in surprise.

Determined to show her just how important she had become to him, he pressed his lips to hers, until she curled against him in surrender, wanting more.

Heart pounding in his chest, he laid her down on the bed. While she watched, he stripped down to the buff, then divested her of every inch of clothing, too. Enjoying the soft, supple sight of her, he lounged next to her. She shivered in delight as he ran his hand over her body, from shoulder to breast to inner thigh, then arched as he found her most sensitive spot.

Closing her eyes, she let her head fall back. "I have to warn you," she purred as he stroked, and adored her with masterful precision, "it takes very little these days for me to go off like a rocket."

Her every quiver was like a match to flame. And

though he sensed she was falling as hard and fast for him as he was for her, he also knew he had not yet enticed her to take their relationship to the next level.

He bent over to kiss her, savoring the soft, womanly taste of her. "Me, too. Which is why—" he kissed her again, even more passionately "—we have to…go slow…"

And go slow they did.

Taking it one step, one caress, one kiss at a time. Until there was no more waiting. Only wanting. Only the mewl of her mounting frustration and the need to be as close as they could possibly physically get, again.

Driven by the same relentless need, he moved behind her. Aware some positions had become uncomfortable for her, he rolled her onto her side, lifted her where she needed to be and slid between her thighs. Kissing the nape of her neck and caressing her languorously with his hand, he possessed her with easy, shallow strokes that were as tantalizing to her as they were for him.

Again and again, until the need to possess her heart and soul built to a fierce unquenchable ache. And still he loved her, slowly and deliberately, until she sighed and shuddered and called his name. And he lost control, too.

Replete with satisfaction, they stayed that way, wrapped up tight in each other's arms.

When the aftershocks stopped, he turned her to face him again. Their breaths catching, hearts beating in unison, she lifted her lips to his. Pleasure sifted through them anew. They kissed, softly and languidly, until both were ready to make love again.

And Nick knew, life just didn't get any better than this.

* * *

June hit Texas with a blast of heat that left the entire state reeling, and continued the entire first week. Air-conditioning helped, of course, but at eight months pregnant, Sage was still sweltering, even when the outdoor temperature hadn't topped 105 degrees every day.

Dallas was equally hot.

Concerned, Nick called every evening to make sure Sage and the baby were okay.

The calls were the highlight of his day.

Even when she only seemed to be half paying attention to him. "What are you doing?" he asked in exasperation, when another clattering noise interrupted their conversation.

"Um… Getting some ice from the icemaker."

She had just gotten ice two minutes ago, for her beloved decaf chai tea.

Before that, she had been standing in front of a fan, trying to cool off. And while he didn't fault her the extra cooling power of an oscillating stand fan, in addition to the central air-conditioning in her apartment, he was aggravated to only hear one out of every three words she was saying to him, due to the background noise.

"Can you repeat what you just said?" Nick asked. "I can barely hear you."

"I'm sorry." Sage sighed. The background noise faded slightly. The heat and complaint in her voice did not.

"I'm. Just. So. Hot. I really can't stand it."

He could imagine her beaded in sweat, the way she had been through most of the latter half of her pregnancy, especially when they were making love. Which they did every chance they got together.

Smiling affectionately, he attempted to tease her into a better mood. "Thought about taking a cold shower?"

"Already did. The minute I finished at The Cowgirl Chef. But, not to worry," she continued with a smugness that enticed, "my latest plan seems to be working."

The victory in her low voice had his senses humming. "And what might that be?" he returned.

"I'm running ice cubes down my body."

Just like that, he was hard as a rock and missing her so badly he could barely stand it. "Seriously?"

"Would I joke about this?" She sounded irritable again.

Wishing he could wrap his arms around her and pull her close, and kiss her until they both forgot why she was piqued, he settled on listening to the sound of her low, sexy voice.

"Why aren't we Skyping or FaceTiming right now?" he teased, already getting a pretty good visual in his mind.

"Because then you would see just how enormous I'm getting this week."

He shook his head, wishing she could see herself through his eyes. "You're beautiful," he said tenderly.

Unimpressed, she harrumphed. "I'm fat."

"Flat-out gorgeous."

"Portly."

"Stunning and amazing—"

She sighed loudly. "Let's go back to what we were talking about before we got sidetracked. What were you saying about your meeting first thing tomorrow?"

"It's a pitch for a group of potential investors for the second store." One they were still working on, as a matter of fact. He had just taken a break to call home.

"The one in Houston?" Sage prodded.

"Denver," he corrected.

An uncomfortable silence fell. Finally, Sage cleared her throat. "Did you say Denver—as in Colorado?"

He'd felt the same way when he heard of the change in venue earlier that day.

For both their sakes he downplayed the inconvenience of the project location. "There's a new luxury mall going up there. It's slated to open in August. One of the original merchants, another upscale Western-wear store, had to drop out, so MR and the partners snapped up the space. Now we just have to find financiers to fund it."

Sage took a moment to process that. "Is it going to be just like the one in Dallas?"

He had shown her pictures of the interior in progress, as well as let her peruse the upscale merchandise set to be in the store.

"MR and the partners have decided that each venue should have a different look entirely, suitable to the overall location. They want more of a boutique feel, instead of a chain." Which meant a whole truckload more work, from the outset. Most of which would likely have to be done on site.

"I see." Sage's tone was cool.

"I'm going to limit my travel there, Sage." That had already been decided.

More silence.

"Sage?" Was she angry? Had they been using Face-Time or Skype, he would have been able to see her expression and have a better idea of what she was thinking and feeling.

"I'm still here."

Yet, Nick noted, her voice sounded weak and thready. He began to panic, the way he always did when he was away from her and she might need him. "Are you okay?"

"Yes, ah…"

His heart stopped at the sound of her high-pitched yelp, followed by a low, tortured moan. "Sage?" Nick pressed again.

Another sound of distress. This one more intense.

"Tell me what's happening!" he demanded.

All he got was more silence.

"Right now, Sage," he warned, adrenaline racing, "or I'm calling 911…" Cell still pressed to his ear, he headed for the MEP office landline.

"No." Sage gasped again, and let out a frantic cry. "Don't do that!"

Nick stopped dead in his tracks. "*Are* you in labor, Sage?" he could tell from the sound of things she was in pain.

He heard her draw a deep, halting breath.

"Yes. I think I am."

"You can't leave," MR said, when Nick went to the conference room where she and Everett were still working on the PowerPoint slides for the next day's presentations.

Did she have a hearing problem? Nick wondered, grinding his teeth in frustration.

"Sage is in labor."

The only reason he hadn't called 911 was because the contraction had passed, and her good friend, and sister-in-law Adelaide was on her way to take Sage to the hospital.

MR took off her glasses. "So? It's a first baby, Nick. Hence her labor and delivery can take anywhere from twenty-four to thirty-six hours on average."

There was nothing average about Sage. Or his baby, Nick thought fiercely.

"Which means—" MR consulted her watch "—since it's close to midnight now, you can still make our 10:00 a.m. meeting tomorrow, drive back to Laramie afterward and still get there in plenty of time."

Nick really did not have time for this. "I'm leaving."

Everett studied him, with his usual poker faced expression. He couldn't be sure, but Nick thought there was a small smile playing around the edges of the assistant's mouth. As if he were enjoying not seeing his boss get what she wanted, for a change.

MR leaped up, momentarily losing her cool. "Nick, if you bail on us again, there will be repercussions," she warned.

Nothing, Nick thought, like the ones that would happen if he missed the most important day in his life to date.

"Goodbye, MR."

He turned and walked out of the room, down the hall and out of the building.

He tried calling Sage again when he reached his car, but his call went straight to voice mail. "Sage, it's Nick, I love you and I'm on my way. I should be there in two and a half hours or less. Call me if you can."

Except, she didn't call.

And all the hospital would tell him was that she had made it to the ER, no problem, Adelaide by her side, and was being treated. And he should drive safely, as things still appeared to be in the *very early* stages. But, the nurse promised, she would call him if there were any changes.

So Nick drove, calmly and safely.

And thought about how much he wished he were already at his wife's side. Instead of miles away.

He reached the hospital at two thirty in the morning.

Walked in through the only doors open that time of night, the Emergency entrance.

And saw, to his surprise, Sage, standing in street clothes near the desk, her wheeled hospital bag on the floor beside her. She was completely red-faced and miserable. His older brother, Gavin, an ER physician, was standing with his arm around her shoulders. "...happens to a lot of people," he was saying.

Nick crossed the distance between them hurriedly. "What's going on?" he asked.

Sage could barely look him in the eye. "I wasn't in labor," she mumbled.

"She was having Braxton Hicks contractions," Gavin explained. "We kept her under observation for a while, just to make sure."

"But it was all a false alarm. Apparently, I'm still a good three and a half weeks away from delivery," she said, then turned on her heel, still shaking her head in abject humiliation, and headed for the exit.

"Take her home," Gavin advised with a meaningful look. "See she gets *a lot of rest and TLC.*"

More than up for that, Nick grabbed the hospital bag Sage seemed to have forgotten and strode after her. He caught up with her as they reached the outside. The air was still stifling hot.

"I've never been so embarrassed in my life," she muttered as he opened her door for her.

"You'll feel better when we get to your apartment," he soothed.

Sage stopped, her mouth open in a round O of further distress.

Nick paused, not sure why she would find fault with that. "I figured you'd want to go there instead of the ranch since it's close, and bound to be way cooler, because I turn the AC way up when I'm away, but if you'd prefer to be at the ranch house…" With all the privacy…

"I'd rather be at my apartment. But…" She threw up her hands in frustration. "We probably shouldn't. Not without ruining everything else."

She was not making any sense. "What are you talking about?" Nick asked.

She shut her eyes, sighed and motioned him on. "You'll see."

When they walked into her apartment and approached her bedroom, Nick could only stare.

"You don't like it," Sage guessed desultorily.

"What's not to like about a king-sized bed?" It was perfect for making love, cuddling. He wouldn't have to worry about taking up too much of the space, thereby exacerbating the back problems that had been plaguing her the entire pregnancy.

As if on cue, Sage put a hand behind her waist, rubbed. "It takes up most of the room."

He stepped behind her to take over the massage, gently kneading until he felt the knotted muscles on either side of her spine began to ease. "But what a way to take it up."

Sighing luxuriantly, she leaned into his touch.

Feeling her start to relax, he turned her to face him. "Why didn't you tell me you were doing this?"

"Because it was supposed to be a surprise for Father's Day, Nick." New misery lit her eyes. "Only I was going to have to give it to you *early*, since we're going to be in Dallas that weekend for the grand opening."

"I gave you the ergonomic kitchen stools a couple days early," he pointed out. Mostly because *he* hadn't been able to wait.

"I know. But when you saw your present for the first time, I wanted it to be completely made up with all the linens. Instead of just with the wrong-sized pillows, plain white sheets and a single blanket. But the accoutrements haven't come in yet, and won't get here until Thursday, so…darn it all—" she balled her fists at her sides "—why are you smiling?"

Joy rushing through him, he wrapped his arms around her. "Because this bed is the best present anyone has ever given me." It meant Sage wanted to get closer to him, the same way he wanted to get closer to her.

She blinked up at him, whispering, "Really?"

"Really," he confirmed thickly, hugging her close.

He cupped her chin and lifted her face to kiss her. Then stopped, when she burst into tears.

"You're sure we don't need to go back to the hospital," Nick asked, half an hour later, when Sage still hadn't stopped crying.

Her silent flow of seemingly unstoppable tears was really starting to worry him.

"It's j-j-just h-h-hormones," she cried, fisting her hands in his shirt. "And the fact that I'm just so tired of being pregnant, and hot all the time, and achy and moody. And the fact that I cry when I don't know why, and laugh when I shouldn't and never seem to get a full night's sleep." She hiccupped. "And I know I have a healthy baby and I shouldn't complain…"

Nick gathered her even closer, loving the feminine feel of her against him. "In your place, I'd complain, too."

"No you wouldn't," she argued, "because you're a saint."

He couldn't help it—he laughed at that. "Oh, Sage," he said, pressing a kiss in her hair as they snuggled together in their new king-sized bed. "If you only knew… how flawed I am."

"You aren't," she insisted stubbornly, beginning to sound a little sleepy now.

But he was.

Otherwise, he never would have pretended that they could be just friends, and then lovers, and then co-parents, and wife-and-husband-in-name-only and want nothing more from her than what she offered.

Because the truth was, he wanted a hell of a lot more from her. And from himself.

He wanted to be able to tell her how he felt without fear of losing her. He wanted them to have it all. Marriage, a kid. Hell, half a dozen kids! And the kind of love that would last a lifetime, just like his parents had, and hers apparently had enjoyed, too.

But if that wasn't in the cards for them—and he had to admit, it increasingly looked like they would never move past the status quo—then he would have to find a way to be satisfied with what they had, and not waste time looking for anything more.

Because to do so could spoil everything. And that was the last thing he wanted.

Chapter 13

"So what do you think?" Nick asked Sage, when he took her to the Galleria after hours for her first look at Upscale Outfitters.

"Very nice," she said.

And it was. The distressed white-and-beige brick walls contrasted nicely against polished floors with the patina of rich aged dark brown leather. The lighting was perfect, the strategically placed mirrors and carpeted dressing rooms of the finest quality. The expensive designer clothes, boots and hats were gorgeous, too.

Nick looked around. Pleased, and yet...

She came closer, inhaling his brisk masculine scent. "What is it?" she asked softly, taking his hand.

For a moment, they stood pensively side by side, linked by so much more than their entwined palms. Then he shook his head, as if kicking himself for looking a gift horse in the mouth. "Nothing."

When they had first become friends, they had told each other everything. Or so it seemed. Since they'd been married they had started censoring themselves from time to time. If it continued, she knew they would lose the intimacy that had bound them together thus far. And that scared her.

She drew a breath, then prodded, "Nick?"

For a moment, he remained silent. Seeming to do battle with himself, even as he studied his handiwork. Finally, he said in that sexy, gruff voice she loved, "There's nothing here of what I envisioned when I came up with the idea of turning Monroe's Western Wear into a chain of stores."

She swiveled to face him. "Maybe that's because the original Monroe's, with its century of service to one community, can't ever be duplicated," she soothed. "Even if the two stores were identical in every way."

His gaze drifted thoughtfully over the dark blue knit maternity shorts and top she wore before returning to her face. "You may have a point there."

Her body tingling with the need to make love with him, she sauntered even closer, glad they had the evening to themselves.

Curious, she had to ask, "Do you wish your family was going to be here tomorrow for the ribbon cutting?" The way hers had been when she'd opened The Cowgirl Chef. She searched his eyes. "Because it might not be too late to get them here, you know."

Nick vetoed the idea with a shake of his head. "MR was clear. No family."

Except mine, with their connections, Sage thought ruefully, glad Nick had never found out about that.

Nick walked over to straighten a display of top-of-the-line boots. "She doesn't want noncustomers taking up space that could be used for paying clientele. That's why only she and Everett will be here tomorrow, representing the other partners."

Doing her best to lighten the somber mood, Sage propped a hand on her hip, adapting a saucy stance. "Are you sure I'm invited then?" She batted her eyelashes flirtatiously. As he began to grin, she pushed on, "Or will it only be okay if I purchase something, too?"

He caught her around the waist and brought her as close as her pregnant shape would allow. He curved a hand over her cheek, then cupping her chin in his hand, he gently rubbed a thumb over her lower lip.

"You are nonnegotiable," he told her, his voice husky with affection. "And for the record, I'm very glad you're here to support me." He bent to kiss her lips. "I know it can't be easy for you, traveling in the last trimester."

Sage waved off the "sacrifice."

"It was no big deal," she insisted cheerfully. "I know I was a little weepy there for a few days earlier in the month," she admitted, playfully wrinkling her nose at him, "but I promise you, I've managed to put an end to the crying jags. In fact, I haven't had a single one since the night of the whole Braxton Hicks episode!"

Nick grinned as she laid her head on his shoulder, and he reached over to massage a hand down her spine. "You really have to stop feeling embarrassed about that."

Sage only wished she could.

Determined, however, to make sure it never happened again, that she would never jump the gun and mistake a few semiregular "practice" contractions for the real thing, she went back to talking about the trip.

"I know you've been a little nervous about me traveling with you, but there's really nothing to worry about." She reiterated what she had already told him, before they'd left Laramie County. "I saw the doctor this morning. He said Little One is still positioned fairly high up in my abdomen, and I'm not showing even a single sign of early labor. Which is what we'd expect, given that my due date is still another two weeks away."

"That's good," Nick interrupted, fiercely protective as ever, "because if you were any closer to delivering our baby..."

He would have eighty-sixed her trip, for sure.

And it would have killed her not to be here with him, on his big weekend.

She brightened as they let themselves out the employees' entrance and walked out into the hallway that led to the exit.

"In any case," she reminded him, "the drive here was only a little over two and a half hours. And we stopped three times so I could get out and stretch and walk around. Plus—" she stopped to make a comical face "—followed every precaution ever known to pregnant women and their doctors."

He laughed at her dramatics.

Wrapping his arm around her shoulders, he tucked her into the solid heat of his body, then leaned down to press a kiss on the top of her head. "We still need to get you to the hotel so you can have a proper dinner and rest."

That sounded good.

Except...

Sage really hated to tempt fate.

She turned to face him as they stepped out into the

heat of the Texas summer night. "Are you sure you want to return to The Mansion?" She drew an enervating breath. "I know the management promised us an amazing experience if we ever chose to return again, but…the last time didn't work out so well." She would hate for a repeat of their wedding night. And though she felt fine now, she was still prone to a little evening sickness, from time to time.

"I've taken pains to make sure everything will be perfect for you this time," Nick said. "Plus, it's near the hospital your obstetrician recommended—in case of any trouble, and right down the road from the Galleria mall, as well."

He'd made his case.

Sage smiled. "Then, The Mansion it is."

They were at the front desk, checking in, when the manager came out to speak to them.

Guessing—correctly as it happened—that she did not want to relive the specifics of her prior humiliation, Nick suggested gently, "Why don't you go on up to the suite with the bellman? I'll be along in a minute."

It had been a very long day for her and the baby, so she quickly relented. "I'll see you up there." She continued across the lobby with the bellman. Turned, as they reached the elevators.

Saw Nick's face.

Whatever was being said, he was definitely not happy.

She hoped that wasn't an omen of another bad night.

Sage was still worrying when Nick walked into the hotel's best suite a good fifteen minutes later. "Everything okay down there?" she asked.

In the penthouse suite, it was just fine.

Both he and the hotel staff had gone all out to ensure that their stay was incredible. Bouquets of her favorite yellow roses adorned every room. There were baskets of fresh fruit and boxes of chocolate. An assortment of beverages. Sumptuous robes and slippers. As well as a complete array of spa services, should they request them.

He strolled toward her, confident as ever, a slow smile tilting the corners of his lips. "It's going to be perfect," he promised.

As if the grim exchange had never happened.

Sage studied him, not sure why he was suddenly shutting her out. Just knowing that he was. And it had something to do with his conversation with the hotel manager.

Unable to help but feel a little hurt, she slid him a look. "You sure?" She splayed her hands across his chest. Aware she didn't want him lying to her, for any reason, she savored the strong, steady beat of his heart. "'Cause you didn't look very pleased earlier."

For a second, his face bore the look of a warrior about to head into battle. Then, he became inscrutable again. Wrapping his arms about her, drawing her in close against him, murmuring huskily, "I was just making sure there would be no shrimp or fish of any kind in the room service dinner they are sending up for us."

Her inner radar told her that while that might be true, it was also a little more than that. But then, given what had happened during the previous visit, she figured he had a right to be overly cautious. Especially since the health of their baby was also at stake.

Not about to let the past calamity keep them from hav-

ing a great time tonight, however, she snuggled against
him. "I'm sure it will all be fine. But if it makes you feel
better," she teased, "I'll let you check everything out in
advance, just to be sure."

He tilted her face up to his. Their lips met and they
kissed, soft and deep and slow, getting their evening
alone off to an excellent start.

An hour and a half later, after what had turned out to
be the most wonderful dinner she'd ever had was wind-
ing down, and they walked out to the penthouse terrace
overlooking the city, Sage could still feel an undercurrent of something going on with Nick.

"Can I ask you something?"

He lounged against the brick wall, the starlit sky and
sea of glittering city lights forming a romantic backdrop behind him. Crossing his arms, he flashed her a
wolfish grin. "Anything."

Sage stationed herself opposite him, as the warm,
dry summer air blew across their bodies. "Why were
you so insistent we stay at a five-star hotel this evening?" she asked curiously. When it was so unlike anything he usually did for himself. "Was it because it's a
big weekend for you? Or was it because you were trying
to please me? And you somehow got the idea that this
was what I required in terms of luxury and comfort?"

He sobered, confirming her worst suspicions. "You
grew up with a lot of money, Sage."

Too much, she often thought in retrospect. "So there-
fore I'm above staying at the kind of modestly priced
chain hotel, where you usually stay, when you're on
your own?"

He paused, as ruggedly sexy as always. Looking

deep into her eyes, he took her hand. "I want you to be happy."

Reveling in the strong warmth of his fingers encircling hers, she reiterated, "Money isn't going to make me feel that way, Nick. My parents realized that, too, which is why they put most of their accumulated wealth into the family's charitable foundation before my father died, and gifted my mother and me and my siblings all with property in Laramie County instead. So we would have a foundation to build our futures on. A future that would require each and every one of us to work and work hard for whatever we have. Just like my parents had to do."

He continued to hold her gaze, the corners of his mouth barely turning up. "We talked about that when we first became friends," he reminded, a veil dropping over his emotions.

Determined to understand him, the way a wife should, she leaned in even closer. "Then why do you think I still need to go back to the old life I had in Dallas growing up, the life where whatever I wanted, whenever I wanted it, was pretty much just given to me, no questions asked?"

He lifted his broad shoulders in a careless shrug, challenging her now. "Because that kind of life is hard to leave behind."

"Who told you that?" she countered irritably, then blurted out before she could stop herself, "MR?"

His manner as composed as hers was irritable, Nick inclined his head. "We had a few talks about downward mobility in general, early on. But to be honest," he said gruffly, "I was thinking about it long before that. Worrying that I might not be able to..." He stopped abruptly, started again, "That *you* might not be content with less, long-term."

Sage thought about the relief she'd felt, when she had left her moneyed childhood existence and struck out on her own after culinary school. Her needing to not be caught up in all that was part of what'd had her chasing her ex all over the West Coast, searching for a simpler version of happiness.

Was the opposite driving Nick now?

Was that part of the reason he'd let those with more wealth and power obliterate his vision for a chain of Western-wear stores, and replace it with their own?

Though he had every reason to be proud of what he had accomplished in getting the Upscale Outfitters chain started, she sensed he still felt frustrated and hemmed in. Maybe even more so than before he had signed a contract with Metro Equity Partners.

Because then he'd still had his dreams.

He hadn't had to cede creative and business control of the venture for greater financial stability in the long run. Just to protect his unborn child. And possibly please her, too…?

He tucked a strand of hair behind her ear. "I want you to have everything your heart desires."

Then that would be you, Nick, she thought wistfully, gazing into his eyes.

As more than friend or lover or husband-for-business-purposes-only. "I want you to have everything you ever wanted, too." She pushed the words through the ache in her throat. "And for the record, I am very happy in Laramie."

She yearned to add, *You could be, too, if you'd just stop chasing the almighty dollar and give it a chance.*

But wanting to support him in whatever he endeavored, she said kindly instead, "But I understand why you'd want something different from what you had growing up, too. Maybe," she added, attempting to look at it from his point of view, "in a way, we all do."

And yet, Nick thought, as Sage slipped into the bathroom to get ready for bed, there were also plenty of things they both wanted. Friendship. An ongoing sexual relationship. This baby. And the sense of family Little One was already providing.

Initially, that had been more than enough to make him happier and more content than he had ever been.

That had begun to change the night they said their vows.

Although they had yet to share space together full-time, occasionally living together as husband and wife added another layer of intimacy to their complex arrangement. Sharing the ups and downs of her pregnancy, attending her obstetrical appointments and anticipating the birth of their child brought them closer, too. She wasn't just the wife in their for-business-reasons-only marriage, she was the wife he had always yearned to have. Sweet, loving, generous.

Definitely worth waiting for, he thought, as the bathroom door opened, and Sage walked out.

She was wearing one of the old-fashioned knee-length nightshirts he adored, with a band collar and a row of buttons up the front. Her face scrubbed of makeup, her cheeks a pretty pink, her just-brushed hair loose and flowing, she looked sweet and innocent, and, as she had been of late, incredibly shy about her body.

Although not about to admit it.

"I know." She rested one hand on her hip, and adapted a pinup girl pose. She fluffed the ends of her hair with her free hand. "I've still got it."

Grinning, he crossed to her side, and took her in his arms. "You better believe you do, sweetheart." He caressed the curve of her cheek with the pad of his thumb, as her lower lip trembled once again.

Then he lowered his mouth to hers, and kissed her long and slow and deep, before dancing her toward the bed. They broke apart long enough for him to gently lay her down.

He opened the buttons on her nightshirt, raining kisses over her face, her throat, her full, sexy breasts. She shivered as he went lower still. As his hands stroked and caressed, he kissed her in a way that let her know there would be no more holding back, no more pretending they weren't as important to each other as life itself.

Valiantly, Sage tried to keep her emotions out of the kiss. With absolutely no success. It didn't matter what deal they had made, long ago. Or how she longed to give him every ounce of freedom and independence he deserved.

When she was in Nick's arms, all she could think about, all she could do, was surrender. To the sensations his lips and hands created. To the hardness of his body, and the tender resolve in the way he made love to her.

She wanted to feel connected to him, not just physically, but heart and soul.

And when sensations ran riot through her, perspiration beading her body, and they finally reached completion and catapulted into oblivion, she had never felt more blissful.

Eventually, Sage's racing heartbeat slowed, and her

body stopped shuddering. Sweet moments passed as they clung together. She sighed with contentment. If this wasn't true love, and she guessed it still wasn't, at least not in the traditional sense, she did not care.

Her relationship with Nick was everything she had ever wanted and needed. And in the end, wasn't that all that really mattered?

Nick smoothed a hand through her hair, down her spine.

He pressed a kiss into her hair. "Think you'll be able to sleep tonight?" he murmured, helping her put her sleep shirt back on and adjust the pillows, just so.

"I hope so," Sage said, yawning, as Nick shrugged on a pair of pajama bottoms and climbed in beside her.

She really needed it.

Chapter 14

The only problem was, Sage didn't sleep. Despite the effort Nick had made to help her relax and get comfortable, she never really did get cozy in the big, wonderful hotel bed. Long after he was sound asleep, she was still staring at the ceiling. By morning, she was not just tired, she was unbearably cranky and out of sorts, too. To the point where every single pep talk she tried to give herself failed miserably.

And though she tried to hide it from Nick, she knew he had seen her unusually intense irascibility, too.

Finally, he asked what they were both thinking.

"Are you sure you want to go this morning?" He stood in the bathroom doorway. "Because I would understand if you didn't want to endure what could very well be a madhouse, if anywhere near the expected customer traffic comes thru."

This is his day. It has to go well. More important still, I want to be there for him.

"Yes, of course, I want to go." Sage slipped on a sleeveless, knee-length black jersey maternity dress that was supposed to be slimming but in reality clung to her enormous stomach, making her look and feel like a beached whale. "I am going to go," she repeated emphatically.

Nick studied her reflection. Zeroing in on her frown, he asked, nonplussed, "What's wrong?"

Nothing and everything, Sage thought, blinking back a new round of unprecedented tears.

She did not know why she was so crazy hormonal this morning. It was one thing to do without a little much-needed sleep. Another to cry in the shower, cry while trying to put on her makeup—to the point where she had to wash her face and do it all over again. All for no reason she could fathom!

Didn't she have the most wonderful man on earth by her side, waiting excitedly to welcome their baby into the world?

Hadn't he pampered her silly last night?

Made love to her with exquisite tenderness?

Helped her feel every bit as important to him as he was to her?

So why, then, Sage thought on a new burst of frustration, as she ran a brush through her freshly blown-dry hair, did she feel on the verge of losing it all over again?

Ducking his searching gaze, she padded back into the dressing area of the luxury suite, in search of the flats that went with the dress. She plucked them from the suitcase, and dropped them onto the floor. "I'm just excited for you," she fibbed.

Nick watched as she toed them into position, then attempted unsuccessfully to slip her swollen feet into them.

Nick knelt before her, like a prince courting his Cinderella. "Need some help, sweetheart?"

Unfortunately, he could not fit her feet into the soft ballet flats, either.

Not sure what she was supposed to do, with them just minutes away from departure, she contemplated her options. The sneakers she'd traveled in were too beat up. The only other thing she had were flip-flops.

Nick followed her gaze. "They'll be okay." He helped her slip her feet into them.

Aware it was supposed to be a brutally hot June day, with the temperature soaring to 104 degrees, but the mall itself might feel cool, she grabbed a lightweight sky blue cardigan and her bag.

Together, they headed out.

"I'm supposed to be there from open to close today, but MR is going to have a driver ready to take you back here, whenever you're ready," Nick said.

"Sounds good," she replied.

What wasn't good was the look on MR's face when she saw Sage walk into the luxury store, in flip-flops. As usual, the venture capitalist recovered quickly. Her disdain slipped into a warm, welcoming smile as she motioned for one of the sophisticated saleswomen. "You know what would go great with that dress? A summery white denim jacket and some black-and-peacock-blue boots."

"Absolutely," the clerk said. "I'll get right on it."

Her lower back aching, the way it had for months

now, Sage let herself be led off. Behind her, she heard Nick tell MR, "I've got a few things I'd like to discuss."

"We'll talk in the back office," MR chirped happily.

The two disappeared, and Sage focused on being the "wife" Nick needed her to be.

Nick held his temper while MR shut the door behind them. Turning, she gave him a droll look. "Why so serious?"

Nick folded his arms in front of him. Curious as to how long she'd play innocent. "I spoke to the manager at The Mansion last night."

MR's expression remained guileless. "And…?"

He'd known for months that his business partner was not the person she purported to be. But for her to stoop as low as she had was still unfathomable. At least for someone like him who had grown up in a rural community where neighbor looked out for neighbor.

"Cut the bull, MR," he retorted, his patience exhausted. "I know what you did."

MR walked over to the mirror she'd installed and checked out the black lace-over-silk dress and knee-high lace-up boots she wore. Adjusting the turquoise-and-leather pendant she wore, she turned back to face him, her countenance calm. "I'm sure I don't know what you're talking about."

Nick was just as sure she did. "Here's the bottom line. I'm done being jerked around like a marionette on a string."

MR paused, an exaggerated expression of sympathy on her perfectly made-up face. Carefully, she began, "I understand you're anxious about today."

Anxious, hell! "My wife and child are not going to be collateral damage in your ambitious schemes."

An unpleasant pause, filled with unexpressed guilt.

MR lifted a discerning brow, her countenance turning ugly. "Careful, Nick, this is a situation that could play out in more than one way." She arrowed a thumb at her sternum. "I'm the one with all the advantages."

Before he could continue, the sales rep knocked and opened the door slightly. At MR's approving nod, she walked in, a flushed Sage at her side. With a sweeping gesture toward Nick's wife, the clerk asked, "What do you think? Hat or no hat?"

MR's gaze narrowed critically, all business once again. "None for Sage. The custom, definitely, for Nick."

He couldn't help but note how beautiful and alluring Sage looked in the fancy boots and jacket. He also noted she had her right hand behind her, discretely rubbing the small of her back. A small bead of perspiration dotted her brow. He crossed to her side in instant concern, and wrapped a supportive arm around her waist. "Are you too hot in that?"

"I'm fine." She flashed a dazzling smile, her brow growing ever damper, as she rested against him. "I wouldn't mind sitting down for a moment, though."

Everett appeared in the doorway. "Several hundred people are already lined up outside the door and the camera crew is here to film the ribbon-cutting ceremony for the grand opening. The mayor just arrived, too."

MR handed Nick the hat they all wanted him to wear. "Nick?" Her shrill voice rang with impatience.

"Sage and I will be right there," he promised, al-

ready getting his wife a bottle of sparkling water from
the fridge.

MR flashed her disapproval. "Five minutes," she
warned.

"No problem."

Once he and Sage were alone, Nick took another long
look at her. She seemed a little unsteady. And very tired,
beneath the aura of flushed excitement. Protectiveness
rose within him. "Are you sure you're up to this?" he
asked her gently.

"Positive." She hesitated, her lip taking on a perplexed curve. "When I walked in, were you and MR
arguing about something?" When he didn't answer right
away, she added anxiously, "It sounded…unpleasant."

It likely would have been, had he gotten to the bottom line. But he figured that could wait. What was important now was Sage and their baby, making sure they
both were okay.

"Nothing you need to worry about," he soothed. He
would take care of this.

For all of them.

Sage wasn't surprised Nick brushed her off. He had
a way of shutting down emotionally whenever their in-
teractions headed into overly intimate territory.

Still, it stung.

Luckily, they had no chance to pursue the conversation, given Everett's repeat appearance in the doorway.

"Showtime!" the assistant said.

Gallantly, Nick offered Sage a hand up.

Obediently, Everett reminded him, "The hat."

With a grimace, Nick settled it on his head.

One hand on Sage's back, he escorted her out to the

front. On the other side of the glass, a big white ribbon had been stretched across the space.

He dropped his hold on her as the mayor and other local dignitaries greeted him and offered their congratulations. The camera crew filmed while Nick and MR jointly held the large pair of scissors and cut the ribbon. Everyone clapped. There were several hoots and hollers and loud whistles. The doors were pushed all the way open and the crowd, buzzing with excitement, surged inside.

It was, Sage noted, both gratifying to see such enthusiasm—even if the mercantile wasn't what Nick had originally envisioned—and a little overwhelming, too. Plus, maybe it was the unusually high heels of the boots she wore, but her lower back was now aching like the jab of a hot poker.

Warning herself that this event wouldn't last all that long, she forced herself to smile through the near rhythmic discomfort.

Nick appeared at her side. "Mayor, I'd like you to meet my wife, Sage Lockhart Monroe."

The handsome politician nodded, extending his hand. "I know your family well."

"Very nice to see you here," Sage returned politely.

Then froze, as a river of something wet and warm trickled down her leg and splattered on the floor.

She looked down in horror and shock, as everyone around her automatically stepped back.

For a moment, she thought she had done the unthinkable and wet herself.

Then she knew.

Oh, heavens.

Oh, no.

Not now.

Not here.

My God…

"Sage?" Nick said, as the water saturated her underwear and dripped down her thighs.

She panicked as she felt her knees buckle beneath her.

A collective gasp filled the air. Nick rushed in and caught her as she fell backward. "It's okay. I got you… Talk to me, Sage. Can you tell me what's happening?"

"I need…to lie down…" she whimpered, and he eased her gently onto the floor. As pain wrapped her middle in a breath-robbing vice, she felt another even more disturbing sensation. She gripped her husband's forearm tightly. That couldn't be…could it? Oh, no. "Nick…" *My God!* "Nick…!"

He grabbed a folded sweater from a nearby display and eased it under her head. "It's all right, sweetheart, I promise. I'm right here with you, and I'm not going anywhere. Someone's already calling 911…"

Too late for that, she thought miserably, as the panic and fear inside her twisted and rose. Tears blurred her eyes. "I feel the baby's head."

Out of the corner of his eyes, Nick saw MR and Everett and their bevy of salesclerks taking charge and waving the crowds back.

Unfortunately, all the commotion caused even more people to gather outside the storefront.

For once glad the venture capitalist had such a take-charge personality, Nick turned back to his wife.

Drawing on everything he had learned about childbirth, he soothed, "You can't, sweetheart. It's way too soon for that."

Her eyes were glazed with panic and pain. "I do, I swear! It…" She moaned, a deep, feral cry for help, and gripped his arms, hard. "The baby is coming!"

Now? Here?

Sage held on even tighter. Wildly, she pleaded with him, "You've got to help me make sure…" She let out another panicked, keening cry. "You've got to look…"

Nick was vaguely aware they were moving racks of shirts around them, to try to block the view.

He got down on his knees, eased Sage's hem up, reached beneath her dress and removed her drenched panties. Easing her thighs apart, he inhaled a bolstering breath and checked.

Sure enough, she was right, it was definitely their baby's head.

Little One was crowning.

There was no time to wait for the EMTs.

"Get me something to put underneath her," he shouted, as Sage sobbed and panted.

Several brand-new extra-large men's shirts of fine soft cotton were ripped off hangers and thrust at him.

"Nick," Sage sobbed. "I've…got…to…push…"

He had no choice but to cede all control. "Then go for it, sweetheart," he said, hastily making a bed beneath her.

She grunted, shoved.

The head came out, into his waiting palm.

"Again," he directed, gently but firmly supporting the emerging infant.

She pushed.

The rest of their baby's body slid out into his waiting hands. Perfect as could be, and covered in a waxy white substance. The cord was still connected to Sage.

Sage lifted her head and shoulders off the floor, trying to see. "Nick...?" she asked anxiously.

"It's a boy," he declared.

And Little One hadn't made a sound, Nick noted in alarm. Didn't seem to be breathing, at all.

Sending up a silent prayer, Nick used the tip of his little finger to wipe the baby's nose and mouth of mucous, then held their infant upright.

Startled into awareness, their son let out a lusty, high-pitched cry.

Sage began to sob, openly now, and Nick felt a surge of love and gratitude as the paramedics rushed in.

The hours that followed were a blur. Sage had only hazy memories of the ambulance ride to the hospital and their time in the ER before being whisked up to the maternity wing.

But she would never forget the moment when she had seen Nick help their son take his first breath. Or the way he had looked as he settled their child in her arms. As if all his dreams had come true, too. Or the incredible miracle of cradling her baby son in her arms for the very first time. And the feeling of the contentment that flowed through her when the three of them were finally settled in one of the hospital's private maternity suites was beyond compare.

Nick sat in the chair next to the bed as she nursed. He watched, mesmerized, as little Shane fed.

Sage could tell he had something on his mind.

She did, too, so she decided to go first before any

more time elapsed. "I'm sorry I disrupted the grand opening."

He shook off her apology. "I'm sorry I let them set the grand opening so close to your due date."

Sage shrugged. "With a 49 percent share, you didn't really have a lot of choice. And Father's Day weekend was a great time to enter the retail market." She expected the weekend sales would be through the roof. Not a bad way to start a business.

Nick, however, did not appear to be thinking about his hard-won success.

Brow furrowing, he let his gaze drift lazily over her. "Did you suspect you might be in labor this morning? Is that why you were so weepy?"

So he had seen her surreptitious tears, she thought, her body warming everywhere his gaze had landed. "My hormones were definitely raging," she admitted self-consciously, appreciating his tender concern, "but I wasn't having contractions. Not like I did when we had the whole Braxton Hicks debacle. Just the kind of lower back pain I've had the entire pregnancy. And I didn't connect that with labor." She grimaced, remembering. "Until my water broke, anyway."

Nick exhaled, his relief as strong as her own. "Thank heaven EMS got there quickly."

She grinned. "Thank heaven *you* knew exactly how to proceed until they *did* arrive."

He chuckled fondly, his attention moving from her to their son, and back again. "It's not like I had to do much," he admitted with an ornery grin. "When our son was ready to make his entry into the world, he came right on out."

They smiled and held hands. Then Sage handed their

son over to Nick, to hold and burp. He had never looked so strong or handsome, or felt so very much an integral, needed part of her life. And Shane's… "We are so very lucky," she told him softly, meaning it with all her heart and soul.

One big hand gently cupping Shane's head and neck, the other supporting his diapered bottom, Nick tenderly cradled Shane against his broad chest. "We are," he admitted happily.

He kissed them both, then drew back, sober now, and looked her in the eye. "Which is why I want to make some changes in my business dealings. And most important, stop all the traveling right now."

Heaven knew, there was nothing Sage would like better than to have her husband around full-time, instead of just on weekends. But…

"Will the partners allow that?" she asked.

Nick's jaw jutted out. "It's not really their decision to make," he said curtly.

Wasn't it?

Sage wondered.

Chapter 15

"Is now a good time?" MR asked, from the doorway of the hospital room, five hours later.

For celebrating it sure was, Sage thought, cuddling her newborn son in her arms. She just wasn't sure she wanted to do so with MR, who continued to annoy her on nearly every level. But with Nick's business partner standing there with a huge basket of baby things in her arms, and a congratulatory smile on her face, there wasn't much she could do but say, "Yes. Of course." With her free hand, Sage motioned her in.

"I won't stay long." MR set the luxurious gift on a chair and perched on the window ledge.

The exec had changed out of the Western wear she'd worn earlier in the day, and was now in the usual sleek business suit and heels. Her hair and makeup looked freshly done, too. In contrast to Sage, who still felt like a sweaty, disheveled mess, after giving birth.

MR continued scanning the room thoughtfully. "Where's Nick?"

"He went back to the hotel to get cleaned up and retrieve our hospital bag." So she could shower and change into something more comfortable than her hospital gown. Maybe do her hair and makeup, too.

She knew it was silly, but she wanted to look good for Nick—and Shane.

MR beamed. "Good. Then you and I will have a moment alone."

Feminine instinct told her this could not be good. Wary of the sweetly sleeping babe in her arms, Sage tried not to tense. "Something wrong?"

"Actually, for once in this process, everything is incredibly right! Shane's dramatic entry into the world has caused a *huge* media splash. We've been fielding calls right and left with news crews wanting to do stories on his birth. The sooner, the better, if we want to take advantage of this publicity gold mine. But Nick, as usual, is refusing to cooperate."

Good for my husband, Sage thought fiercely. *Family first. Always.*

Deciding it best to be honest, she admitted calmly, "I don't think it's a good idea, either." Sage shifted little Shane higher in her arms. His little rosebud lips worked soundlessly for several seconds, before he let out a soft sigh, stuck his thumb in his mouth, just the way he had in her womb, and promptly fell back asleep. "Shane went through an incredible trauma, being born in the middle of a mall store."

"A luxury Western-wear emporium," MR corrected. She gave the infant a dismissive glance. "And he's fine!"

Technically, yes. But that didn't mean Sage wanted to

trot her newborn son out like a pony on parade in front
of a bunch of strangers. For mercenary reasons, no less!

But knowing MR would not understand that, she
simply said, "I'm exhausted, too."

MR went over and shut the door to the hall. Their
privacy ensured, she strode back to the foot of Sage's
hospital bed. "I don't think you understand what an
incredible opportunity this is to promote not just the
opening of the first Upscale Outfitters store, but Nick as
modern-day Western hero and all-around Renaissance
man. Ruggedly handsome, sexy. Rancher-businessman.
Loving husband and protective dad, who also turned
out to be very good in a medical emergency."

That he had been, Sage thought proudly.

In fact he was so good, she was beginning to think
she just might have finally disregarded all her heartfelt internal warnings and fallen head over heels in love
with him, anyway.

Meanwhile, MR waxed on enthusiastically, "I mean,
there he was, catching his son in his bare hands—on
Father's Day weekend, no less!—and then wrapping
him in one of our shirts, which, by the way, we have
already sold out of. The partners will be *very* upset if
Nick does not take advantage of this phenomenal stroke
of good luck and publicize the heck out of what happened this morning."

Sage imagined that was the case. Her father had felt
the same way about making money. Only to figure out
in the end that in doing so he'd missed out on an awful
lot along the way, particularly with his family.

"The news stations are promising to run Nick's in-
terview and story all day tomorrow, in honor of the
holiday." MR rubbed her hands. "All we have to do is

get Nick to cooperate, pronto." She leveled a hard, expectant look at Sage.

She thought about the way MR had treated Nick the
last few months, with her endless demands and constantly disregarding his decisions. Sage decided that
deal or no, she did not owe MR anything. At least not
of this import.

"I'm sorry, MR, but if Nick has already said no…"

MR's expression turned unpleasant. "Then overrule
him! As his 'wife' you certainly have that prerogative.
There are two breaking news crews downstairs, waiting for my call. I can have them up here in five minutes
to do a quick story with you and the baby, and then we
can add Nick in, when he gets here. By then, it will be
a done deal, so there will be no reason for him not to
cooperate."

Sage had dealt with reporters during her family's
scandal the previous summer. It was never that short,
or easy, or uncomplicated. "I can't and won't override
Nick on this," she reiterated firmly.

MR looked furious. "You understand this will be a
deal breaker for the partners."

Sage doubted that.

If there was big money at stake, and if Nick was es-
sential to make that cash, the partners would remain
all-in.

Able to bluff as well as MR, she shrugged. "I can't
help the way you and your partners feel."

MR tapped her foot impatiently. "No, but you can
keep Nick from making a rash decision that will ruin
his life."

Tired of the veiled and not-so-veiled threats, Sage

looked the venture capitalist in the eye. "What are you trying to say?"

"If Nick wants his business dreams to come true, he's going to have to live up to his end of the deal he made. And be the face and driving force behind Up-scale Outfitters."

"You can't be serious."

"Oh, but I am." MR went on, sweet as pie, "Because I'll tell you right now, the partners will either pull the funds on the rest of the projected stores, or force him to resign and give up his interest in the company. And that's if they don't sue him for breach of contract. And while Nick might think doing this his way, in his own time, is what he really wants right now, eventually he will realize what he gave up, Sage. He'll recognize that this was a once-in-a-lifetime opportunity. And he blew it out of some misguided notion of being there for you and your son.

"And when that happens," MR continued vindictively, "he'll go back to feeling as trapped as he was the day I met him. And it won't be me he resents, Sage. It'll be you and your son."

Sage stared at the executive. Wishing she could refute everything MR was saying, yet knowing in her heart it was true. Nick was just like her late father. Made for bigger things. No matter how much he loved his family and wanted to be with them, he would never be happy running one small store, in a small town. No matter what he said now.

And a Nick who was miserable would not be a good father, good friend or lover. Never mind husband…even if in name only.

Sage sighed in defeat. "What do you want me to do?"

"Make him do what he has to do. For all your sakes." MR paused. Looked down at Shane, then back at Sage. "You owe Nick this."

Much as Sage wanted to disagree, she could not.

Sage's hospital bag in one hand, a bouquet of flowers and a teddy bear in his other, Nick burst out of the hospital elevator. Frowning, he stopped at what he saw. One camera crew going into the hospital room where Sage and Shane were supposed to be resting, another coming out.

MR walked out, and waved him toward them. "Here comes our hero now!" she gushed.

Nick strode forward, the fury and resentment inside him building. The knowledge he'd made a mistake, ever getting involved with MR and Metro Equity Partners, was stronger than ever.

A microphone was pushed into his face. "Nick! How does it feel to have delivered your own son on such an exciting day, no less!"

He might not want to be doing this. On the other hand, if he snarled, that would make headline news, too. He did not want that to be the lasting legacy of this amazing moment in his life.

Nick summoned the feeling of catching his son in his hands. Seeing little Shane take his first breath, and let out that strong, indignant cry. "It felt great!" Nick smiled, pushing on into the room.

Sage was propped up in her hospital bed, their infant son cradled lovingly in her arms. He wasn't sure which one looked more sweet and vulnerable, he just knew they were the center of everything good and solid and wonderful in his life.

He crossed to her bed, bent down and kissed her temple. Not for the cameras, but because he sensed she needed his support right now more than ever.

For a second, she relaxed into his touch. Her yearning to be alone, just the three of them, seeming as strong as his.

As he drew back, he saw her lower lip quiver.

"I think Little One is starting to get hungry again," she warned.

Which probably meant, Nick thought, there'd probably be a little crying again, and a huge need for privacy.

The news reporter motioned her camera crew closer. "Then we'll make it quick," she promised with a smile.

With MR looking on triumphantly, they went over the events of the morning. "And your baby's name is...?"

"Shane Lockhart Monroe," Sage and Nick said proudly together.

"Lovely! That's a wrap. Thanks so much, guys."

The crew exited. The other TV crew came back in briefly, asked a couple of questions specifically of Nick, got a thirty second film clip of the new family, and then departed.

No sooner had they cleared the portal than MR pulled out her smartphone. "Nick, we need to go over the calendar of events in Denver later this week."

Nick saw his wife deflate. "Not now," he said, as his son wrinkled his nose and began to shift and fuss.

MR stepped closer and folded her arms pertly in front of her. "I understand you'll have to take the baby back to Laramie when he's released tomorrow or the following day," she said kindly, "but after that, we're still going to need you in Colorado."

MR was right. They did have a lot to talk about. But he needed to speak to Sage first.

"I'll call you as soon as I can," he told the venture capitalist.

"Tonight?" MR pressed.

Nick wanted this done, too.

More than he ever could have imagined.

"I'll let you know where and when," he said.

Her emotions in turmoil, Sage waited until Nick had closed the door, then draped a blanket over her shoulder and eased the gown down to expose one breast.

She cupped Shane's downy-soft head in her palm, and teased his lips with her nipple, until he latched on. Seemingly as adept at everything he tried as his father, he fed like a champ.

"You don't have to stay, you know," she said.

Especially when you're looking at me—and Shane— like that. As if we're everything you ever wanted or dreamed of having. Because it's moments like these, when I'm tempted to believe that the baby and I could be enough to make you completely happy, that also make me want to go off the rails and tell you how much I feel. In my heart and soul. And how much more I want in this life we're building together.

But she couldn't do that, Sage reminded herself sternly. Not without breaking the promises they had made to each other at the outset.

She knew Nick deserved better than that.

He flashed her a sexy, sidelong grin. "If you're shy, I don't have to watch," he volunteered kindly, moving a slight distance away. "I can sit over here. Or even head out to get you a decaf chai iced tea, if you like."

Sage blushed and shook her head as the unprecedented awkwardness between them increased. "It's not that." He was as familiar with her body as she was with his.

He turned to squint at her expectantly. "Then…?"

Ignoring the ache in her heart, Sage forced herself to do the right thing. With effort, she met and held his gaze. Reminding herself they were on the brink of having something truly wonderful, but only if they didn't get in the way of each other's dreams.

She swallowed, reining in the tremor in her voice, and looked him right in the eye. "You have business. This is still opening weekend and the new store will be open for several more hours." He had been slated to be there all day, as well as from 1:00 p.m. to 6:00 p.m. on Father's Day.

Nick pulled up a visitor chair, turned it around backward and sat down, legs straddling the seat, arms folded along the top. She noted he had put on the usual American-made shirt and jeans, instead of the Italian-made brand he'd been wearing for the grand opening.

He smiled tenderly, watching as she moved Shane to her other breast.

"That's what I want to talk to you about," he said quietly, as she began to nurse their son again. His expression sober, he continued, "I've been mulling my options for a while now, but when you went into labor this morning, and I realized that the only reason you weren't at the hospital in Laramie, where you should and would have been, was all my doing, I also realized a lot had to change." He paused and compressed his lips together tightly. "I can't put family second, Sage. Not anymore."

* * *

Nick had expected his decision to be met with great joy. Instead, Sage looked like he had delivered the worst news possible.

Her soft lips took on the stubborn pout he knew so well.

"Except we're not a traditional family, any more than we're a traditional married couple."

Feeling as if his life was about to be blown to smithereens, he forced her to spell it out. "You don't want more?"

She paused, all cool elegance once again. "Of course I do."

Was this about the difference in the way they'd grown up? The fact that he'd never known the kind of luxury she had enjoyed before moving to Laramie, and might possibly want to savor again. Now that they had a baby to care for.

Sage inhaled sharply, abruptly looking as miserable deep down as he felt. "But…" She kept her eyes locked on his with effort. "We had a deal. Friends first. Lovers second. Co-parents third."

He remembered, and he regretted conceding what he had really wanted, in favor of expediency, and an alternate route to happiness.

"And then we became husband and wife," he reminded her.

She tensed, all the color leaving her face, then returning in a riotous bloom of color.

He didn't have to be a rocket scientist to see she was about to push him away again. "As was going to be required by your new business partners," she reminded him matter-of-factly.

Noting that Shane had fallen asleep again, she lifted him onto her shoulder and covered her breast with the edge of her hospital gown. "But we also agreed that wouldn't change anything between us. You would still have your goals and ambitions and I would have mine. We'd go our own ways and come together when we could."

Shane slept on.

Reining in the pain and disappointment he felt, Nick asked, "What are you trying to say?"

"That the mistake this morning was not yours, it was mine. I shouldn't have come on this trip with you at all. Not this close to my due date. Even if my OB gave me the go-ahead, with plenty of conditions, I should have realized the potential dangers and been a lot more cautious."

So this was it? She blamed herself for the chaos surrounding the medical emergency? "Come on, Sage. There was no way you could have known this would happen. You were a little over two weeks from your due date, and you weren't the least bit dilated when you saw the doctor yesterday."

"Actually," she admitted ruefully, "I think there might have been a sign or two."

He narrowed his eyes. "You told me that since the Braxton Hicks catastrophe you'd hardly felt even the slightest warm-up contraction."

"That's true. It was the lower back discomfort that kept getting to me, and last night, into this morning, it was pretty awful."

"Is that why you were so weepy and out of sorts when we were getting ready to go this morning?"

"In retrospect, I can see I was probably in labor all

night. I just didn't think my inability to get comfortable was all that different from the usual, because as you well know, my back has bothered me the entire pregnancy."

He took a moment to reflect on that. "Well, I'm glad you went with me today. Because if you hadn't," he continued gruffly, "I might not have been there when you did give birth."

"So it all worked out. I got to be there to support you this morning, and witness the excitement of the grand opening of your new business venture. And you got to personally be the first to welcome little Shane into the world."

"But…?" he prodded, sensing there was more.

Sage sobered. "I still should have known better. And next time…if there is a next time…" Blushing, she stumbled over her words uncertainly, and for a moment, had to look away from him entirely.

She squared her slender shoulders determinedly. "And I don't mean having another child necessarily… but just the next time a choice like this has to be made." Once again, she met his gaze. "I'll make sure I do what's right for Shane first, and me second. And I'll step back and let you worry about you."

Her vow encompassed everything they had originally promised each other. Yet it hit him like a sucker punch to the gut.

He took her free hand in his. "And that's good enough for you?" he asked, savoring the soft and silky warmth of her skin, the sweet womanly scent of her.

He moved onto the hospital bed so he could sit beside her. "You don't want more?" he asked quietly, as her thigh pressed intimately against his. "A traditional marriage and family? Or true, abiding love?" *The kind I could give you, if you'd only open up your heart and soul to the possibility?*

She stared down at their entwined fingers, thinking, deliberating. "Of course I do, theoretically," she responded in a low voice edged with resentment. "But realistically, Nick? I don't want you giving up anything for us that you're going to regret later, out of some misguided momentary notion of romantic love," she confided, her lower lip quavering.

Seeming on the verge of tears, she withdrew her hand from his and said, "I don't want you and me to make the same mistake that Terrence and I did, thinking we could rewrite the foundation of our relationship just through strength of will or because we thought that was what was expected of us. I don't want to risk everything we've had for something that might not pan out, that could ruin everything. For you, for me, for Shane. Especially now—" she inhaled a deep, shaky breath, looking protectively down at the baby cuddled against her "—when we're still caught up in the miracle of giving birth."

They were still in a daze over that, Nick thought, albeit—at least for him—a truly happy one.

Sage, on the other hand, seemed a lot more conflicted. Still, she had been through a lot in the last twenty-four hours, so he tried to rein in his hurt feelings and be patient.

Oblivious to his mounting frustration and dismay, she continued, "It's not surprising you'd want to give our son everything. Because I do, too. But we have to be levelheaded and think about how this all began."

"Casually," he recollected, wishing like hell he'd told her the truth about his feelings in the beginning.

She nodded, accepting that. "With distinct, well-outlined limits."

Silence fell.

Nick thought about how much he had always hated being constrained—by anything. Especially rudimentary rules made long ago that had no bearing on what they were currently experiencing.

Treading carefully—he was dealing with a wife who had just given birth after all, a wife who might be experiencing a storm of mood-shifting hormones—he stifled his own soul-deep disappointment long enough to ask, very quietly, "What if that's not enough for me?"

For a moment, a defeat similar to what he felt flickered on her face. Then the fiercely independent Sage he'd first met returned. Her heart as guarded as ever. "If we want to make this all work long-term, if we want all our dreams to come true, it's going to have to be enough, Nick," she told him resolutely. "For both of us."

Chapter 16

"For someone who just had a son, you're looking awfully blue," his older sister Erin said from the other side of the Triple Canyon ranch house kitchen. She set out glasses, ice and cold beverages for the Welcome to Our Two Families party for little Shane. Then paused to watch Nick set up the party-sized coffeemaker and hot water dispensers for tea and cocoa.

Her expression worried, she checked on the potluck casseroles warming in the oven. "And Sage doesn't look as happy as I would expect her to be, either."

Glad she was upstairs nursing the baby, and not privy to any of this—it was hard enough for him to hear it—Nick set out the platters of ham, brisket and chicken. "Shane was up most of both nights that they were in the hospital."

"You were there, too," Erin challenged. "Walking the floor with him."

Life was not as simple as his sisters sometimes thought. Nick swallowed. "Yes, I've lost sleep." *Over the mess our life is suddenly in.* "But Sage is the one who is nursing so I think it's harder on her."

Erin paused sympathetically. "What else is going on?"

Together, they set out the silverware and napkins. "I need to ask you something and I don't want you to get offended."

She grinned in amusement. "Well, that's a great start for a heart-to-heart."

"I'm serious." What he was about to broach was delicate, to say the least.

She sobered, too. Knowing they wouldn't have too much time before the rest of both clans started arriving, she touched his arm and encouraged softly, "Fire away. After all, what are big sisters for?"

Nick drew a breath, aware having one woman in the family disappointed in him was more than enough. He lounged against the counter, hands braced on either side of him. "Mac's made some jokes about the fact that when you had the twins, your hormones were way out of whack."

Erin laughed and rolled her eyes. "Ah…yeah. I cried at the drop of a hat."

Nick remembered.

Yet no one had seemed to think anything of it. It had all seemed so normal. What was happening between him and Sage wasn't. At least as far as he could figure, thus far. "Did that affect how you felt about things?"

Erin looked at him with perceptive eyes. "Like what, exactly?"

He swallowed around the tight knot in his throat.

Pushed on resolutely. "Your marriage. Or what you wanted in the future or even the present."

"No. I know Mac is the one for me."

Pushing into more difficult territory, Nick presumed, "And that's different from your first marriage?"

"Yes. That was a mistake," Erin reflected candidly. "I mean, I can't regret it, because that union gave me Sammie and Stevie and Angelica, but I also know even if Angelica hadn't been diagnosed with leukemia, and our relationship hadn't been strained by her long illness and death, that our marriage never would have lasted."

Nick had been in middle school when they'd divorced. "How come?"

"We wanted different things. He needed his freedom. I needed someone I could count on to be there through thick and thin." Erin set out the appetizer trays. "Are you and Sage having problems?"

Nick shrugged. "I want things that she doesn't want." He'd thought time would fix it, allow them to finally get on the same page. But it hadn't. And now they seemed to have come full circle. To the strangers they had initially been to each other. With so much still out of reach. And he didn't know what in the hell to do about any of it. All he knew was that he didn't want to hurt Sage. Never had. Never would. And if that meant putting his own needs and desires on the back burner once again...

Erin's gaze narrowed speculatively. "Can you compromise?"

"I'm not sure," Nick admitted.

Abruptly, the sister who had raised him from age ten on looked as sad and concerned as he felt, deep down. "It's that serious?"

Reluctantly, Nick nodded.

Silence fell.

Finally, he said, "She still wants to raise Shane together and so do I."

"But not be married?" Erin guessed, her lips twisting in a troubled moue.

Nick went back to setting out the buffet. "We haven't spoken about divorce."

"But," Erin said, "you're worried that talk is coming."

Nick nodded stiffly.

Doing his best to pull it together, he said, "On the other hand, the two of us have both been through a lot the past few days. Heck, make that the last five months. And as you've confirmed, her hormones are out of whack." Although his gut told him, not that out of whack...

"You want my advice?"

Not trusting himself to speak, he looked Erin in the eye.

"You've never been afraid to take risks in business. Or encourage me to do the same. It's why I spun off my boot-making business and moved with Mac to the Panhandle so he could continue taking Wind Energy to that part of the state, without having to be away from us all the time. Yes, I worried that all the change would be hard for us, but in the end our love for each other and our children saw us through."

And they were happy, Nick knew. Blissfully so. He forced the words out. "You're saying Sage and I have the same potential."

Erin clasped his shoulders. "If you take a good hard look at what's really going on with the two of you. And then take the kind of risks in your personal life that you're all too willing to take in business. Yeah, little brother, I really do."

* * *

"How much is Nick going to be traveling now?" Lucille asked as Sage finished nursing.

Sage handed Little One to her mother for burping. "I'm not sure." She walked into the adjacent bath to remove her robe and put on her party clothes.

Lucille paced, Shane on her shoulder. "You haven't discussed it?"

Sage slipped on a pair of white capris and walked out, still buttoning a sleeveless buttercup yellow blouse. Aware she needed her mother more than ever, she replied, "Not recently. But initially, Nick wanted to take six weeks paternity leave, and then travel sporadically after that."

Her mom drew back and looked her in the eye. "And the venture capital company underwriting Upscale Outfitters?"

She wandered over to the mirror and frowned at the shadows beneath her eyes. "They want him back on the road by the end of the week." In Denver, no less!

"What do you want?"

Sage applied concealer beneath her eyes. Aware her mother was still awaiting an answer, she said, "I don't want to be the 'ball and chain' holding Nick back."

Lucille watched Sage put on foundation and blush. "Isn't there some compromise?"

"I wondered the same thing, but when I broached it on the way back from Dallas, Nick didn't want to talk about it." She frowned. "To me, anyway." After applying lipstick, then mascara, she spun back to her mom, who was in seventh heaven cuddling baby Shane.

"Has he talked to anyone?" Lucille asked.

Sage jerked in a breath. "He spent several hours yesterday afternoon at Metro Equity Partners office, meeting with MR and the team while Shane and I remained in the hospital, recuperating from the birth."

"And...?"

Sad and confused, she related how shut out she'd felt. Then and now. "Nick didn't want to talk about what was said then, either."

Her mother arched a brow in surprise.

"All I know for certain is that papers are being sent out this afternoon, for signature. Apparently, they couldn't get it all ready before he left Dallas."

Aware Shane had fallen fast asleep, her mother settled him in the beautiful wooden cradle that had been in Nick's family for generations.

Finished, Lucille straightened. "You think they gave him an ultimatum?"

Sage sat down to put on her shoes. "MR told me, in the hospital, he was going to have to be fully committed to being the spokesperson for Upscale Outfitters. Or else."

"That's why you did the local news interviews," Lucille ascertained.

While still in her hospital gown and robe, looking like heck. Sage forced herself not to grimace at the memory of being pressured by Nick's business associates. "The publicity was too good to pass up," she fibbed.

Her mom scowled. "Your father and I might have felt that way, in our heyday, but not you and Nick."

Sage edged closer, working to keep her voice low. "What are you saying?" she asked a great deal more casually than she felt.

"That maybe the real problem is, you're not being true to yourself. Or him, honey."

Tears pricked her eyes. "I don't want to pressure him," she admitted miserably. Which would certainly happen if she spilled everything. "He's been through enough recently, seeing the dream he had for expanding the legacy of Monroe's turn into something else entirely."

Lucille handed her a tissue. "I thought the grand opening of the new Dallas store went very well."

Sage dabbed the corners of her eyes. "In terms of sales, the reports were outstanding." Her throat clogged with suppressed emotion. "In terms of making Nick feel proud or triumphant?" she whispered hoarsely. "Not so much."

Lucille took Sage's arm and drew her over to sit side by side on the bed. "So you're walking on eggshells around him."

"I want to support him, Mom, but not back him into a corner."

Lucille patted her hand. "The way the venture capital group is."

Sage nodded. "I'm afraid if I don't give him the room he needs to make all his professional dreams come true, he'll end up feeling trapped, and walk away from me, too." Just like Terrence had.

Her mother stood, thinking, and began to pace. "You're right," she said softly, turning back around. "It is a very tenuous situation. It won't, however, be the first and only crisis the two of you face as a married couple."

Sage looked at her mom uncomprehendingly.

"For everything that brings you and Nick together,

there will be someone or something else just as power-
ful threatening to tear you apart."

*Like MR and her partners. The relentless demands.
The fact that I'm still afraid to tell Nick how I really feel.*

Sage knotted her hands together on her lap. "If that's
the case, what should I do?"

Lucille sat down beside her once again, and gently
advised, "You have to have ask yourself, just how committed are you?"

*More than he could ever—or maybe will ever—
know,* Sage thought.

"How much are you willing to let outside factors
wedge distance between you and Nick?"

Not willing at all!

"Now for the most important question of all…" As
usual, Lucille saved the biggest zinger for last. "Are you
going to open up your heart—the way I've *yet* to see
you do, honey—and *really* go after what you want?"

Which was Nick.

To be all hers.

All the time.

Sage thought about what her mom had said while she
finished dressing for the party. She was just about to go
downstairs and join the gathering of the Monroe and
Lockhart clans, when she saw an unfamiliar sports car
coming up the drive. It stopped behind the long rows
of family vehicles. Everett emerged, thick yellow envelope in hand.

Realizing this was her opportunity to get started on
her Rescue Our Marriage project, Sage slipped out the
back and came around the side of the ranch house to
intercept MR's assistant. Before she made a final decision on exactly how she was going to proceed next,

there were a few things she had to know. She sensed he could help her.

She motioned the smartly dressed assistant over to where she was standing, out of view of the front windows. Brow arched curiously, he approached.

"I want to ask you something."

"Okay."

"That comment you made to me, the morning after Nick and I got married. When you told me that I hadn't gained a husband, and had instead lost my best friend." She searched his face. "What prompted you to say that?" What had MR's assistant known then, that she might still not?

A beat of silence fell. Finally, Everett held the envelope against his chest and allowed, "Look, I probably shouldn't have butted in that way. But I felt sorry for you."

Sage struggled to understand. "Because I had been ill?"

Grimacing, he corrected, "Because you were being played."

So maybe her intuition that MR wanted her out of the way had not been so off-kilter, after all. "In what way?"

"MR has a way of taking over people's realms without them ever knowing it. I'm a case in point. I haven't had a life since I started working for her."

"Then why continue?"

Everett let the package fall to his side. "She's going places. I want that kind of success, too. Being her sidekick is the fastest, surest way for me to climb the ladder myself."

Sage studied him closely.

"You really think MR's that single-minded?" In the

hospital, although the venture capitalist had manipulated Sage to help her get what she and her partners wanted, she'd also seemed concerned about Nick's long-term happiness and future.

A terse nod. "Whatever she does is always for her own gain. If someone else benefits along the way, great." He shrugged. "If not, doesn't matter."

In retrospect, Sage could see that, too. "And I come in where...?"

For a moment, Everett seemed to battle with himself. Finally, he allowed, "You were the one thing standing in the way of Nick's triumph at Upscale Outfitters."

Were, Sage thought, focusing on the past tense of the statement. Not *are*... Her chest tightened. "So your boss was out to split us up from the get-go?"

He briefly inclined his head. "Let's just say she had her ways of making sure things did not go smoothly for the two of you, starting with the honeymoon."

"The shrimp that was ordered," Sage guessed.

Everett lifted a staying hand. "I don't know anything for sure. All I can assert is that she is the one who spoke to the hotel management. Every time."

Sage blinked. "But I thought the hotel took responsibility for the mistake."

"Of course they did."

Because the customer was always right, never more so than in a five-star hotel.

What Everett was intimating all made sense. And yet... "MR was the one who insisted Nick and I get married before he ever officially made a deal with Metro Equity Partners. Why do that," Sage continued curiously, "if she didn't want me around?"

"Because, as she said, a deadbeat dad would not have

made a good spokesperson, and she didn't want a PR nightmare." Everett exhaled. "And because she also knew that the moment Nick had a ring on his finger, he would feel…"

"Trapped," Sage guessed.

He nodded. "Whereas if he hadn't made an honest woman of you, he would have felt guilty, and then been even more tied to you, trying to prove to everyone that he was a good guy."

"But, on the other hand, if he married me…" Sage said.

"Even briefly," Everett added.

"His being a good person would be assumed."

Everett continued, "Since he had done the honorable thing and had been responsible for you and the baby."

"MR told you all this?"

"She called it a teachable moment."

"So she wanted Nick for herself," she stated.

He exhaled. "She knew the two of you'd divorce if it eventually didn't work out due to Nick's heavy travel and work schedule."

Which MR had machinated every step of the way, Sage thought indignantly.

Everett continued with a poker face, "By then, of course, Nick would be filthy rich as half owner of six luxury stores, and she could step in, reap the benefits. Go from being his boss/partner to boss/partner/wife."

Sage stared at him, amazed at the depth of the duplicity. "She said that, too?"

"Of course not, but I know how her mind works. I saw the way she pored over the publicity photos of Nick. I've seen her work with other clients. With Nick it was different." Everett paused to reflect. "But in the end, I guess I was really the one who was naive to think my giving you a heads-up would make a difference in the way things eventually worked out."

It had, and it hadn't, Sage thought, aware things weren't necessarily as "over" as Everett—and perhaps MR—thought. "Would you mind if I took the papers to Nick?" she asked, suddenly ready to do battle herself.

The door opened before Everett could reply and Nick stepped outside to join them.

"Not necessary. I'm here." He took the envelope from Everett. "Got a pen?"

Sage began to panic. Nick looked so determined. So grim. So ready to put it all behind him. Which was the last thing she wanted! "I really think you and I should talk," she said hurriedly.

Avoiding her eyes, Nick shook his head and said heavily, "Not about this, we don't."

Sage stood with Nick, watching Everett drive away, hastily signed documents in hand. "Is Shane still doing okay?"

Nick nodded. "He's still sleeping but I brought him downstairs, so everyone can quietly admire him. Your mom said she'd text us if he wakes and needs to be fed, but in the meantime, how about you and I take a walk?"

"Sounds good," Sage said softly. She wanted the privacy. The chance to get everything back on the right track.

Although it wasn't clear from the implacable expression on Nick's face that this was what he wanted.

He led her down the gravel path to the pasture, where the ranch horses were grazing. "Those papers I just signed severed my relationship with Metro Equity Partners. I'm no longer a co-owner of, or the face of, Up-scale Outfitters."

His news rocked her to the core. "That's a pretty big decision."

"And the right one." He rested his arms on the top of the wooden fence and gazed out at the land that had been in his family for generations. "I've known for some time it wasn't a good fit, either business-wise or personally." He flexed his broad shoulders resolutely. "I'm relieved to be out of it."

She could see that. And yet...there were other parts to his dreams. Ways he could be hurt. She moved closer still, inhaling the brisk masculine scent of his aftershave. "What about financially?"

He turned a level look her way. "Since I never put any of my own money into the start-up, most of what I lost was my time and effort." His sensual lips thinned ruefully. "But I can't complain given all I learned about what I don't want in a career path. I'm happy to be my own man again."

Sage could see that. She was happy for him, too. But scared that a change this huge in attitude and outlook could mean more in his personal life, too. Aware that the numbness she'd felt for the last several days was gone, the ache in her heart back full force, she forced herself to remain calm as she asked quietly, "Now what? Are you going to go back to just running Monroe's?" *Back to just being my friend, and lover, and nothing else...?*

Pivoting toward her, he rested an elbow on the top of the fence. He inclined his head, his emotional barriers still intact. "I still want more. But on my terms this time."

Unable to fault him for that, after all he'd been

through, Sage hitched in a breath and told him sincerely, "I hope you get what you want."

"I'm sure I will in business." He flashed his most impersonal smile. "It's the rest of my life that's up in the air."

Hers, too.

His expression turned formidable. He looked her in the eye. "I don't want to travel anymore, Sage. I don't want to be away from you, and I don't want to be away from Shane."

Sage's pulse pounded. She felt on the verge of tears. "I don't want that, either," she admitted, aware it was now or never.

She took his hands in hers. Holding them tightly, she gazed up at him and admitted, "I never have."

Expression gentling, he pressed his forehead against hers. "Why didn't you say something?"

She hitched in an enervating breath. "Because I didn't want you to end up feeling robbed of anything, Nick. I didn't want you to feel trapped."

Lifting his head, Nick's gaze drifted over her, as if he were memorizing every detail. "The way you've been?"

The lump in her throat was back. Another wave of anxiety slid through her. Ignoring the sudden wobbliness of her knees, she tried to figure out where this was all going.

She knew if they ever had a prayer of making things work, she had to be completely honest with him. Tears blurred her vision. "I admit I regret marrying when and why we did."

The silence stretched between them, emphasizing all that was at stake. His jaw clenched. "So do I."

Calling on every ounce of courage she had, Sage

pushed on. "I regret the way we started our family, too."
She studied their entwined hands, then looked deep into
his eyes, admitting tremulously, "I wish we had done it
out of love, not practicality."

He squinted.

"Are you talking about your feelings now—or
mine?" he demanded gruffly.

Here was her chance. To open up her heart. Go for
broke. "Yours. But it's okay," she rushed on, as he
wrapped an arm about her waist, and would have drawn
away, but held fast. She splayed her hands over his chest.
"You don't have to view our relationship romantically."

"I don't?" he echoed in shock.

"No," she said. "Because I have enough in my heart
for both of us."

"Except I do feel that way about you, Sage. I have
from the very first. I just didn't tell you how I really
felt because I knew you weren't in a place where you
could take a risk like that."

"So you opted to be my friend instead."

"And then lover. And then father of our hoped-for
child," he recollected rustily, wiping away her tears with
the tip of his fingertip. "The night we married was one
of the happiest times of my life."

"Mine, too. At least," Sage amended ruefully, "until
we got to the hotel."

"And MR had a surprise waiting for us."

She paused in shock, asked warily, "You know about
that?"

He nodded curtly, his disillusionment and disappointment as sharp as her own. "I talked to The Mansion
hotel manager the evening before the grand opening. He
felt terrible about what had happened before, about

the fact that the order was written up to specifically request shrimp, instead of exclude it. He assumed it was
a data entry error from the room service department."

"But you knew better?"

"I had been there when MR pulled a similar stunt
with one of the suppliers, blamed it on one of their
younger sales reps and then used the mix-up to leverage
a lower margin on their goods. So I figured it was her."

"Did you confront her?" she asked.

He nodded. "It was what we were talking about, in
the office, when we got to the store that morning."

"Right before I interrupted."

"And then later, at the MEP office the next day. MR
said she was only helping me out. Speeding the process
of me discovering you were all wrong for me." Anger
simmered in his eyes. "The ironic thing is that I had
already realized that I could not continue to be in partnership with someone that manipulative and deceitful."

He paused, grimacing, and her heart went out to him.

Soberly, he continued, "I knew I had to go through
with the grand opening, and make sure I did my part
in publicly launching the new venture. I owed the other
partners that. But I planned to tell you I was going to
end things as soon as I could."

"Only I went into labor before any of that could happen..." Sage recollected.

"And little Shane was born." He paused, sharing the
happy memory of their son's tumultuous but ultimately
victorious entrance into the world, via his daddy's help.

Sobering, Nick went back to the reasons behind his
decision. "The worst thing is I had a sixth sense that
MR was trying to undermine the two of us all along."

"Apparently, Everett thought so, too." Sage went on

to reveal the gist of her conversation with MR's assistant the morning after the wedding. "Unfortunately, instead of trying to avoid that pitfall and talk to you about what he'd said to me, and the need for us to keep the lines of communication open and make our friendship—which is the foundation of our entire relationship—even stronger, I let the seeds of doubt grow. Jeopardizing our potential to stay close and happy, at every turn."

Nick reflected soberly, his gaze as sincere as it was tender. "Seems like we should have done a lot more talking."

Sage nodded. "About what was really in our hearts and on our minds." She wreathed her arms about his neck and stood on tiptoe. Her heart brimmed with happiness. "Because I'm crazy in love with you, Nick. I want to be all in, all the time, from here on out." She kissed him.

He pulled her close and kissed her back, passionately and evocatively. Until her toes curled and her knees threatened to buckle. "I'm crazy in love with you, too," he admitted thickly.

Their gazes locked as readily as their smiles. At last, it seemed, they were as committed to their relationship and each other as she had always wanted to be.

"So," she prodded softly, "what do you say we make ours a real marriage, in every way?"

Nick grinned broadly. "Sweetheart, I'm all in. And one more thing…" He reached into his pocket and withdrew a velvet jeweler's box. "I haven't yet given you your push present."

Sage lifted the lid. Inside was a stunning diamond solitaire. "Oh, Nick…" she breathed.

Hoarsely, he told her, "It can double as the engagement ring you never got but should have had."

She slid it on her finger, next to her wedding band, and watched as it sparkled in the sunlight. She sighed in delight. "It's perfect."

He smiled down at her adoringly. "I'm glad you like it."

Her heart bursting with all the joy she felt, Sage laughed. "Like it? I love it!" She pressed her lips to his. "Love you. Our son. Our life…"

Epilogue

"It's amazing, what a difference the right business plan can make," Sage murmured two years later, as she and Nick took one last look around the satellite store, before calling it a night.

The first Monroe's Outpost was set to open the following morning. Located on Main Street, in the county seat of a rural county just west of Laramie, the brand-new mercantile bore the same distinctive Texas atmosphere as the original Monroe's Western Wear.

Although much smaller in scope, it was well-designed and well-outfitted with every necessary item a cowgirl or cowboy could need. The boots, jeans, shirts, chaps, jackets, hats and belts were both high-quality and reasonably priced.

Nick looked around with a pride she and his family all shared. "I think Mom and Dad would be proud to know we were bringing a needed service to this community."

Sage nodded happily. "And the other rural community stores that will come in the next decade."

All without requiring any outside capital, or interference.

The clatter of little cowboy boots sounded on the wood floor. Sage followed Shane as he raced curiously down the aisle. "Trust me," she teased, over her shoulder, "if there is one thing every busy parent knows, the less time it takes to get any task accomplished, the better."

In her life, and many others, convenience was key.

"And that's only going to be truer five months from now," she said, as Nick caught up with them.

"I imagine that's so," Nick predicted, tenderly wrapping one arm around her shoulders. "Although—" he curved a hand lovingly over her blossoming tummy "—Shane doesn't seem to mind going places now."

Sage leaned against her husband's chest. She rested her head on his shoulder, as their little boy took his pint-sized hat off his head, let out a whoop worthy of a rodeo cowboy and tossed it in the air. He hooted again as it clattered to the floor. "Because we're letting him run around and explore, unfettered. The minute we strap him into his car seat…"

Nick chuckled. "He'll let us know he would much rather be free."

Sage grinned as Shane caught sight of himself in the mirror, then resettled his hat and paused to reflect.

She turned back to Nick, splaying her hands against the solid warmth of his chest. "Think he comes by his independent spirit naturally?"

"Probably." Nick kissed Sage's temple and smoothed a hand through her hair. "But he also has a boundless ability to love."

They all did, Sage thought contentedly.

Shane stopped just short of them. He lifted his hands, signaling his desire to be picked up.

Nick obliged.

Shane smiled happily, then leaned over and put his hand on Sage's tummy, as he had seen his daddy do. "Baby. In there," he declared.

Nick and Sage smiled. "There sure is, little dude," Nick said proudly.

Shane's smile broadened. "I like babies."

Her heart overflowing with gratitude and joy, Sage bussed the top of her little boy's head. "We all do."

Shane grabbed a fistful of each of their shirtfronts and pulled them in for a group hug. "I love Mommy and Daddy, too," he said adamantly.

"We love you, too," Nick and Sage said in unison.

Shane squinted comically. They squinted mischievously back. Then they all began to laugh. Life, Sage thought, did not get any better than this.

* * * * *

Patricia Thayer was born and raised in Muncie, Indiana. She attended Ball State University before heading west, where she has called Southern California home for many years.

When not working on a story, she might be found traveling the United States and Europe, taking in the scenery and doing story research while enjoying time with her husband, Steve. Together, they have three grown sons and four grandsons and one granddaughter, whom Patricia calls her own true-life heroes.

Books by Patricia Thayer

Harlequin Western Romance

Count on a Cowboy
Second Chance Rancher
Her Colorado Sheriff

Harlequin Romance

Tall, Dark, Texas Ranger
Once a Cowboy...
The Cowboy Comes Home
Single Dad's Holiday Wedding
Her Rocky Mountain Protector
The Cowboy She Couldn't Forget
Proposal at the Lazy S Ranch

Visit the Author Profile page at Harlequin.com for more titles.

DYLAN'S LAST DARE

PATRICIA THAYER

To Nora.

Acknowledgments

Thank you, niece, for your expertise in getting my hero back on his feet. And to my model, Daniel. I couldn't have done it without you both.

Thanks to Colin Anderson for sharing your bull-riding experiences. I know your wife and mom are happy you are retired.

And always to Hence, my friend and true Texas cowboy.

Chapter 1

Dylan Gentry's life would never be the same again.

He gripped the arms of his wheelchair, trying to fight off the panic that threatened to take over his already battered body.

It was all gone.

He'd never again be able to do what he loved. He'd never be able to feel the rush from a wild ride, the thrill from the cheer of the crowd as he broke out of the chute. He'd ended up a cripple for life, all because of one mean son-of-a-gun bull, Red Rock.

Dylan's hands fisted. He hated himself more for the self-pity. But dammit, hadn't he earned the right? He'd spent the last two months in the hospital. He'd had three surgeries, one to close up the wound in his gut from being hooked by the bull, and two more on his crushed leg.

Hell, it was January. He'd spent the entire month of December in the hospital. A month that he'd planned to spend at the national finals in Las Vegas. Now he was stuck in a two-bedroom cottage at his brother Wyatt's ranch in San Angelo, Texas, waiting for the next physical therapist to show his face.

In the past two weeks, he'd already sent six packing within hours after their arrival. Today, he was going for number seven. At least it gave him something to look forward to. He glanced around his new home. There was a state-of-the-art television and sound system, a bookcase filled with every top-selling novel.

There sure as hell wasn't much else for him to do.

He picked a book off the coffee table and threw it at the door, hating what he'd become and feeling sorry for the next person who walked in the door to face his wrath.

Brenna Farren stepped onto the small porch and raised her hand to knock on the door, when she heard something hit the other side. Startled, she paused, recalling what Wyatt Gentry had told her about his injured brother. No doubt the past months had been difficult for national-champion bull rider Dylan Gentry. As a physical therapist, Brenna knew she wasn't her patients' most popular person. She had known this was going to be a difficult job when she applied for the position, but she wasn't about to turn down the excellent pay and the bonus, which was she could live right here in the cottage.

Another object hit the door with a thud. Sounded as if her new patient was having a bad day. Even with her limited experience she knew that was to be expected.

Brenna gripped the knob. "Let's see if we can change that, Mr. Gentry," she said, then released a breath as she swung open the door. She walked inside and caught a surprised look from the good-looking man sitting in the wheelchair.

Midnight-black hair hung over his ears and forehead. His square jaw showed more than a few days of scraggly beard, but that didn't take anything away from his handsome face. Yet it was his eyes that caused her to pause. They were a pale blue, mixed with silver. His gaze was cold as stone, yet triggered a sudden warmth within her.

She jerked away from his hold and smiled brightly at his irritated look. "Good morning, Mr. Gentry."

"Who the hell are you?" he growled.

"Brenna Farren."

"Well, if you're here to clean I don't need the sheets changed or any fresh towels."

She figured the towels didn't need to be changed, because he looked as if he hadn't bathed in days. She glanced around the mess in the cozy room. "The place could stand to be tidied up, but not right now. I'm here to help you get back on your feet. I'm your physical therapist."

He couldn't hide his surprise. "The hell you are."

"That's correct, I've been recommended by Dr. Morris, the orthopedic surgeon who took over your case when you moved here. Your brother hired me."

"Well, you can just tell Wyatt to unhire you because I don't need you."

"You need me more than you think, Mr. Gentry." Her gaze moved over him. Dressed as he was in a T-shirt, she could see his upper-body muscle tone was incredible. Her attention went to his cutoff sweatpants that allowed her to see the long scar running down his left calf. She tried to remain expressionless, but she knew that this man had had his share of pain, since his cast had been removed only three weeks ago. She also noticed that his inactivity from being in a wheelchair showed in his flaccid lower limbs.

"Not a pretty sight, is it?" he hissed.

He was a beautiful sight, just his leg was scarred. "I've seen worse," she admitted. "Besides, the scars will fade more as time passes."

"I don't give a damn."

"Well, I'm here to help change your mind about that."

"I don't need anyone," he snapped at her. "I'm doing just fine." He tried to move away, but the wheel caught on the end of the coffee table. Brenna watched as a frustrated Dylan fought to turn. Finally he broke free and rolled his chair across the room.

"First thing tomorrow I'll have some of this furniture removed to make it easier for you to move around," she called to him.

Dylan Gentry stopped at the wide bedroom door. "Don't waste your time, Ms. Farren. You won't be here tomorrow." His large hands worked with the wheels and he rolled himself inside the room and slammed the door.

Brenna released a long breath. "That went well."

She walked though the living area. There was another door that led to the second bedroom. That was to be hers. She peeked inside. Although small, there was plenty of room for the double bed with a multicolored quilt and a tall pine dresser. The bathroom was roomy, and the doorway had been widened to accommodate a wheelchair. On the side of the tub was an attached whirlpool. Great.

She returned to the living room, then to the small dining area. At the table there was an empty spot for a wheelchair. Everything had been newly renovated to accommodate a handicapped person. Past the breakfast bar, she went to the refrigerator and opened the door, finding it fully stocked with food. More than likely Maura Gentry had brought meals in for her brother-in-law, but by the looks of it, he hadn't been eating much. She would have to change that since Dylan couldn't keep up any kind of strenuous exercise without some nutrition.

If he would cooperate with her. That meant somehow she had to get him to agree to do therapy. Her job depended on it. Even though her family was close by, she needed this job…and a place to live. As a recent graduate and with her present…circumstances, she didn't have the time to wait around for other offers.

Her mentor, Dr. Morris, had sent her to the Rocking R Ranch to talk with Wyatt Gentry about his twin brother who'd been seriously hurt during a bull-riding accident. Even after hearing that Dylan Gentry had driven off a half-dozen therapists in the past weeks, she hadn't been scared off. She couldn't afford to be.

Still, she knew this had to be rough on the two-time world-champion bull rider. She should add the best-looking man she'd ever seen. Those grainy black-and-white pictures in the paper hadn't done him justice. No doubt his reputation with the ladies wasn't an exaggeration. Now he was confined to a wheelchair.

It was Brenna's job to help change that.

Even when Wyatt had been reluctant to hire a woman, she had convinced him that she could handle the man and his therapy, promising she could get his brother back on his feet.

And Wyatt was giving her two weeks to get Dylan started on his exercise program.

Brenna was a West Texas native, had grown up on a ranch with brothers who'd ridden in a few rodeos. She could never figure out what drove some men to danger. The thrill of an eight-second ride, a ride that could be the last. Memories of Jason came rushing back as she recalled his fatal hang-gliding accident, and their argument that had been the last words spoken between them. Tears flooded her eyes, knowing he'd chosen the thrill of danger over her…and their unborn child. Now she was alone, pregnant and trying to survive the best she could.

Several loud thuds from somewhere in the cottage had Dylan burying his head under the pillow. He hadn't slept much last night, not when a picture of Brenna Farren appeared every time he closed his eyes. Hell, what did he expect? He hadn't been with a woman in months. So the first good-looking one to come along was bound to arouse him. The noise grew louder. He raised his head and glanced at the clock: 7:00 a.m. What was going on?

He grabbed a pair of sweats off the floor and dragged them on. Scooting to the edge of the bed, and with one arm on his wheelchair and bracing his weight on his good leg, he made it into the seat. He lifted his damaged leg onto the footrest, released the chair's brake, then headed to find the ruckus. He opened the door to discover that the red-haired vixen had returned.

Kneeling in the corner, Brenna Farren was attempting to pull out some shelves. The business suit she had on yesterday had been replaced with a pair of faded jeans that hugged her shapely bottom and two long… lovely legs. A pale pink blouse didn't hide her other generous curves, either. Her long hair was pulled back into a ponytail, showing off a slender neck and creamy skin. He shook off a sharp tingling that suddenly added a different kind of pain to his lower body. Dammit, she wasn't supposed to be back.

"I told you yesterday I didn't need your services, Ms. Farren."

She swung around, the look of surprise widening her huge whiskey-brown eyes. "Oh, good morning, Mr. Gentry."

"There's nothing good at this hour."

"Oh, really." She sat down on the floor. "I love the early morning. It's so quiet…peaceful." Her voice was soft and throaty, reminding him of dim morning light and whispered demands of lovers… He shook off the thought.

"That's because everyone is asleep," he argued. "That's what I want to be."

"You can sleep in later after we get you on a routine."

"When hell freezes over," he said and nodded toward the door. "Now, would you mind leaving?"

She stood up and placed her hands on her hips. "As a matter of fact, I would mind. I promised your brother that I'd give this job a chance—that I wouldn't let your rude attitude run me off. So you'll have to do better than shout at me. I grew up with three brothers. I've been yelled at by the best."

Dylan's fists clenched. He loved Wyatt but he was

getting pretty tired of his interference. "Then I'll pay you for the month and fire you."

She shook her head. "You can't do that. I took this job and I made a promise. Now, you've already spent too much time in that chair without working your muscles. It's going to be even harder to get you up and walking—but not impossible."

"You don't seem to understand, Ms. Farren."

"Brenna," she corrected.

He sighed. "Brenna. I can't get back on my feet. I'm going to be in this chair for the rest of my life."

Brenna could see the fear in his eyes and heard it in his voice. She had a strange impulse to reach out and touch him, to give him comfort. She pulled back. "How do you know that, Dylan? I've conferred with your physician, and he said you haven't given therapy enough of a chance."

"You discussed my case?"

"With Dr. Morris," she said bravely. "We've gone over your X-rays and I talked with Dr. Ratner, the surgeon in California who did the reconstruction. He did a remarkable job."

"Then why the hell aren't I walking?"

"Because the damage was severe. Besides a rod put in to repair your tibia, pins were added to the talus bone."

"Speak English."

"All right. Your left calf and ankle were crushed by a two-thousand-pound bull. Not only the bones, but there was some muscle and nerve damage. It's important you do therapy to help with circulation and to strengthen the muscles. I also know the bull's horn punctured your abdomen and you sustained rib damage, but you healed nicely. So that pain shouldn't stop you."

"Well, I'm stopping you," he argued. "I've heard it all before by several specialists. Bottom line is they couldn't guarantee that I could go back to riding, or even that I'll walk again. Okay, okay, I should consider myself lucky to be alive. But lady, I don't call this living. And I'm not going to bust my butt for nothing—not if I can't be like before." He turned his chair around and returned to his bedroom.

Brenna wanted to call him back, but Dylan clearly wasn't ready to hear anything she had to say. Not now. It was her job to get him to want to give therapy a chance. How was she going to challenge this man? Somehow she had to make him want to fight to walk again.

There was a quiet knock on the door and Wyatt Gentry peeked his head in. He smiled and, although the two men weren't identical twins, she could see the close resemblance.

Wyatt walked in. "Should I ask how things are going?"

"Not bad," she lied. "Your brother hasn't thrown anything at me."

"Give him time." Wyatt grew serious. "Brenna, if you've changed your mind and think this job is too much, I'll understand."

Oh no, she couldn't lose it before she got a chance. She shook her head. "Trust me, I can handle anything that Dylan dishes out. I just have to figure out a way to make him want to try therapy."

"Well, I hope you make it. Oh, by the way, the parallel bars are being delivered within the hour. Just tell me what you want removed from the room."

"We can do without the bookshelves, the recliner chair and coffee table. If it's not too much trouble. That will give us room for the weight bench and bars."

"This is the easy part," he assured her. "Dealing with Dylan's temper is the difficult task. Maybe I should be here when he sees what's going on."

"No. That's why you hired me. I have to be the one he communicates with. Your brother is used to getting what he wants. He has to learn that if he wants to walk again, he has to work at it."

Wyatt grinned. "I'm beginning to believe you can do it. It's been a long time since Dylan hasn't been able to sweet-talk a woman into getting his way."

Brenna tensed. The man was hard to resist, but not for her. Right. She knew if Dylan Gentry wanted to, he could make her forget her own name. She just had to keep that fact from him. "You don't have to worry about me being charmed by your brother. I'm his therapist… that's all." It would be a long time before she would allow herself to be interested in any man, much less a danger-loving man like Dylan Gentry.

By 11:00 a.m. the furniture had been removed and the parallel bars and weight bench had been set up in the living area, leaving just enough space for the TV and sofa. Brenna decided that her patient wasn't going to have enough energy left after therapy to do anything else but watch TV.

Speaking of her patient, she hadn't seen Dylan since earlier in the morning. Well, it was time he came out of hiding. She went to his bedroom door and knocked.

There was only silence and she knocked again. "Dylan," she called.

No answer.

"Dylan? I'm fixing some lunch. Is there anything special you want?" Her job description also included making meals and some light housework. She didn't mind, since she was living here, too.

No answer.

"Dylan?" She knew he had to be hungry, because he hadn't had breakfast. "Are you all right?" She turned the knob and pushed open the door to find a large bed with Dylan Gentry sprawled across the center. A colorful quilt covered part of his body, but his glorious chest was bare. No red-blooded woman would deny that the man was beautifully built.

Surprised at the sudden rush of feelings, she refocused her thoughts and moved to the bed. He was her patient. That was all. She called his name again. When that didn't wake him, she touched his foot. "Dylan, you need to get up."

The man opened his eyes, revealing mesmerizing silver-blue pools that immediately locked on her. A hint of a smile creased his sensual mouth.

"Well, hello, darlin'." He stretched his arms over his head, lazily. "I was just having this great dream, but you're so much better."

The husky tone of his voice sent a warm shiver though Brenna as she saw the true side of the charming bull rider that all the ladies drooled over. Well, she didn't have the time or the desire.

Brenna pushed away from the doorjamb and moved to the bed. "Well, you're not dreaming now," she said. "It's reality time."

His smile only grew as he rolled to his side and reached out to touch her arm. "The real thing is so much better." His voice turned husky. "Why don't you climb into bed and let me show you."

If his sexual advances were supposed to scare her off, he was wrong. She had heard similar words so many times before. Jason used to sweet-talk her every time he wanted his way. "I have a better idea. Why don't you get up and eat something, then do a short therapy session."

"The only place I'm headed is the bathroom, then back to bed." He sat up and the covers dropped to his waist as he reached for the wheelchair. Brenna was quicker and pulled it back, away from his reach.

"What the—?" His dark eyebrows drew together as he frowned at her. "What do you think you're doing?"

"You've been spending far too much time in this chair. You need to get ambulatory. You're weakening your good leg by not using it."

"So what if I am?" he said. "That's my business."

"And *you're* my business."

"You're fired. Now get out."

She folded her arms. "Make me," she challenged.

Pain flashed across Dylan's face and Brenna wondered if she'd gone too far. She went into the living room, grabbed the walker and returned to the bedroom. "Here. From now on you'll use this to get around."

"You've got to be kidding," he said, disgust in his tone.

"If you can balance on the back of a bull, Mr. Dylan 'The Devil' Gentry, surely you can manage a walker."

He dropped backward on the bed. "I'm not using any damn walker... I'll crawl first, so you might as well give me back the chair."

"Physical therapists are a stubborn bunch. And since

you're the one who has to use the bathroom, I think I can wait you out."

He pulled the quilt over his head and let out a string of colorful curses.

Brenna knew if she was going to work with Dylan, she couldn't let him get away with sleeping all day. She also knew that if he complained enough, Wyatt would fire her.

"You're behaving childishly, Mr. Gentry," she said as she took hold of the edge of the covers and yanked them away. She bit back a gasp, discovering the man was naked underneath. Quickly she diverted her eyes to his face, only to catch a satisfied grin from Dylan.

The man had absolutely no problem with his nudity. "Since we're getting so familiar with each other, don't you think you could call me Dylan? *Bren.*"

She dropped the blanket on him. "I'll call you what-ever you like as long as you get up and attempt to co-operate."

He looked thoughtful. "All right, I'll get up, but only if I can use crutches."

"But your balance…"

Another grin. "Lady, like you said, my livelihood was dependent on my balance. Besides, I've used crutches a few times over the years with other minor injuries. So if you want me up, just bring me the damn things."

She left the room and by the time she returned with lightweight crutches, he'd managed to put on a pair of sweatpants. "This is against my better judgment," she told him. "You could fall."

"Darlin', I've been falling all my life," he said as he scooted to the edge of the bed.

"Not on my watch," she argued, then braced herself in front of him, planted her legs and helped pull him onto his good leg. Surprisingly, he did the task easier than she had expected. She helped him with the placement of the crutches, and walked along with him to the bathroom. She started to go in with him, but he stopped her.

"Whoa, this is where I draw the line. Sometimes a man has to go it alone. This is one of those times."

"What if you fall?"

"Then I pick myself up." He took another step inside and closed the door in her face.

"Just call out when you're finished, I'll come get you," she said through the door.

"I'm sure I can figure it out," she heard him say.

"You just think you can, Mr. Dylan 'The Devil' Gentry." She pivoted and marched to the kitchen, praying that she could survive this next month...and this man.

Dylan cursed as he stumbled coming out of the bathroom. Although he wasn't very good at it, he liked to be up, at least on his *one* good leg, but he wasn't going to let Ms. Farren know that.

With the crutches securely in place under his arms, he slowly made his way to the kitchen, still peeved he hadn't scared her off with his seduction routine. He found her at the stove, humming a song. Well, she wouldn't be singing for long, not after he tossed her out.

"As soon as you finish here, you better go pack your bags because you're not staying."

She turned and came to his aid. "Let's get you to the table, Dylan. The soup is nearly ready."

It did smell good, and he discovered he was hungry.

He thought about telling her he didn't need any help, then her hands were on him. Although her gesture was clinical, he liked her gentle and warm touch. He also liked her nice scent, fresh…feminine. At the table, she was careful of his injured leg, and helped him into the chair. Then she came back with two bowls and placed one in front of him and took the seat across from him.

Brenna placed a napkin on her lap and looked up. Dylan couldn't help but notice how pretty she was. Not in a traditional beauty-queen fashion, but with startling warm, honey-brown eyes that seemed to hold such wonder and innocence, and her mouth had him wondering how it would taste. Her skin was flawless, despite a soft sprinkling of freckles across her pert nose.

No, he couldn't have her around. He didn't need anyone seeing him like this, especially a woman. "Look… you've got to face it, this isn't going to work. I don't want you here. So why don't you just leave?"

"I can't." She placed her spoon on the table. "To be honest, I need this job. But more important, Dylan, you need me. If you ever want to walk again, you need my determination, my drive to push you hard. You need someone who won't let you bully them. Who won't let you slack off. Oh, you need me all right—that is, if you ever want to regain the use of your leg."

Her optimism was contagious, but he couldn't let himself hope. "But I'll never climb back on a bull again."

She huffed out a breath. "Aren't two national championships enough? Besides, aren't you a little over the hill for a bull rider?"

Even though her comment was true, it still stung. Over thirty, everyone knew a rodeo rider was pretty much used up. He'd planned that this would be his last year. Of course, if he'd won the championship again, he probably would have gone another year on the circuit. "I was on top this year. I was headed to the national finals in Las Vegas." He paused, realizing his frustration. "How would you feel if you couldn't do your job?"

"It would be rough. But I'm trying to build my career, you've had years of success. Isn't being on top a good time to get out? Look at Michael Jordan, he retired."

"Then he returned to basketball."

She thought again. "How about football players John Elway and Troy Aikman? They retired because of injuries that threatened their lives," she added. "They found other things that were important to them. Surely you've made enough money to start over with something else. Besides, Dylan, you can't even walk right now. How can you think about going back?"

"That's what I mean," he stressed. "So, what's the use of me killing myself if it's all for nothing?"

Brenna's eyes flashed as she got up from the table. "The use is that you have other things to walk for. Your family. Your brother, his wife and their children."

Dylan was never one to do much with family. Wyatt had been the only relative he had had, until last year when they'd learned their father's true identity. A bronc rider named Jack Randell. After the discovery, Wyatt immediately had to come to San Angelo, Texas, even bought the old Randell family ranch, the Rocking R. Dylan had wanted no part of the Randells, but Wyatt had gotten close to his half brothers, Chance, Cade and Travis, and their other illegitimate half brother, Jared Trager.

And since the accident, Dylan had been stuck here. "That's Wyatt's family, not mine."

"It's yours, too," she insisted. "Family can be important to your rehabilitation."

He didn't want to hear any more. "What is it going to cost me to get rid of you?"

Brenna crossed her arms over her breasts. Just the simple movement was erotic. Oh, God. He couldn't have her living here.

"Why don't I make a deal with you," she began. "How about you cooperate with me for two weeks?" She raised her hand to stop him. "Just hear me out."

He hesitated, then gave a nod.

"If there isn't any progress by that time, I'll leave." She lowered her hand. "Now, I have terms. I want you to get out of bed every morning by seven o'clock, you'll need to spend the allotted time on the parallel bars and work twice a day with weights. And I will work you hard, Dylan. Harder than you've probably had to work in your life, but I also believe that together we can get results." She looked him in the eye. "You can walk, Dylan. I believe it. So, how much are you willing to do for that? How much are you willing to do so you can get out of the wheelchair, to walk on your own?"

Dylan didn't want to just walk, he wanted to go back to what he had loved to do: bull riding. He wasn't afraid of work. Hell, he grew up with hard manual labor, handling rough stock for rodeos. But this was all he'd ever wanted. And even if he was retiring, he wanted to go out on top. He was Dylan "The Devil" Gentry.

"I want to get back to rodeoing. Can you help me do that?"

He watched her hesitate and his heart sank into his

gut. Then her eyes darkened with determination. "It's going to cost you extra, but I feel if the desire is there, you can do anything."

"I know I have the desire, but do you, Brenna? Can you put up with my nasty attitude and bad days, and make me the man I used to be?"

"I hope by the time I'm finished you'll learn that being a man has nothing to do with the size of the bull you ride."

She made him want to do a lot more than just walk. He shook away the distracting thought. "Can you do it?" he challenged. "Will you do it?"

Brenna's gaze locked with his. There was a flicker of vulnerability before she masked it and nodded. "Why do I feel like I just sold my soul to the devil?"

His face split into a beautiful smile that set her heart aflutter.

Because she had.

Chapter 2

Early the next morning Brenna stepped outside on the porch, hoping the brisk air would help her recent queasiness. What she didn't expect was to find Wyatt Gentry's four-year-old daughter, Kelly, sitting on the step.

"Well, good morning."

Smiling, the cute little blonde stood. "Hi, Miss Brenna." Under a heavy nylon jacket, she wore a pink sweater with blue corduroy pants and a pair of boots. She came up another step. "You remember me? Kelly. I live in that house." She pointed to the large ranch house about a hundred yards away.

"Yes, Kelly, I remember you." Brenna hugged her own heavy sweater closer to ward off the January cold. "What are you doing out so early?"

"I'm going for a ride on my pony, Sandy. My daddy is going to take me." She frowned. "But I don't know where he is." She glanced at the cottage door. "Is he inside with Unca Dylan?"

"No, but your uncle is awake. You want to come inside?"

The girl shook her head, a mixture of fear and sadness in her eyes. "No. He doesn't like me."

"Oh, sweetheart. Your uncle was hurt in a bad accident. He's just having a rough time trying to make his leg work again. I bet soon he'll be happy again."

"Then will he like me?"

"I think he already does," Brenna tried to assure her. "But let's give him a few weeks and when he's feeling better you can come by for a visit."

The child smiled. "I like you," she said as she studied Brenna. "You're pretty. Do you have any little girls who are four?" She held up the same number of fingers.

Brenna shook her head as she held a protective hand over her stomach. "No, I don't," she said, feeling a sudden yearning. "Not yet." She prayed that the baby growing inside her would be born healthy. If she survived the next few months, this job paid well enough to guarantee that she could stay home with her child for those first few months, but she still couldn't give her baby a father.

A man's voice drew their attention and they both looked toward the barn to find Wyatt. Kelly's face lit up and she took off running. Brenna waved and watched until the girl jumped into her father's arms. The scene reminded her of her own father, Sean Farren. There was nothing like the secure feeling parents gave a child. Brenna was a little ashamed she hadn't told her parents about the baby—the baby she had conceived out of wedlock—with a man they'd never met.

Brenna knew they'd be disappointed with their oldest

child and their only daughter. She was the first Farren to bring home a college degree. She also thought she'd be bringing a husband, but that had changed with Jason's hang-gliding accident and death. Just days later she'd discovered she was pregnant. With no other options, she had to come home to her family's ranch.

That was the reason she needed to have a job that paid enough to allow her to raise her child and not have to depend on Mom and Dad. Tugging her sweater around her, she knew she had to tell them. She'd seen the subtle changes in her body. At three months, she was beginning to lose her waistline. It wouldn't be much time before her secret was out.

Brenna walked back inside the cottage. This was to be her home for a while. But what would happen with her job when Dylan Gentry discovered her condition? Would he send her packing or would she be given the chance to help him back on his feet?

She hoped the latter. At least she didn't have to worry about the man being attracted to her. Most men ran from women with children. Too bad she couldn't say the same. The handsome bull rider was dangerous in more ways than one. She would definitely have to keep her head, and her distance.

Brenna glanced around the small but comfortable room. The cottage had been recently remodeled by Wyatt and Jared Trager. There were new windows, kitchen cabinets and countertops. The doorways had been widened and new hardwood floors had been laid throughout, making it easy to get through with a wheel-chair.

Suddenly Dylan's bedroom door swung open and he came out with the aid of his crutches. She stayed rooted to the spot, waiting to see if he needed her assistance. By the looks of his sure, smooth movements, he was handling them very well. She figured he did everything well. There was one problem she thought, eyeing his perfectly proportioned body, his broad shoulders and bare chest. How could she get him to wear more clothes? Pregnant or not, her hormones were racing full speed, especially with a good-looking man around all the time.

"What's for breakfast?" he asked.

"So you're hungry?"

He made his way to the table. "If we're going to work this morning, I'm going to need some food. I've done enough weight training to know that."

A thrill rushed through Brenna. Her job had just become a whole lot easier. She walked into the kitchen and took the lid off the skillet that held the scrambled eggs and bacon she had prepared a short while ago. Taking out two plates, she scooped up the food and took them to the table. She went back for two glasses of juice. During the meal the conversation was kept at a minimum as her patient concentrated on his food.

Dylan paused from his eating and glanced across the table at his new drill sergeant, for the moment. Brenna looked a little tired and there were dark circles around those striking brown eyes. Of course, he was probably the reason. He hadn't exactly been agreeable since her arrival. He still didn't want her here and had planned to get rid of her, but she'd managed to find his weak spot.

She'd challenged him. And he'd never backed down from a challenge.

Besides, she was the only therapist who'd showed up at the door who seemed sure he would walk again. He still wasn't certain that she could pull it off. Although she wasn't very big in size, he knew she was strong. He'd felt the toned muscles across her back and arms when she'd helped him stand at the parallel bars yesterday.

Of course, she had to be strong to lift patients. What had surprised him was her embarrassment when she'd stripped off the blanket and discovered him buck naked. Hadn't she seen patients naked before? Hadn't she seen a man without clothes? He couldn't help but wonder if there was someone in her life.

She definitely was attractive enough. Although he preferred blondes, he wondered how that glorious rust-colored mane would look down. She smelled good, too. He remembered the soft citrus scent whenever she'd gotten close to him.

His attention turned to her figure. Although she was wearing bulky sweats now, he recalled the sweet curve of her hips and long slender legs. He had no doubt she would fill out a pair of Wranglers to perfection. Just the way he liked...

Whoa. He didn't need to think of Ms. Farren as anything short of Attila the Hun. He was already too vulnerable with his battered and bruised body. There were scars that would never go away. His leg was the worst, a road map of red lines from the accident and the numerous surgeries. Not a pretty sight.

There was a time when women had admired his physique. After every successful ride, he could almost guarantee there would be women who'd be willing to share his celebration, even the night, with him. Since the accident, they hadn't been exactly lined up at his door. Yesterday morning, for a flash of an instant, Brenna had looked at him as if he were a man. And he definitely saw her as a woman.

Man, she was going to be a killer on his sleeping schedule.

He downed his orange juice, then reached for his coffee mug and leaned back in his chair while watching her. She picked at her food. "At the rate you eat, I'll never get to the bars."

She set down her fork. "I guess I put too much on my plate." She stood. "You're right, we should get started." She carried the dishes to the sink.

"Hey, we have time for you to finish."

"I've had enough," she told him. "Drink your coffee and we'll get started on the weights."

"Why don't you join me with a cup?"

She shook her head. "Caffeine makes me jittery. But enjoy yours while I clean up the dishes."

"Can't we take a few minutes to talk?"

Brenna set the dishes on the counter and turned around. She knew it wasn't unusual for a patient and PT to get personal. "What would you like to know? My credentials?"

He shrugged. "Where are you from?"

"I grew up here. My parents own a small ranch on the other side of San Angelo."

"Does everyone around here ranch?" he asked.

She shrugged. "It *is* cattle country." She knew he was new to the area. "Your own family has done very well in the business." Everyone knew the affluence of the Randells.

"What family is that?"

"The Randells."

"Does everyone know my business?"

Brenna wiped her hands on a towel and came to the table. "No, I only know the story because Wyatt told me. If you're worried about what people think…"

"I don't give a damn, but my business is my business."

"Seems to me you gave up your privacy when you become a national bull-riding champion." She had seen Dylan Gentry's exploits written up in the news the past years. "You draw a crowd wherever you go…especially women."

She saw a flash of pain in Dylan's eyes before he masked it. "That's over," he said. "I just want to be left alone."

Good. Brenna didn't feel like fighting off a bunch of women to get him to do his therapy. "That's fine with me." She pointed to the equipment in the living room. "We're going to be concentrating so hard on your rehab that you aren't going to have a chance to think about anything else."

He made a snorting sound. "There isn't enough therapy in the world to do that."

Brenna knew that dealing with a patient's depression was part of the job. Silently she went back to doing the dishes, knowing that she had to keep Dylan Gentry distracted with hard work.

Thirty minutes later, after a series of warm-up exercises, they got busy at the weight bench. Brenna was spotting Dylan as he lay on his back lifting the barbells up and down to help improve his upper-body strength. She was impressed at how easily he did each repetition. She also saw the strain on his face and knew he was pushing himself—too hard. Maybe he was just trying to impress the new PT, but she didn't want him to burn out. Finally she called a halt and handed him a towel to wipe off his sweaty chest. After a few minutes, she crouched in front of him and began strapping small weights around his ankles.

"We'll take this slow…and easy." She held on to his leg before he started. "We're not going all out on your first time, or tomorrow you'll be worthless. So take it easy," she warned. "Just lift your leg a few inches, hold it, then lower it."

A cinch, Dylan thought. But the light weight felt like a ton. By the time he finished five reps, beads of sweat had formed on his face. Even though she told him that was enough, he did five more. He wouldn't give her the satisfaction of seeing how hard the exercise was on him, but his leg had other ideas. The muscles fatigued from being sedentary for so long suddenly went into spasm.

Crying out, Dylan grabbed his leg. "Damn, damn…"

"Lie back," Brenna ordered as her sure hands went to work, kneading and soothing the knotted muscles in his thigh.

Dylan draped his arm over his eyes, hating his weakness but letting her magic fingers take over and ease his pain. Soon the pain turned to pleasure. What had soothed him was now beginning to arouse.

"That's enough." He sat up and tried to push her hand away. "My leg feels better."

"Just let me finish working out the stiffness."

He groaned and tightened his hold on her hand. "That's never going to happen if you keep this up," he said honestly.

She glanced down and suddenly her face flamed red.

"Oh… Then we should take a break." She handed him a bottle of water and walked out of the room.

Dylan fell back on the weight bench and closed his eyes. Somehow, he had to find a way to stop seeing Brenna Farren as a woman. He thought about the long-legged, auburn-haired vixen and realized that was never going to happen.

Four days later, taking a break from his workouts, Dylan sat on the sofa, remote in his hand, flipping through the channels, when his brother peered in the door. "Hey, Dylan," Wyatt said. "Got a minute?"

"It's your house."

His brother frowned. "I told you when I bought the ranch months ago I want you as my partner, just like we'd always talked about."

"Didn't plan on me being a cripple."

"Temporary situation," Wyatt said assuredly.

"And I told you I want no part of the Randell place. Besides, if I had a choice…"

Wyatt raised his hand. "You wouldn't be here," he finished his brother's sentence. Wyatt sat down on the sofa. "Just so you know, this ranch didn't start with Jack Randell. Our grandfather, John Sr., started the Rocking R and was well respected in the community. At one time this spread was one of the biggest in the area until Jack ran it into the ground."

"And you're putting it back together." At his brother's nod, Dylan went on, "And you're even running a herd."

Wyatt nodded again. "Hank Barrett suggested I give it a try. The Rocking R's herd is for the Mustang Valley Guest Ranch's cattle drives and roundups." He folded

his arms. "You can't believe the big demand for working cattle ranches."

Dylan saw his brother's excitement and envied him.

"Chance, Cade and Travis will be helping out,"
Wyatt continued. "I'd like you to meet them."

"Thanks, I think I'll pass."

Dylan had heard more than enough about his three
half brothers and Hank Barrett, the man who raised
them when Jack Randell was sent off to prison for cattle
rustling. Dylan felt the same about Jared Trager, another
illegitimate brother who'd showed up last year. Seemed
their daddy enjoyed seducing women, then when he got
tired of them, he moved on. And no one had seen anything of good old Jack for years.

"Maybe when you get back on your feet you'll feel
differently," Wyatt suggested. "How is the therapy coming?"

Dylan frowned. "You should know since Ms. Farren
has been reporting to you."

"Brenna and I haven't spoken since the day I hired
her. I thought you should handle this business on your
own."

Dylan gave a sarcastic hoot. "That would be a first."
His brother had always tried to manage his life.

"Look, Dylan. A few months ago, I wasn't sure you
would even survive the accident, let alone ever walk
again," he said, emotion lacing his voice. "You've been
given a second chance, but it's up to you what you do
with it." Wyatt gave him a long look, then stood and
walked to the door. "Call if you need anything." He left,
closing the door quietly behind him.

Dylan suddenly felt like a heel. Deep down, he knew
his brother was only trying to help him.

"Wyatt!" he called as he struggled to get up, one hand gripping the back of the chair as he reached for his crutches. He made it to the door, but when he pulled it open he was surprised when he was forced backward as someone slammed into him. It wasn't Wyatt, but Brenna. He fought to regain his balance but the attempt was futile. He dropped his crutches, reached out to grab the door frame for support, and in the process managed to sandwich Brenna between himself and the wall.

She gasped and her arms immediately went around his waist. He tried to shift his weight, but the action only seemed to increase the friction between them, shooting heat throughout his body.

"Dammit. Hold still," he demanded.

She froze. Only the sound of the TV in the background and their ragged breathing filled the room. Then her gaze raised to meet his and the startling color of her whiskey eyes mesmerized him. He couldn't seem to manage his next breath, but he managed to inhale her arousing scent. Only inches from her tempting mouth, he could easily bend forward and take a taste of her. Suddenly realizing where his thoughts were heading, he gripped the door frame and hopped backward on his good leg.

Now free, Brenna moved swiftly to retrieve his crutches. She helped slip them under his arms but didn't move away.

"You okay?" she asked.

He managed a nod, wishing she would stop asking him that question.

"Here, let me help you." Her hands touched his arms.

He jerked away. "I can do it," he insisted, and planted the base of his crutches on the floor, then turned and headed to the privacy of his bedroom. There he could deal with a different kind of pain.

Dylan didn't come out of the bedroom for the next hour. He didn't want to, at least not until he could find a way to fight his reaction to this woman. She was his therapist, she was going to have her hands on him…a lot. He groaned, thinking how much he wanted her touch…how he ached for it.

What the hell was wrong with him? No doubt Brenna was pretty, but she had commitment written all over her. And he definitely wasn't a forever kind of guy. Maybe in that respect he was like his old man. He had no desire to settle down with a wife and kids. He'd never known anyone who'd set a good example for him to follow.

All his life he and Wyatt had been known as Sally Gentry's bastard kids. Still, that hadn't been as bad as when they were ten years old and Earl Keys came into their mother's life. He'd convinced her that he'd make a good home for her and her boys. The truth was, Keys only wanted free laborers for his rough-stock business. Every summer both he and Wyatt had worked the rodeo circuit. During the school year, they'd lived on the man's Arizona ranch, but the work hadn't been any easier. Just as soon as the two had turned eighteen, they were gone.

No, neither Randell nor Keys were the best examples of what a father should be. Dylan had no doubt he'd inherited a few bad genes. He'd traveled the circuit and he was damn good at whatever he tried, starting out calf roping with Wyatt. Later, he'd discovered the excitement of bull riding. And the money for his talent and all the endorsements hadn't been bad, either. He was somebody. Then.

He rubbed his leg. Now he was a cripple.

A knock sounded on his bedroom door, then it opened. Brenna stepped just inside. She'd changed into a pair of jeans and blouse that had his juices flowing once again.

"Are you hungry?" she asked. "Or you going to stay in here all night and pout?"

"I'm not pouting," he insisted. "I'm just tired."

She came farther into the room. "You're in good shape. And your stamina has increased, so we can go longer, starting tomorrow."

"What if I don't want to go longer?"

She crossed her arms. "Look, Dylan, we agreed to a work schedule. If I let you slide now, you'll never get back on your feet. If you're worried about what happened with the cramps, we can work on that."

This woman was unbelievable. "I can handle the cramps." *It's you I can't seem to handle,* he thought silently.

"Good, because more than likely they'll return. But I can help. There's the whirlpool bath and I can give you a massage."

He tensed. Oh yeah, that was going to help a lot.

Brenna just stood there for a few more moments.

"Is there something else you want?" he asked.

"Staying closed up in here isn't good for you, Dylan. Not when you're used to having people around."

"I don't have a problem with it."

"As your therapist, I do. Your sister-in-law called and asked if you want to come up to the house for dinner."

Oh boy, the whole family all at once. He thought about Wyatt and the way he'd handled things earlier.

"If you are worried about the children, I know little Kelly would love to get to know you better."

"I'm not good with kids."

"Kelly is female. No matter what her age, I bet you can have her charmed in minutes." Brenna wrinkled her nose and Dylan knew she was trying to hide a smile.

"If I'm so good with the ladies, how come it hasn't worked on you?"

Her easy laughter filled the room. "I don't think you've been trying to charm me, only drive me away. Besides, I'm not a lady. I'm your therapist."

Ooh, she was definitely a lady. "Just out of curiosity, what would it take to get your…attention?"

"More than sweet words…or a cocky smile. I have three brothers, and they've inherited a bit of the blarney along with their Irish genes." She sobered. "Besides, I learned a long time ago to believe only half of what men say, and the other half is probably exaggerated."

"Whoa, someone must have done you wrong, lady." He scooted to the edge of the bed and placed his legs on the floor. "Who was he? Want me to go beat him up?"

A sadness transformed her face. "His name was Jason. And you can't beat him up…he's dead." She started to leave, when Dylan reached out and grabbed her arm. She pulled away as tears formed in her eyes.

"Look, I'm sorry. I didn't know." The urge to take her into his arms and hold her was overwhelming.

"It's okay." She moved toward the door. "I guess if you aren't going to your brother's for dinner then I better fix you something."

He shook his head. "No, don't cook, Brenna. We're going to supper at Wyatt's."

"I'll help you get there," she said, "but it would be better if you go to dinner on your own."

"Look, for the past week we've been living in pretty close quarters. And it's been hard to stay out of each other's business, much less their space. I've let you handle me at will, strap me in contraptions, and cause me considerable pain. Now, I'd say you owe me. Please, go with me."

She hesitated. "Okay, but don't think you're going to get your way all the time."

He wanted his way, all right. With her. "I'll take what I can get." He got to his feet. "Give me ten minutes to shower." Using his crutches, he grabbed some underwear and a pair of jeans from the bureau drawer.

"You be sure to use the bench in the tub," she warned.

"Or what? You're coming in and joining me?" He grinned. "Maybe that's not such a bad idea."

He watched her blush, but she didn't back down. "Be careful, remember I can hurt you."

He wasn't thinking pain, only pleasure as he headed off to the shower, a cool one. And for the first time in a long while, it was good to feel alive.

Fifteen minutes later they were both seated in one of the golf carts that belonged to the Mustang Valley Guest Ranch. With Brenna behind the wheel, they headed up to the main house. That was the easy part. The three steps to the porch were much more of a challenge to Dylan.

"You're getting to be pretty good with those crutches," Brenna said.

"Now, who's trying to charm who?" he asked, trying to relax his labored breathing.

"If that's what it takes, I'll do my part."

He smiled, enjoying the easiness between them. "Just how far will you go, Ms. Brenna?"

Even under the porch light, he could see she was flustered, but before she could give a retort the door opened and Kelly appeared. The child looked a little apprehensive, then relaxed seeing Brenna. "Hi, Unca Dylan," she said. "Hi, Brenna."

"Hello, Kelly," Brenna said, and she pulled open the screen door allowing Dylan to go in first. Then she followed.

Dylan's gaze swept around the huge sunny-yellow kitchen. There were pine cabinets and white-tiled countertops. At the stainless-steel stove, his sister-in-law stood cooking. His brother had always talked about having a home. It looked as if he'd gotten his wish.

Maura turned and smiled. "Dylan and Brenna, I'm so glad you both came."

"Thank you for inviting us," Brenna said.

Maura walked over to greet them, surprising Dylan with a hug. Then she stood back and gave him the once-over. "Well, look at you, Dylan, getting around so well." She turned to Brenna. "Thank you for helping him."

"Oh, Dylan is the one who did the work," she insisted. "I only gave him a little push now and then."

"Using a bulldozer," Dylan said, and they all laughed.

The sound of voices drew their attention to the doorway where Wyatt and seven-year-old Jeff walked into the room. He and Wyatt weren't identical twins, Dylan thought, struck once again by their differences, but they were pretty close, with the same height and build. Their hair color was the same, but their eyes were different—his brother's were blue while his were more gray. Wyatt was the more sensible one. Dylan had always been attracted to trouble.

The young boy's face lit up. "Wow, Dad, Uncle Dylan came."

Wyatt smiled. "Yes, son, I'd say he did." He walked up to Dylan. "Glad you could make it, bro."

"I didn't have much choice," Dylan lied as he leaned on his crutches. "This was the only way to get a taste of Maura's meat loaf. You've certainly bragged about it enough."

"Well, come and sit down," Wyatt coaxed. "Dinner shouldn't be too long. Would you like something to drink? Soda? Iced tea? Milk?"

"Iced tea sounds good."

"I'll get it." Jeff ran to the refrigerator, then came back with a full glass. "Uncle Dylan, Dad said you're the best bull rider in the world."

A sadness moved through him, but he pushed it aside and smiled at his nephew. "Well, I had won the national championship, but someone else won the title this year."

"I told Benny Roberts you did, but he said that I'm lyin' 'cause you aren't really my uncle."

A strange protectiveness came over Dylan. "I guess you just have to prove him wrong. As soon as I locate my things, I'll dig up one of my championship buckles and you can show him."

"Oh, wow!" His eyes rounded. "Can I, really?"

Dylan ruffled the boy's hair. "Yes, you really can."

A smiling Jeff went to his seat across the table, next to Kelly. The little girl looked like her mother, pretty as a picture. When he winked at her, her face lit up with a smile, and a funny feeling circled Dylan's heart.

Brenna leaned toward him. "I think you got yourself a couple of new fans here." She looked him in the eye and whispered, "You've still got it, Dylan 'The Devil' Gentry."

Chapter 3

Two hours later, Wyatt walked Brenna and Dylan out to the porch. She noticed he was careful not to hover too close to his brother, letting him move by himself. Although tired, Dylan seemed to want to show off and made easy work of getting down the steps and into the golf cart.

"Thank Maura again for the great meal," Dylan said.

"Anytime," Wyatt said. "And if you'll let me know where your national championship buckle is, I could get it."

"Impossible. It's in my trailer and that's parked in Arizona."

Wyatt shook his head. "No, it's here," he said. "So is Cheyenne Gold."

Dylan tensed. "You brought my trailer and horse here?"

Wyatt glanced at Brenna, then back at his brother,

and nodded. "Yeah. You spent so much time in the hospital, and since you were coming here anyway... I thought you might need your things close by. No sense you paying a fortune to store your trailer and board your horse. Here it's free."

Brenna got in the cart, feeling more than the January chill. There was new tension between the brothers.

"We should get back," she suggested. "You two can hash this out when it's warmer. Wyatt, thank Maura again." She pressed her foot on the pedal and they shot off down the path.

Once at the cottage, Dylan got out without her help and went up the single step with ease. Inside, he started toward the bedroom, but Brenna caught up with him.

"Dylan, why don't you watch television out here? The screen is bigger. We could put a movie in the VCR."

"I don't feel like a movie."

"Then stay and talk?" She should keep out of this situation, but this situation could interfere with her patient's recovery. "I can fix some coffee."

"I know what you're trying to do, Brenna, but it isn't going to work. I'm mad as hell. So let me be."

She took hold of his arm and got a fierce look as his silver-blue eyes locked on her.

Somehow she managed to find her voice. "No. Not until you tell me what was so bad that it ruined the end of an enjoyable evening with your family."

"I didn't ruin it, my brother did."

Brenna watched as he started to pace a path to the door then back again. "Tell me what he did that was so terrible."

"What Wyatt has always done for the past thirty-one years—try to run my life. He's older than me by five minutes, and believe me, he has let me know it all our lives. He's always felt he knows what's best for me. Just like my coming to the ranch. I agreed to stay here, only until I recovered from my injuries. But he still couldn't leave things alone. It was his idea to get a therapist. I never wanted one. I just wanted to be left alone.

"Now he thinks he had the right to drag my trailer and horse here. Without asking me, I might add. He's just looking for a way to keep me here permanently."

Why did Dylan's words hurt so much? Brenna had known from the beginning that he didn't want a therapist. Over the past week, he'd gotten past that and had accepted her, but hearing the bitterness in his voice now she wasn't so sure. Her own anger flared. She'd be damned if she'd stay where she wasn't wanted.

"You're right, Dylan," she agreed. "Your brother had no right to push you into anything you didn't want. At least one of your problems can be easily solved."

He cocked an eyebrow. "Which one's that?"

Her chest was tight. "Your therapist. I'll have my bags packed and be gone in thirty minutes."

He had blown it big-time.

Dylan knocked on Brenna's bedroom door, but she didn't answer. He knocked again. "Brenna, can we talk?"

No answer.

"Please, Bren. You misunderstood. Open the door and let me explain."

No answer.

He couldn't let her leave, not like this, not at all. He tried the door. It was unlocked. He pushed it open slightly to notice a suitcase on the bed and Brenna placing her clothes inside. "Brenna, will you stop? I don't want you to leave."

She didn't look up. "You said you didn't want me."

"I was only angry with Wyatt for how he'd manipulated me. How he's always been able to get me to do what he wants."

"I don't think he put you on top of that bull, or caused your accident."

"Of course he didn't. But it's a fact that he wanted me here. He wanted me as his partner in this ranch, wanted me to meet the Randells and become part of one big happy family."

She paused and glared at him. "And you want me to sympathize with you for what again?"

"Okay, so it isn't a capital offense. But he won't butt out of my life."

"It's called being part of a family," she retorted. "Deal with it, Gentry. Not everything is always about you. Don't you know that your brother loves you? He's trying to help you the only way he knows how. And all you've done is to get angry and be disagreeable."

"I agree," he admitted.

"And blame everyone else for your misfortune," she continued, not hearing him.

"Hey, I said I agree."

"You may be used to getting everyone's attention while you're perched on a bull, Dylan Gentry, but there are others to consider now."

She had scraped off another layer of his hide. "What do you want?" he asked. "My blood? I said you're right."

She stared at him. "I am?"

"Yes. I've been a rotten bastard. Hard to live with and worse to deal with." He sank down to the edge of the bed and looked at her. "Now, will you stay? Will you help me change? Help me walk again?"

Brenna was caught off guard by his sudden change. But from day one this man had had a tendency of doing just that…and more. If she was smart, she'd take this opportunity to get far, far away. But she couldn't. She knew she could help him get back on his feet, help give him back a life. Hopefully, it wouldn't be on the back of a bull.

"What about your brother?" she asked. "I think you two need to sit down and work this out."

"We will," he promised. "So, you'll stay and continue my therapy?"

Brenna told herself that it was only for the money, for her baby. "I'll stay."

He grinned at her and she nearly melted to the floor. She was in deep trouble if she didn't find a way to shield her heart from this man.

Early mornings had been Dylan's time. Over the past ten days he'd been pushing himself as hard as he could with the weights and on the parallel bars. In ten days, he'd not only changed his attitude but increased his strength. He had more energy now, more stamina.

Brenna tried to hold him back, warning him that he could do damage if he rushed it. But he wasn't quitting until he was on his feet. On the parallel bars, with Brenna's close attention, and the gait belt for safety, he'd managed to put weight on his bad leg and hold it. The pain was bad, but worth it as he took that first, shaky step. He still needed more strength in his legs…a lot more, and he was getting tired of waiting. That's why he worked overtime with the leg weights.

He'd also talked with Wyatt, apologized for his behavior, but asked his brother to check with him before making any more decisions about his life. Dylan wanted to make those on his own.

With his progress, he was thinking it might be possible to get back on the circuit. He missed the travel, the crowds and yeah, the female attention… He thought about how long it had been since he had kissed and caressed a woman, had one in his bed. He closed his eyes and Brenna's face came into focus. He released a groan and sat up at the bench. It infuriated him that his reaction to her was so strong. He wiped the sweat from his face and got up to head to the shower. A long, cold one.

A soft knock sounded on the door. "Come in," he called.

The door opened and little Kelly poked her head in. "Hi, Unca Dylan. You busy?" She smiled brightly.

He found he'd looked forward to her visits before heading off to school.

"Not for my favorite niece." The cute blonde wasn't a blood relative, but Wyatt had adopted both Jeff and Kelly when he married their mother. That was close enough for him.

She giggled. "I brought you something." She held up a picture that looked like a bunch of scribbling.

"That's very nice."

"It's Mommy, Daddy and Jeff and me." She pointed off to the side. "That's our house. It's for you to hang up. That's so we can be with you all the time."

"That's real nice, Kelly. I'll tape your drawing to the refrigerator so I can look at it whenever I want."

She walked up to him and whispered, "I know a secret, too."

"You do?" The child's eyes were wide with excitement. He played along. "You want to tell me?"

She shrugged. "You have to cross your heart and promise not to tell." She ran her small hand over her coat.

He did the same. "I cross my heart."

"Mommy has a baby in her tummy."

Dylan didn't expect to feel the rush of emotion. Was it true or just wishful thinking on the child's part? "She does? How do you know?"

She rolled her eyes. "'Cause the pink stick says so. That's how you know."

"Oh." How did a four-year-old know about a pregnancy test?

"Mommy and Daddy were whispering about it in the bathroom. Mommy was cryin', but they were happy tears. And Daddy was kissin' her." She sighed. "They kiss a lot."

No doubt, Dylan thought as a pang of jealousy hit him. "Well, maybe we shouldn't say anything. I think they want to surprise everybody."

Kelly placed a finger against her lips. "I won't tell."

"That's good because if you do, you know what will happen?"

She shook her head, causing her ponytail to swish back and forth.

"The tickle monster will come and grab you." He lifted her onto his lap and began to tickle her ribs, making her giggle. Just then Brenna came into the room.

"Help me," Kelly cried in between fits of laughter. "Unca Dylan won't stop tickling me."

"Is that so? Well, we have to do something about

that." Brenna came up behind Dylan on the bench and
went after his ribs.

Dylan didn't know how it happened but he was soon
the one under attack by both females. He managed to
release Kelly and grabbed for Brenna. Somehow she
ended up in his lap, her cute little bottom fitting nicely
against him. That was when he looked up and saw
Wyatt and Maura standing in the doorway.

"Don't let us interrupt…your therapy," Wyatt said.

Brenna felt heat rush to her face, realizing what she
was doing. Her behavior was so unprofessional and
so unlike her. She scrambled off Dylan's lap. "Wyatt,
Maura, please come in."

"You want to help me, bro?" Dylan said. "Seems the
girls have outnumbered me."

"Looks like fun, but I'll have to pass." Wyatt glanced
at his daughter. "Kelly, you didn't tell us where you
went. Your mother was worried."

"Sorry. I brought Unca Dylan a picture." She pointed
to the one on the sofa.

"Well, next time tell us when you leave the house."

"'Kay. Am I in trouble?"

Brenna watched as the wide-eyed child looked up
at her daddy, her lower lip forming a pout. Kelly was
good. Brenna knew because she used to do the same
with her father. "Wyatt and Maura, why don't you sit
down and I'll make some coffee."

Maura shook her head. "No, thank you. I need to
get to work. Besides, I'm off coffee for a while." She
glanced up at her husband and smiled. "Come on, Kelly,
we need to get going."

The girl took her hand, then smiled back at her uncle
before walking off with her parents.

Brenna looked at Dylan. "You two looked thick as thieves."

"That's because we share a secret."

She smiled. "It's great that you and Kelly are getting along so well."

She started to walk away. He reached out and pulled her onto the weight bench, his strength tumbling her backward. He ended up leaning over her, causing his black hair to fall over his forehead. There was a sexy glint in his eyes. "I bet you want to know what it is."

The pressure of his hard body against hers was far too distracting. "Not really. Now, let me up."

A playful grin appeared across his handsome face, and she knew how he'd gotten his nickname.

"It's different when I have the advantage," he teased.

"Just let me up," she insisted.

He only shifted closer. When his eyes met hers, the mesmerizing silvery-blue gaze ended her futile struggle.

"Aren't you the least bit curious?" he asked.

Brenna suddenly realized that his question had nothing to do with any secret. Unable to stop herself, she gave a surrendering nod. Dylan lowered his head and his lips met hers in a gentle caress. She should have resisted, but she only managed a faint whimper as he began to take tiny nibbles from her lips. Finally his mouth closed over hers, so gently and searchingly, as if he was trying to savor her.

Then without warning, the kiss changed as Dylan ran his tongue over the seam of her lips, teasing and probing until she opened to him. With a groan, he delved inside to taste her. Brenna's body grew aroused and instinctively she moved against him.

"Bren..." He breathed her name, then captured her

mouth once again. The kiss was deep and thorough, driving her desire higher and higher. She couldn't think about anything but this man. Suddenly there was a ringing sound.

Dylan drew away with a curse and reached for the cordless phone. "Hello," he growled.

Brenna sat up quickly and tried to pull herself together. She took a calming breath, but nothing eased the anger and shame she felt for her behavior. If she was to continue this job, she had to somehow stay away from Dylan Gentry.

Dylan hung up the phone. "Sorry about the interruption. It was my manager." He reached for her hand as she tried to stand. "Hey, where are you going?"

"I need to fix breakfast." She tried to keep the trembling out of her voice, tried to break his tight grip. "I'd say it was a good thing it happened—the interruption, I mean."

"Now, that's where we disagree," he told her. "I'd say it's a good thing the kiss happened."

Brenna drew back. "No, Dylan. That wasn't a good thing. I'm your therapist."

"I'm also a man and you're a woman and we were both curious about what it would be like if we kissed."

And I'm pregnant with another man's child, she reminded herself. "Okay, so now we know," she relented. "And we can forget about it."

He hesitated a moment, then nodded. "All right. If that's the way you want it. But if you change your mind—"

"This isn't a joke," Brenna interrupted him. "And I'm not going to be one of your conquests." She broke free and took off into the kitchen. How could she so easily have forgotten Jason and jumped into this man's arms?

It wasn't long before Dylan came up behind her. "Look, Brenna, I didn't mean to upset you. I overstepped, but it was only a kiss." There was a long pause, then he spoke again, "And you're wrong, never once have I never thought about you being a...conquest. If you've been reading up about me you would know that I prefer blondes."

She turned to him and glared, but he was grinning at her. Darn the man. "So you can't handle us feisty redheads? Too much fire, ah?"

He started to speak, then stopped. "I'm not going to touch that one."

"Chicken," she teased, finally starting to relax.

"You're damn straight. You can cause me a lot of pain."

She smiled this time. "You're learning."

"So we're friends again?" he asked.

"Friends," she agreed, knowing it was a dangerous move.

Dylan leaned on his crutches and studied Brenna's flushed face. He had to admit that he reacted more strongly to her than he wanted...or needed. But the feel of her body against him drove him to do irrational things. And the last thing he needed was to get involved with this woman. She was the type who would be hard to walk away from...and that was all he'd been good at. Except this time he wasn't even able to walk. Yet.

With another look, he noticed there were blue shadows under her eyes. Dammit, he didn't want to worry about her, either. "Are you okay?"

She nodded. "I'm just a little tired."

No wonder, when she wasn't getting much sleep. He'd heard her moving around before dawn. "That's because you're up before the sun."

She opened the refrigerator. "I'm used to little sleep." She took out the bacon and began placing strips in the warming skillet.

"Bren, I don't want to argue with you. I'm just concerned you're working yourself too hard."

"I'm used to hard work," she insisted. "I had two part-time jobs in college, while I was carrying a full load of classes. Before that, I lived on my parents' ranch. Being a girl didn't mean my chores were any easier. Believe me, I can handle this job, Dylan." Her gaze met his. "Unless you have any complaints."

Dylan sighed. Only that she was too pretty not to notice, that he wanted to kiss that sassy mouth of hers again and again.

He shook away the thought. "Not a one, Bren. You've convinced me."

"Well, praise be, I think you're catching on."

"Okay, so I'm a slow learner."

"I'd say you learn pretty fast. Your progress has been remarkable."

He waved his hand. "Let's not talk about me anymore." He smiled. "Want to know my secret?"

"I thought you said you were good at keeping secrets. If you tell me then it's no longer a secret." She got two plates down from the cupboard, took out flatware from the drawer and carried it to the table.

He followed her. "It's good news."

"So, keep it to yourself." She went back into the kitchen.

He wasn't listening. "Okay, I'll give you a hint. Someone is pregnant."

Chapter 4

Brenna's heart skipped a beat, then began racing. Oh God, how did he find out? "How did you know?" she gasped.

Dylan's smile widened. "I wasn't sure at first. You never know how reliable kids are. But when Wyatt and Maura walked in here earlier I was pretty sure it was true. I mean, Maura had a glow about her—"

"Maura?" Brenna interrupted, confused as to what he was saying.

"Yeah, she's pregnant."

Brenna sank against the counter with the unexpected reprieve. "Maura's pregnant?"

"Is there an echo in here?" He frowned. "Isn't that what I just said? That was Kelly's big secret. Seems she overheard her parents talking about a pink stick and a baby. And seeing the grin on my brother's face, I'd say it was true. You knew, too?"

"Huh...yeah," she lied, trying to be convincing. "Just don't let on, okay? They probably wanted to wait until the time was right to tell everyone."

"I can keep a secret."

Her mouth twitched.

"All right, you caught me at a weak moment," he admitted.

Dylan wasn't talking about the secret anymore. Brenna glanced away, but was lured back by his infectious smile. Then that smile disappeared and his blue eyes searched hers. She knew that he was thinking about the kiss, too. Brenna tried to erase it from her mind, but she could still feel the imprint of his mouth on hers, still taste him. Her chest suddenly tightened, her breasts grew heavy and sensitive. Dylan noticed it too as he shifted his gaze to her T-shirt. His bold inspection instantly caused her nipples to harden.

She drew a quick breath. "Are you hungry?" she asked and immediately regretted her choice of words. "I mean, you should have some protein."

Dylan was trying hard not to break his promise, but Brenna Farren was a tempting woman. Damn, he never should have kissed her in the first place. She was his therapist, for God's sake. She was the one who was going to get him back on the circuit. So that meant he had to find a way to curb his desire for her. But there was no way he could change things back to the way they were before, before he got an intriguing sample. He started to answer her but was interrupted by a knock on the door.

"Sure is busy around here this morning." With the aid of his crutches, he headed across the room. He pulled open the door expecting to find Wyatt. Instead, there was an older man standing on the porch. He was in his midsixties with a head of thick gray hair. His face was weathered with lines, especially around the eyes.

"Good mornin'." He smiled. "I apologize for bothering you so early, but Wyatt said you'd be up." He offered his hand. "I'm Hank Barrett. I wanted to stop by and welcome you to San Angelo."

Dylan was caught off guard as he took the man's hand. "I'm Dylan."

"I guessed that. You look too much like your brother not to be." Barrett's smile faded. "We're all sorry to hear about your accident, but I'm glad to see you're doin' so well." He fiddled with the black Stetson in his hands. "Do you mind if I speak with you a moment?"

Dylan nodded and moved aside. "Come in."

"Thank you," Hank said as he stepped into the cottage and glanced around at all the equipment. "I see you're busy, so I won't keep you long," he said. Then he spotted Brenna in the kitchen area and grinned. "Is that you, Brenna Farren?"

Brenna came forward. She wiped her hands on her sweats. "Hello, Mr. Barrett."

"Oh, I think you're old enough now to call me Hank. Aren't you a sight for these old peepers." He examined her closely. "Land sakes, I haven't seen you since before you took off for college."

"I graduated last summer."

"I know. Your daddy has been shoutin' the news to everybody. He's sure happy his girl is home."

Dylan watched her blush.

"I'm happy to be here, too."

Hank looked at Dylan. "She must be good at her job if she got you on your feet."

"Brenna's a real slave driver," Dylan said, finding it easy to talk to the man.

"*Someone* has to get you to do your therapy," she insisted.

"Sounds like you're both what each other needs." The older man glanced back and forth between the two. "Look, I didn't mean to interrupt you. I just wanted to stop by and invite the two of you to supper this weekend."

Dylan tensed. He'd bet his favorite pair of chaps that he'd be seeing the Randell brothers at this supper. "I don't know if that's such a good idea."

"Look, Dylan. I don't want to put any pressure on you. But you've been pretty much holed up here the past month. Thought you'd like a night out. And maybe you're just a little curious about Chance, Cade, Travis and Jared."

"Not really," Dylan said, realizing he was curious… a little.

Hank nodded, but didn't look as if he was about to give up. "Then how about you come as a neighbor accepting an invitation from another neighbor? I doubt the boys are going to force themselves on you. I think right now they're more interested in your ability to ride a bull than the fact that you're a blood relation."

"I'm not much interested in any part of Jack Randell's life."

A wide grin appeared on Hank's face. "Well, you see, you already have something in common with them after all. Chance, Cade and Travis want no part of Jack, either."

Dylan glanced at Brenna. She gave him a hopeful

look. "I could drive, and if it gets to be too much for you, I could bring you home."

What did he have to lose? He turned to Hank. "What time?"

The older man sighed. "Anytime after five will be fine. With my housekeeper, Ella, it's hard to tell when everything gets put on the table." He looked at Brenna. "As I remember correctly, your mother, Maggie, was a pretty good cook. I bet you inherited some of her talent."

"I'm not bad," she said. "I would love to bring something."

"That sounds great. See you both Saturday." With a wave, he walked out and closed the door behind him.

Brenna turned to Dylan. "Well, you are a surprise, Gentry."

He shrugged. "I'm just keeping my promise."

She folded her arms over her chest. "And which promise is that?"

"That I would work on changing my attitude if you'd stay."

"So you're okay with the possibility of meeting your brothers?"

"Whoa, there." He raised a hand. "I only have one brother and that's Wyatt. As far as I'm concerned, these Randells are just neighbors." He wasn't about to admit to her that he was curious to meet them, too.

"Well, that's a start," Brenna said, and headed back to the kitchen.

He followed her. "What is that supposed to mean?"

"Nothing. Just that you're at least meeting them. The Randells are pretty nice people." She smiled. "But then you'll find that out all by yourself."

* * *

Three days later, Brenna drove Dylan to the Circle B Ranch. She used the twenty-minute trip to fill him in on the history of the Circle B and how Hank recently had turned the running of the ranch over to the brothers.

Now it was part of the family business. Hank's Circle B, Chance and Joy's ranch, Cade and Abby's ranch, along with a small section of Jared and Dana's property that all met together at the valley, were all part of the Mustang Valley Guest Ranch. Even Wyatt's place was included in the package, expanding the operation with a working cattle ranch. At this time of year the place was closed until spring. The Randells loved having the chance to spend time with their families.

Brenna looked across the seat at Dylan. He hadn't said a word since he got into the truck. No doubt tonight was going to be difficult for him.

"You know, the Randells aren't going to push you into anything. I think they just want to get to meet you. Like Hank said, they're in awe of the fact that you're a world-champion bull rider."

"I guess I should have brought my buckles," he said sarcastically.

"Dylan, don't be this way. The Randells are trying to reach out to you. Remember, they were as shocked as you must have been at finding out they had three half brothers."

"You're right." He released a long breath. "I'll behave."

She turned off the highway onto a gravel road and headed past the rows of white-fenced pastures where cattle grazed in the high grass. They drove under the wrought-iron archway that read Circle B Ranch. Soon outbuildings came into view, a barn, then a large two-story gray house with white shutters.

Brenna continued past a row of cars and trucks until she reached a long white building with the name over the door reading, Circle B Chuckwagon. She parked and turned off the engine.

"Hanks says now that the family is so big, they have to eat their meals here in the guest-ranch dining hall when they all get together."

Dylan remained stone-faced. "I guess we should get this over with." He raised the door handle and started to get out.

"Wait, Dylan." Brenna stopped him. "I'm telling you right now, I don't want you to have a good time. If that starts to happen, you let me know and I'll get you the heck out of the there."

"Very funny," he said, but she could see he was fighting a smile.

She released his arm, climbed out and went around to his door. He didn't need her help, but she was standing nearby just in case.

Dylan eased out, set his crutches under his arms before heading for the entrance, where he was met with the sound of laughter and children's voices coming from inside.

Wyatt came out to greet them. "It's about time you showed up." He glanced at Brenna. "He giving you trouble?"

"Nothing I can't handle," she said.

"Well, you're officially off duty for the evening. I'll take care of this guy. I want you to enjoy yourself."

Brenna knew the Randells, but not well. They had all

been ahead of her in school. She reminded herself being invited was part of her job. Wyatt could have brought his brother, but she doubted Dylan would have come if she hadn't offered to take him back home whenever he wanted to leave. She took her rice-and-mushroom casserole out of the truck and followed the men inside. Already several people had surrounded Wyatt and Dylan. She paused and decided to stay back. He needed to deal with this himself.

Brenna started across the pine floor, skirting several children and the long tables with high-back chairs, toward the kitchen area. A stainless-steel counter already held several dishes of food, including a huge bin of fried chicken.

She set down her dish and started to turn around when she heard her name.

"Well, if it isn't little Brenna Farren."

She looked up to find the Circle B's housekeeper, Ella. She was a tall, big-boned woman dressed in a plaid blouse and black jeans. Her gray hair was cut short and combed back from her handsome face.

"Hello, Ella. How are you?"

The housekeeper gave her a big hug. "I'm the same, but you've grown into a real beauty. I heard you were home. I bet your mama is happy about that."

Brenna nodded. "Although I haven't been able to spend much time with Mom and Dad. I've been working."

Ella raised an eyebrow. "I know those Gentry men are easy on the eyes, but take the time to get home and see your folks."

"I promise. It's just that Dylan needs most of my attention these first few weeks."

Ella glanced at the crowd across the room. "Looks like he's standing on his own pretty good."

Brenna couldn't deny that, and he was growing stronger day by day.

A short time later, Joy and Abby Randell came up to Brenna and introduced themselves. Joy was married to the oldest brother, Chance. They had a daughter, Katie Rose, and a three-month-old son, Dane. Abby was married to the second oldest brother, Cade. They had two boys, a ten-year-old, Brandon, and a two-year-old, James Henry.

The next to arrive was the pretty, dark-haired Josie Randell. She was married to the youngest brother, Travis. They had a little girl nearly two years old, Elissa Mae. Josie was also Hank's biological daughter who he'd only learned about a few years ago.

Another arrival to the group was Dana Shayne Trager. She was married to Jared, the first of Jack's illegitimate sons. He'd been the one who had a picture of Sally Gentry and Jack Randell together. Dana had a five-year-old son, Evan, and another baby on the way. Finally Maura joined the group of women and made her announcement that she and Wyatt were expecting a baby in September. The Randell family was certainly growing.

Brenna couldn't resist any longer and asked to hold Dane. Joy relinquished her tiny son, who looked so much like his father, Chance. Surprisingly, he also looked like his uncle Dylan. Brenna couldn't help wondering who her baby would resemble. Would he be the image of Jason?

The biggest problem was how to explain her situation to her family. Would they accept the news of their first grandchild with enthusiasm? How would Dylan take it? Would he let her continue being his therapist? He had made so much progress in the past month. The last thing she wanted was for him to quit. She glanced across the room and saw him talking with the Randell brothers. He was making a different kind of progress now. And he seemed to be fitting in just fine.

The other ladies in the group noticed it too. "Would you look at that," Joy said in amazement. "All six of them. The brothers are finally together."

Dylan sat at the table as Chance, Cade and Travis took turns telling him about their childhood. Dylan quickly learned how hard it had been on all of them—that being a legitimate son of Jack Randell hadn't been easy. Although Hank had taken them in, they hadn't had an easy time. They'd had to do a lot to convince people they weren't like their father.

"Our lives must sound pretty boring compared to yours," Travis said. "I bet you miss the rodeo."

"Yeah, I miss it," Dylan admitted, absently rubbing his leg. "But as you can see, I got pretty banged up. I still have a long way to go before I can compete again."

"So you're plannin' on going back to the circuit?" Travis asked.

"I'd like to," Dylan admitted. "I don't know anything else."

Wyatt interrupted. "I've been trying to get Dylan to stay and be my partner."

"I'm not ready to retire yet," Dylan insisted. "If I continue the therapy and if the doctor releases me, I figure I have a good year where I can still be competitive."

Cade laughed. "Boy, can tell you're single." He was

the tallest of all the brothers, and the darkest, with his brown eyes and black hair. He was a part-time rancher and financial adviser. "Abby would kill me if I tried anything that dangerous."

"As would Joy and Josie," Chance added with a grin. He was a quarter-horse breeder and trainer. "But I wouldn't have it any other way. The right woman excites me more than sitting on an ugly bull for the thrill of an eight-second ride. No offense, Dylan."

"None taken," Dylan said. "Everyone needs to do what they love."

"You're right," Jared said. "I get to be a carpenter. Chance, you have your horses. Cade, you play the market and Travis still works in computer security. And even Wyatt's got his rough-stock business." He smiled. "I'd say we're all following our hearts."

Dylan nodded in agreement, but he wasn't like these guys. They all had homes and families…a special woman. He'd never wanted any part of that. So why was he envying these men?

Dylan was grateful when his attention was drawn to questions from the kids. He answered them the best he could and promised to bring his championship buckles the next time. Feeling a little closed in, he looked around, hoping to find Brenna. He finally spotted her standing with the other women. She turned and his breath caught. She had a baby cuddled against her breast. The tiny infant's fingers were latched on to one of hers. Brenna was beaming as she cooed at the child.

Then, as if she sensed someone was watching her, she raised her head and their eyes met. Blood pulsed through his body, causing a searing heat to pool low in his gut.

Chance said something, but Dylan couldn't make it out as he tried to focus.

"I think the man's distracted," Chance said, and laughter broke out. "He hasn't heard a word we're saying."

"What?" Dylan asked. "Did you say something?"

"Nothing important," Chance commented, smiling.

"Well, I have some important news," Wyatt said. "Maura is pregnant."

Wyatt got slaps on the back and congratulations from the group. Dylan was happy for his brother, too.

Dylan's attention was drawn back to Brenna. Damn. She looked like a natural with the baby. That alone should be reason enough to stay far away from her. Easier said than done, especially since he'd kissed her. All he could think about was doing it again. Not a good idea when he was determined to go back on the circuit.

"Admit it, the Randells aren't so bad," Brenna coaxed as she drove them back to the cottage.

Dylan kept his gaze on the glow from the truck's headlights lighting the dark road. "No, they aren't, but that doesn't mean I'm going to fit in here."

"Dylan, Wyatt didn't fit in at first, either. You should give yourself some time, get to know them."

"All right, I will. But that's not going to change the fact that I'm going back to the circuit. If I remember correctly, that was how you convinced me to let you keep the job. You promised to get me on my feet. Are you going back on your word?"

She stiffened. "No. I'm not going back on my word." She turned on to the driveway, then drove past the main house to the cottage.

She shut off the engine. "It just seems crazy to me that you're risking your life for—"

"Brenna, it's my life," he interrupted and clasped his hand on her arm before she could get out of the car. "And that makes it not your concern."

It was too dark to see her face, but he inhaled her scent, reminding him of her softness, her kiss.

"Fine," she whispered. "Like you said, my job will be over once you get back on your feet." Brenna climbed out of the cab and slammed the door. She came around to help him, but he'd already gotten out. Seeing he didn't need her help, she walked up to the porch and went inside the cottage. By the time Dylan got there, Brenna was already in her room with the door closed. He didn't blame her, he wasn't fit company for anyone.

Brenna paced her small room, trying to relieve some of her anger. Damn that man. Hadn't she learned her lesson? Dylan Gentry was a bull rider. He wanted life with the rodeo rather than any family.

No more attempts to try to save a man who didn't want to be saved, she vowed. Jason had taught her a bitter lesson. She wasn't important enough to him to stop his dangerous lifestyle.

She lay down on the bed and placed her hand over her slightly rounded stomach. Tonight, seeing how protective the Randell men were with their wives made her feel more alone than ever. She knew none of the couples had had an easy time finding love, but eventually it had all worked out, with happy endings for each one of them.

Guess that wasn't meant to be for Brenna and her child. Jason was gone and her baby was without a father. And soon she wouldn't be able to hide the fact that she was pregnant. Her parents had to be told. She prayed for a little more time, a few more weeks, just so she could finish her job here. But she couldn't stay away from her parents much longer. And Brenna knew the second her mother saw her, she would know something was up. Brenna didn't want to see the disappointment in her eyes.

There was a knock on the door. She pulled down her bulky sweater and sat up. "Come in."

The door swung open and Dylan stood in the doorway. "I want to apologize. I shouldn't have gotten angry with you."

"And maybe I shouldn't have pushed you. You did a good thing going to the Circle B tonight. I know it made Wyatt happy."

"I don't think it takes much these days to make my brother happy. Maura and the kids and the ranch are doing a pretty good job of that."

Brenna couldn't help but see the obvious love between the couple. "Yeah, it shows."

Dylan took one step inside, then sat down on the end of the bed. Brenna started to protest, but they had lived in such close quarters during the past weeks, it would be silly to get prissy now.

"Were you that happy with… Jason?"

Startled by the question, her gaze darted to his. But she couldn't lie. "No. Maybe that's the reason I see how special Wyatt and Maura's relationship is."

"It seems like an epidemic around here. Every couple tonight was gushing. I felt like I was intruding." He looked at her. "How did you feel?"

She nodded. "The same," she admitted. "I even saw sparks between Ella and Hank."

"Damn, I thought it was just me." They both laughed, then Dylan sobered. "I need to get out more."

She smiled. "Shows you're on the mend and getting impatient. Besides tonight, the only place you've gone is to the doctor's and Wyatt's."

"I can't drive."

"This ranch is pretty big. You can go out with your brother. He'd probably get a kick out of showing you around. You have a golf cart at your disposal. Why not surprise him tomorrow?"

"I think I will." He glanced back at her. "You look tired. Why don't you take tomorrow off?"

"Whoa, I'm the one who says when you can stop your therapy." She stood. "You're at a critical stage, Dylan."

"Bren, I'm not slacking off. You know how much I want to get back on my feet. Look at me." He stood and put weight on his injured leg. "I've been adding more and more weight every day." He wasn't even leaning on the crutches. "Maybe I can start using a cane."

She knew he'd advanced way ahead with his therapy. "Why don't we wait until you see Dr. Morris?" He nodded then went to reach for his crutches and lost his balance. Brenna tried to help but they both ended up on the bed.

He raised his head and grinned. "Thanks for the help, Bren. But in the future, I can handle it."

Brenna needed to keep the situation light, but she couldn't think when his body was pressed into hers, his heat burning every inch of her. She swallowed hard. "It's a reflex. I don't usually let my patients fall." His face was inches from hers, his breath caressed her cheek. Somehow she managed to push him off of her and stood, offering her hand.

He waved her off. "It's been a while since I needed help getting out of bed."

Brenna felt her cheeks flame, remembering that first morning and Dylan's nude body. She stood back and watched him get to his feet, knowing she wasn't going to be needed much longer. "You've come a long way, Dylan. You've got to be proud of your progress."

"I'll be much happier when I walk out of here under my own power." He grabbed his crutches and headed to the door, then turned around. "Brenna, thanks for going with me tonight."

She nodded. "You're welcome. I had a good time."

"I could see that when you were holding the baby."

She glanced away. "They're hard to resist."

He stood there as seconds ticked by, making Brenna aware of the small room. "I'm sorry that things didn't work out between you and Jason." He paused again. "You deserve better."

Brenna didn't know how to respond, but Dylan didn't seem to expect a response as he left. She sank onto the bed. "I don't know if I do, but my child does."

Chapter 5

The next morning, Dylan was up by six-thirty and drove to the main house. Careful to balance his weight on his good leg, he climbed out of the golf cart, and reached back into the cart for one crutch. He was determined to start walking again. Hopping around on one foot wasn't getting him anywhere. The doctor had said it was all right to put weight on the injured leg, just be sensible.

Using the railing, Dylan made his way up the four steps to the back porch. He shifted the crutch under his right arm, then placed his foot on the floor. Adding some weight, he tested the leg's strength. It felt stiff but not too bad. With a slow, limping gait, he made his way to the door and knocked, then stepped into the warm kitchen.

That's where he found Wyatt and Maura standing

at the stove locked in a loving embrace. His brother's arms were wrapped around his petite wife as he gazed down at her. The intense look exchanged between the two was sizzling…and intimate. Finally the couple noticed their intruder, but it was he who was embarrassed.

"Hey, don't you two ever stop?" he said. "Remember, there are innocent children around."

"Not at this hour," Wyatt said. "Only annoying brothers."

"Stop it, Wyatt," Maura declared. She was dressed in a pair of dark pleated trousers and a white silky blouse. Her long blond hair lying against her shoulder was a little mussed, no doubt by Wyatt's hands.

Escaping her husband's hold, she came to greet him with a hug. "Dylan, you are always welcome here. Anytime. Please, come sit down, you're just in time for breakfast."

"Now, that's what I call a welcome." He smiled brightly. "Thank you, Maura," Dylan said as he limped his way across the room.

"Hey, don't look now but you're missing a crutch," Wyatt pointed out.

Dylan collapsed in the chair. "It's outside in the cart. I thought it was time I try out this bum leg and see how things go." He thanked Maura as she set two mugs of coffee on the table.

His brother sat down across from him. "How does it feel?"

"Not too bad, but I'm not planning on running a marathon, either."

Wyatt nodded but held Dylan's gaze. "Did you just stop by to show off, or was there something else that brought you out so early?"

He shrugged. "Is there anything wrong with a brother coming by to visit?" He smiled at Maura. "And maybe sharing some breakfast."

"So Brenna threw you out, did she?"

"No. She just *suggested* that I get out of the house for a while. Besides, she hasn't had a day off since she started working with me." Dylan couldn't help but notice how tired Brenna had been looking the past week.

"Oh, man, that's cruel and unusual punishment."

Dylan glared at his brother. "Are you trying to tell me I'm hard to get along with?"

Wyatt's grin widened. "Yeah, you're a real pain, but we love you anyway."

Just then little Kelly came into the room still dressed in pink pajamas. "Unca Dylan!" she cried and ran to hug him. "Are you going to eat breakfast with us?"

He pulled his niece onto his lap. "If it's okay with you."

She nodded. "You can eat here every day if you want."

They all laughed. "I think your mom and dad would get a little tired of seeing me."

"I won't. I love you." Her tiny arms went around his neck in a hug. Dylan's chest grew tight. In the short time he'd known them, both Jeff and Kelly had worked their way into his heart.

"I love you too, darlin'," he confessed. "You want to be my best girl?"

Kelly nodded, then laughed. "I can't. Brenna is your girlfriend."

Dylan was caught off guard. "Honey, Brenna is helping me walk."

"But you like her, don't ya?" Kelly asked.

"Yes," he admitted. More than he should.

"My mommy likes my daddy and they're going to have a baby, maybe you can make a baby with Brenna—"

"Kelly Ann!" Maura interrupted her daughter. "Honey, it's time for you to get dressed for school. I'll be up in a few minutes to brush your hair."

"But Mommy, I wanna talk to Unca Dylan."

"Later. C'mon," she said, holding out her hand.

"'Kay." Reluctantly the child climbed off Dylan's lap and went to her mother. Maura scooted her out of the room as she sent an apologetic look Dylan's way.

"Sorry," Maura said. "As you can see, children have a pretty vivid imagination."

"Don't I know it," Dylan joked. "You better watch out for that one."

"Why, because she sees something going on between you and Brenna?" Wyatt asked.

Dylan wasn't going to let his brother bait him. "No, because Kelly told me last week she overheard you two talking about a pink stick and a baby in her mommy's tummy."

Maura gasped, her face reddening. "Oh, Wyatt, she must have been listening at the bathroom door. That little stinker."

Wyatt's eyes rolled. "I'm more concerned about what else she's been hearing between us."

The red deepened on Maura's face as she smacked her husband on the arm. "I think you should talk with her."

"Me?" Wyatt choked. "Ah, come on, Maura. You know I can't handle her tears."

"You're such a pushover, and don't think the kids

don't know that." Maura walked back to the stove and served up two plates of ham and eggs. She glanced at the clock. "Oh, I better get going. I need to get to the Yellow Rose flower shop. I have a special shipment this morning from the flower wholesaler. The Stanley wedding is this weekend." She looked at Dylan. "Don't be a stranger." She kissed Wyatt's cheek. "Don't forget to take Jeff over to the Lazy S so he can spend the day with Evan."

"Promise." Wyatt kissed her again, then let her go.

"Looks like a certain female around here got your number." Dylan picked up his fork and began to eat.

Wyatt shrugged. "Hey, there are worse ways to live. Now, tell me what's going on between you and Brenna."

"Nothing. She's my therapist. That's all." He took a bite of ham.

"So you're immune to the fact that you're living with a beautiful redhead?"

Oh, yeah, he'd definitely been aware. "You're the one who hired her. I thought you'd be happy that things are strictly business."

"Does she have someone else in her life?"

"She did." He remembered the sadness in her voice as she spoke of Jason. "That's beside the point. Soon I'll be going back to bull riding, and she'll go on to another job."

"Let's just say—if you weren't going back and wanted to settle down—could you be interested in Brenna Farren?"

Dylan knew a trick question when he heard one. "Of course. Like you said, she's a beautiful woman. But you know I don't do permanent relationships." He needed to change the subject and fast. "Hey, how about showing me around the ranch this morning?"

Wyatt raised an eyebrow. "Really? You want to see the operation?"

"Sure, I want a look at those bulls I'm going to be riding."

Wyatt grinned. "I got a few young ones that are promising, but Bud and the crew took the Gentry rough stock to a rodeo in Arizona."

"Why aren't you with them?"

Wyatt picked up his mug and leaned back in his chair. "That's what's great about being the boss. I've done enough traveling over the years. Besides, I have three good reasons to keep me home—and keep me happy." Then he added, "Make that four with the baby."

Thirty minutes later, Wyatt and Dylan were in the cart and driving to the pens where the rodeo stock were kept. The facility was impressive with top-of-the-line metal fences and pens, along with a new barn where Wyatt kept his champion bucking horses. He had a lot invested in the new business, and with the recent contracts for the coming season, they would show a profit this year.

Next, they went by Dylan's trailer so he could pick up more clothes and some more rodeo trinkets to give to Jeff and Kelly. He also stopped at the barn and checked on his horse. They pulled up right next to the animal's stall. Ignoring the crutch, Dylan got out and grabbed the rail to brace himself as he looked in to see Cheyenne.

"Hey, fella."

The big, golden-yellow chestnut horse whinnied and

came to greet him. Dylan stroked the animal's head playfully and at the same time tried to keep his balance, but the horse was too excited. Dylan staggered backward, but Wyatt caught him, then handed him his crutch.

"I guess you can say he's missed you."

Dylan laughed. He knew Cheyenne wasn't going to stop pestering him until he got to run. "I can't give him what he needs—a good run."

Wyatt tried to ease his concerns. "He's out in the corral most of the day, I bring him in at night. One of the ranch hands takes him for a run every few days. Is there anything else you want us to do?"

Just that Dylan would have liked to be the one to ride him. "No, looks like you got everything covered." He was going to check with Brenna to see when he'd be able to ride Cheyenne himself.

Dylan pulled his cowboy hat down lower. The February wind was frigid as Wyatt continued the tour and drove out to the pasture. Even his sheepskin coat didn't keep out the chill, but it felt wonderful. His brother stopped on a ridge and pointed to a large herd of Herefords grazing in the valley.

Dylan shook his head. "I can't believe you're in the cattle business."

"Why? Our paternal grandfather was a very successful cattle rancher."

Dylan turned away.

"Look, bro, we may not want to acknowledge our biological father, but John Randell had nothing to do with the circumstances of our birth. He was a well respected man around this area and I'm proud to carry on his legacy with the Rocking R. Besides, the cattle business is profitable." He looked at Dylan. "I'm a partner in the Mustang Valley Corporation."

"Sounds like you and the Randells are pretty tight." Dylan found himself envious of their relationship. All his life, it had just been him and his brother.

"Yeah, we've become friends. You saw last night, the brothers have accepted us—you, me and Jared. They didn't have to, either. If you hang around a while, you'll discover their strong sense of family. Something we never had."

"Well, nothing against the Randells, but that's not going to happen. My life is out on the circuit."

Wyatt nodded. "Okay, but when you do decide to retire, will you think about settling down here? We can split the Rocking R."

"What would I do on a ranch?"

"What you do best," Wyatt said. "Teach bull riding. Open a school. Your name alone would bring people in. And you could help me. You've ridden more bulls than anyone I know. You could probably look at one and know if he's going to be any good on the circuit."

Dylan couldn't believe he was actually intrigued by his brother's suggestion. "Thanks, I appreciate the offer. Let's see how I do when I go back."

Wyatt nodded as if satisfied with the answer. "That's good enough for the time being. Now, I better get you home before Brenna sends out a search party."

Dylan arrived back at the cottage about nine o'clock. He'd enjoyed spending time with his brother, but knew that he had to get to his weight bench. Brenna should be up by now, but just in case, he was quiet when he came though the door.

The living room and kitchen were both empty. He headed for his room, noticing that Brenna's bedroom door was open, but she wasn't inside. That's when he heard the strange sound coming from the bathroom. He went closer and listened to the retching. After about ten seconds it happened again. Dylan decided that Brenna had to be pretty sick.

"Hey, Bren, you all right?"

Her answer came in a moan.

"Bren, I'm coming in," he warned, then opened the door to find her lying on the rug next to the tub. Still dressed in her pajamas, she had one hand across her stomach, the other across her eyes.

He managed to sit down on the lip of the tub. "Are you all right?" he repeated.

She groaned. "Please, just leave and let me die in peace."

"You feel that bad, then I'm calling Wyatt and we're taking you to the doctor." He braced his hand on the sink and started to stand, when she reached for him. The motion was too much and she lay back down.

"I'll be fine," she whispered.

"Like hell you will." Not knowing what else to do, Dylan took a damp washcloth, then leaned down and placed it over her face. He didn't like her ashen look.

Using his crutch, he went to her room and pulled the blanket off the end of the bed. He started back when he spotted the box of soda crackers on the nightstand. Soda crackers...vomiting... Suddenly he remembered the time a few days ago when he'd teased Brenna about knowing someone who was pregnant. She had looked so panicked over the discovery. It was beginning to add up.

Grabbing a stack of saltines, Dylan returned to the bathroom. He stood in the doorway and studied Brenna's slender body lying on the beige-tiled floor. Automatically his gaze was drawn to the slight curve of her stomach. A baby. The realization made him feel as if he'd been sucker punched in the gut.

He sat down on the tub's edge and covered her with the blanket, then made a towel into a pillow. He leaned down and offered her a cracker. "Here, this might help, too."

They exchanged a look that confirmed what he already suspected. "Thank you." She took a small nibble, then another.

"How far along are you?" he asked with a flicker of hope that she would deny it.

She didn't even flinch. "Three and a half months."

"So you knew you were pregnant before you took this job."

She bit off another section of cracker. "Yes."

"I take it Jason is the baby's father." It hurt to state the fact, knowing that Brenna cared deeply for someone.

A lone tear ran down the side of her face. "Yes."

"Oh, God, you've been practically carrying me. Dammit, Brenna, you should never have taken this job."

This time she glared at him. "It was because of the baby that I had to. I need to be able to support my child, Dylan. And I've been doing my job."

"That's not the point," he argued. "You've been doing hard physical work. What about your parents? I should call them."

She grabbed his arm. "No, you can't. I haven't told them yet."

"Why the hell not? Surely they would help you with the baby."

"My parents have enough to deal with. They went into debt to help put me through college. I can't ask them for any more." She reached out and gripped his arm. "Please, Dylan, you can't call them."

He couldn't stand to see her upset. "Okay, okay, but you can't keep this a secret forever. Pretty soon they'll discover they're going to be grandparents just by looking at you." He was still having trouble handling the news himself.

"I will, but I need a little more time." Another tear fell. "If you want to fire me, I'll understand—"

"Stop talking crazy." Did she really think he was such a cold bastard? "Besides, you promised to get me back on my feet."

She looked up at him with those golden-brown eyes. "Thank you."

Unable to resist, Dylan slid off the tub and down onto the floor beside her. He pulled her into his arms and cradled her head against his chest. Brenna didn't resist as his hands moved over her back, trying to soothe her fears.

"Did Jason know about the baby?"

"No," she began, her voice soft. "He died just a week after… I got pregnant."

A strange feeling of protectiveness came over him. "So you've been carrying this burden on your own?"

Brenna pulled away. "This baby isn't a burden. I love her." She was fierce as a lioness protecting her cub.

He refused to let her go and drew her back into his arms. "C'mon, darlin'. You can't act tough all the time. Let me help you," he whispered against her silky hair. "Together, we'll figure out something. I promise, you and the baby are going to be fine."

An hour later, after a warm shower, Brenna managed to pull herself together. She couldn't put it off any longer, she had to face him. In the kitchen, she found Dylan at the stove, stirring soup in a pan.

He turned to look at her. "Go sit down. You need something in your stomach." He poured the soup into a bowl and with the aid of his crutch, he carried it to the table.

Brenna didn't budge as she noticed how well he was moving around. "Hey, look at you." She pointed down at his leg.

"Oh, yeah, I've been testing putting a little weight on it this morning."

"How does it feel?"

"Not bad."

"Just don't overdo. If your leg starts hurting, get off it."

"Yes, ma'am. Now, I'm going to boss you around for a change. Sit down and eat. That kid of yours has to be starving."

"You don't need to take care of me, Dylan," she insisted. "I'm pregnant, not helpless. I got sick this morning because I ate too much at the party last night. I've been feeling pretty good lately."

He didn't look convinced. "You still need to eat. Sit." He wasn't listening to her. "Okay, I'll let you do this, but let's not make a habit of it," she said and took a place at the table.

The last thing she wanted was to start relying on this man. She'd only end up getting hurt again. No, first she had to find out her fate. Did she still have a job?

"Dylan, now that you've had time to think about it, I need to know if you truly want me to stay." She began to eat her soup, the chicken broth surprisingly good.

Dylan sat down across from her. "Why wouldn't I? Like you said, you haven't slacked off in any of your duties, but I'll tell you right now, there's no heavy lifting. If I start to fall, let me fall."

"Anyone ever tell you that you're bossy?"

"Nope." He wiggled his eyebrows. "Sexy, maybe."

No doubt about that, Brenna thought as she broke out laughing. "Whoa, it's getting pretty crowded around here. I'm not sure there's enough room for you, me and your ego."

He started to answer, when a knock sounded on the door. Suddenly feeling a whole lot better, Brenna got up to answer it. She had one problem resolved; she had her job for a while longer. She pulled open the door only to find Sean and Maggie Farren standing on the porch.

Another problem had just popped up. "Mom! Dad! What are you doing here?"

"Well, we're happy to see you, too," her mother said as she gave her daughter a hug.

Her father did the same. "Aren't you going to invite us in?"

"Oh, sure." Brenna stood aside trying to calm her racing heart. "I was just surprised to see you."

Petite Maggie Farren was forty-eight years old. She

was a beautiful woman with amber eyes and brown hair. Her slender build was covered by a pair of jeans and a blouse. She looked around and her gaze stopped at Dylan. "Actually, we were over at the Circle B and Hank suggested we stop by. He said Mr. Gentry wouldn't mind."

"But Mom, I'm working right now."

Dylan got up from the table, leaning on it briefly for support. "It's all right, Brenna. Of course you can visit with your parents." He reached for his crutch and made his way across the room. "Hello, Mr. and Mrs. Farren. I'm Dylan, not Mr. Gentry. It's nice to finally meet you."

"It's nice to meet you, too," Maggie said, then sent an approving glance toward Brenna.

"Same here, son," her father said. "Call me Sean and she's Maggie," he answered as he shook Dylan's hand. Her father was a tall, slender man. All energy and muscle, with an easy smile and quick wit. "We've been pretty worried about you. Glad to see you're on the mend." He grinned and his blue eyes crinkled. "Of course, I bet my Brenna had something to do with it."

Dylan nodded. "She was a big part of it. She refused to let me give up. I owe her a lot."

"Brenna has always been strong-willed," Sean said. "I think that's because she has three brothers."

"I have no doubt she can handle herself just fine." Dylan looked at Brenna. "I'm going to take a shower. You stay here and visit with your parents as long as you want."

Brenna tried to keep the panic out of her voice, but it wasn't easy as she watched Dylan desert her. She turned to her parents. "I was planning on coming home this weekend."

Her mother frowned. "Brenna, are you feeling okay? You look a little pale." Maggie Farren's eyes were the same color as her own, and right now they were searching for answers.

Self-consciously, Brenna fiddled with the front of her sweatshirt. "How would you like some coffee, Mom?" She went to the kitchen, and her mother followed.

"Are you sure you're getting enough sleep?"

She busied herself scooping coffee into the coffee-maker. "Yes, I'm sleeping fine."

Maggie didn't take her gaze off her daughter and Brenna knew she wasn't fooling her mother. "Sean," Maggie called to her husband. "Would you go to the car and bring in the muffins that I baked?"

Her father left them alone. Once he was out the door, Maggie placed her hands on Brenna's shoulders. "Okay, missy, tell me the truth."

"Mom, there isn't anything…"

Her mother's gaze once again traveled over her daughter, then suddenly stopped at her slightly thicker waistline. She gasped as her trembling hand touched the growing curve. "You're pregnant."

Brenna felt light-headed as her mother gripped her by the arms. She'd never been able to lie, and what was the use? Everyone would know sooner or later. She nodded. "I'm sorry." She collapsed into her mother's arms. "I'm sorry," she cried.

Maggie's eyes filled, then she hugged her tightly. "Ssh, don't cry. Everything will be okay."

"I never meant for this to happen."

"I know." Maggie held on tighter. "But you've been

blessed with a precious gift." When she finally released her daughter, she asked, "What are you planning to do?"

"Work, and support myself and the baby."

"And what about the child's father? Is he going to be involved in your lives?"

Before Brenna could tell her mother about Jason, her father came into the cottage carrying a basket of muffins. Immediately, he saw their tears. "What's the matter?"

Telling her father would be a lot harder for Brenna, but she had to do it. Her mother took her hand in a show of support. "Tell him, Brenna."

"I'm…going to have a baby, Dad."

Her father's eyes widened in surprise. "Oh, Bren…" After a second or two he frowned. "Are you okay?" He walked to her and drew her into his arms.

Brenna nodded against his chest. "Yes, I'm fine. The baby's fine."

He pulled back. "Good. Then you tell me who is responsible for this. He should do right by you."

"Dad, you don't understand—"

"I understand that the man has a responsibility to you and his child. Now, who is the father?"

Brenna didn't know how to tell him that the father was dead, that their first grandchild was going to be born out of wedlock.

She opened her mouth to speak, when she heard Dylan come into the room.

"That would be me, sir," he announced. "I'm responsible."

Brenna gasped at the lie, but was too stunned to speak. Sean Farren walked to Dylan. Seconds ticked away as both men eyed one another. Then her father spoke. "If this is true, I expect you to do right by my daughter. And soon."

Chapter 6

"Are you crazy?" Brenna asked as she sank against the closed cottage door. The Farrens had just left for home.

Dylan wondered the same thing himself, but at the time it had seemed like the right thing to do. When he'd come out of the bedroom and heard Brenna's father grilling her, his protective instincts kicked in and he'd stepped forward.

"Probably, but it wouldn't be the first time."

She groaned and began to pace the room. "Now I have to go and tell my parents the truth." She started toward the kitchen then suddenly swung around to face him. "Didn't you realize that they would expect you to take care of us—to marry me?" She waved her hand as tears filled her eyes. "I'm sorry. I know you were trying to help me."

Dylan couldn't stand it any longer and he went to her. "Bren, don't cry. I'm the one who's sorry. I didn't mean to make things worse."

Somehow in the past weeks he'd come to care so much for Brenna, and it broke his heart to see her like this. He reached for her and she resisted momentarily, then crumbled into his arms, sobbing against his chest. For the first time, he realized how fragile she was. Brenna Farren wasn't weak by any stretch of the imagination, and no doubt she could handle this situation alone, but no way was he going to let her. There was a baby to think about. An innocent child who didn't deserve to start out this way.

"Bren...just listen to me for a minute." He continued to hold her, not wanting her to break the intimate contact. "I have an idea that might work. I want to go with you to talk to your parents." He shifted his weight on the crutch as his arm tightened around her back. "I want to assure them they don't have to worry about their daughter and grandchild...because we're getting married."

This time he couldn't hold on to her. Brenna jerked back. She swiped at her tears and glared at him. "This isn't funny, Dylan. And I don't appreciate the joke." She started to walk away, when he reached for her again.

"I'm not joking, Bren, and if you'll just listen to me—"

"Why should I, Dylan? I can't play this game. This isn't just my life we're talking about...it's my baby's, too."

He knew that all too well. "It's the child I'm thinking about. I know firsthand what it's like growing up with a father who doesn't want to claim his child. I know if Jason had lived things might have been different, but either way, it's not your baby's fault." He raised an eyebrow. "I take it your parents never knew about Jason."

Brenna shook her head, recalling the excuse she'd made to her mom and dad because Jason never showed on her graduation day. Later, she'd learned that he'd let her down to go canoeing on the Colorado River. "They were supposed to meet at my graduation, but he wasn't there. I told them we'd broken up."

"So they won't suspect that there had been another man in your life. I could be the little one's daddy."

"No! Everyone will know when the baby's born. Dylan, I'm over three months pregnant. I've only been here six weeks. Even if we were together the first night…" Her face flushed, realizing what she'd implied.

"Hey, I've been known to sweep women off their feet." He tossed her a sexy grin and more heat rose to her face.

Brenna realized that wouldn't be hard to believe. "But that's not me," she stressed. "I'm not like you. I'm not as casual about sex. I've only been with one man."

His smile faded. "Unlike me who's been with hundreds of women. Damn, it's a wonder how I ever had the time and energy to become a world-champion bull rider."

Brenna knew she'd hurt him. "I didn't mean it like that."

"Yes, you did," he said. "It might surprise you to know that bull riders are athletes. And with all the competition out there, you have to train and work out constantly. And even then you can get injured. On good days you still have trouble just getting out of bed, let alone partying all night." He raised a hand. "I'm not saying that I haven't shared some time with women, but they've all known I wasn't about to settle down. My focus has always been bull riding."

"All the more reason for you to forget this crazy idea."

"I disagree. If we're married, I don't have to worry about distractions on the circuit."

This was insane, she was actually thinking about it. Was she losing her mind? "What about the time difference as to when we met?"

He shrugged. "We can tell your parents that we met last summer at a rodeo."

"I can't lie to them."

"Bren, you haven't been honest with them as it is, or you would have told them about Jason and the baby when you first came home."

She blinked back the tears. Her mom and dad had already done so much for her. "I can't put this on them. They'll want to help, and also the ranch has been a big strain financially the past few years. I can't add to it."

"Then let me help you." He raised a soothing hand. "And think about your baby before you decide. I'm not suggesting a real marriage here. I know that's not what you need or want. This is so your parents will have the reassurance that you and their grandchild will be taken care of."

"I can take care of us," she insisted.

"Okay, so you don't need me financially," he conceded. "But what about taking my name? Unless you have something against it. I mean…because of Jack Randell."

She was shocked that he could think such a thing. "I thought you knew me better than that. Of course not. But you can't want to be saddled with a wife and child."

"Look, Bren. Unlike Wyatt, I never planned to marry…ever. I'm too much like my old man. But like I said before, being married has its advantages."

She bet it did, Brenna thought. Dylan "The Devil" Gentry could use his wedding ring to keep women from getting too attached to him. As she had.

"The real reason I want to do this is because of you." Those silvery-blue eyes bore into hers. His hand touched her cheek. "It was you who made me want to get up and walk. If I make it back on the circuit, it's because of you. Because you wouldn't give up on me, even when I wanted to give up on myself."

She shook her head. "You wanted to walk, Dylan, or you never would have worked so hard to get this far."

He hugged her. "Oh, Bren, let me help you now. You and the baby can live here in the cottage. I plan to be traveling the circuit. When I'm home, we can keep the same arrangement we've always had these past weeks."

Brenna was in big trouble. She was seriously considering his proposal.

"You can continue to work, or go back to school and maybe you can get your master's. In a few years when I retire, Wyatt has invited me to open a bull-riding school here at the Rocking R."

Brenna walked across the room. Being so close to him made it difficult to think. "With all these long-range plans, you forgot one thing, Dylan. What about the baby? He or she will get attached to you and then one day you'll walk away."

He looked as if she'd struck him. "I wouldn't do that, Bren. If we get married, I will always be there for the child."

Brenna realized that she wanted him to be there for

her, too. Deep inside she knew this was a bad idea. Dylan was the type of man who loved danger and would never settle down. Could she handle him walking in and out of her life? Probably not.

"If we decide to go through with this, I think there should be a timetable. That way we both have an out, if we happen to find someone else. If we agree on this from the start, then no one gets hurt?"

"How much time?" he asked.

Once again, nothing seemed to deter him. "Say, six months after the baby is born. Then we should talk about continuing on…or ending it. We could let people think things didn't work because of your profession."

"If that's what you want," he said. "There's one more thing, Bren. I want as few people as possible to know the circumstances. As far as I'm concerned, this baby is mine. That means the kid thinks of me as his father. No matter what happens between us, I will always take care of the baby. Do you have a problem with that?"

His promise brought more tears to her eyes. She shook her head. "No. I don't have a problem."

Dylan smiled at her and something tightened around her heart. "Good." He limped across the room to her, leaned down and brushed his mouth across hers. She sucked in a breath, then all too soon, he pulled away.

"Now, I think we'd better go talk to your father before he comes back here with a rifle."

The next morning, Dylan got up before dawn. He finished his workout in record time, then Brenna supervised his therapy as if nothing between them had changed, despite the fact that a whole lot was about to.

But yesterday had changed everything else between

them. That afternoon, they'd gone to visit the Farren Ranch and talked with Brenna's family, including her younger brothers Michael, James and Connor.

Surprisingly, Dylan found he had hated to fabricate the details of their first meeting and their so-called relationship. It was Maggie Farren who had the most questions and reservations. None of that seemed to matter to Sean Farren, not when Dylan told him their plans to marry. Since the Catholic church had a six-month waiting period, the couple had no choice but to opt for a civil ceremony. Arrangements would be made when he and Brenna went into town later that day for the license.

After a quick shower and some breakfast, Dylan headed down to the barn to tell his brother the news. He found Wyatt with his champion bucking horse, Rock-a-Billy, in the corral. The animal had hurt his leg in the last rodeo and had been sent home to heal.

Dylan pulled the golf cart up beside the fence, got out and grabbed his crutch. "How's it going?" he called to his brother.

"Pretty good," Wyatt said as he walked out of the corral. "The vet said Billy should be able to travel again by next week."

"That's good news," Dylan answered. "Speaking of news, I've got some. Brenna and I are getting married."

Except for the sound of Billy's restless whinny, there was only silence. Finally Wyatt looked at him. "How long has this been going on?"

"Long enough," Dylan said, not knowing what else to say but feeling he owed his brother the truth. "And another thing, Brenna is pregnant."

That got Wyatt's attention. "That's some therapy." He stopped. "There's more, isn't there?"

Dylan shrugged. "It's not anybody's business."

"I hope you don't bunch me into that category? I'm your brother. Now, tell me the rest of the story."

Wyatt had always been overprotective, and the last thing Dylan wanted was for his big brother to try to talk him out of this marriage. "This isn't for anyone else, but Brenna was pregnant when you hired her. The baby's father was killed in a hang-gliding accident three months ago. When her parents learned about the pregnancy two days ago, I more or less told them I was the father."

Wyatt made a whistling sound, then surprised him when he smiled. "You still dive in with both feet, don't you?"

"When I have to," Dylan admitted. "Look, bro, it was Bren who helped get me back on my feet. I couldn't let her handle this situation alone."

"So you offered to marry her and raise her child."

"Yeah. It doesn't change my plans, though. I still plan to ride again. But that baby needs a father. So they'll be staying on in the cottage, if that's okay."

"As far as I'm concerned, that's your place for as long as you want it."

"Thanks. If the doctor okays me to ride, I want the Rocking R to be my home base. I want to come here in between rodeos."

"I'm liking the sound of this," Wyatt said, grinning.

"I've also been thinking about that bull-riding school you mentioned. Maybe in the future we can talk about it some more. Sounds like something I might like to do."

"That sounds real good." Wyatt lifted his cowboy hat and reset it on his head. "Funny how a woman can get you to look at things...differently."

"I'm not changing my goal," Dylan protested. "It's

still to get back on a bull. But a man needs to think about investing in his future."

He had plenty of money in the bank, but it wouldn't last forever if he didn't make plans. He should start a college fund for the baby, and if Brenna wanted to go back to school.

"When is this wedding taking place?" Wyatt asked.

"Brenna and I are going today to make the arrangements. Probably next week sometime. Will you be my best man?"

"I'd be happy to."

Wyatt put his arm across Dylan's shoulders. "Looks like the last of the brothers is about to get hitched. I guess when we find the right woman, we don't waste any time."

"This isn't like that," Dylan insisted.

"Yeah, that's what we all said."

She didn't remember saying yes.

Now, two days later, Brenna stood in front of a three-way mirror in a local bridal shop, admiring the ivory, tea-length dress she was going to wear when she married Dylan.

The fitted, off-the-shoulder bodice had a scalloped neckline and long sleeves that ended in points at her wrists. The skirt was gathered at her waist and draped softly around her. Brenna touched her slightly rounded stomach, trying to calm the butterflies.

"Oh, Brenna, you look beautiful," her mother cried. She grasped her hands together, gazing lovingly at her daughter. "And your grandmother's pearls will be perfect. Simple, yet elegant."

Brenna wanted to call a halt to this madness. It was

all going too fast for her. How did things get so out of control? That she knew. When she and Dylan had gone to her parents' house, everyone just took for granted that they'd be married. In fact, her brothers had played her protectors, practically threatening Dylan if he didn't do his duty.

She didn't want to be anyone's duty.

Now she was marrying a man she barely knew. A man who wasn't good husband and father material. A man who would never give up his dangerous profession for her.

"I think this dress is beautiful," Maggie Farren said. "Although the dress with the antique lace was also pretty. What do you think?"

Brenna didn't want to think. She wanted to run away, but she couldn't. There was her baby to think of. A baby she already loved, and couldn't wait to hold in her arms. And as much as she wanted to handle her life on her own, she couldn't deny her child two parents. She glanced at her mother's glowing face. She knew she couldn't burden her parents again. There was only one way, and that was to accept Dylan's generous offer.

The salesclerk walked up. "You look absolutely breathtaking," she said. "That dress is made for you."

Brenna glanced at the price tag and gasped. There was no way she or her parents could afford to pay this amount. "Is there something a little more...reasonable?"

The salesclerk smiled. "You don't have to worry about the cost. Mr. Gentry left instructions with us to let you pick any dress you want. That price wasn't a problem."

"But I can't..." Brenna hesitated and looked at her mother.

"I think we'll take this one," Maggie said. "And we'll need shoes and undergarments." With a nod, the saleswoman walked away.

"Mom!" Brenna gasped. "What are you doing?"

"The man loves you. If he wants you to have a beautiful dress, then let him buy it for you."

"But you don't understand…"

"I understand more than you think. There is nothing wrong with letting your future husband give you a nice wedding." She blinked back sudden tears. "I'm sorry that your father and I can't."

"Oh, Mom, I didn't exactly give you any time to plan one." They both laughed.

"We're getting a double bonus. A grandchild."

Brenna was becoming excited. "So you're happy?"

"I'm so happy that you've found a man who obviously loves you."

Brenna had to fight her own tears. Her mother was so wrong. She was marrying a man she barely knew, but worse, one she was quickly falling in love with. Someone who could never return that love.

That alone could be disastrous.

Six days later, with the aid of his cane, Dylan stepped off the elevator followed by Wyatt, Maura and the kids. He wore a new navy suit, a crisp white shirt and a blue silk tie that felt as if it was strangling him inch by inch. He'd even had his hair trimmed, and when Brenna came into view, he knew all the hassle was worth it. She stole his breath away.

Today, she was all soft and feminine…and beautiful in her ivory dress. He felt a sudden stirring and had to shake away the feeling. Gripping a florist box, he started toward her.

Brenna looked up as he approached. Her auburn hair was pulled up on her head with tiny flowers tucked into the curls. Her golden-brown eyes were wide and fearful as a skittish filly.

"Bren…" He stopped in front of her. "You're beautiful."

She released a breath. "Thank you. You look handsome."

He noticed the crowd of people growing, then took hold of her hand and nodded behind him. "You think we can go over there so I can talk to you?"

If possible, she looked more nervous than he did. Together they started off toward a little alcove at the end of the hall.

"You're doing real well with the cane," she remarked. "Just remember not to overdo."

"Stop playing therapist, Brenna," he said. "I feel fine."

"Sorry, it's a habit." Her gaze finally met his. "Look, Dylan, if you decided not to go through with the ceremony, I'll understand. I mean, it was a crazy idea."

Dylan's finger covered her lips to quiet her. "I'm not changing my mind, Bren. I brought you over here so I can give you this." He leaned his cane against the wall, then opened the box revealing a bridal bouquet of ivory roses and orchids, trimmed in lavender and surrounded with greenery and white ribbon.

"Oh, Dylan. It's beautiful." Her hands trembled as she lifted the flowers from the box. "Thank you."

"You need to thank Maura. She put the bouquet together. She told me what each flower means, but I forget, so you'll have to ask her."

Brenna could hardly believe Dylan's sweet gesture. "I will when I thank her." The elevator chimed and more of the Randells stepped off. "This is turning out to be a little bigger than I expected."

Dylan glanced toward the crowd. "Once I told Maura, things got out of control."

It was all so overwhelming. "There's still time to back out," she said.

"How can I convince you I don't want to back out?" He smiled. "Maybe there is a way." He took her by the arm and drew her close. Dylan's gaze locked on hers just as he lowered his head, then his mouth touched hers, gently. Slowly the kiss deepened as his arm came around her, drawing her against him. The contact drove every rational thought from her head and she grabbed hold of his jacket to keep from sliding to the floor. Finally, hearing someone calling to them, they broke apart.

They looked around to find Wyatt. "It's time," he said.

"Good." With a wink, Dylan retrieved his cane, then took her hand, and they headed to the judge's chambers.

Somehow everyone managed to crowd into the room. "Seems these family weddings are becoming a habit," Hank Barrett said. "This makes number six in the past few years."

Dylan took Brenna's hand as the judge directed them to stand in the front of the room. Beside the groom was Wyatt, and next to the bride was her matron of honor, Maura. Her parents stood behind them along with her brothers.

Brenna took a long breath and released it as Judge Clark began with, "Dearly beloved…"

During the ceremony she kept her attention on Dylan. Finally she heard, "You may kiss your bride."

When Dylan turned to her, she thought she was prepared for his kiss. Then his mouth captured hers and she was swept away once again. All she could do was put her arms around his neck and hold on. Finally her new husband pulled back and winked at her. Before she could say a word, they were being pulled apart with offers of congratulations.

They were swept away to sign the wedding certificate, then Wyatt invited everyone back to the Rocking R where Maura, and the rest of the Randell wives, had planned a reception for the happy couple. Brenna wasn't sure she could carry this off. Then she looked at her mother's face and saw how happy she was. She knew she had to keep playing the game.

It was too late to turn back now.

The wedding guests broke out in cheers as Dylan walked his new wife into Wyatt and Maura's house. He was a little taken aback by all the attention they were getting over this simple ceremony.

Dylan glanced at Brenna and saw her smile and he was glad that he'd let Maura go all out for this day. He was a little surprised by how much he'd been enjoying himself, especially kissing his new wife. Things might change when they were alone, so he was going to take advantage of all the opportunities. Like now. He pulled her close and pressed his lips against Brenna's and the crowd cheered once again.

"I'll get even with you, Gentry," Brenna threatened with a smile. "Your therapy is going to double."

His mouth captured hers once again, causing her

to swallow the rest of her words. Brenna forgot her thoughts, forgot even to breathe. This had to stop. She pulled back. "Aren't you overdoing it a little?"

He grinned. "We want to convince everyone, don't we?"

"I think getting married is convincing enough," she said as her mother came up to her.

"Oh, Brenna, you were beautiful." She had tears in her eyes. "I know it wasn't the church wedding we wanted for you, but the ceremony was lovely just the same. You two look so happy."

Dylan hugged Maggie. "I'm going to do everything possible to keep your girl happy."

"I know you will, Dylan." The older woman smiled, then walked off to greet other guests.

"You're making an awful lot of promises," Brenna said.

"And I'm going to keep them. Can't you stop worrying for just a little while?" He pulled her close. "It's going to be okay, Bren. Trust me." He kissed the end of her nose. "Will you?"

She knew she was crazy but she nodded anyway.

"Good. Come on. I believe there's a cake with our name on it waiting for us in the dining room."

He took her into the next room where they posed for pictures before cutting the cake, then they went around and visited with everyone, thanking them for coming and for all the gifts.

Wyatt then quieted the crowd as he stood next to Maura, both holding a champagne glass.

"To my brother and his bride. Dylan, I never thought there would be a woman who could put up with you, let alone make you want to settle down. Brenna, welcome to the family. May your life together be filled with happiness, joy and most importantly, love." He raised his glass. "To Dylan and Brenna."

Next, Chance Randell took the stage. "Since I'm the oldest, I'm speaking for my family." He turned to the bride and groom. "Dylan and Brenna, we would like to welcome you as neighbors. We hope we to get the opportunity to get to know you both better. We got together and thought the best wedding gift we could give you is a honeymoon." He reached into his pocket and pulled out a key. "The family would like to give you the bridal cabin in Mustang Valley. It's stocked with food and enough wood to last you at least a week." He grinned. "The best part is that the guest ranch is closed for the season, so you'll be totally alone."

Brenna could barely swallow, but she somehow managed to thank Chance and the brothers for the wonderful gesture. Soon after, the party broke up and everyone headed home. Brenna offered to help Maura clean up.

Her new sister-in-law smiled. "You can't, you and your husband will be leaving soon."

Brenna wasn't planning on going anywhere near the honeymoon cabin. "We can go later," she said.

"No need. We've taken care of everything." Just then Wyatt came in, pulling a suitcase for Brenna and a duffel bag for Dylan. "Your mother packed your clothes, Brenna. Now you two have no excuses. Just follow Wyatt to his truck and he'll drive you to your honeymoon destination."

Brenna's pulse pounded. She hadn't planned on going anywhere. She looked at Dylan.

"Then I guess we're ready," her new husband said. "Come on, honey, it looks like they're trying to get rid of us." With cheers from the Randell family, he took her hand and walked her outside to the truck.

There was definitely no turning back now.

Chapter 7

Twenty minutes later, Wyatt let the newlyweds off at the narrow dirt road that led to the cabins. Since there were no vehicles allowed in Mustang Valley they had to use a golf cart for the three-minute drive to the isolated cabin.

"Looks like we're here," Dylan announced as he pulled up to the one-story split-log structure. He climbed out and retrieved their bags. Brenna didn't move as she looked around the secluded area. About a hundred yards away there was a rocky-bottom creek. Although most of the trees were bare, the view of the valley was still spectacular. A feeling of serenity washed over her as she turned toward the lone cabin surrounded by shrubs and trees.

This was a perfect place for a couple who didn't want to be disturbed.

She got out and came around to help, feeling a little of the calm leaving her just in time to see another cart heading away over the rise. Someone had probably come here to check out the cabin. She took her suitcase from Dylan so he could handle his cane. He made his way to the small porch and used his key to unlock the door. Suddenly when he held out his hand to her, all of today's events hit Brenna. She'd married this man. For real—but not real. Now she was on a not-for-real honeymoon. Great.

With a tight grip on her suitcase handle, she walked across the threshold, but nothing could have prepared her for what she found inside. The main room was aglow with dozens of candles and a fire in the hearth. Two love seats were across from each other; in between sat an old steamer trunk. There was a small kitchen area and a round table with two place settings of china and a centerpiece vase of white roses and candles. In the alcove sat a huge four-poster bed, draped in a wine-colored satin comforter adorned with dozens of pillows, and rose petals scattered about. More candles and flowers lined the area.

This would be anyone's dream honeymoon, but not hers. She turned to Dylan. "Okay, what now?" she asked.

He sank against the door. "Believe me, this place gives me plenty of ideas, but I don't think you want to know what they are."

No, she didn't. "How long are we expected to stay here?" She eyed the king-size bed. *One* bed. The only other place to sleep was on one of the short sofas.

"I don't think it's safe to show our faces for at least a few days."

Dylan was going to kill Wyatt. He knew that his brother had a lot to do with this setup. In other circumstances he wouldn't mind spending the weekend with a beautiful woman, but this wasn't a good idea. Not if he was going to keep his hands off her.

"Look, Brenna," he began. "I had no idea they were planning to give us the cabin. If I had, I'd have made some excuse for us not to come here."

"Dylan, it's all right," she assured him. "It's not as if we haven't been living together the past six weeks. We can handle the next few days."

Sure he could, he told himself. "Okay. Why don't you take the bed. I'll sleep on the sofa."

"You can't possibly fit," she argued. "I'll sleep there."

"No way. You take the bed," he insisted.

"But your leg will cramp up."

He shifted his weight onto his good leg. "You and the baby need room too, and sleep."

"I'm not that big…yet. Besides, the baby is comfortable and we get plenty of sleep."

"Any suggestions?"

He eyed the huge bed. "We can…share the bed," he said.

"What?" She looked startled.

"Why not, it's big enough," he reasoned. "We can put pillows down the middle of the mattress so neither of us will…infringe on the other's space. I'll even sleep on top of the covers. We won't even know we're in the same bed." Right. Who was he kidding? He'd been so aware of Brenna that he hadn't been able to think rationally since that first kiss.

She looked unconvinced and tired.

"Are you feeling okay?"

"Just a little tired…and hungry."

He smiled. "How about some supper?"

She nodded. "That sounds good. I was too nervous to eat at the reception."

"We had cake." How could he forget feeding her, then kissing her, tasting the sugary frosting off her lips. He went to the refrigerator and opened it, hoping the frigid air would cool his jets. "Oh, man. Will you look at all this food?"

Brenna came up beside him to see several casseroles and salads crowding the shelves, plus a big platter of fried chicken. There were cheeses and olives, a cheesecake and two pies, some wine and fruit juices.

"Looks like the family has been busy," Brenna said. "This must have been what that person was doing here."

Being stuck here might not be so bad, he thought. "What would you like for your wedding supper, Mrs. Gentry?"

Her brown-eyed gaze shot to him. "Anything is fine."

Dylan saw her nervousness and closed the door. "Brenna, you have to stop looking at me like I'm a stranger trying to have my way with you."

"But…we were married today."

He grinned. "I know, I was there."

"And so was my family," she said. "They think this marriage is for real."

"It's as real as you want to make it," he said, leaning on his cane. His leg was beginning to ache from standing so long. Brenna noticed his discomfort, too.

"You should be off your feet." She urged him toward the table.

Dylan didn't argue as he collapsed into a chair. "I guess I overdid it a little today," he said as she began massaging his leg. It felt heavenly, maybe too much so. "That's enough," he told her, stopping her hands. "I'll be fine if I'm off it for a while. After I fix us supper."

She started to argue about that.

"You need to relax, too," he insisted.

"I've been getting plenty of rest."

He shook his head. "You're not cooking tonight." He got to his feet. "Now, you sit and I'll call you when things are ready."

She opened her mouth, then closed it. "Fine. But I'm going to help you. Just let me change out of my dress and I'll be right back."

She started to walk away, when Dylan took hold of her hand. "If I haven't said it already, you looked beautiful today."

She flushed. "You mentioned it earlier, but it's nice to hear. Thank you. And thank you again for this dress and the flowers, though you spent too much money."

He shook his head. "Seeing you today made it worth every penny."

Dylan's grip on her hand tightened, and he fought everything inside him not to lower his head and capture her sweet mouth, to pull her soft body against him. He bit back a groan and finally released her.

Silently Brenna retrieved her suitcase and disappeared into the bathroom. He hissed out a long breath and made a beeline to the refrigerator, praying the cold and the sight of food would change the direction of his thoughts.

When Brenna returned ten minutes later, her hair was down and she was wearing jeans and a bright pink sweater. Dylan still had on his suit pants, but had removed his jacket and tie and rolled up his shirtsleeves.

They sat down at the small table in front of the window overlooking the valley. The sun had gone down, but soft moonlight silhouetted the large trees. They ate cold chicken, Caesar salad and some of the cheesecake.

Afterward, Dylan added logs to the fire and they sat on the sofa, talking about the day. The tension between them began to fade away but that only lasted until it was time for bed.

Once again, Brenna went into the bathroom to change. Dylan quickly undressed in the alcove, hanging up his suit and some clothes in the closet. He searched his bag, found a pair of pajama bottoms and silently thanked his brother. After one last check around the cabin, he secured the locks and checked the dying flame in the hearth. He still avoided the bed as he anxiously paced around, realizing he was actually nervous.

This was ridiculous. He hadn't been this edgy since he'd tried to cop a feel with Becky Phillips when he was sixteen. He wasn't a teenager anymore, and this wasn't a game. He'd married Brenna today to protect her and the baby, not to take advantage of the situation.

That didn't change the fact he wanted her…badly.

At least at the cottage they had their own rooms to go to for privacy. Here they were practically in each other's pocket. Worse, they were about to share the same bed—a honeymoon bed surrounded by soft candlelight and the sweet fragrance of flowers.

He went around and blew out candles, then turned on the lamp beside the bed and sat down on the mattress. He heard the bathroom door open. His breath caught as Brenna stepped out from the shadows.

"Sorry, this was all my mother packed for me."

She was wearing a champagne-colored gown. The

straps were thin, exposing her delicate shoulders. The satin material draped over her full breasts, revealing the hard points of her nipples. His gaze raked over the slight swell of pregnancy, the curve of her hips until the fabric stopped midcalf, showing off her shapely legs. He swallowed. He was a dead man. There was no way he was going to survive this night.

Dylan was having the best dream ever. He opened his eyes to find sunlight shining through the cabin window and discovered he wasn't dreaming.

Brenna's soft, warm body was curled against his. A throaty moan escaped her mouth as her fingers skimmed over his chest. He sucked in a breath, trying not to respond to the wonderful torture. And she wasn't finished. She moved closer, rubbing herself against his already aroused body. Another moan.

His heart raced in his chest. He had to put a stop to this or he was going to explode—or die.

Reluctantly, he placed his hand on her arm. "Bren," he whispered, but she didn't open her eyes. He shook her a little harder. "Bren, wake up."

Her eyes still remained closed. She made another throaty sound and moved on top of him, her mouth inches from his. "Kiss me."

His heart nearly came out of his chest and his groin tightened painfully. This was more than any man could tolerate. He surrendered.

"If that's what you want." His arms wrapped around her and pulled her upward so his mouth could meet hers in a hungry kiss. He didn't hesitate and slipped his tongue past her lips and delved inside to sample her sweetness. She groaned again, pressing her body closer.

Her satin gown only stimulated him more, heightening his pleasure.

Damn, she was pure temptation and he wanted her. Bad. But not like this. He gripped her shoulders and pushed her back.

"Bren," he breathed. "Wake up!"

Finally her amber eyes blinked open. Another shot of need surged through him and he wished he had kept his mouth shut.

When Brenna realized where she was and what she was doing she scrambled off him. "Oh!"

She tried to move away, but he kept her from going too far. "Please don't go."

She hugged the blanket closer as she tried to calm herself. She couldn't look Dylan in the eye. "How did I end up on your side of the bed?"

"You were probably cold and seeking warmth."

Oh, sure. She was definitely warm. "I'm sorry."

He rolled to his side, resting his head on his hand. "I wasn't complaining, but I didn't want things to go any further when you weren't…aware of what was going on."

"Nothing is going on. I was asleep. I had no idea what I was doing."

He smiled. "There's nothing wrong with us wanting each other. In fact, it's natural."

She couldn't let that happen. In the end, he was going to leave her. She couldn't let another man hurt her, especially when it involved her child. "If you married me hoping to get someone to warm your bed then we better end this now."

"Just hold it right there," he said and climbed out of bed. "I can't deny I want you, but I don't take advantage of women." He went to his bag, pulled out some clothes, then limped to the bathroom, but paused before going in. "If you would stop lying to yourself, you'd realize that you want me as much as I want you. For your information, I wasn't the one who initiated the kiss this morning." He went into the bathroom and slammed the door.

Oh, God, Dylan was right. She'd been all over him. Her body was still tingling from the aftereffects. What had gotten into her? Better yet, what was she going to do now? How could they live together like this? She heard the shower go on. She closed her eyes and pictured a naked Dylan stepping into the stall. She didn't have to imagine much since she'd already seen him without clothes.

Pushing away those thoughts, she got out of bed intending to get dressed, then realized her suitcase was in the bathroom. Looking down at her revealing gown, she knew she had to put on something else. She went to the closet and found Dylan's white shirt and slipped it on. After buttoning it, she rolled the sleeves up as she walked into the kitchen.

First, she started the coffee, then took eggs and milk out of the refrigerator. After putting bacon in the microwave, she made up the mixture for French toast. Somehow she had to make amends to Dylan, and hoped that a hearty breakfast would help smooth things between them.

Dylan had handled this morning all wrong. He dipped his head under the showerhead. Now he had to figure out a way to bring things back to the way they were. He turned off the water and stepped out of the shower. Reaching for a towel, he knew he had to stay focused on his goal: to get back to bull riding. Brenna was helping him, and in return, he was helping her. He had to remember that.

He pulled on underwear, then his jeans and zipped them up. He wiped the steam off the mirror and stood in front of one of the two sinks in the oversize bathroom. This place had been well thought out by the designer. There was a double shower stall. Off in the corner was a large Jacuzzi tub. No doubt meant for newlyweds' bathing needs. He pictured Brenna sitting in the deep tub, with watery bubbles dancing over her breasts. He groaned. Don't go there, he told himself as he ran the razor over his face.

She doesn't want any part of me. Not that way. He rinsed off the rest of the lather and realized he hadn't brought in a shirt. Great, she'll think he did it on purpose. He opened the door, glad to discover she wasn't in bed. He grabbed a shirt from the closet and put it on. Then, using his cane, he headed to the kitchen and the enticing smell of coffee.

When he turned at the counter, he stopped and so did his heart, then it began pumping like crazy at the sight of Brenna Farren Gentry dressed in his shirt. He took another breath, but it didn't help. She had the longest, smoothest and shapeliest legs he'd ever seen. He never had been interested in women's feet, but hers were… slender and delicate, each toe polished a rosy pink.

He shook his head. Oh, Lord. He was losing it.

Finally she swung around and blinked in surprise. "Oh, Dylan. I didn't hear you come out of the bathroom."

How could she not hear his heart drumming? "I just

got here." He walked to the coffeemaker and poured himself some needed brew. After several sips of courage, he decided he had to face her. "Bren, about this morning—"

"No, Dylan, you were right," she said. "I made too much out of it. Besides, I was the…guilty one. I was on your side of the bed."

Hell, she was on top of him, but he wasn't going to bring that up. "I still shouldn't have gotten so angry." He stepped closer. "But believe me, Bren… I would never do anything you didn't want. Ever."

Her amber gaze met his. "I know. But you were also right about us being attracted to one another." Tears swam in her eyes. "I don't want…"

It was natural to go to her and take her in his arms. "Ssh, Bren. I swear, nothing will happen. If we make it through this…honeymoon, things will be easier back at the cottage."

"What do we do?"

He didn't have a damn idea. He nodded toward the frying pan. "How about some of that French toast?"

She laughed. "I think *that* I can handle." She turned back to the stove.

Dylan went for his coffee, knowing the last thing he needed was more caffeine. He'd better concentrate on something else, like his therapy. Exhaust his body with exercise so he would stop having carnal thoughts about Brenna.

He doubted that he'd ever forget how she looked in his shirt.

Without regular exercise equipment, they had to improvise the therapy session. For a bench, Brenna directed Dylan to the trunk in front of the fireplace. Using a blanket to pad the table, she began the stretching exercises for his hamstrings, working her way to his thighs. They usually carried on a easy conversation during the routine, but not this morning.

"We'll go light today," she said. "But I don't want your leg to stiffen up."

"We can't let that happen," Dylan grunted, knowing that wasn't the part of his anatomy he was worried about.

He had never been so aware of Brenna's touch as she worked his damaged leg to regain more range of motion. Then came the resistance training as she used her body weight to press against his bent leg. After each series of reps, she massaged away any stiffness. The time went by agonizingly slow until finally they finished the session.

"I think we can stop for now." She stood over him. "But I want you to sit in the whirlpool for fifteen minutes."

"You never give up, do you?"

She raised an eyebrow, looking bossy and cute. "Do you want me to?"

"No." He wiped his face with the towel, then managed to get to his feet. He got his cane and followed her to the bathroom. She turned on the water and adjusted the temperature and jets.

Dylan had stripped off his shirt, standing next to the tub in his jeans. When Brenna stood, her gaze went to his chest, then moved upward. He couldn't miss the yearning in those whiskey-hued eyes. Damn, he was dying here.

"I don't think it's too hot," she said, changing the

subject. "But you might want to test the water before you get in."

Dylan glanced down at the large tub. "You know, there's plenty of room. Want to join me?"

"No! No, thank you." Her voice was breathy.

"Come on, Bren...it's like a hot tub. And you worked out just as hard as I did. Besides, who will know?" he teased. "I'll stay on the other side."

She went to the cupboard. "I'll be just in the next room if you need me." She took out a towel and put it on the counter. "I don't have a swimsuit." She turned and walked out.

"Great! Now that's a picture that's going to help me relax. Brenna naked," Dylan grumbled as he stripped out of his sweats and climbed into the bubbling water. He laid his head against the back of the tub and closed his eyes and this morning flashed into his head. The feel of Brenna's body tucked against him. Her hands on him, wanting him. He groaned and sank under the water in frustration.

So far, marriage was hell.

That afternoon they ventured outside. The day was sunny and warm and perfect for a walk. Brenna was dressed in black stretch pants and a long, blue pullover sweater when she walked out of the cabin. She wanted to take the golf cart, but Dylan insisted that he could make it down to the creek on his own power. She didn't argue, figuring she could come back and get the cart if the walk turned out to be too much for him.

Brenna packed some food and her camera, hoping to get a glimpse of the mustangs. She found herself excited about the excursion. Over the years she'd heard about the ponies that roamed this valley.

Slowly, with Brenna keeping a constant eye on Dylan, she led the way down the rise and they began a lazy stroll along the rocky bank.

"Would you stop?" he asked as he made his way over the uneven ground. "I told you I could handle this." He stopped by the water. "See, I'm still in one piece."

She ignored his sarcasm. "Why don't we find a spot and sit a while. I could stand a break. We've walked a long way."

He grinned. "I know."

"Pretty proud of yourself, huh?"

"Wait until you see me toss away this cane."

She couldn't wait. But when that happened, he wouldn't need her any longer, either. "We'll have a party," she promised.

They came to a grove of trees and a clearing where she spread the blanket, then sat down and glanced around. If she looked closely she could make out the other cabins marking the edge of the valley, but the structures were not so noticeable that they disturbed the valley or the inhabitants. There was also Travis and Josie Randell's house tucked away in the hills over the other side, but several trees hid most of the structure from prying eyes. She sighed. It must be paradise to live here.

She looked up at Dylan. "You should sit down."

"Yes, Mother."

Okay, so she was being a little protective. She told herself it had nothing to do with the fact the man was now her husband. "That's 'Mother sir.'"

He laughed and sank to the blanket. He, too, seemed

to be caught up in the valley's beauty. "Who'd ever think a place like this still existed?"

"It's so peaceful," she said. "No wonder the mustangs come here."

"Speaking of which, I think they're about to make an appearance."

Dylan scooted up behind her and pointed in the direction of a small group of horses that were walking their way. A white stallion led the group, followed by a buckskin mare and a foal scurrying to keep up. There were several others, a chestnut, a paint, all distinct in looks due to the mixture of Spanish ancestry and many other breeds.

"Oh, they're beautiful," Brenna breathed as she reached for her camera. Without moving from her spot she snapped several pictures of the animals. Finally the horses moved on.

"They don't seem to be bothered that we're here," she said, feeling Dylan shift closer to her. She knew she should move away, resist the temptation of starting something. "My dad said that Hank has protected them for years. As you can see it's as if they know that they won't be harmed by us."

"What happens when the herd gets too large?"

"Hank and the Randells round up some of them and hold an auction. Mustangs make good saddle horses."

"I know. My first horse was a little chestnut mare. I was eleven years old. It took me weeks to catch her, but I finally got her eating out of my hand."

Brenna didn't doubt that. There wasn't a female alive that could resist this man. She raised her camera and snapped another shot.

"That's a pretty nice camera you've got."

She held up her gift to herself. "I did splurge a little. There was a time I dreamed of being a professional photographer. I wanted to see the world and work for CNN or some other big news company."

"What changed your mind?"

"Reality hit. I needed to make a living and support myself. It would have taken years to get established."

"You can't give up on your dreams."

"I haven't. They've just changed. I'm doing what I love to do. And I can take fabulous baby pictures. Who's to say I can't be the next Anne Geddes?"

"I have no doubt you could be, whoever she is." His arms were around her, pulling her into an embrace, and she wasn't resisting. And she should be, especially when his mouth went to her ear and he whispered, "Your baby is lucky to have you as its mother."

A shiver went through her as his hand rested against her stomach. "I... I'm going to try to be the best mom possible."

"I want to help you," he said. "I want to be a part of the baby's life."

How many times had she heard similar promises? How many times had Jason disappointed her? During the four months they'd lived together, she had learned not to expect anything from him.

She turned toward Dylan. His silvery-blue eyes were mesmerizing, sending her heart racing. "Please, Dylan, you don't have to make me promises. We both know you'll be going back to the circuit." Her problem was, she wanted this man to come home to *her*.

"But I'll be coming back to the ranch."

"Dylan..."

He placed his finger against her mouth to stop her words. "Don't say anything."

Then he lowered his head and his lips touched hers. Any rational thought fled from Brenna's head as Dylan worked his magic.

Chapter 8

Dylan wanted to keep touching Brenna, kissing her, tasting her, but he knew he had to let go of her. Reluctantly, he pulled away. When he raised his head and saw the desire in her eyes, he nearly changed his mind.

"Damn, you're a tempting woman." He placed another light kiss on her lips.

She blushed.

"There's a rider on horseback who just came over the rise," he said. "We should make sure he gets an eyeful and make this look real."

"I guess we should," she agreed, then surprised him as she moved forward and kissed him.

Dylan gripped her by the arms and turned her in his lap, giving him better access to her delicious mouth. When he heard her soft whimper, he broke off the kiss, before things got too far out of hand. Since someone was about to interrupt them, he needed to keep his head. He drew back and saw her stunned look.

"We'll continue this later," he whispered, seeing Hank Barrett ride up. "In private."

He turned toward Hank as the older man climbed off his mount. Dylan got to his feet and Brenna followed his lead. She straightened her hair and her clothes as the rancher made his way to them.

"Hank, good to see you," Brenna said.

Dylan offered his hand. "Hello, Hank. We can't thank you enough for letting us stay here. This place is wonderful."

"Glad you like it, but I doubt if you two are any more anxious to see me right now than I am to be here. I drew the short straw and I'm here to relay a message. The weather people are predicting a storm coming in tonight. I figured you wouldn't care, but I was sent to warn you so you can pack up and head home if you want. I told everyone that neither of you could care less about a little rain."

Dylan glanced up at the clear, blue sky. "When is the storm supposed to get here?"

"Around midnight, maybe earlier." He pulled a small cell phone out of his pocket. "Just in case things get bad, you can call and we'll come and get you out. All the family numbers are in the phone." He paused as he cocked an eyebrow. "Unless you want to leave now? Think about it." With a nod, Hank walked away, then climbed up on his horse and rode off.

"I guess we should go back to the cabin and call your brother to come and get us," Brenna said.

"Hold it just a minute," he said. "Do you really want to leave?"

She knew she should say yes, but after the kiss they'd shared she was having trouble thinking clearly. "It's probably for the best. I mean with the rain and all… what if we're stuck here?"

Dylan tossed her one of his drop-dead-sexy grins. "Well, we don't have to worry about starving to death."

We could get into so much trouble, she thought, unable to get the idea of sharing the whirlpool tub with him out of her head.

"Come on, Bren…let's stay. We have a right to relax and enjoy ourselves. We've both been working hard the past two months, especially you. And what about all that food in the cabin? We can't let it go to waste." He stepped closer, lowered his head, and his mouth touched hers, gently.

"What was that for?" she asked.

"Just because you look so damn sexy." He took another nibble. "Tell me if you want me to stop."

"You don't play fair, Dylan Gentry. I'm in a weakened condition and you're taking advantage."

"You're right. This could lead to a lot of trouble. Trouble that neither one of us is ready for." His expression was serious. "I would like to stay the night, and I promise that I won't lay a hand on you. You're safe with me, Bren."

Now *that* was just what every girl wanted to hear.

Around midnight, as predicted, lightning lit up the dark sky. Then came the thunder rumbling through the valley. It seemed to rattle the cabin. Brenna lay in bed wide-awake, listening to the soft snores coming from Dylan's side. How could anyone sleep through all the noise?

Usually, Brenna wasn't afraid of storms. When you lived in Texas, thunderstorms were a fact of life. She just didn't care to be all alone during a severe storm. This one promised to be a doozy. The wind whistled and rain pelted the windows. The building was sound, but that thought didn't comfort her at all.

All of a sudden Dylan turned to her. "You okay?"

"Yeah, I'm doing fine." She sat up. "But I'd like to know what's going on. Do you think you can find a weather report on the radio?"

"Sure." He threw back the blanket and got up. He grabbed his cane, went to the radio and turned it on.

"It's a good thing the cabin is powered by a generator, because I doubt this area has electricity." As the wind and rain continued to pound the cabin, he finally found a station and soon heard that there were two tornadoes spotted outside San Angelo.

Just then the cell phone rang. Dylan grabbed it off the table. "Hello." He listened, then said, "You're sure? Okay, we will. Bye." He punched the off button and frowned. "That was Chance. There's a tornado headed in this direction."

She jumped up. "Are they coming to get us?"

"No time. We need to take cover now!"

Brenna grabbed another of Dylan's shirts. "Where do we go?"

He glanced around. "Chance suggested the bathroom…the tub." He grabbed the blanket off the bed and took her hand. "Come on."

Inside the dark bathroom, Dylan led her to the tub. "Get in," he ordered.

She did as he asked, then helped him get over the

side. Shivering, she huddled on the bottom. Dylan pulled her to him and wrapped the blanket around them.

"Dylan, I'm afraid," she confessed.

"I'm not going to let anything happen to us," he promised as he laid her down in the large tub and eased himself beside her.

The sound of the wind intensified, almost deafening to the ear. Suddenly a sharp crackle sounded, then a crash against the cabin wall. Brenna gasped.

Dylan pressed his body to hers. "Ssh, darlin'. It's going to be okay." His lips touched her forehead, then her cheek as the wind continued to howl.

Brenna had never been so scared. She couldn't stop trembling. She burrowed her face into Dylan's chest, trying to absorb his warmth, his strength. Then came a sound like a speeding train and they both froze. He drew her underneath him, using his body to protect her as the noise grew louder and louder and the cabin began to shudder.

"Dylan!" she cried.

"Hang on, love. I'm not going to let you, or our baby, get hurt." He pulled the blanket over them as they huddled in the tub. Brenna began saying a litany of prayers to keep them safe, to let her baby be born so she could have a chance to love it, not to let anything happen to Dylan.

The cabin shook as if it was going to explode, then came the sound of glass breaking, but Dylan never let go of her.

She hoped he never would.

There was quiet. Wonderful silence, only the sound of the pouring rain as it came through the window, soaking him.

Dylan pulled back the blanket and looked down at a frightened Brenna. "You okay?" He was almost afraid to ask.

When she nodded, he smiled and broke the heavy tension.

"Oh, God. That was close." He managed to sit up and glance around, but he couldn't see a thing. It was pitch-black and rain was coming in everywhere.

"Come on, we better find out the damage." He climbed out of the tub and helped Brenna.

"What if it isn't safe?"

"I figure the tornado hit pretty close." The cell phone rang and Dylan pulled it out of his pocket. "Hello," he said.

"Dylan, it's Chance. Are you and Brenna all right?"

"Yeah, but the cabin isn't in very good shape."

"I could care less about the cabin. It's you and Brenna we're worried about. Cade's on his way over in the 4x4 to pick up the two of you. Just hang on a few more minutes. I'll call Wyatt and let him know you're safe and on your way home."

"We'll be here." Dylan found he was shaking when he hung up. "They're coming to get us. Let's go see if there's anything left of the cabin."

He took Brenna's hand and managed to open the bathroom door and lead her into the main room of the cabin. She gasped as they eyed the destruction. A tree had come through the window and part of the roof was gone. There was water everywhere.

"Oh, this is awful," she gasped. "What if we had been in here?"

"But we weren't," Dylan assured her. "And we took cover. You're safe, I'm safe, our baby is safe."

Just then a horn honked. "That's Cade. We'll leave everything. Wyatt and I can come back tomorrow."

He went to the cupboard, pulled out a dry blanket and wrapped it around her. He wanted to carry her to the car, but no way could he manage that. Instead, he put his arm around her just as Cade's headlights lit their way through the door.

"Man, am I glad to see you two are all right." Cade climbed out and glanced around at the destruction. "Damn, looks like Jared is going to be busy a while. Come on, let's get out of here and find a drier place."

"Just take us back to the cottage," Dylan said.

"Sure you don't want to go by the house? It's closer."

Dylan shook his head. "We're anxious to get home."

"I don't blame you."

The trip seemed to take forever, but they finally made it to the cottage. After thanking Cade, Dylan limped heavily on his cane as he helped Brenna inside.

"You're going to take a warm shower. You're shivering."

Brenna couldn't argue, just headed for the bathroom. As if still dazed, she stripped off the shirt and the nightgown her mother had sent for her honeymoon. Her honeymoon. How close they'd come to…

She couldn't help thinking about what could have happened to her, to the baby and Dylan. Everyone she cared about. She stopped herself. She didn't want to care about the man. Tears flooded her eyes as she climbed into the steamy shower, then a sob racked her tired body and she gave in to her emotions and began to cry in earnest. They could have died tonight…the baby, too. The brutal reality made her knees weak. She sank against the tile wall for support, then felt herself being lifted as a pair of strong arms wrapped around her. She opened her eyes to see Dylan.

"It's okay, darlin'. I've got you." He pulled her into his arms.

"I… I thought we were going to d…" She cried, not caring that she was naked, only that Dylan was with her, holding her.

The shower spray plastered his hair against his head, his clothes were soaked. "I know," he soothed. "We're safe now. All three of us." His hand moved to her protruding stomach.

She leaned into his gentle touch, never wanting him to stop.

"Let's get you out of here." He shut off the water, then led her from the shower. She stood on the carpet as he leaned against the counter and wrapped a towel around her, keeping her close to him.

"You need to be in bed," he whispered, doing the best he could to help her to her bedroom.

Practically hopping on his good leg, Dylan turned on the small lamp on the dresser. He took out a long T-shirt from the drawer and returned to Brenna. Easing her grip on the towel, he quickly dried her, trying to be fast and efficient, trying not to linger over her shapely curves. But nothing he did stopped her shaking. Maybe he should have Wyatt take them to the emergency room. He pulled the shirt over her head and began drying her hair.

"I'm so cold," she whispered through chattering teeth.

"I'll get you warm," he promised as he pulled back the blanket and helped her climb in. Covering her up, he leaned over her and began rubbing vigorously over the blanket. He forced a smile. "How's that? Any better?"

She shook her head. "I'm...still cold."

Dylan knew he had to call Wyatt. He started to leave when Brenna reached for him. "Please, don't leave me. Hold me..."

He looked down at his wet jeans and shirt. "I'll get you wet."

"Take them off," she said, her eyes showing her need. "Please."

He quickly pulled off his boots, then stripped off his shirt and jeans. Leaving on his damp briefs, he climbed in beside her.

Brenna went into his arms. "Oh, you're so warm," she breathed.

Dylan lay still, only holding her, but Brenna had other ideas. She shifted against him. Every soft curve of her body became intimate with his as her smooth legs moved against his rough ones. He groaned.

"Brenna...you need sleep."

She raised up, her gaze locked on his. "I need...you," she confessed.

Dylan brushed her hair away from her face. "We shouldn't do this," he said halfheartedly, aching to kiss her. He couldn't remember wanting anyone so much... ever. "I don't want you regretting anything in the morning."

"I would never regret being with you."

He was only a man. He bent his head and took her mouth in a slow, yet deliberate, kiss. He pulled back slightly, then started nibbling gently on her lower lip, trying to control his desire. He felt a lurch of excitement as Brenna returned his enthusiasm. Their kiss intensified as he forced her lips apart with his persistent tongue. She tasted like heaven. Hearing her purr, he moved against her, wanting more…needing more. He wanted to know the pleasures of her body. He cupped her breast in his hand, then ran his finger over the hard nipple through the soft cotton material. She arched closer, offering him more.

He broke off the kiss and gasped for air. "God, Bren… I want you—"

His declaration was interrupted by a loud pounding on the front door. "Damn. That's Wyatt. I'll be right back," he promised. He kissed her, then climbed out of bed. After grabbing a pair of sweats from his room, he slipped them on and had just finished tying the drawstring before he opened the door.

Wyatt pushed his way into the room. "Nice of you to give me a call to let me know you and Brenna are okay."

"Sorry. I needed to get Brenna settled," Dylan said. Hell, he kind of got distracted.

"She okay?" Wyatt asked in a quiet voice. "The baby?"

Dylan nodded. "They're both okay. Damn, but it was a rough few minutes." He shivered, trying not to think about the close call. "I don't think things could have gotten much worse."

"I know. That twister came right through the valley…" Wyatt eyed his brother closely and released a long breath. "Only you could end up in a tornado on your honeymoon."

"Yeah, right. Tonight was a little too wild, even for me." He raked a shaky hand through his hair. "Brenna was pretty shaken. I made sure she took a warm shower and got into bed."

Wyatt studied him a while. "I'm sorry that I interrupted you two."

Dylan wasn't about to tell his brother anything. Not when he didn't have a clue as to what was going on, either. "You didn't. But it has been an exhausting night. I need some sleep."

"I should get back home, too. I don't want Maura to worry." He reached out and punched Dylan in the shoulder. "Man, I'm glad you're okay. Now, go back in there and take care of your wife," he said and winked. "I'm going back to mine."

The thought echoed in Dylan's head. Brenna was his wife now. He had promised her he was going to take care of her. "Good idea. I'll tell you all about it in the morning."

Wyatt nodded. "I'll be at the rough-stock pen till noon. Now get some rest, too. 'Night," he said, then walked out.

Dylan shut the door and returned to the bedroom. He sat down on the edge of the bed. "That was Wyatt, playing big brother."

"He cares about you," Brenna whispered, unable to meet his gaze.

Dylan touched her cheek and made her look at him. "What about you? Are you okay?"

He knew she was having second thoughts about what had almost happened between them. Hell, so was he.

She hesitated. "It's just earlier… I didn't plan for that to happen."

He laughed. "I don't think either one of us did." God, he still wanted her.

She groaned. "I bet you didn't plan on getting stuck with a weepy wife one minute, and one that jumps you the next."

"Tonight shook us both. We reached out to each other. We needed to feel…alive."

A tear rolled down Brenna's cheek and something tightened around his heart. Bending down, he kissed it away. "Ssh, Bren. It's okay." He pulled her into his arms and held her. He ran a soothing hand over her back and listened to her heart beating against his chest. A few minutes later he heard her even breathing return. She had fallen asleep.

This is the first time I put a woman to sleep, he thought, knowing it was for the best. He gently laid her back down on the pillow. Unable to resist, he brushed Brenna's hair away from her face, touching her cheek. She turned into his hand. The simple act caused a yearning deep inside him, and even though he should have turned away, he couldn't seem to leave her now. But the time would come soon when he had to pack up and hit the road.

Dylan stretched out next to her on the bed and she automatically curled against him, making him yearn for sharing more than just a space in bed. He closed his eyes and released a long breath. This wasn't going to be as easy as he thought. If he knew what was good for him, he'd get the hell out of town.

Before it was too late and he couldn't leave at all.

The next morning the world was sunny again. Besides a few downed trees and the wet ground, there was no sign of the severe storm that had hit the previous night. Dylan stood on the porch and inhaled the early-spring smells. He'd been up for hours. He had to. He hadn't wanted a repeat performance with Brenna this morning. She was curled up against him when he'd awakened two hours ago. He'd decided it would be safer if he got the hell out of there. He'd busied himself with his exercises and fixed some breakfast. Brenna was still asleep, and he wasn't about to wake her.

She needed rest. His therapy could wait until later. He stepped off the porch and headed to the barn. He had his cane, but he was trying not to use it unless he had to. If he was ever going to get back on a bull, he needed to push harder. Starting today. He was going riding, and not in the damn cart. His doctor had told him he could try things, just use good judgment.

This morning, Dylan decided he was going to saddle up Cheyenne, and he and Wyatt were going to ride out to the valley. He'd been wanting to do this since his horse had arrived six weeks ago. After being in the valley the past two days, he wasn't about to stay locked up in the cottage. No more. If he was ever going to get back on his feet—and on a bull—he had to push himself, hard.

He walked through the barn and greeted the ranch hands busy doing their morning chores. He approached

Cheyenne's stall and discovered it empty, then went to find Wyatt. His search ended in the corral where his brother was checking the tack on two mounts.

"Hey, I thought the rules were you don't ride unless you saddle your own mount," Dylan repeated one of their stepfather's strict rules.

Wyatt ignored him. "Just don't get used to it. From now on, you do it yourself. I was trying to save some time." He handed Dylan Cheyenne's reins. "You sure you're up to this?"

"We'll soon find out."

"Come on then, let's get going. The guys are probably already in Mustang Valley." He climbed onto his horse, a gray gelding, and waited.

Dylan swallowed and patted his horse. "Okay, boy. Be easy, I'm not ready to dance around this morning." He grabbed hold of the horn, raised his left leg to the stirrup and pushed his booted foot through, then pulled himself up into the saddle with a grunt.

Cheyenne shifted sideways, eager to get going, and Dylan had to work to calm him, taking the time to see if his leg would work the commands. He felt stiffness in his right thigh, but he didn't give up and got Cheyenne under control.

"Ready?" Wyatt asked, giving him a questioning look.

Dylan grinned. "You better believe it."

"Well, what the hell are we waiting on?" Wyatt swung the reins around and his horse turned toward the trail. They started out slow, just an easy walk, but neither horse would put up with that.

The wind and the sunlight across Dylan's face was

exhilarating. Nothing had felt so good in a long time. It had been months since he felt this free. He wasn't restricted, his movement wasn't hampered at all. Flexing his leg muscles, he gave Cheyenne commands. His injured leg ached a little, but he definitely had the strength needed to control the stallion.

When they reached the open field, they began to trot, then finally broke into a flat-out run. He glanced over his shoulder and saw Wyatt trying to keep up. Finally he pulled back on the reins and eased the animal to slow down. By the time Wyatt came up beside him, he didn't look any too happy.

"Couldn't you just take it easy your first time out?" He shook his head. "Brenna's going to have my hide if anything happens to you."

He thought about Brenna and leaving her in bed. "Nothing is going to happen. Did you see me, bro? I can ride."

Wyatt smiled. "Yeah, I'd say you can ride. But can you slow it down a bit? I'd like to get there in one piece." Wyatt walked them through the grove of trees, then the clearing as they approached the valley…and the damage.

They were silent as they rode through the high grass. Right down the middle of the valley a section was stripped bare from the tornado. Dylan looked up toward the cabin to assess the damage that was too dark to see last night. A tree had fallen over the back side and part of the roof was gone. He shivered, not wanting to think about what could have happened to them. He looked farther up the rise and saw a line of five men on horseback. Chance, Cade, Travis, Jared and Hank. The family was here.

"Come on, they're waiting on us."

Cheyenne easily made the trek up the soggy ground to the top of the rise. "'Morning, boys," Hank greeted with a nod. He directed his attention to Dylan. "I'm sorry about yesterday. I should have gotten you two out of here." He shook his head. "But there weren't any tornado warnings in the afternoon."

"Don't worry about it."

"Glad to see you're okay," Chance said to Dylan. "How is Brenna this morning?"

"She's sleeping. I thought it was better to let her rest after last night."

"It was a helluva night," Travis joked as shook his head.

"Sorry about the cabin," Dylan said.

"Hell, it's only wood," Cade said. "We're just glad you and Brenna are all right. Besides, Jared needs something to do until May."

"Hey, speak for yourself," Jared said. "I'm not going to be getting any sleep when the baby arrives."

"I hear you, bro," Chance chimed in. "I haven't had a full night in the last three months."

"Hey, stop whining like little puppies," Hank broke in. "You love every minute of it and you know it." He looked at Dylan and winked. "Don't you and Brenna wait too long to start a family, these guys already have a head start on you."

Dylan felt the heat rise to his face. Did Hank know their situation? He doubted it. "We'll see."

"Hey, Dylan, glad to see you on horseback," Jared said. "How soon before you test out a bull?"

"Not sure. But I'll let you know."

"Hey, maybe you can invite us over to watch," Travis said, looking hopeful.

"We'll see." He found he was looking forward to it, and to spend more time with these guys. Not that he was ready to join the family, but maybe it wouldn't hurt to be friends.

Chapter 9

She was going to kill him.

How dare he go and risk hurting himself? Brenna paced the cottage, ignoring Maura's scrutiny. She drew a breath to calm herself. It didn't work. Not when Dylan was out there doing something foolish. Well, what did she expect? The man would do anything on a dare.

"You said he went with Wyatt?" she asked.

Maura nodded. "Wyatt will make sure Dylan's careful. They wanted to see the tornado damage in Mustang Valley."

"Aunt Brenna, are you mad at Unca Dylan?" little Kelly asked.

"I'm not angry, honey, just worried. His leg isn't as strong as it should be."

"Mommy gets mad at Daddy sometimes, but then he kisses her and makes it all better. Maybe you should do that and you won't be mad anymore." The child looked hopeful.

"Aren't you just a busy little bee," her mother said. She looked at Brenna apologetically. "And here all this time I thought she was playing with her dolls."

Just then the door opened and a smiling Dylan walked in, followed by Wyatt.

"Brenna...you're up."

She folded her arms over her breasts. "I usually am at this time of day." She glanced at the clock. It was nearly eleven. "I didn't know you were planning on going out."

"I didn't think I would be gone too long."

Maura stood and took her daughter's hand. "I think we should head back to the house, Kelly."

"But Mommy," the girl began, "I want to tell Unca Dylan something."

"What is it, sweetness?" Dylan asked as he knelt down and pulled the child to him.

Kelly's blue eyes grew large as she caught her mother's warning glare. "I gotta whisper it in your ear."

"Okay." Dylan leaned forward and listened intently as the child relayed her message. He then whispered something back that made Kelly giggle.

Then each of her parents took one of the child's hands and walked out toward the door, where Maura paused. "Why don't you two come up for dinner tonight? Jeff and Kelly will have eaten and will be upstairs watching a movie. That leaves the adults to enjoy their enchiladas."

"Sounds good," Dylan said, wishing he wasn't left alone to face Brenna.

"Don't forget, Unca Dylan," Kelly called from the porch. "Kiss her for a really, really long time like Daddy does Mommy—" The child's words were cut off when the door closed.

They were alone. Dylan waited for Brenna to say something. She didn't, just walked into the kitchen, poured some water from the kettle into a cup and added a tea bag. She did look rested, her complexion fresh, and the color back in her cheeks. Her fiery locks lay in thick curls against her shoulders. She had on her usual baggy sweats, but now he knew what was underneath. He recalled his trip into the shower, holding her naked body in his arms.

He quickly shook away the direction of his thoughts and focused on saving his butt. "I was going to tell you, but you were sleeping so soundly," he said.

She took a sip of her tea. "You could have left me a note."

He wasn't going to waste time arguing. "You're right, I should have."

"Or maybe you knew I'd be upset that you got on a horse." She glared at him.

He raised a hand. "Hey, the doctor said I could start doing more, just not to be foolish."

"So you didn't go for a run, you walked Cheyenne all the way to the valley? Right?" She cocked an eyebrow. "What if you'd fallen?"

"I fall all the time," he said. "Remember, it's what I'm good at. Getting off an animal, fast."

Brenna knew she was being foolish. Of course Dylan had to start doing more. She recalled a time when he wouldn't even get out of his wheelchair. The reason she'd been hired had been her promise to get him back on his feet. His determination to get back on the circuit had helped them both make their goals. "You missed the therapy session."

"I know, but I thought we would make it up this afternoon."

She shook her head. "I have a doctor's appointment."

"Okay, then we go to the doctor's, come back here and do the therapy."

She couldn't believe it. Since when was he going with her? "You don't need to go with me."

He looked hurt. "I know. I'd like to though, unless you have a problem with me tagging along."

There were a hundred reason why he shouldn't, but right now she couldn't think of a single one. "I also have an ultrasound scheduled."

He smiled, and it stole her breath. "Well, hot damn. We're finally going to get a look at this little one." He walked up to her and pulled her into his arms, then placed a kiss on her mouth. She didn't have a chance to resist as the kiss quickly intensified and swept her away. When he finally pulled back, her legs could barely hold her up. He leaned his forehead against hers.

"You still angry with me?" he asked.

Unable to speak, she shook her head.

His grin broadened. "I guess Kelly was right. But maybe I should convince you a little more." He lowered his head once again and covered her mouth.

Oh, this man definitely wasn't playing fair.

That afternoon Dr. Sara Parks studied Brenna's chart. "Well, it looks like you're doing just fine," she told her. "You put on three pounds last month. Is the morning sickness easing up?"

Brenna nodded. "Yes. I haven't had any in almost two weeks."

"Good. Now that you're in your second trimester it should subside altogether." The doctor smiled. "I see here that you got married. Congratulations. Is the father here today?"

Brenna nodded, then corrected the doctor's assumption. "Dylan is going to be my baby's father, but the biological father is dead."

"I remember you telling me that." She scribbled something on the chart. "Well, I hope you and Mr. Gentry will be happy."

"Thank you, Doctor."

Just then there was a knock on the door and Dylan peered in. "How's she doing, Doc?"

"She's perfect."

He walked in. Playing the attentive husband, he stood next to the exam table and took Brenna's hand. "I think so, too, but she has a tendency to be a little bossy. Can you do something about that?"

The forty-something doctor apparently wasn't immune to Dylan's charms. "Why not let her have her way then?"

He laughed. "Good idea. Thanks."

Another knock and a pretty, blond technician wheeled in the ultrasound machine. "Picture time," she said with a bright smile aimed at Dylan.

"That's just what we've been waiting for," Dylan said and glanced at her name tag. "Renee. Our baby's first picture."

"Well, let's get started then," the tech suggested. "Lie back, Mrs. Gentry."

Brenna did as she was asked, using the pillow to prop herself up so she could see the screen.

"Mr. Gentry, you go around and stand beside your wife so you get a good view." The tech reached for a tube of cream. "Just to warn you, this cream will be a little cold." She pulled down the sheet and tugged up Brenna's gown, exposing her rounded stomach for the world to see. Well, that bit of reality should repel Dylan.

Dylan stood there stunned. He had touched her every curve last night, every time she pressed against him. But this was the first time he actually saw the changes in her body, saw the baby growing inside her.

The machine began to make a swishing sound. "What's that?"

Renee smiled. "That is the baby's heartbeat."

Dylan's gaze went to the screen as he gripped Brenna's hand in his. The image all seemed fuzzy to him, then slowly the outline of a tiny figure came into view. He swallowed hard. It was the baby.

The tech talked with the doctor and adjusted knobs on the machine. "By the looks of it, you have yourself a very active baby."

Dylan felt Brenna trembling and he looked down and saw the tears in her eyes. "Are you okay?" he managed to ask, his own throat a little tight.

She nodded. "This just makes it all so real." Her voice was filled with awe.

"Yeah, it does." Unable to resist, he leaned down and placed a soft kiss on her forehead. His pulse raced and he wanted more, but resisted. He turned back to the machine as the technician pointed out vital parts of the baby.

"Do you two want to know the sex?" Renee asked.

Brenna looked up at Dylan and nodded. "Yes, we want to know."

"Well, let me do some investigating here. I'll go around back and in between the legs. Oh my, yes, it looks like you have yourself a girl. What do you think, Doctor? You see any equipment I've missed?"

Dr. Parks leaned toward the screen and after a few seconds smiled. "No, Renee, I have to agree with you. A girl. She should arrive sometime in mid-August."

Dylan couldn't find his breath. "We're going to have a daughter." He glanced at Brenna, then placed a soft kiss on her lips. "Just what we wanted."

"It's a girl."

Dylan swept into the kitchen of his brother's house. Maura stood at the stove and Wyatt was setting the table for supper.

"We're having a girl." He waved the picture in the air.

"Hey, that's great." Smiling, Wyatt slapped Dylan on the back and hugged Brenna. "Let me see." He took the printout from the ultrasound. "She's a real beauty, bro. You got a name picked out?"

Dylan snatched the picture back. "Don't make fun of the kid."

Maura walked over. "He's just jealous because I don't have an ultrasound scheduled until next month," she said as she hugged them both. "I'm so glad everything is okay. All mothers worry about having a healthy baby."

Just then there was a loud crash upstairs. Wyatt groaned. "Come on, Dylan, you might as well get some practice handling kids. I need you to help me straighten this out." The two men left the room.

Brenna felt a little awkward. Her sister-in-law hadn't

said much about the quick wedding followed by an even quicker baby announcement.

"Is there anything I can do to help with dinner?" Brenna asked.

"You can sit down. The past few days had to wear you out."

She sank into a chair at the kitchen table. "I feel fine."

Maura frowned. "Let's see, in less than a week you've planned a wedding, gone on a honeymoon that was interrupted by a class-four tornado, not to mention you've been working nonstop with Dylan's therapy. I know being newly married is a strain in itself." She smiled. "And with a Gentry man, to boot."

"I didn't plan on marrying Dylan," she said. "He's the one who—"

Maura sat down across from her. "Brenna, you don't owe me any explanation. I know that your baby's father died. Nothing else is any of my business. All that matters is you're married to my husband's brother and that makes you my sister." She patted Brenna's hand. "And I'm here if you ever need to talk."

A tear ran down Brenna's cheek. She'd never had a sister to talk to. "Everything happened so fast. Dylan married me because my parents demanded to know the man responsible for my baby. Before I knew it, Dylan had told them he was. He just did it because he's grateful that I'm helping him walk again." She brushed her hair away and sank back into the chair. "You must think I'm the worst person in the whole world."

Maura shook her head. "I'd never judge you. Not with my past. When I met Wyatt, I had just come from a woman's shelter. I was running away from my abusive ex-husband. You can say Wyatt rescued me and the kids. I resisted him for a long time. And in the process there're a few things I learned about Gentry men. One is they're stubborn, and another is their feelings run true and deep. They don't do things unless they want to. Brenna, Dylan cares about you…and the baby. I can see it in his eyes and I think you're perfect for him."

"I know he never wanted to get married."

"What man does? We have to convince them they can't live without us."

"What happens when Dylan goes back to bull riding? I don't know if I can handle that."

"We make a lot of sacrifices when we love someone. You gain a lot of strength, too. Dylan may surprise you and change his mind. He may find what he has here is a lot better than what he has out there on the circuit. You've seen him with Kelly. He turns to mush. Can you imagine him leaving his own daughter?"

Around nine-thirty that night Dylan and Brenna arrived back at the cottage. She was tired but too keyed up to sleep. Dylan seemed the same. She went into the kitchen and busied herself with preparing the coffee-maker for the morning. And she filled the teapot for herself.

She tried to stifle a yawn.

He came up behind her. "You should have told me you were tired. We could have come home sooner."

When Brenna turned around, he was right in front of her, looking gorgeous in his Western shirt and jeans. His hair lay in waves and was tucked behind his ears. There was still the faint scent of aftershave lingering on his skin. Her gaze raised to his silvery-blue eyes.

She swallowed. "I enjoyed spending time with Maura and Wyatt. I'm fine."

"We did have a nice time, didn't we?" He smiled. "The whole day was great."

"You should be tired, too. You were up at five and on a horse for two hours, then a trip into town and waiting at the doctor's."

He leaned closer, placing an arm on either side of her head. "Best day I've had in a long time."

Brenna knew she should turn away, but she was weak where Dylan was concerned. She wanted to be in his arms, to be held by this man, to be loved by him.

"I don't want it to end," he said in a husky voice as he lowered his head. He touched her lips tenderly, then touched them again and opened his mouth over hers and drank deeply. She whimpered.

"Easy," Dylan said, trying to rein in his eagerness. "Unless you want more?" He cocked an eyebrow. "I should warn you, if this keeps up, it's going way past kissing. Tell me you want the same."

She nodded as her arms went around his neck and her lips raised to meet his. She was an intoxicating blend of tastes and textures that left him aching for more.

"I want you, Bren… From the first day you walked in here, I've wanted you." He dug his fingers through her hair, then across her shoulders, then down her arms, eager to touch her everywhere. Her lips parted on a moan and he swallowed the sound, and his tongue thrust inside. He felt her arch against him, trying to get closer. Her eagerness nearly pushed him off balance, making him remember his vulnerability. But he couldn't get past his need for her.

He cupped her face. "I want to make love to you."

"I want that, too," she whispered back.

Silently, he took her hand and walked her to his bed-room, then closed the door. Inside, he drew her against him and reveled in the feel of her body against his as he took her mouth in a hungry kiss. It wasn't enough. His hands went under her shirt and unfastened her bra, then cupped her breasts in his hands. She shivered as he toyed with the sensitive tips until they grew hard against his fingertips. He pulled away long enough to tug off her shirt and bra, and dropped them on the floor. Then he bent down and sucked the nipple into his mouth and she groaned again as she clutched his head.

"You like that?" he asked, happy he was pleasuring her.

"Yes," she breathed.

"Then you're going to love what else I have in mind." He moved her to the bed, removing his own shirt as they went. He kissed her again and helped her kick off her shoes, then he unfastened her slacks. With an impatient tug, he let the rest of her clothes drop to the floor. To-gether they sank to the mattress and he laid her back against the cool sheets.

"You're beautiful," he breathed as he leaned down and stroked her breasts, then moved down to her stom-ach, taking great care of the new life growing inside. "You're sure it's okay for us to do this?"

She nodded. "The doctor said everything is fine. That sexual relations are good for expectant mothers." She reached for him, her mouth eager. He wrapped his arms around her, unable to get enough. He inhaled her sweet fragrance and couldn't wait any longer.

He managed to pull off his boots and socks, then stood up and worked the zipper on his jeans. "If you have any doubts, Bren…tell me now." He'd beg if he had to, but he couldn't walk away.

She reached out to him. "Make love to me, Dylan."

He was naked and beside her in no time. He drew her against him and closed his lips over hers in a shivering sigh. His hand moved over her body, touching, stroking her, wanting to bring her pleasure.

Dylan was trembling when he parted her legs. His fingers moved in between and found her ready for him. In the dimly lit room he watched her eyes widen, then she gasped as he pushed inside her. He joined their hands as he began to move, deep, deeper until he felt he was becoming part of her.

Brenna's breath caught in her throat as Dylan's hips rocked against hers. Heat shot through her, searing her skin, burning her throat. Her body responded naturally, as if they'd made love a hundred times before. His pace picked up and she lifted her hips, searching for more as she moved with him. She wrapped her legs around his waist and arched to meet him, straining toward the pleasure.

A sob broke from her throat as he whispered sweet words against her ear and a light flashed behind her eyelids. She cried out his name as a burst of sensation swept her away. Then a low guttural sound erupted from Dylan and he collapsed on top of her.

Brenna was still floating when he drew her to his side. She never wanted to let go of him and held on tight as sleep took over.

The sun was bright the next morning. Brenna squinted as she sat up in bed. Naked. And not in her bed. Memories of last night flashed through her head.

She'd made love to Dylan. Her betraying body tingled in remembrance.

It never should have happened. He was going to leave and take her heart with him. But how could she regret making love? He had been so tender, so caring. She'd never known those feelings. Never with Jason. He'd never held her after, never cared about her needs or desires.

Suddenly the door opened and Dylan came into the bedroom carrying a breakfast tray. He wore a pair of jeans and a smile. She sucked in a breath as her libido rose.

"Good morning, Mrs. Gentry."

She held the blanket against her breasts. "What time is it?"

He put the tray at the end of the bed, sat down beside her and kissed her. Not just a little peck either. A long, searing, wake-up-and-turn-you-on kiss.

Her arms went around his neck and held on. When he finally pulled away, he grinned. "Now, good morning, Mrs. Gentry."

"Good morning."

"That's better, but I'm willing to keep working to put you in a better mood."

"I'm not in a bad mood. But I just overslept. I need to get up so we can get started on your therapy."

"We can take a few minutes for breakfast." His eyes searched hers. "And for a talk. I take it you have regrets about last night."

Her chest tightened. She wanted to scream, no, that last night was the most perfect night in her life. "Looking for compliments?"

His smile died. "No, just a little honesty." He started to get up, but Brenna reached for him.

"I'm sorry, Dylan. I'm just not very good at this."

"We're married, Brenna. There's nothing wrong with what happened between us."

What about when you leave me and break my heart? she cried silently. "You know our marriage isn't real."

He looked as if she'd slapped him. "I guess you're right. My mistake." He stood. "I thought we had something special here." He grabbed a shirt and limped out of the room. A few seconds later she heard the front door slam.

Brenna wanted to go after him, but she didn't know what to say, how to explain how she felt. Who was she kidding? It was already too late to protect herself—she was totally, completely in love with the man. She looked down at the tray at the end of the bed and saw a cup of her tea and dry toast, with a dab of her favorite strawberry jam.

Brenna felt a tear slip down her cheek. Was she brave enough to take what he had to offer her? She was still afraid, but she couldn't let go of him. Not yet. They might have only a short time together, but she wanted to spend it with Dylan. She got up and headed for the shower. Now she had to convince him of that—that she and the baby both needed him.

An hour later, Brenna set out to find Dylan. He was angry with her and he had every right to be. She'd gone willingly to his bed last night and asked him to make love to her. Now she needed to tell him why she'd pulled away in the morning.

Inside the barn, the air was cooler and she had a

little trouble adjusting to the dim light. Once her eyes focused, she moved through the row of stalls, seeing several horses, knowing that Dylan's horse, Cheyenne, was boarded here.

At the end of the row in the large corner stall she found the beautiful chestnut stallion. He sensed her too, and immediately stuck his head over the gate to investigate. She had to smile as she came up to him.

"Well, hello, good-lookin'. Where have you been all my life?" She reached out so the animal could sniff her hand, then she began to stroke his head. He was greedy and pushed against her, wanting more. She'd been around horses all her life, so she wasn't afraid of his aggressiveness. In fact, if she wasn't pregnant, she'd love to ride him.

"You'd better be careful. Cheyenne isn't a gentleman."

Hearing Dylan's voice, she froze, then turned around. "It's okay, I can handle him."

Carrying a bucket of feed, he moved past her, opened the gate and went inside. He finished filling the stallion's trough, patted the animal's rump and came out to face her.

"What are you doing out here?" he asked. "Do you need something?"

"Can we talk?" She glanced nervously up and down the aisle. They were alone.

His face was like stone. "What about?"

"This morning."

He shook his head. "I think you pretty much let me know how you feel—"

"No, I didn't. I got scared, Dylan." She fought hard to keep the tremble out of her voice. "I don't regret what happened last night." She sighed. "I just didn't... I didn't know how to handle it. Everything has happened so fast..." She glanced away. "But I've never once regretted marrying you, or your making love to me... even if it's the only time." She started to leave, when Dylan grabbed her arm, then backed her up against an empty stall.

This woman had Dylan at the end of his patience. "You can't say something like that and just walk away." His face was inches from hers. "I don't think so." He took her mouth in a slow, drugging kiss. She tasted heavenly, and he needed her more than his next breath. "You know how to turn me every way but loose, don't you?"

"I'm not trying to."

"The hell you aren't." He pressed against her, his mouth on her neck, then moved to her ear, feeling her squirm. "Come on. We need some privacy to finish this discussion."

He took her by the hand and they walked back to the house. When they reached the cottage, Brenna pulled away and crossed to the other side of the living room. "Stay there," she ordered him. "First, I need to finish what I came to tell you."

He did as she asked.

She raised her chin. "I didn't plan on last night happening."

He had. "It was inevitable from the first kiss."

She looked surprised at his comment. "The point is, things have changed between us. Do you want to stay married to me?"

He blinked. If she only knew. "Yes."

She nodded. "And I want to stay married to you, but

I want you to know that I won't try to stop you from going back on the circuit. And as we agreed, in six months we can decide if we want to continue or…dissolve the marriage."

He nodded. "But, Bren, no matter what happens between us, I will be there for the baby."

She stared at him. "You don't have to be if—"

Dylan was across the room and enfolded her in a tight embrace, his hand on her stomach.

"This baby—this little girl is going to have a father. So stop being so stubborn. We can make this work, Bren. Trust me."

Oh, she wanted so much to believe him. But trust? That was the problem.

Chapter 10

Two weeks later, Dylan awoke with Brenna's naked body pressed against his side. For never having shared a bed with a woman for longer than a few hours, he was getting pretty attached to having his wife next to him, and couldn't imagine not having her there.

He placed his palm over her rounded stomach. They'd been married just three weeks, and in that time he'd watched her body change daily. He'd gotten to know her, too. Her moods, her stubbornness, her tenderness. Also where she liked to be kissed, the sounds she made when he pleasured her, and he couldn't seem to get enough of her.

Brenna shifted in her sleep and her hand stroked his chest, arousing him. He resisted the urge to turn into her touch, knowing she needed her rest, and he needed to get up.

It was time to make some plans, he thought. His agent had called him about an offer from Tom Jarvis of Extreme Thrills, a company that handled promotion for rodeos. Tom had heard about Dylan's quest to return to competition. Jarvis wanted him to make personal appearances for the upcoming rodeos and would pay him top dollar just to shake hands and sign autographs. Dylan wasn't sure he wanted to sell himself that way. And he wasn't too eager to leave home right now.

He looked down at his wife. Oh, no, he was happy right where he was. Brenna moaned and moved against him, then finally opened her eyes and smiled.

"Good morning," Dylan said and bent down and kissed her.

She wrapped her arms around him. Slowly she came to life, her legs shifting as he moved against her.

"Mmm," she sighed. "I love how you say good morning."

He kissed her again. "Oh, I'm only getting started," he said, erasing everything else from his mind.

An hour later, Dylan walked toward the rough-stock pens. As he arrived, he heard some commotion. He quickened his step and found his brother, his stock manager, Bud, along with a half-dozen hands around the corral gate looking into the pen.

"What's going on?" Dylan asked.

Wyatt turned and smiled. "Dylan, just the man I want to see. Bud bought a new bull."

Dylan stepped up to the railing and glanced at the new addition. The jet-black Brahma circled the dirt area nervously, snorting and shaking his head. The bull stood still as his ebony eyes locked with Dylan's, then he began clawing his hoof in the ground as if sending out a challenge.

Dylan was mesmerized by the huge beast. For the first time in a long time, he felt a familiar stirring inside him. The chance to ride, to try to conquer this guy.

"What do you think of him?" Wyatt asked. "You think Tornado Alley will be any good?"

Dylan cocked an eyebrow. "Who gave him that name?"

Wyatt raised a hand. "I swear, he was already named when I got him."

"Has anyone ridden him?"

Wyatt shook his head. "We were going to try today."

Just then Brenna's younger brother, Connor, the youngest of the Farren boys, came out of the barn. Wyatt had hired the eighteen-year-old to work weekends with the horses while he finished high school.

"Hey, Connor, how's it going?" Dylan asked.

The tall, lean teenager smiled, reminding him of Brenna. "Hey, Dylan." He strolled over with a lanky gait. "Good to see you. Where's Brenna?"

"She's up at the cottage." He'd left her in bed after they'd made love. He'd hated to leave her, but she could use the extra sleep.

"You come to take a look at the new bull?"

Dylan's attention was once again drawn to the huge animal in the pen. "Yeah, I did."

"I bet you'd love to ride him," Connor teased.

Wyatt stepped in. "Ah... Dylan isn't ready to get back on a bull yet." He looked at his brother. "Don't you need to get a doctor's okay to ride?"

That could happen soon. Dylan had an appointment with his doctor that afternoon. He was tired of playing the invalid. "No, I feel fine. I wouldn't mind finding out if Tornado is worth what you paid for him."

Brenna was used to having more to do, but Dylan seemed to think that she needed a lot of sleep. She didn't. And staying cooped up all day in the cottage was making her crazy, especially since her husband didn't need her help as much anymore.

He could drive his truck now. Besides, he had been riding Cheyenne nearly every day. Because of her pregnancy, she couldn't ride a horse with him. Finished with the little housework there was, she was pretty bored by the inactivity. Maybe she'd ask Dr. Morris about taking on another patient. Part-time, of course.

Brenna knew all too well that her future could change suddenly. Dylan had never promised her he'd settle down and she found she needed more of a commitment than just that he would hang around for six months.

What about after?

Would he go out on the circuit and she'd stay at home and discover that she couldn't take it? What about all the beautiful, willing women who chased after rodeo stars? Could she compete when her stomach was so large she couldn't tie her shoelaces? How could he still desire her then?

She thought back to just hours ago when he'd made love to her, and last night he'd been just as eager. A shiver went through her body at the memory. She had to stop with the doubts. Dylan was here with her now and he had promised that he would always be there for the baby.

Brenna grabbed her coat and left the cottage. She

needed some fresh air, and since her brother, Connor, was working for Wyatt today, she could go visit him. She walked through the deserted barn wondering where everyone was, then she heard the loud voices and cheers coming from the rough-stock pens.

That was probably where she would find both Dylan and Connor. She smiled, thinking about the time her husband had spent with her family. Her brothers all looked up to him. Her happiness suddenly evaporated when she came out of the barn and saw Dylan at the top of the chute just about to climb onto a bull. Her heart lodged in her throat and her entire future began to fade away. He was joking with the other ranch hands, when he abruptly glanced over at her.

She couldn't handle this, not again. She couldn't just stand here and watch as something happened to him. She swung around and marched off, ignoring Dylan calling to her, and kept walking until she made it back to the cottage.

Once inside, she wanted to hide, wanted to forget what she'd seen at the pens. But the image of Dylan sitting on top of the bull wouldn't go away.

The door opened and Dylan walked into the room. "Brenna, you can't ignore me."

"I don't feel like talking."

"That's exactly what we need to do. Let me explain."

"You don't owe me any explanation," she told him. "From the beginning, you said your goal was to go back on the circuit. Well, congratulations, it looks like you're about to make it."

"I didn't do anything," he said. "I wasn't going to

ride, I was just showing another rider some tips on how to grip the rigging."

She blinked rapidly. "And you *needed* to climb into the chute on top of a bull to do that?"

"Maybe not," he hedged. "But, dammit, I needed to get up there for myself. To see if I could do it. It's been seven months since my accident. Maybe I wanted to know if I'd lost my nerve."

She wished he had.

"Dammit, Bren, you always knew my plans were to get back on a bull."

Oh, yes, she knew. But she was hoping she would matter more. Wrong again. "Fine, then why don't you stop talking about it and just go?"

He looked as if she had slapped him. "Is that the way you want it?"

She didn't have a choice. "That's the way I want it."

That afternoon Dylan sat in Dr. Morris's exam room while Brenna stayed at the cottage.

"Well, it looks good," the white-haired doctor said as he clipped the film onto the lighted viewing screen. "You've healed nicely. I can't believe you're the same man who was wheeled in here months ago. I'd say your recovery is nothing short of remarkable. And I'd also say that your excellent physical therapy is the reason why." He smiled. "Of course, I don't have to tell you how vital Brenna's been to your success. You married her. Where is she today?"

"I can drive now, so she stayed at home," he lied. He hadn't asked her to come along.

"I guess I don't need her here since I have her chart on

your progress." He shook his head. "You know, Dylan, I didn't have much hope for you when I got your case. Especially with your attitude and your ability to chase off therapists. Brenna was just about your last hope. She was the only one who wouldn't give up on you. I can see why you wanted to keep her around."

Dylan felt as if a knife had pierced his heart. "Yeah, she's been a real workhorse, and kept me in line." He couldn't talk about her anymore. "Doctor, I want to know about going back on the circuit. Am I ready?"

The older man studied the chart again. "You've regained close to eighty-five percent of your leg strength, but most likely you'll always have a slight limp. That could get better, or worse, especially when the weather gets cold." He sighed. "I'm not crazy about you bull riding, but there's no medical reason why you can't return."

Dylan nodded. After waiting so long, the day had finally come, and now he wasn't sure it was what he wanted to hear. He stood and shook the doctor's hand. "Thank you for giving me back my life."

The older man smiled. "You're welcome, but I'm not the person you need to thank. Save your gratitude for your wife."

Yes, he owed Brenna a lot. And wished he could give her what she needed—a husband who would be around all the time.

Dr. Morris signed the chart, then added, "There's one more thing, Dylan. I need to stress that if you go back to bull riding, that steel rod in your leg doesn't make you a superhero. You could fall or land at a funny angle and there is a chance that you'd injure your leg again.

And you may not be so lucky the next time. Maybe you should think about what's more important."

The doctor left and Dylan went to the waiting room and Wyatt.

"Well, how did it go?" his brother asked.

"Fine. I'm good to go."

"And just where are you plannin' to go?"

"Where I've always planned. Back on the circuit."

Wyatt raised an eyebrow. "What about Brenna and the baby?"

"Brenna and I have discussed this and she knows the score. In fact, she encouraged me to go. So I'm heading out on a promotional tour on the Texas circuit."

"Are you going to ride?"

"I haven't decided yet." He definitely needed practice before that happened.

"You don't have to, bro. I think Brenna would be happy if you told her you'd decided to stick around. I know I would be. The partnership offer is still on the table."

Dylan laughed as they walked out of the medical building. "Hey, remember I'm like our old man, Jack. I'm too restless to be cooped up. I need excitement. I need to be out there on the road, doing what I'm good at."

Even though Brenna had become important to him, how long could he stay at the ranch? What if he couldn't give her what she needed? God, he couldn't stand seeing disappointment in her eyes, knowing he wasn't the man he wanted to be. Until he climbed back on a bull, he was still in limbo.

Wyatt stared at him. "You've never tried anything else. You might surprise yourself."

"Yeah, and I could fail, too."

Six days later, Dylan sat in his hotel room in Lubbock, Texas, staring at the telephone. He'd been gone nearly a week and he was miserable. He was back in the limelight, but it wasn't the same. He hadn't gotten on a bull. He was only on display. So far, the promoter had used his name and past championships to help bring in the crowds. Years ago, Dylan would have loved the attention, the women and the free rounds of drinks everyone wanted to buy a world champion.

And there were the endless questions from reporters. The first and foremost was, "Are you coming back?" The second one was, "Are you as good as before?" A lot of the other bull riders asked the same things. For the first time in a long time, he wondered if he could survive the eight-second ride. Did he even have the determination and courage to get back on a bull?

Not when all he could think about was Brenna. Was she eating and taking care of herself? She'd had a doctor's appointment yesterday. How was the baby? Growing, no doubt. Brenna would be, too. He remembered her rounded stomach, the feel of her soft skin under his hands. Suddenly frustrated, he stood and walked to the window. Dammit, he had to stop thinking about her. All she had to do was ask him to stay. Instead, she'd pushed him away—out of her life, out of the baby's life.

He had talked with Wyatt, but his brother hadn't been real forthcoming in giving him any information. He just told Dylan to call Brenna. What if she wouldn't talk to him? Oh hell, he'd be back home in another week.

Home.

It surprised him how much he had begun to think about the Rocking R that way. Especially since Wyatt's offer to sell him part of the ranch kept nagging at him. Kept him thinking about building a home, a place for Brenna and the baby. What if he failed? What if he couldn't be what she needed? Be the man she deserved? He had to prove to himself he could be the man he once was.

There was a knock on the door. He got up and looked through the peephole to find Ty Andrews, one of the young, up-and-coming bull riders on the circuit. He opened the door.

The guy grinned. "Hey, Dylan."

"Hi, Ty. Nice riding today."

"Thanks to you. I drew a good bull and remembered a few tricks you taught me."

"It's your talent. What can I do for you?"

"Just wonderin' if you want someone to help you with practice. If you're not busy tomorrow morning, my dad's place is a few miles west of here. He has a few Brahmas and a practice chute. He helps coach me and maybe…you might want to try to ride."

Dylan froze. Here was the chance he'd been waiting for. "I'm not sure," he hedged. "I didn't plan on riding this trip." Yeah right, then why had he brought his rigging?

"Okay. I understand if you're not ready." He turned to leave, when Dylan called him back.

"Hey, wait a minute." He took a breath. "Why don't we talk about it over some dinner."

"Sure," Ty said.

"A steak sounds pretty good and I'm going to let you buy." Dylan slipped into his boots, then grabbed his wallet off the dresser.

Ty countered. "Then you buy the drinks."

Dylan agreed. Maybe a few drinks would chase a beautiful redhead out of his mind.

"Are you sure you're okay?" Wyatt asked. "Do you need anything?"

The following weekend Brenna sat at the kitchen table at the ranch house. Both Maura and Wyatt insisted she come up for supper. "Yes, Wyatt, I'm fine. And no, I don't need a thing." Except for her husband to come home, she thought.

"Then why are you working in your condition?"

"I'm pregnant, Wyatt, not helpless. Besides, I'm only helping out Dr. Morris a few hours a day. I have a lot of time on my hands."

"Dammit, Brenna. Dylan should be here to take care of you."

"No. I don't need to be taken care of. And Dylan is where he wants to be."

"How long is it going to take before you two realize that you belong together?"

How she wished that were true. "Look, Wyatt. I went into this marriage knowing the rules."

He shook his head. "The rules can change. I've never seen Dylan as happy as when he's with you."

She'd thought he was happy, too.

"You should have said you didn't want him to leave. Told him how you feel."

"Wyatt," Maura called as she walked into the kitchen. "The kids want you to come upstairs to say good-night."

"I'll be there in a minute."

"Honey, I think it's best to go *now*," Maura stressed as she came to the table. "I'll get Brenna some tea and keep her company while you're gone."

Reluctantly, Wyatt got up and left the room.

Maura carried two cups to the table. "Sorry. He's been like this since Dylan left. He feels responsible for allowing it. Since it was his bull…"

Brenna didn't blame anyone. "I knew from the start that Dylan was going back to rodeoing. Oh, Maura, I never should have let this get out of control. I should have told my parents the truth from the beginning. Dylan only married me because he thought he could help my situation." Her voice lowered. "He was grateful that I got him to walk."

"You did get Dylan to walk when the rest of us failed, but I don't think most men marry out of gratitude. From the beginning, Dylan has been attracted to you."

Brenna glanced down at her protruding stomach. "Yeah, I'm a real sex goddess."

"To him you are."

Brenna knew that was true. Dylan had been fascinated by the baby growing inside her.

Maura smiled. "A lot of men think pregnant women are sexy. Besides, I think Dylan isn't as shallow as he's let everyone believe. He says he doesn't want to settle down, or to have a permanent home. Have you ever thought that was because he's never had one? Wyatt and Dylan lived out of a single-wide trailer until they were ten. Their stepfather let them know from the day he married their mother that they weren't welcome in his home. Then just this past year, they learned that a womanizing jerk named Jack Randell was their biological father."

Brenna's chest tightened as she listened to the sad story.

"No wonder Dylan is so crazy about the rodeo," Maura said. "Everyone there loves him, but at the same time, he doesn't think he has any worth unless he risks his life and climbs on a bull to give them an eight-second thrill."

Wyatt returned to the room and sat down next to his wife. "And I'd give anything to get Dylan to retire and come work with me. Chance, Cade and Travis have approached him to open a bull-riding school and be a partner in the Mustang Valley Guest Ranch." Wyatt frowned, and Brenna realized how much he looked like his twin. "All my life, all I ever wanted was a home." He took hold of Maura's hand. "But Dylan ran from it. Then you came along…and the baby. When he told me he was going to marry you, I was floored. This is a man who's never made any kind of commitment. But he was ready to be your baby's father. Does that give you any idea how he must feel about you?"

Brenna swallowed.

"Now," Wyatt continued, "getting him to admit it is another thing, but he was making a start."

Maura looked up at her husband and smiled. "The Gentrys are a little hardheaded."

"I beg your pardon," Wyatt said. "If I remember,

you were the one who needed convincing. I wanted to marry you. You ran off and I had to chase you down."

She kissed him, then turned back to Brenna. "So I was a little afraid to trust again. But as you can see, Wyatt did finally convince me."

"It's different with you two," Brenna said. "Dylan doesn't love me."

Maura's eyes lit up. "The man is crazy about you and your unborn child."

Brenna wanted to believe her. "Then why did he leave?"

Wyatt was the one who answered. "It has nothing to do with you. He needs to prove something to himself."

Brenna didn't need Dylan to prove anything to her unless it was that he loved her. In return, maybe she needed to show him that she would stand by him, too. But was she strong enough to handle Dylan being a bull rider? Could she watch her husband as he did what he loved to do?

There wasn't the slightest doubt. Yes, she could. She wanted to be with Dylan. Or was it too late?

"Wyatt, where is Dylan now?"

"He's headed for Fort Worth this weekend."

She sighed. "So far."

"Not too far. If need be, I can get you there."

"How?"

"Cade Randell has a plane," Wyatt said. "I bet he'd fly us to Fort Worth, unless you can't because of the baby."

"That shouldn't be a problem, but I'll call the doctor and check. And you call Cade to see if he'll take us."

"There's something else," Wyatt began. "Dylan's entered in the bull-riding event tomorrow. Can you handle that?"

Brenna tensed. She didn't know that Dylan was going back so soon. She was suddenly sad that he felt he couldn't share that with her. "If the doctor says I can fly, I'm going."

Wyatt grinned. "You're making the right decision."

She sure hoped so. Dylan might already think she wasn't worth all the trouble. Somehow she needed to convince him that no matter what, she'd be there waiting for him when he came home.

Chapter 11

Saturday morning, Dylan wasn't at the rodeo just to sign autographs. He was entered in the bull-riding event. A year ago, he would have loved all the attention from the fans for his attempted comeback—especially from the women—but today he just wanted to be left alone. He needed to concentrate on the job he had to do. The last thing he wanted was to play celebrity.

So many things had changed since he'd met Brenna. The main thing was they were married. And right now he wanted desperately to talk to her, just to hear her voice. So much so he wanted to pack up and go, but he couldn't think about the future until he dealt with the past.

The last five days, Dylan had been at Ty Andrews's family's ranch to see if he could get back into competitive shape. He'd started out bad, then it got worse. He couldn't stay on the bull, Doctor Dread, much past the gate opening. It hadn't been easy, and he'd felt every jar and buck, but Dylan needed to get his strength and balance back. Mainly to see how his leg handled the landings. Maybe he was past his prime. But he couldn't walk away yet. He had one more thing to do.

Since today's rodeo was small, and not many of the big names were there, it gave Dylan the perfect opportunity to check his ability. This was his chance to see if he still had it. To see if he could still handle a real competition.

Dylan heard the announcer start the bull-riding event and he headed toward the chutes. Before he got there, he heard his name called out. He turned around and saw a woman who looked familiar. It took a moment, then her name came to him. Lisa Sue Hartley. The pretty blonde showed up at lot of rodeos. She particularly liked bull riders. They'd hooked up a few times, but it had never been anything serious.

With a big smile she strolled toward him, dressed in tight Wranglers and a multicolored Western shirt. Her Stetson sat perfectly on her blond head. She wasn't shy, either, and planted a kiss on his mouth. He managed to back away, but she was persistent and wanted to meet him later. Not long ago he would have been eager to party with her, but the invitation was no longer appealing. All he could think about was Brenna and his up-coming ride.

"I need to get to the chute, I'm up soon." He took off for the pens and found Ty waiting for him. He handed Dylan his rigging and wished him luck. Dylan felt the nerves as he adjusted his chaps, but he liked knowing that the adrenaline was flowing.

"You'll do just fine." The young rider slapped him on the back. "Just remember, you're the best in the world. You don't need to prove anything."

Yeah, he could walk away now, but he knew he couldn't go back to Brenna if he wasn't whole. Not until all his demons were conquered. "I need to prove something to myself."

Dylan worked rosin along the rigging, then climbed up the outside of the chute and straddled the top rail. He'd drawn a gray bull named Ornery Critter. Dylan hung the bell-weighted rope down the side, then the worker across from him hooked and pulled it up around the animal's flank and tied it. Dylan tugged at his gloves and sucked in a breath, then swung his leg over and took a seat on the back of the bull.

Ignoring the snort of the thousand-pound animal under him, Dylan went on with the ritual and slid his hand up and down under the rigging, then wrapped the rope around his hand and made a tight fist. He shoved his hat down on his head and shut out the crowd noise when they announced his name.

This was it. It was all or nothing. And he wanted it all. He wanted his life back. He sat up straight, raised his hand in the air, then called out, "go" and gave a nod. The gate swung and Ornery shot out.

The bull immediately went into a tight turn, then stopped and reversed direction. Dylan anticipated the move, but only for a split second. Ornery was known for his high kicks and Dylan wasn't disappointed as he fought to keep his balance and not fall forward. He'd lost his hat, but not his seat. Miraculously, he landed square on the bull's back and stayed with the animal as he changed direction once again. Ornery went into a series of high kicks and still Dylan kept his balance.

Then the buzzer went off.

The crowd roared as Dylan hit the ground and rolled away from danger, then scrambled to his feet. The clowns went to work and waved their arms to attract the bull's attention. Dylan ran to the fence, where he was swept through the gate to safety.

The announcer came over the loudspeaker. "Looks like 'The Devil' is back." Then a score of ninety-three was posted by the judges and a loud cheer erupted through the crowd.

Dylan hadn't even caught his breath when Ty came up. "Nice goin'." He handed him his hat. "We both made the final round."

None of that mattered to Dylan. All he cared about was he'd gotten back on the bull and rode the full eight seconds. He didn't need any more buckles or championships.

Just then Lisa Sue reappeared next to him, bringing along the newspeople eager to get pictures of the two of them. Dylan wanted to be by himself. Lisa felt differently and placed a kiss on his mouth. He jerked back. "Don't, I'm married."

She looked surprised. "Why isn't she here to see you ride?"

A longing tugged at him, and he wished Brenna were here to watch him. "She's pregnant. And it's better for her to stay home." That's where he wanted to be, too.

The blonde's hands went up the front of his shirt. "Then I say you could use some attention." He gently removed her hands. "No, thanks," he said just as he heard his name called out.

Dylan looked up and saw Wyatt coming through the crowd of people. What was his brother doing here? Oh, God. Was something wrong with Brenna? The baby? Then he saw her. Brenna. Dylan's breath caught in his throat. It had only been two weeks, but he was hungry for the sight of her. She looked so pretty with those big brown eyes and pert nose.

He pulled free from Lisa and went to his wife. "Bren," he called. "What are you doing here?"

"I came see you. But I can see you don't need me here."

"Bren, that's not true." Dylan reached for her, but she pulled away. "Let me explain. I did know Lisa from before, but there's nothing going on…" He forced a smile. "You really came here to watch me ride?" That thrilled him.

"It was a mistake."

"No, don't leave," Dylan said. "We can go somewhere and talk."

She shook her head, then turned to Wyatt. "I'll meet you at the car." She walked off.

"Bren…hear me out."

Wyatt grabbed him before he could leave. "Just let her be, Dylan. She isn't ready to listen right now."

"But I need to tell her I didn't do anything. I know I had a reputation, but I swear, Wyatt, since I married Brenna I've never so much as looked at another woman. I'm crazy about her."

"Then you should have let her know how you felt before running off."

"Hell, I didn't even know how I felt until I left. I didn't know how much I'd miss her. Is she okay?"

"She's miserable." Wyatt glanced over his shoulder.

"Look, I need to go after her. Cade flew us here, so I'll have her home in a few hours." He started off, then stopped. "Just so you know. Brenna came here to support you. She realized how much you love bull riding and she wants you to be happy."

Dylan couldn't feel any worse. And it was his own fault. He'd gone after what he wanted, hadn't he? It was all he'd been working for. The rodeo was his life. Then he'd found Bren... God, she was beautiful, stubborn, sexy, bullheaded and he loved her. He blinked at the realization. When had it happened that he couldn't stop thinking about her, couldn't stop wanting her every night, wanting to see her smile every morning.

Ty appeared. "Want to grab some food before the finals?"

Dylan came out of his reverie. "No, I'm not going to be around for the finals."

Ty cocked an eyebrow. "Why? You get hurt?"

Surprisingly his leg felt pretty good. "No. I found something I want more. I just need to convince her of that."

Ty grinned. "Good luck." He shook Dylan's hand. "It's nice that you could go out on top."

Dylan didn't feel on top. In fact, he'd never felt so low.

Brenna hadn't slept all night. That morning she called Dr. Morris and told him she couldn't make it in to work. She really needed to get her things together so she could be gone before Dylan returned. With no other choice, she had to live with her parents. Not for long though. She had money saved and if she could continue to work, she should be able to make it.

She took her clothes from the dresser and placed them in a suitcase. Dylan could file for divorce, and of course, she wouldn't contest it, or hold him to any promises. A tear found its way down her cheek. Then that part of her life would be closed…for good.

She sank to the bed. She couldn't do this anymore. Once again, she'd allowed another man to break her heart. This time was even worse than before. What she'd felt for Jason had been infatuation. She truly loved Dylan. But no more. From now on, it was going to be her and her baby.

"Bren…"

At the sound of her name, she jerked around. Dylan stood in the doorway. Oh, God. Why did he have to see her like this? "If you give me ten minutes I'll be out of here."

"So you're just going to walk out on us?"

She gathered her pride and looked at him. "We both know this marriage was a mistake. You don't need a wife tying you down. And by the looks of the way you rode yesterday, you'll be back doing what you love." She straightened. "It's what I promised you, it's what you paid me for."

Dylan was so tired. He'd driven all night to get back. He hadn't had any sleep, and he was wearing the same clothes from his ride. But seeing Brenna packing, he didn't care a damn about how he felt.

"Look, Bren… I left the rodeo right after you did and I drove all night. Have mercy on a guy and let me take a shower. Then we can talk."

"We've talked, Dylan. It hasn't done us any good. Just admit we made a mistake so we can move on. Maybe we can remain friends."

"Friends?" Dylan shot across the room. "You want to forget everything that's happened between us?" He grabbed her by the arms and pulled her close. Before she could protest, his mouth covered hers. The familiar hunger was there as her lips parted and he tasted her, praying it wouldn't be the last time. She whimpered and slipped her arms around his neck and his desire soared higher. She was his. He couldn't let her go.

He broke off the kiss. "Please, Bren…just let me clean up and get some coffee down me so I can think straight."

Brenna nodded. She couldn't speak. She'd already shown him too much of her feelings. She was weakening and that was bad. This man could talk her into anything and promise her anything except what she truly needed from him. His love.

He kissed her again and selfishly Brenna let him, savoring the feel of him against her, her body responding eagerly, knowing this was the last time. Then when he went into the shower she gathered up the rest of her clothes and walked out the door, wondering how she was going to survive not seeing him again.

An hour later, Dylan rushed through the back door of Wyatt and Maura's house to find his brother sitting at the table with Jeff and Kelly.

"Is Brenna here?"

Wyatt shook his head. "No, should she be?"

Dylan glanced down at a concerned Kelly. "Hello, sweetie."

"Hi, Unca Dylan. Did you lose Aunt Brenna?"

"Yeah, honey. I sure did."

"Hi, Uncle Dylan," Jeff greeted. "Did you win a buckle at the rodeo?"

"Not this time, buddy." He tousled the boy's hair, then looked at his brother. "I need to find her."

Wyatt looked at his kids. "Jeff, why don't you and Kelly go watch some television."

"You need to talk, huh?" The four-year-old nodded, then climbed down from the chair and hugged Dylan. "I hope you find her so you won't be so sad." The little girl took her brother's hand and they walked out of the room.

Dylan raked his fingers through his hair. "Wyatt, you've got to help me. Brenna left me."

"Did you tell her you wanted her to stay?" Maura stood at the kitchen door. "Sorry, I shouldn't interrupt."

"No!" Dylan gasped and went to her. "Please, I need help to get Brenna back."

"Then you have to decide what you're going to offer her. Is it going to be her waiting here while you're off rodeoing and kissing other women?"

"Lisa Sue kissed *me*," he insisted. "I didn't kiss her. My only objective was getting on that bull yesterday to see if I could ride him. Afterward, I discovered that I didn't need that anymore. I want Brenna and the baby. I want us to be a family."

"Then convince *her* you're going to stick around, not us."

Suddenly an idea stuck Dylan. He looked at his brother. "You got time to go for a drive?"

"Sure," Wyatt said. "Where we headed?"

"Could you show me that land you offered to sell to me? Unless you've changed your mind about us being partners."

Grinning, Wyatt got up, headed for the door and

grabbed his hat. "Come on, there's a sweet spot that would be perfect to build you a house."

"Just what I want." Inside he was praying that Brenna would want his love. Because he'd decided he couldn't live without her.

Brenna didn't feel like getting out of the house, but her mother insisted that they go into town for lunch. So Brenna had gotten dressed in the only pants that fit her expanding waistline, her black stretch pants and an oversize blue shirt. She didn't mess with her hair, just pulled it back into a ponytail, and put on some makeup for the trip.

It had been a week since she'd left the cottage and not a word from Dylan. Brokenhearted, all she wanted to do was stay in her bedroom, but as painful as it was to think about a life without Dylan, she had to make some plans for her and her baby's future.

"Mom, would you go with me to look for an apartment?"

Maggie Farren reached across the truck seat and took hold of her daughter's hand. "Brenna, you know you don't have to move out. At least wait a while before you do anything rash."

"Mom, I need to do this," she said, knowing how easy it would be to stay. She glanced out the window and realized they were driving by the road to the Rocking R Ranch. Her home. She shook off the thought. "I need to be in my own place. I can't expect you and Daddy…" When she came home she'd told her parents everything about Jason…and Dylan.

Just then Maggie Farren turned off the highway onto a dirt road. "Hang on, it might be a little rough."

Brenna grabbed the handle over the door. "Where are we going?"

"I'm picking up your father."

"Daddy's here?" What was her father doing on Wyatt Gentry's land?

Just then they came to a clearing where Brenna saw the trailer. Dylan's trailer. The canvas awning was pulled out, shading the structure from the sun. His dusty black truck was parked under a tree. About fifty yards away, she saw two men, her father and… Dylan. Her mother pulled to the side of the road, then looked at her daughter. "Go tell your father we need to get home."

Brenna didn't want to leave the safety of the truck. "Mom, please."

"Brenna, you can't keep running. You have to face Dylan sooner or later."

Reluctantly, she climbed out of the cab and started down the slope of the hill toward the two most important men in her life. They both turned to her as she approached. Her dad smiled, but when she glanced at Dylan her breath caught in her throat as she felt his hot gaze on her.

"Bren…" he whispered.

"Hello, Dylan." She turned away. "Daddy, Mom says we need to get home."

The tall man looked up the hill, then turned back to Dylan. "Give me a minute." Before Brenna could do anything, her father took off jogging to the truck, leaving her alone with Dylan.

She didn't think she could hurt any more, but she was wrong. At the sight of this man, her chest tightened painfully. He looked so good. His Wrangler jeans were creased down the front. His colorful Western shirt of blue and white brought out the azure hue in his eyes. His cowboy hat tipped low on his head, shading the sun.

She started to go, but Dylan stopped her.

"Please, Bren, don't go," he pleaded.

"I have to." She waved her hand. "My parents need to get home." Just then she glanced toward the truck and saw her mother turning around. They were leaving her. Oh no, her parents had set her up.

She began to hurry up the slope, but by the time she reached the road, they were gone. "Darn it. Why did they leave me?"

"Because I asked them to," Dylan said from behind her.

She glared at him, then turned away. She wouldn't cry.

"Okay, Bren, I'll take you back. I only asked your parents to give me a chance to talk with you. I would never hold you here against your will."

She closed her eyes. It hurt to look at him. "We've said everything, Dylan."

"No, we haven't." He blew out a long breath. "Can you at least tell me how you're feeling?"

"There's no need for you to worry, I'm fine."

"But I do worry. You're carrying my baby." His gaze went to her stomach and she felt a warmth spread through her.

She gasped. "Don't say that."

"Why not? I told you that I was going to be here for her. I don't go back on my word."

She couldn't listen anymore. "Will you please take me home?"

"Yes, but after I show you something." He raised a

calming hand. "I promise it won't take any longer than two minutes. It's right over here."

When she nodded, he took her by the arm and they walked past the trailer. Curiosity got her and Brenna couldn't help but ask, "You're not living at the cottage?"

"No, I decided to move out here a few days ago."

Dylan had fallen in love with this spot the second Wyatt showed this land to him. The view had sold him. Together they walked to the edge of the rise that looked over the green valley trimmed with rolling hills. Several trees covered the area, which would give them plenty of shade from the summer heat.

"Do you like it?"

Brenna sighed and began taking in the scenery. "Oh, Dylan, it's spectacular."

That made him smile. "I can't tell you how happy that makes me."

"Why? Why should that matter to you?"

Hunger rose in him, and longing. He stuffed his hands in his pockets to keep from reaching for her. Once he touched her, he was gone. He needed to keep his distance, at least for now.

"Because I'm planning on building a house here. Wyatt sold me part of the Rocking R."

She blinked those incredible whiskey-colored eyes. "You're going to stay here in San Angelo?"

He nodded. "And build a permanent home." He glanced over the property. "I've been thinking about it for a while now. Wyatt has been trying to get me to move here for the last year. The Randells want me to open a bull-riding school and be part of the Mustang Valley Guest Ranch. I decided it's time."

Her eyes widened. "But you're back on the circuit. To compete."

He shook his head. "I've decided to retire."

"But your leg is fine."

"My leg isn't the problem, it's my heart. Oh, I'm not saying that I didn't need to get back on the bull. I needed to prove that I hadn't lost my edge, or my courage. Winning was important, but not as important as trying again. Can you understand that?"

She nodded. "Why didn't you say anything?"

He shrugged. "I didn't know until I'd actually climbed back onto the bull and rode, until the eight-second bell went off. Then I realized that I could walk away. No regrets."

Tears filled her eyes. "Oh, Dylan."

He wanted to go to her, but he couldn't yet. He still needed to plead his case. "I discovered I wanted something else more. You."

Brenna shivered at his words. "Oh, Dylan. For how long? Until another blonde comes along?" She hated sounding so jealous.

"If you're talking about Lisa Sue—"

"Like I care what her name is," Brenna interrupted.

"Well, I knew her a long time ago. But since you, Bren, there hasn't been another woman. I hadn't even been tempted. I only want you. I want to be married to you. I want us to be a family. I want our baby to grow up, knowing she has a mother and a father."

Brenna thought she would die from the ache in her chest. She wanted so much to believe Dylan, but she needed more from this man. She wouldn't settle for anything less than love. "It won't work, Dylan. We can't keep pretending everything is perfect between us."

"We didn't have any trouble getting along before," he protested.

"But you don't need me now. Your leg is almost a hundred percent. It's just gratitude you're feeling. Please, take me back to my house." She had to get away from him. She started toward the truck.

Dylan came after her. When he turned her around, she could see the desperation in his eyes. "Bren, you have to listen," he insisted, then released her and took a step back. "Damn, I'm no good at this... I want to say all the right things, but it's hard to know how to start." He raked his fingers through his hair and his shoulders slumped. "Ah, hell, here goes. You want to know why I was so desperate to get back on the circuit? It was because it was the only place I felt like I belonged. People didn't judge me as long as I stayed on the bull the full eight seconds and scored high. I gave them a show.

"But sometimes I couldn't outrun the loneliness. And sometimes it got bad, too. When our mother ignored the fact that her husband degraded and abused her sons. Wyatt handled it better than I did. He'd always known what he wanted, then went to find his family. I ran off to the rodeo. That was the only place I felt important. Then my accident happened. I thought I'd lost everything. I wanted to give up." His gaze locked with hers. "Until you walked through the door. Stubborn and bossy... and beautiful." His voice softened. "You made me realize how miserable I was." He sucked air into his lungs.

"God, Brenna, you have no idea how much I need you. I didn't know myself until I messed up. You're more important to me than my next breath. I... I can't stop thinking about you. I didn't know how wonderful it would be to lie next to you, just watch you sleep, wish-

ing there was a way that I could tell you how I felt...
but not knowing how. Afraid that you'd push me away."

Brenna stayed rooted to the spot, unable to move,
aching to wrap her arms around this precious man.

His eyes searched hers. "God, Bren... I love you...so
much I can't stand it." He came to her, placed his hand
against her stomach. "And I love this baby. I promise
you I'll do my best to be a good father." His eyes filled.
"Damn, I wish I could say it right... I brought you here,
to show you that I was going to put down roots. That I
wasn't going to risk my life anymore."

Brenna's body grew light. "Oh, Dylan." She touched
his face. "Oh, you said it perfectly. You said everything
I needed to hear. I love you, too."

He smiled then. "You do?"

She nodded. "I've never felt about anyone the way I
feel about you. No one—"

She was silenced when his mouth covered hers in
a kiss that quickly grew intense. He tried to show her
how desperate he was for her. He'd realized in the last
week that she was the woman he was meant to love.
When he broke off, they were both breathless. "So are
you going to give us another chance?"

She giggled with excitement. "I don't know. I thought
blondes were your type."

He pulled her against him. "You're the only type I
want...forever."

"That's a long time. Sure you won't get bored?"

Before he could answer, he felt something against
his stomach. He pulled back, looking amazed. "Was
that the baby?"

She nodded. "She's been moving a lot lately."

"Oh, man, and I missed it."

"You're here now. And we'll share it all now... Daddy."

He cupped her face. "And I'm going to love her as much as her mama. And I love you a lot." He kissed her again and again. This time his hands skimmed over her stomach to her breasts. She moaned and moved against him.

"I want you, Bren," he breathed.

"I want you, too," she said. "I wish we were back at the cottage."

"I may just be able to accommodate the lady." He lifted her up in his arms.

"Dylan!" She gasped. "You shouldn't carry me."

He started up the rise toward the trailer with a grin on his face; his leg felt great. "Thanks to you, I can do a lot of things I never thought I could. The best is loving you. Did I ever thank you for making me whole again?"

"Many times," she said. "Now, stop wasting time talking, I want to see 'the devil' in action."

He grinned. "Believe me, it will be my pleasure."

Epilogue

"Hello, little darlin'," Dylan crooned at the new baby daughter in his arms.

Sarah Ann Gentry had been born just an hour ago. And with her daddy coaching her mama, she came into the world with a loud wail. She weighed a respectable seven pounds and two ounces and measured eighteen inches long. The gorgeous little girl had her mother's big brown eyes and a crown of red hair.

"She's so tiny," he whispered, then glanced at Brenna lying in the hospital bed. She looked tired, but more beautiful than he'd ever seen her.

"You wouldn't say that if you were the one who'd delivered her." Brenna smiled as she took her daughter from him. "And I'd do it all over again to get this one."

Dylan sat down on the bed. He couldn't stop looking at the miracle in her arms. He shook his head, feeling tears fill his eyes. "I've got to be the luckiest guy in the world."

"I think we both are, especially now that the house is finished. We can take our daughter to her new home."

Yes, their two-story, five-bedroom home had been completed just last week and the furniture had been arriving daily. In a few days when they'd left the hospital with Sarah, they would all truly be going home.

"And the first thing I'm going to do is to carry my bride over the threshold." He leaned forward and kissed her. "I love you so much," he said. "Even more than I thought possible."

She touched his cheek. "And to think I once had to compete with a bull."

"Never again," he told her.

In the past months since Dylan had confessed his feelings to Brenna, he'd never once regretted his decision to leave the rodeo circuit. Of course, he'd had plenty to keep him busy with building the house and opening the bull-riding school at the Rocking R. Already full, he had to turn applicants away. Best of all, he was only working a half mile away, and he could go home and see his wife and daughter anytime.

He placed another kiss on Brenna's lips. "It's sure going to be tough to stay away from you for the next six weeks."

"It's good discipline for you," she teased.

Before Dylan could argue, a knock sounded on the hospital-room door and Brenna's parents peeked in. Wyatt followed, helping his pregnant wife, Maura, who was expecting twins, a boy and a girl, in eight weeks.

"Can we see our new granddaughter?" Maggie Farren asked.

"Sure." Dylan's chest puffed out. He stepped aside so his in-laws could get a look at Sarah. All the aunts and uncles crowded around, too. If Dylan had learned anything in his six-month marriage to Brenna, it was that family was everything.

Dylan thought about his own family, his wife, daughter and his half brothers. A year ago he had been alone. Never again.

Hank sat in the saddle and looked over Mustang Valley, as he had nearly every day of the past forty years. The serene valley hadn't changed much. The herd of wild mustangs still roamed the pasture.

But Hank wasn't alone anymore.

Since the widower had taken in three wild boys twenty-five years ago his solitude had disappeared, and he liked it that way. Now, his family had grown more than he'd ever dreamed. Three more Randell boys had come to the valley to live, expanding the family to six sons. All the brothers had married beautiful wives, giving him ten grandchildren with the recent arrival of Sarah, and Dana and Jared's baby daughter, Cassie. And two more were due to arrive soon.

"Oh, Jack, you've missed so much with your sons." Hank thought about the man who'd taken off, leaving three young boys. A man who'd selfishly used women. "Your loss was my gain. Thank you."

The sound of voices and laughter brought Hank back to the present. The older grandchildren came riding in on horseback, led by Brandon. Soon to follow were the younger ones in the horse-drawn wagon they used for the guests.

Chance, Cade and Travis were on their mounts and

came up beside Hank. Chance spoke. "Jared and Wyatt are setting up the barbecue. You ready to fire it up?"

"We probably should start it before the kids get restless."

The brothers rode off to take care of the task. Hank turned to see Ella come out of the newly repaired honeymoon cabin. He climbed down and walked to her.

"Is everything ready?" he asked.

"Everything is perfect," she told him. "All the repairs are completed. We brought in food and flowers and the rest is up to the couple."

She smiled and he suddenly realized how much he'd depended on this woman over the years. Whatever would he do without her?

"It was a good idea you had, surprising Dylan and Brenna with the cabin for the weekend," he said.

"Well, their honeymoon was interrupted rather abruptly by that tornado. And after six weeks of parenthood, it's a great time for a couple to rediscover each other."

"You're such a romantic," he teased.

She made a snorting sound. "So, after all these years you finally noticed."

"I notice a lot of things." His gaze met hers. "Especially when they pertain to you."

He watched as emotion clouded her eyes. "Why, Hank Barrett, don't you go getting all mushy on me. I wouldn't know how to handle it."

He surprised himself, and her, when he pulled Ella into his arms and kissed her gently on her shocked mouth. "I just needed to tell you that I care about you. The boys think of you as a mother. And all the grandkids call you Grandma. I'd call you one special woman, Ella. Thank you for coming into my life."

She relaxed in his arms momentarily, then pulled back. "It was my pleasure." Ella's eyes watered, but there was a smile on her face. And Hank realized that smile had been something he'd been looking forward to for years.

"No, it's been mine." He took her hand and together they turned and watched the children running up and down the rise. The adults were busy spreading out the blankets, arranging things for the picnic. The brothers were talking and joking with each other. They weren't just family, they were also friends.

"You know, Hank, we are awfully lucky to have all this."

"I know," he began, not wanting to let go of Ella's hand. He wanted to share this moment with her. "I was just sending up a thanks to good old Jack Randell for letting me raise his boys. I wouldn't even mind if there were more of his kids out there."

She groaned. "Well, if that happens, I hope it's a girl who comes to Mustang Valley."

Hank didn't care. He'd been blessed with so much. He had it all. All he could ever want or need was right here in Mustang Valley. His family.

* * * * *

Daisy went over to the bassinet and lifted out Tony,
cradling him against her. "Of course. There's lots
more video, but another time. The footage of what the
ranch looked like before Noah started rebuilding to the
day I helped put up the grand reopening banner—it's
amazing."

Harrison wasn't sure he wanted to see any of that. No,
he knew he didn't. This was all too much. "Well, I'll be
in touch about that tour."

*That's it. Keep it nice and impersonal. "Be in touch"
was a sure distance maker.*

She eyed him and lifted her chin. "Oh—I almost
forgot! I have a favor to ask, Harrison."

Gulp. How was he supposed to emotionally distance
himself by doing her a favor?

She smiled that dazzling smile. The one that drew him like nothing else could. "If you're not busy around five o'clock or so, I'd love your help in putting together the rocking cradle my brother Rex ordered for Tony. It arrived yesterday, and I tried to put it together, but it has directions a mile long that I can't make heads or tails of. Don't tell my brother Axel I said this—he's a wizard at GPS, maps and terrain—but give him instructions and he holds the paper upside down."

Ah. This was almost a relief. He'd put together the cradle alone. No chitchat. No old family movies. Just him, a set of instructions and five thousand various pieces of cradle. "I'm actually pretty handy. Sure, I can help you."

"Perfect," she said. "See you at fiveish."

A few minutes later, as he stood on the porch watching her walk back up the path, he had a feeling he was at a serious disadvantage in this deal.

Because the farther away she got, the more he wanted to chase after her and just keep talking. Which sent off serious warning bells. That Harrison might actually more than just like Daisy Dawson already—and it was only day one of the deal.

Don't miss
Wyoming Special Delivery *by Melissa Senate,*
available April 2020 wherever
Harlequin Special Edition books and ebooks are sold.

Harlequin.com

Love Harlequin romance?

DISCOVER.

Be the first to find out about promotions, news and exclusive content!

 Facebook.com/HarlequinBooks

 Twitter.com/HarlequinBooks

 Instagram.com/HarlequinBooks

 Pinterest.com/HarlequinBooks

ReaderService.com

EXPLORE.

Sign up for the Harlequin e-newsletter and download a free book from any series at **TryHarlequin.com**

CONNECT.

Join our Harlequin community to share your thoughts and connect with other romance readers!
Facebook.com/groups/HarlequinConnection

HSOCIAL2020